The Lavender Ladies

Detective Agency.

ESCAPE FROM
SUNSET GROVE

The Lavender Ladies
Detective Agency:

ESCAPE FROM
SUNSET GROVE

Translated by Kristian London

Minna Lindgren

PAN BOOKS

First published 2014 by Teos Publishing, Finland

First published in the UK 2017 by Pan Books
an imprint of Pan Macmillan
20 New Wharf Road, London N1 9RR
Associated companies throughout the world
www.panmacmillan.com

ISBN 978-1-4472-8938-8

Originally published 2014 as *Ehtoolehdon Pakolaiset* by Teos Publishing, Finland.

135798642

A CIP catalogue record for this book is available from the British Library.

Typeset by Ellipsis, Glasgow
Printed and bound by CPI Group (UK) Ltd, Croydon, CR0 4YY

Visit **www.panmacmillan.com** to read more about all our books
and to buy them. You will also find features, author interviews and
news of any author events, and you can sign up for e-newsletters
so that you're always first to hear about our new releases.

The Lavender Ladies
Detective Agency:

ESCAPE FROM
SUNSET GROVE

Chapter 1

Siiri Kettunen woke up to such a dreadful racket that she thought she was in hell. She heard booming overhead, banging from beyond the wall, and battering somewhere in the distance and remembered that Sunset Grove had been threatening its residents with a plumbing retrofit for some time now. Scaffolding had surrounded the retirement home in May, followed by a swathe of plastic; the only thing missing was a moat. Windows were to be kept shut, and that went for balcony doors, too; not a ray of sunshine made it inside. Spring had been sunny and unusually warm in Helsinki, but indoors it was pitch-dark and as stuffy as a studio-apartment sauna.

Siiri glanced at her clock radio. The time was seven minutes past six on a Monday morning, and her home was threatened with imminent ruin. Very dedicated they were, these construction workers, although some of Sunset Grove's residents had had their doubts when they discovered that the contractor carrying out the retrofit was foreign and most of the workers were Polish, Russian, or Estonian.

The noise grew increasingly intolerable. Someone was

hammering on the wall so violently that Siiri was afraid the building would come crashing down around her ears. Did these demolition men think all senior citizens were deaf? And that that gave them the right to run riot in the middle of the night like a bunch of lunatics, without a thought to the residents' comfort? Slowly she pulled herself up, lowered her old feet to the grey linoleum, and paused to let the thrumming in her head subside. When she was a girl, her ankles had been so lovely that men had always paid her compliments, but age had turned her legs to fat stumps. She gazed at her feet and listened to the blood rushing through her head. Odd. One would think that the din from tearing down walls and drilling up floors would drown out the hum in her calcified veins, but, on the contrary, it seemed that her head wouldn't be quietening down at all today.

She snatched her robe from the foot of the bed, jammed her feet into her slippers, and stood. She didn't care for the slippers; it was Irma who had made her buy them. But if she went traipsing about in stockinged feet, she was bound to slip and bump her head, and Irma had no interest in tending a paraplegic. Thinking about Irma brought a smile to Siiri's face, and she wished it were ten already. Then she could pop down the hall for a cup of instant coffee and the paper. But Irma wouldn't be awake at this hour, demolition or no demolition, because she took the strongest sleeping pills money could buy.

'They're perfectly safe,' Irma would say, gold bracelets jangling as she waved a hand dismissively through the air.

'My bedtime candies. I never feel groggy; they just give me a good night's rest. When you're old, it's important to get your rest and to be able to sleep soundly. I always wash them down with whisky; it has such a lovely calming effect, too.'

After stretching her aching limbs, Siiri padded into the kitchen and forced herself to drink two glasses of water. The second one proved a challenge. She drank three gulps, rested a moment, took a deep breath, and drank one more. It was important to get your liquids. Dehydration was an inevitable part of aging, which was why even seventy-year-olds, young as they were, couldn't tolerate alcohol the way they used to. Dehydration also meant all sorts of cramps. Your gums swelled, your skin itched, and your bowels stopped up, and then doctors would prescribe you all sorts of pills instead of telling you to drink more water.

Today, her usual two glasses required Herculean effort. But at long last she completed the task and stood there panting for a moment, as if she had just performed some major athletic feat. The pounding and buzzing intensified. The noise was coming from all directions: from inside her head, outside it, and, now that she thought about it, from her front door, too.

She cast a doubtful eye at the door, as if it would be able to explain what was going on if she glared at it demandingly enough. Apparently, there truly was someone out there, trying to batter their way in with a sledgehammer. Siiri started looking around for her handbag. It wasn't on the telephone table or in the living room, nor was it on her bed or nightstand. It turned up on the wicker chair in the

3

entryway, right where it was supposed to be. She slipped it over her arm, a defence against any and all misfortune, and cautiously cracked the door.

'Cock-a-doodle-doo!' rang out so high and shrill that the boring and bashing momentarily ceased. Irma was awake!

'Isn't it dreadful? It's like we've gone to hell! Which is where we'll find ourselves if this keeps up, since we refuse to die like decent people. A little mass euthanasia might be the just thing now. *Döden, döden, döden.*'

'Irma! What are you doing up at this hour?'

'Are you deaf? My apartment is being smashed to bits by a sledgehammer. A fellow with a beard showed up in the middle of the night, marched into my bathroom, and started work. I was so startled I just threw something on and dashed down here for refuge. Do you have any breakfast for me?'

Irma certainly was energetic. Despite the hour, she was wearing a stylish blue summer dress and a white crocheted shawl over her shoulders. Her footwear, however, was pink and peculiar. Plastic shower shoes of some sort.

'Crocs. They're the latest craze,' Irma explained, as she opened Siiri's fridge to see if there was any cake for breakfast. 'Did you hear those construction workers talking to each other? Blathering like the Tower of Babel outside my front door before six in the morning. I'll tell you, though, one of them could swear quite proficiently in Finnish. The "fucks" were flying; that's what woke me up.'

Siiri had never heard the word cross Irma's lips before. She looked in surprise at her friend, who blithely continued rummaging through the fridge, humming a song from her youth: 'Life's a gas and we'll be fine, now that I'm yours, now that you're mine . . .'

Siiri pointed Irma towards the foil-wrapped pound cake on the bottom shelf. It was two days old, or, rather, she had bought it two days ago. In all likelihood, it had been baked a month ago somewhere in the Baltic countryside. What difference did it make? It still tasted delicious. Siiri turned on the tap, but nothing happened. The water had been turned off, and without warning! Luckily there was still some in the kettle from yesterday. Siiri put it on to boil and took the instant coffee from the cupboard. She knew Irma thought cake tasted best when it was dipped in coffee.

'Yum, cakesies,' Irma said. 'And cakesies always need a good dunking, that's what makes them so good. Oh my, luckily noise doesn't deafen the taste buds.'

They sat at Siiri's table, enjoying their cake and coffee and browsing through the newspaper. An incessant thunder rumbled overhead, as if someone were jackhammering Siiri's ceiling. A counterpoint was provided by arrhythmic blows from next door, where someone appeared to pounding on the floor or wall of Irma's apartment. As usual for a summer Monday, there was precious little of interest in the paper. There were only two obituaries, both equally dull. They scanned the titles of the deceased: *Beloved engineer, grandfather and brother. Dearly missed director of public sanitation.*

'Is Olavi Edvard's family really trying to say they loved him for being an engineer?' Irma said, and she cackled so hard that she choked on her cake. She coughed for a while, coughed and cackled, swatted the air and dabbed at her watering eyes with her handkerchief. 'Oh my! Shall we put "beloved typist" in your obituary?' She took a big swig of coffee and chuckled some more. Then she sighed deeply, eyed the grey plastic covering the window, and pulled a flat green object out of her handbag.

'This is an iPad. It's spelled little i big P-a-d and Anna-Liisa says you should pronounce it like you're Swedish.'

'You bought it?' Siiri cried in horror. Irma had murmured vague threats about her intentions, but Siiri hadn't imagined the day would actually come when a tablet computer would appear in Irma's handbag. Or among the cake crumbs on Siiri's kitchen table, for that matter. 'Didn't it cost a fortune?'

'Not at all,' Irma said, stroking the gadget as if it were a pet. The machine started purring, and pictures appeared on the screen. It really did come to life at a touch, a caress. 'Actually, I haven't the foggiest idea what it cost. I put it on my Stockmann card, and when I do that nothing ever seems to cost much. The bonus points just pour in. The salesperson assured me it was a good buy. Durable, high quality, and pretty to boot, don't you think?'

Irma went back to petting her gadget. It obeyed her commands: a deck of playing cards appeared on the screen, and Irma demonstrated how handy it was to be able to play solitaire without actual cards. Siiri thought it was stupid. She had no interest in watching Irma fraternize with the contraption at her breakfast table. They were supposed to be finishing the newspaper and discussing current events, so they could keep up with the times.

'The paper's in here, too, in my tablet!' Irma crowed, and her bright soprano rose above the cacophony of the demolition. She jabbed and swatted at the screen, which seemed to upset it. Now it was refusing to follow any of her orders.

'I know I saw it here yesterday,' Irma said, breaking into 'The Robber's Song' and bossily tapping at her computer. 'Listen here, you scamp!'

Her gesticulations took the form of increasingly expansive arcs, and Siiri was afraid that Irma would break her expensive toy. She folded up the paper and set it next to the front door in a paper bag. She could hear pounding from the corridor, too, not just from Irma's apartment, and she caught snippets of Slavic grumbles amid the thuds.

'Well, I can't find today's paper on this iPad now, but I know for a fact it's stashed away in there somewhere. The boy at Stockmann showed me, one swoosh and you can read the same articles you have in that rubbish bag over there. Actually, I'm not sure about the obituaries. No, they must be there, since they've started publishing them on the Internet, too.'

'Is that the Internet?' Siiri asked sceptically. Irma had lowered her toy to her lap and was running a forefinger and thumb across it as if she were searching a cat for fleas.

'No, you silly goose!' Irma squawked, still swiping the screen. 'This isn't the Internet, it's how you get to the Internet.'

'Where is it, then?'

'The Internet? Why, it's ... it's everywhere ... and nowhere, really, there's a special word for it. I'm sure Anna-Liisa remembers ...'

'Outer space?' Siiri suggested.

'Oh, for goodness' sake. This isn't rocket science; a child can use a computer and so can I, now, although this machine doesn't want to behave at the moment. I was going to show you something I knew would tickle you. They taught us in class that you can use a computer to track trams, but for the life of me I can't find the app. These things are called apps, did you know that? I wonder if that's it? Agh, now it wants to play Sudoku! Why didn't you come to the computer class with me when you had the chance?'

The very thought had been enough to terrify Siiri. She had never cared for classes and hobbies that required a regression to the school desk. That's why she hadn't learned a thing during her French course at the community centre all those years ago. After that, she had given up, despite the fact that her friends had started taking classes of all descriptions once they retired, and it had been ... goodness, almost thirty years since then. There was no end to the dance steps and knitting styles she could have learned in that time, if she had been so inclined. But Siiri had just ridden the tram, watched TV and read the same books over and over. She felt like a lazy underachiever, and stupid, too, as she observed the determination Irma brought to her battle with her recalcitrant gadget.

'This is impossible. That's it, I'm turning this thing off. Where's the power button? Oops – OK, so that's where it is.

But believe you me, it has a map where you can see the location of every single tram in Helsinki at this very moment. *In real time*, as they say. You can plan your little jaunts much more handily. Or could, if you bothered to develop an interest in the conveniences modern life has to offer.'

Irma sounded so melodramatic that Siiri felt even guiltier about being such an underachiever. How had she let so many years of her life go to waste? Could she still make up for all the squandered moments?

Suddenly, there was a blood-curdling howl from the bathroom, followed by a smash. Then everything was dreadfully still. Siiri and Irma stared at each other in horror.

'*Saatana! Saatanan paska!*'

The cursing was cut off by another crash. Irma clutched her green flaptop to her chest. Her eyes were as wide as plates and she tried to whisper as softly as possible: 'I told you! They know how to swear in Finnish.'

An agonizingly long silence was followed by several sequential crashes and an unpleasant tinkling from the bathroom, as all the mirrors and glass objects tumbled to the floor and shattered. The bathroom door was ajar, and Siiri saw smoke billowing out into the living room. Irma started hacking and swatting it away; Siiri jumped up but was too panicked to move. Maybe the smoke was simply dust, yes, that was it. Demolition dust; there was so much of it around these days that several residents were afraid they'd contract asthma.

Then a brawny, bearded fellow wielding a sledgehammer emerged from the bathroom. He wasn't wearing noise blockers or a neon vest, just a pair of overalls sprouting pockets and loops and other curious extremities. Irma squawked and gripped her flaptop more tightly, as if it were a shield against extraterrestrial invaders.

'*Perkele*,' the man said in unmistakable Finnish. He didn't look their way; perhaps he thought he was alone. Siiri gawked at him, paralyzed with fear. She felt a stabbing pain in her head and didn't dare breathe.

'*Vittu saatana*,' he continued, roughly slamming his sledge-hammer into Siiri's floor. Siiri was afraid it would punch a hole through to the apartment below. She couldn't recall who had moved in after the fat lady had moved on – died, that is. And that had been a year ago, at least. Maybe more.

Siiri looked around and focused on breathing. The dirty, demolition-dusted ogre was standing stock still in her living room. Irma surreptitiously shifted her most precious possession into her handbag, which she then protectively lifted into her lap. When Siiri could breathe normally again and the stabbing pain in her head had subsided, she decided to get a grip on herself. She strode up to the man briskly and extended a hand.

'Good morning, I'm Siiri Kettunen. Please excuse the robe, but I wasn't expecting visitors this early.'

The man gaped at this white-haired ninety-five-year-old in her threadbare bathrobe, her faded, pale eyes taking him in with a cheerful curiosity. Uncertainly, he took Siiri's hand in his grimy paw and started speaking in crude English. Scratching his gut, he explained that there had been a mistake. He wasn't supposed to come through the wall into

Siiri's apartment. Then he told Siiri and Irma to calm down, although they felt they had behaved with admirable poise under the rather surreal circumstances, and looked around to determine where the exit was.

'This way,' Siiri said, opening the front door for the disoriented sledgehammerer. He stalked out in his big, filthy boots, leaving behind crumbs of concrete and a gaping hole in the wall between Siiri's and Irma's apartments. A faint whiff of perfume drifted from Irma's bathroom into Siiri's, which just a moment ago had been as neat as a pin.

'Goodness gracious,' Siiri said to herself as she examined her bathroom. The shower had a hole big enough for a man to walk through, rather round and beautiful, actually, and the floor was strewn with hunks of concrete, tile shards and other detritus. A pair of pipes and a length of electrical wiring protruded nastily from the jagged wall. The sink was still in place, but the cabinet above it hung askew and its contents had dashed to the floor. Broken bottles, jars, and the rest of Siiri's toiletry paraphernalia were scattered among the wreckage.

'How horrible!' Irma wailed, peering over Siiri's shoulder. She had finally roused herself from her chair to see what sort of destruction the devil of a demolition man had left in his wake. 'Shameless!'

They could look right into Irma's apartment. It was hard to make out much of anything because of the debris, but Siiri could see that Irma's sink had been yanked up from the floor and lay just beyond the hole, cracked. They huffed and harrumphed until they wore themselves out. The fact was, no matter how much they cursed immigrant labourers and plumbing retrofits and Sunset Grove, where the staff was incapable of doing anything properly, it wasn't going to change a thing. Irma was the first to step away from the threshold. She paced Siiri's living room before collapsing to the sofa. And then she started to laugh in the lovely way only Irma Lännenleimu could laugh: starting from a high, tinkling chime and gradually dropping like a bel canto singer, gliding from falsetto to a chest-voice staccato. Soon she was slapping her thighs, and finally, after she had settled down, she still jiggled as she dabbed at her tears with a handker-chief. Siiri smiled at her friend, moved a couple of cushions aside, and plopped down next to her.

'Oh dear, oh dear,' Irma wailed, still laughing. 'At least no one can say our lives are boring!'

'Did you wet yourself?'

'I did now!' Irma squealed, starting over again from her high, tinkling chime. Siiri was laughing too, even though she wasn't sure there was much to laugh about. But at least Irma knew how to have fun.

'*Döden, döden, döden,*' Irma said huskily and sighed. 'Well, I have to say, this is one convenient remodel. A couple of sharp blows to the bathroom wall, and whoops, a studio and a one-bedroom are suddenly one big flat. We're flat-mates now, don't you see? We don't have to look for our keys for half an hour to pop over for a cup of coffee.'

'I suppose you're right,' Siiri said, considering the possi-bilities presented by the new circumstances. 'And when you use the bathroom, I'll be able to hear everything in my kitchen.' Irma squealed in delight and started laughing again. Siiri rose to dress. All the signs were that it was going to be a busy day, and she had no intention of receiving any more visitors in her nightshirt and bathrobe.

After waiting for what seemed like an eternity for the cursing sledgehammerer to return, as they were certain he'd promised to do, they grew restless. Irma wanted a glass of red wine, and Siiri wanted to go down to the office to see if anyone intended to do anything about the hole in her wall.

They collected their bits and bobs, which, in this case, meant their handbags and keys, and made for the stairs, having blissfully forgotten that it was still only a quarter to seven in the morning.

Chapter 2

The lobby at Sunset Grove was a seething hive of activity.
The fluorescent lamps glared brightly, as no sunlight could
penetrate the building. A crowd of elderly residents, each
more disoriented than the last, shuffled through the stale air
to the sounds of banging and drilling. Some, like Irma and
Siiri, were dressed appropriately – if you didn't count Irma's
ridiculous rubber shoes, that is – but many had sallied forth
in their nightshirts. No one knew what time it was, or what
season, or why they were there. Director Sinikka Sundström
had not shown up for work yet, and the task of calming the
restless residents fell to the young nurse who had worked the
night shift and the Filipina foot masseuse, Elelibeth Bandong.

'Is the Soviet Union attacking?' a hunchbacked old man
asked Irma and Siiri. He was the one who had moved into
the fat lady's apartment over a year ago: he wore a flat cap,
day in day out, even indoors, and propelled himself along
at a peculiar forward lean, rocking his arms at his sides and
making little in the way of progress. Siiri laughed merrily at
his joke, but the poor fellow was dead serious. He genuinely

believed the time for digging foxholes had passed and he was needed at the front. He was followed by three women asking where the nearest bomb shelter was. Neither Elelibeth Bandong nor the Spanish night nurse understood what *Soviet Union* or *bomb shelter* meant.

'There's nothing to worry about,' Siiri said, taking the Second World War veteran by the arm. 'They're just replacing the plumbing.'

'Why, the Soviet Union doesn't even exist any more!' Irma cheerfully announced, to a look of disbelief from the man. The women still wanted to find the bomb shelter, but they didn't believe the enemy was coming from the East this time. They thought living at Sunset Grove posed a risk to life and limb.

'It even smells funny. Maybe someone used chemical weapons. Or a nuclear bomb went off,' they mused. Irma and Siiri spent some time assuring them that the annihilation around them was the result of a mundane retrofit, not some catastrophe, but the women wouldn't relent. Suddenly, Irma assumed an officious tone and raised a hand: 'Ladies, I'm going to have to ask you to move on. You'll find the temporary bomb shelter this way. Rations will be distributed there shortly.'

She indicated the dining room, where the doors had just opened. The women scurried along to await further orders as quickly as their walkers and osteoarthritis allowed.

'That worked like a charm,' Irma said in satisfaction, then scanned the chaos for familiar faces. The veteran was still clinging to Siiri's arm and seemed to be waiting for orders, too. Even while standing in place, he fanned one arm and swayed so violently that he was on the verge of toppling over and taking Siiri with him. The more wildly he rocked, the more tightly he clamped down on Siiri's bicep. Siiri patted him on the shoulder and tried to think of what to say. She had to remove herself from his clutches somehow, but giving orders didn't come as naturally to her as it did to Irma.

'Perhaps you . . . Sir . . . Perhaps you could also go over to the bomb shelter to wait for breakfast. You don't want to be marching on an empty stomach.'

Three men in neon vests and noise blockers stomped past, hauling electricity cables on yellow spools. They bulldozed through the elderly residents as if they were heaps of rubbish and growled something which sounded Slavic and very beautiful. No wonder the more senile among them thought they were witnessing the continuation of the Continuation War with the Soviets. The decampment of the veteran and trio of bomb-shelter hopefuls prompted a mass exodus of sorts. Everyone made their way to the dining room, thinking it was a safe spot where field rations would be handed out. On normal days, breakfast wasn't served until eight, but now the beleaguered Sunset Grove staff realized that they might want to start pouring the coffee early. Elelibeth Bandong and the Spanish night nurse shepherded the terrorized residents of Sunset Grove over to the canteen tables.

'Cock-a-doodle-doo!' Irma trilled shrilly, waving a hand high in the air. She had spotted Sunset Grove's young lovebirds, Anna-Liisa and the Ambassador, stepping out of the elevator. The Ambassador was snazzily dressed in his day-wear: grey trousers, a brown smoking jacket and a pair of nicely polished brown leather dress shoes. He was leading Anna-Liisa by the arm, as a gentleman should. In her right hand, Anna-Liisa carried her cane, a wedding present from her husband, as married life had proved so invigorating that she no longer used a walker. She had combed her hair up into a bun and donned a brown dress, even though she had generally favoured trousers during her decades as a bachelorette. A wedding ring adorned with ten brilliant-cut diamonds glittered on her left ring finger, and she had rather boldly tossed a green scarf around her neck. They looked happy and handsome as they made their dignified approach towards Irma and Siiri.

'Isn't it awful!' Siiri huffed before Anna-Liisa and the Ambassador had even seated themselves at the card table.

'How's that?' the Ambassador asked. The racket was ear-splitting.

They still gathered every day around the baize-topped mahogany table in the corner of the common room to play cards or simply enjoy each other's company. Many of the original members of their canasta club had passed away, most recently Reino the printer, the Hat Lady, and the fat woman from wing A, but new people had taken their place. Margit joined them whenever she could spare the time.

'This is worse than the Winter War!' Irma shouted.

'Let's not exaggerate, Irma,' Anna-Liisa said frostily, dropping her cane to the floor as she took her seat. She looked even more peevish than normal, rather fatigued, in fact. The Ambassador retrieved the cane with some effort and seated himself. 'What do you know about the Winter War, anyway? Didn't you spend it in indoor comfort arranged by your papa while the rest of us thawed out frozen bodies in jury-rigged saunas while the temperature dropped below—'

'That's enough, dear,' said the Ambassador. He didn't care for reminiscing about the war, although he happily pinned his oak-leaf veterans' insignia to his tux.

'I was in a military hospital. I cared for the wounded,' Irma said, offended. 'One man mistook me for an angel, since I was the first person he saw when he came to. I was rather pretty, you know, with blond curls like the girl on the oatmeal box, and when I wiped his brow with a cool rag he opened his eyes and thought he'd gone to heaven.'

'That's enough, Irma,' Anna-Liisa said in turn. She was eager to get to the burning questions of the day.

'Oh, have I told you that story before?' Irma asked innocently, rummaging through her handbag for playing cards or a handkerchief. 'I'm such an old fuddy-duddy, that's what I always tell my darlings. They get so riled up if I tell the same story twice, although a good story never suffers from being retold, quite the opposite. Children like hearing the same bedtime story dozens of times. And they repeat the same news on the radio every hour on the hour, word for word. Besides, I tell my darlings, there are so many of you that there's no way I could ever keep track of whom I've told a story to, and it's perfectly natural to have to listen to the same story twice now and again.' Irma had numerous children and grandchildren, whom she always referred to as her darlings. 'Have I told you about the time my husband was drilling a bookshelf into the wall and the anchor gave, so the entire shelf came crashing down around his ears, books and all?' she continued.

'Yes!' the others cried in unison.

'Yes, well, all right. But then, perhaps, you can tell me why my husband was drilling a shelf into the wall, books and all. Wouldn't that be impossible, as a matter of fact? My point is that I've probably been telling you made-up stories all these years, a little embellished, you know, but my mother always said, who can be bothered to tell a dull story? By which she meant—'

'Irma!' Anna-Liisa shouted with a force only accessible to the vocal cords of an experienced teacher, drawing a passing construction worker up short. 'You may go,' Anna-Liisa said to him benevolently, as if he were a well-loved butler at her manor. Then she rapped her knuckles in agitation against the baize tabletop, until she'd collected her thoughts and corralled them back onto their original path.

'This plumbing replacement,' she began, 'is impossible.'

She was right, of course. The project had lasted less than two hours and Sunset Grove was in utter turmoil. What would happen when the bathrooms were off limits? Or when the dining hall closed its doors? Everyone had heard horror stories about plumbing retrofits; they were somehow in vogue these days. Irma's cousin had been exiled to some cramped cubbyhole on the far side of town for eight months and the project still hadn't gone as planned. The wrong tiles had appeared in her bathroom, and the shower had been installed sloppily, and far too high.

'My cousin couldn't reach the shower, and she's an average-sized woman. Our family does tend to be short, too, but that's on the eastern Finnish side, and I have nothing to do with them. Except for my cousin Greta, of course; she lives in Punavuori, and she's the tiniest creature. Punavuori, or Rööperi, as they called it, used to be working class, but nowadays anyone at all can live there. The old buildings there are just lovely! Have you been to Punavuori? Siiri, you must have ridden through it on one of your tram rides. Have you noticed how many beautiful buildings there are?'

Irma inevitably started babbling when her nerves got the better of her and she didn't know what to do with herself. But they all understood that this dreadful retrofit, reminiscent as it was of a bombing, had hurled them all into a state of discombobulation. Siiri was glad Irma was keeping spirits up with her chatter; it was soothing. But Anna-Liisa's mouth had tautened into an impervious line, and her brilliant-cut diamonds flashed as she drummed her fingertips vigorously against the tabletop. It was only now that Siiri noticed Anna-Liisa had started using nail polish since joining the ranks of the wedded. Her nails were blood-red with a tinge of violet; in Siiri's view a tad too dramatic for the decidedly mundane ambience of the retirement home.

'Did you get a manicure? Or do you know how to paint your nails so neatly yourself?' she asked Anna-Liisa.

'Siiri, we're in a crisis; can't you think of anything else to say?' Anna-Liisa wailed, her voice quivering with disappointment. 'This cannot go on. I have tried discussing the matter with Director Sundström, but she claims that residents who are renting are responsible for making alternate living arrangements. She insists that she has her hands full with the residents from the dementia unit. She also had the gall to tell me that this is the normal practice in any building association. But Sunset Grove is far from a normal building association; it's a retirement home. We pay through the nose because it's supposed to be a . . . community where we'll be safe. And the one time we need help, there's none to be had.'

Siiri and Irma couldn't quite figure out what sort of help Anna-Liisa expected. The residents of Sunset Grove had received numerous notices about the retrofit and its timetable, the type of work involved at every stage, and its effects on residents' living conditions. As well, of course, about the costs, which were to be recovered through increased rents and service fees. The shrink-wrapping of the building had coincided with the emptying of the basements. The Ambassador was the only one of their little circle who had a basement storage unit, and he hadn't cared to sift through its contents. He had hired a trusted friend to move them to a shipping container somewhere in the fields of Vantaa for the duration of the renovation. Anna-Liisa was convinced that the Ambassador's belongings had been sold and would never been seen again. Next week, plastic sheeting would be distributed to every apartment so that residents could protect their belongings. Residents were encouraged to take down any pictures and pack small objects in boxes. The demolition dust got into everything, which was why it was recommended that furniture be covered in plastic. This reminded Irma of how they always used to go to the villa for the summer and how they covered the furniture to protect it from the sun, and she spent a considerable amount of time wondering out loud why no one ever did that any more. Didn't people go to villas, or was upholstery more tolerant of sunlight these days?

Director Sundström had encouraged everyone to store their valuables in a secure place, for instance a safe deposit box, because, Anna-Liisa said, even though the contractor responsible for carrying out the project, Muhuväe Fix 'n' Finish, was a reliable partner, you could never tell what sort of questionable thoughts were going through an individual construction worker's head. Siiri thought this had sounded a little risqué coming out of Anna-Liisa's mouth, and now she and Irma had started teasing each other: 'You can never tell what's going through a construction worker's head.'

Many of them thought Muhuväe Fix 'n' Finish had a familiar ring to it, and it had turned out to be the same company that used to provide Sunset Grove with janitorial services: the one whose invoicing was rife with irregularities and whose prices were scandalously high; the one they all imagined had ended up in receivership or its owners in prison in the aftermath of last year's dramatic events at Sunset Grove, when financial improprieties were exposed in court and head nurse Virpi Hiukkanen resigned the moment she recovered from her nervous breakdown.

'Focus!' Anna-Liisa said emphatically, interrupting the others' fumbling account of the information that had been disseminated. 'These first two hours have already demon-strated that the line we were fed about dust-free methods and restricting noisy activities to daytime hours was pure poppy-cock. All of Sunset Grove was roused in the middle of the night by the thundering of drills while Director Sundström was snoozing away contentedly in her suburban home. There's dust everywhere; it's impossible to breathe.'

'It's always rough at the beginning, but the kinks will work themselves out,' the Ambassador said gently, stroking Anna-Liisa's clenched fist.

'I'm getting this funny feeling that the name of the con-struction company isn't Muhuväe Fix 'n' Finish after all,' Irma mused out loud, and she started digging through her handbag.

Siiri eagerly took up the gauntlet Irma had thrown down, since it was a simpler nut to crack than Anna-Liisa's. 'Yes, maybe it was just Fix 'n' Finish? Sometimes these companies change names when they get into trouble.'

'I'm sure my iPad knows what the name is. Give me a minute, while I warm it up.' Irma started stroking her flaptop with big, arcing swipes.

Anna-Liisa disapproved of Irma's theatrics. She sniffed so volubly that the Ambassador offered her his handkerchief and patted her comfortingly on the shoulders.

'Everything's going to be fine, dear,' he said, following Irma's manoeuvring out of the corner of his eye.

'I'll just type in "Sunset Grove plumbing". No, I'll put "Sunset Grove retrofit". And you'll see, in just a moment we'll have the answer!'

Anna-Liisa stopped her audible sniffling and cast a dubious eye on Irma's progress. Photographs and text appeared on the screen, and Irma jabbed at one box with a jangle of her bracelets. Voila, her tablet spit out the answer.

'Demolition and construction is being carried out by the Estonian company Fix 'n' Finish, that's what it reads here. What did my instincts tell me?'

'Yes, I already knew that,' Anna-Liisa said sourly. 'As far as I'm concerned, that's of secondary interest.'

'But it's the same company that made a mess of everything before, just under a different name,' Siiri reflected thoughtfully. Irma clenched the tablet to her bosom with both hands, her face glowing in jubilation.

'My little gadget makes me smart and improves my memory. Whenever I forget something, I look it up here. And if a computer's memory starts slowing down, you can buy more. It won't be long before they'll be able to do that for people, too. Just think, what fun! We won't need communal homes and there won't be any demented old ladies around, draining the country's coffers, because the doctor will just insert a little more memory whenever you need it!' Irma laughed, her round body jiggling, and paid no mind to the others' disapproving silence. She tenderly slid her machine back into her handbag and laid the playing cards on the table.

Anna-Liisa looked at Irma, eyes flashing: 'A computer's memory is empty. Information is loaded into it; only then does it have anything to offer. That iPad isn't going to make you one iota healthier or wiser.' The retrofit had done a number on Anna-Liisa; she was typically quite indulgent when it came to Irma. Now she was agitated and peevish, which elicited an unusual solicitousness in the Ambassador.

'Everything's going to be fine, just fine, Anneli,' he said in his soft baritone. Irma and Siiri exchanged glances at this novel term of endearment but didn't laugh, because poor *Anneli* was so upset.

'Be fine!? Do you actually believe that a few caresses from you are going to turn this purgatory into paradise?' Anna-Liisa rose from her seat. She shot a look at her husband that he correctly interpreted as a command to offer her her cane, followed by his arm. 'We're going for a stroll. I'd prefer to rest for a moment, but it's impossible in this hell-hole. Come, Onni.'

They turned and left; Anna-Liisa augustly and the Ambassador her stylish support; he briskly piloted his wife through the spools of electric cable, bags of cement and scaffolding. Irma announced that she had a class reunion today and was in a hurry to get to town.

'Are you going to your class reunion in those beach slippers?' Siiri asked in horror.

'How many times do I have to tell you? These are Crocs. They're perfectly acceptable for wearing to a restaurant on a summer day.' And with that, Irma went, cheerfully and without a care in the world, as if the wholesale gutting of Sunset Grove were but a charming bagatelle in her amusing existence.

Siiri returned to her apartment and threw herself on her bed to listen to the sounds of the demolition echoing through the building. She mused that it might be nice to be in the dementia unit, because then she would be oblivious to the atrocities inflicted by this plumbing project. But then she came to her senses and decided she was happy, because she remembered who she was, could stand on her own two feet, and knew what she had to do today, which was nothing. And because she had friends who played with tablets and allowed their husbands to call them Anneli.

Chapter 3

Sinikka Sundström, managing director of Sunset Grove, had called an emergency meeting in the dining room, which was, for once, overflowing with residents. Director Sundström's untamed mop was frizzy from the humidity, and although she wore nothing more than a gauzy, brightly coloured caftan with an ample neckline and loose sleeves, she appeared to be wilting in the heat. A wooden cross drew the eye to her glowing bosom, and she strained mightily to offer her residents a sunny smile. The gutting of a retirement home was not a project that she, with her degree in social services, had foreseen ever having to shoulder. Fortunately, she was able to rely on the assistance of Project Manager Jerry Siilinpää, who was responsible for managing the retrofit and who would be at hand in person today to update the seniors on the project's progress.

'. . . so now I'm going to need a positive attitude from each and every one of you,' Sundström said, with a clap of her hands.

Nearly every ambulatory resident was in attendance, as Sunset Grove had suffered from drilling and banging for well over a week now. The protective plastic had not been delivered yet; water was liable to be cut off without warning; and rumours of disappearing belongings and damage to personal property were mounting by the day. The physiotherapist had shut her doors, and the activity centre displayed a distinct lack of activity.

'Let's reach into our positivity pouches and pull out a big fistful of good cheer, there we go, another fistful, and another! After all, we're all in the same boat!' Director Sundström cried, spreading her arms like Luciano Pavarotti receiving applause; the only thing missing was a handkerchief the size of a tablecloth dangling from her left hand. 'A great big energizing hug to all of you!'

'What's that?' shouted the veteran in the flat cap. He refused to sit, and flapped his arms in the doorway in his peculiar forward hunch. He couldn't hear anything over the shrieking of the drills and could make neither head nor tail of the director's gesticulations.

'Grab some good cheer from your pouch and throw it around,' Irma yelled at him, followed by a tinkling laugh. She reached into her handbag, pulled out fistful after fistful of good cheer, and flung it around. The others took inspiration from Irma's play-acting, and before long the entire room was sprinkling good cheer, laughing heartily – everyone except Anna-Liisa and the Ambassador, that is, who sat, stunned, in the front row.

'This place is a madhouse,' Anna-Liisa said, fixing her baleful eyes on Director Sundström. The director was thoroughly discomfited. She hadn't had the faintest idea that her inspirational speech would take such concrete manifestation. She wrung her perspiring hands, and when the mayhem showed no signs of abating, she started clapping rhythmically and raised her voice.

'Eyes up here, my dears! Let's remember that this retrofit is an opportunity we don't want to slip through our fingers! Since the walls and the yard are going to be torn up anyway for the new pipes, we're going to be fixing a lot of other things, too. The façade is being replastered as we speak, and when this is all over, each and every one of you will enjoy a brand-new bathroom and kitchen, complete rewiring, improved air conditioning, and the new bushes and trees which will be planted in the yard. We're collecting funds for a garden swing, and you all have the opportunity to contribute to that, too. So if I could ask you . . .'

This speech did nothing to quell the prevailing restlessness, and Sundström's voice stumbled here and then faded feebly into nothingness. All seemed lost. But then a young man in a tightly cut grey suit and rubber sneakers strode through the door. When she saw him, Director Sundström nearly sprouted wings of joy, and her pink cheeks burned even more brightly than before.

'Jerry, thank God! Welcome, Jerry Siilinpää! Could everyone please . . . could you please listen to what Project Manager Jerry Siilinpää has to report on our shared adventure?'

'Who the hell names their kid Jerry?' asked a nearly bald woman, a new resident from C wing, from her wheelchair.

'Siilinpää? Hedgehog Head? Do you suppose that's a transliteration of a Swedish name?' Siiri asked Irma.

'What's hedgehog in Swedish?' Irma asked so loudly that many of the older people nearby started pondering the question. Someone suggested *utter*, but that was clearly the word for otter, as someone else pointed out. 'Oh, how I wish I had my green flaptop; it would tell me in an instant.'

'*Igelkott*,' Anna-Liisa bellowed, to bring a stop to the babble. 'But I rather doubt it's a finnicized name.' She shifted her penetrating eyes to the young man standing at Director Sundström's side. 'You may begin.'

'Cool. Hey, everybody! Sinikka over there just said "adventure", and adventure's a great way to put it.' The project manager's unbuttoned collar was flopping about, and he wasn't wearing a tie. An identification card with his name and photograph plastered to it hung around his neck. Such a thing might be useful in the locked unit, home to dementia patients who couldn't remember their names, but for a healthy young man to be wandering about in public with a name tag looped around his neck, well, this struck Siiri and Irma as downright silly. Siilinpää's hair looked greasy, but Irma knew this was because of the wax he'd smeared on his head.

'My darlings tell me it's quite typical these days for men to fuss over their hair and even use hairspray. And salts and gels are . . . how did they put it . . . "hella normal", I think that was it.'

'Our adventure has got off to a pretty exciting start, don't you guys think? How's everyone feeling here at the Sunrise Grove nursing home?'

'Did you say Sunrise?' Anna-Liisa asked in disbelief. Her hearing was very sharp. Margit was sitting on Anna-Liisa's other side, but hadn't heard a thing because she'd left her hearing aid on her nightstand again. Margit's head nodded, and she struggled to stay awake.

'Yup, exactly! Sunset. I said Sunset Grove,' Siilinpää said, adjusting the tie that wasn't there. His hands found his name tag and held it for a moment, apparently to soothe himself.

'It's like a pacifier, that name tag,' Irma said.

'He'll be putting it in his mouth before long,' Siiri added, and she and Irma chuckled inappropriately.

'Sunset Grove is not a nursing home. This is a full-service retirement community,' Anna-Liisa corrected the young Mr Siilinpää. She eyed him as if he were a student trying to fake his way through an oral report without the necessary preparation.

'But there aren't any services! What if this is a nursing home after all?' shouted the veteran in the flat cap, rescuing Mr Siilinpää. He had advanced up the aisle and was now standing next to Anna-Liisa and the Ambassador.

'Have a seat, Tauno dear,' Director Sundström said in a low voice, giving the irate old man a pleading look. An enormous pearl of sweat ran down her forehead to the tip of her nose and hung there, refusing to drip to the floor.

'I'm not your dear! Don't you dear me!' Tauno growled and he remained standing.

'Jiminy!' Irma squawked. Scattered titters were heard

from around the room. Tauno's arms were fanning faster than ever, but now he was standing still, like some aggressive question mark.

'Why don't you stop waving your arms about, dear, and sit down,' Director Sundström said, her voice quivering. Her throat was blooming with red and white splotches, and the wooden cross at her bosom was bathed in sweat. You could hear a pin drop, until Margit let out a loud snore and started. Confused, she had no idea of where she was. The expectant silence continued.

'I can't,' Tauno said finally. The room pricked up its ears; the old man's voice was barely audible. 'My spine is so twisted that it hurts to sit. A wound from the war. I can't sit properly and even when I stand, it's like this; I have to move my hands to keep my balance. So if you'll please excuse it. The rocking.' After a brief, effective pause he spat between his teeth in a voice so low that few heard: 'Witch.'

At this point, Director Sundström tried to pass off responsibility to the project manager, who was still holding his name tag and couldn't get a word out: 'Yes, of course. Jerry, can you take over from here?'

But Tauno the twisted veteran was trembling. 'Telling a sick man to sit down, ordering old people around like they're children! Doesn't even know who lives here, the bloody cow. And now she's spoiling our final days with these war games. Goddamned bitch!'

Tauno's arms fanned the air furiously as his croaking voice rose, and before long he was shouting such obscenities that his removal from the room proved necessary. Miisa

Sievänen, the pro tem head of residents care, rushed off and returned with two fearsome-looking construction workers to escort Tauno out. They took hold of the gnarled, roaring man as if he were a length of concrete pipe and carried him off until the thunder of the demolition drowned out his raging. Jerry Siilinpää buried his face in his hands, and when finally he restarted his pep talk, it seemed to Siiri that he was holding back a smile. Or tears; it was hard to say which.

'Yup, I see there's lots of spirit here, that's great.'

Siilinpää sighed deeply, took two brisk steps towards the flip chart and grabbed a fat marker. 'OK, guys, so let's say you have a pretty intense situation that's gradually escalating. If we do a little survey of the challenges you're facing here, what's the first thing to come to mind?'

The residents of Sunset Grove stared silently at the boy with the waxed hair, who seemed to view the hellishness of their present circumstances as some semi-amusing challenge they could solve by drawing off-centred ovals on a flip chart with red and green marker pens.

'This here is our project, exactly,' Jerry Siilinpää said, scribbling a P in the middle of the big circle. 'If you guys could just take a look up here at the flip chart, please. Let's map these problems out together first, and then we'll look for action items and paint in the desired landscape. So some of you already have the asbestos removal thing going on in your apartments. Did any critical interfaces emerge during that?'

'Will you look at that; Anna-Liisa isn't commenting on

his language,' Siiri said, and was rewarded with an irate glance from the front rows.

'Why on earth is that easel called a flip chart?' Irma asked.

'Right. Excellent question. It comes from English. Flip because the paper flips over and chart because . . . umm, well. In any case. This is your, I mean our project, and you see these arrows here, these red ones, these are the critical risk clusters. Noise is probably the first one here. I'll put a letter N here.'

Panicked cries echoed from around the room: 'What? How's that? What did you say?' No one understood what the man at the flip chart was talking about.

'Noise! I'm thinking it's a buffer risk during the kick-off phase! But no prob, I can promise you that as the project continues, you'll get used it.'

'What's that?'

'Another – shall we say – critical challenge is dust. It's being taken care of. I'll put a D here. There we go. The moving boxes will arrive tomorrow and then you just pack your things in them and keep them safe and sound so they aren't damaged by the dust, right? Of course it would always be better if the apartments were completely empty, but hey, come on, you guys have to live somewhere, right? So let's just pack up what we can so it's not in the way. This second arrow here is an action item. Let's put A1 on the roadmap, and this box here under the arrow is a box, a moving box. It's an action item. Another action item is plastic, transparent plastic and masking tape. Together these action items form a point, an action point. You guys wrap that plastic around your television and any other electronics you may have. And then tape it so tightly that the dust can't get in and play dirty tricks on your devices. Pretty simple, right? Let's just take it one step at a time, nice and easy, right?'

Jerry Siilinpää jabbed red dots around the arrow to represent dust that wasn't getting into the box.

'Who's going to pack our stuff?' shouted a woman in a purple tracksuit whom Siiri had never seen before.

'Why moving boxes? Where are we moving to?' asked the ancient woman from A wing who was strapped to her wheelchair.

'I'm not packing anything myself, no way,' said the tattooed woman sitting next to her, a recent retiree whom Irma had met over lunchtime porridge a couple of weeks earlier.

'She's perfectly healthy and only sixty-seven years old. Apparently, she's a doctor. She could be my daughter!' Irma whispered to Siiri, and the tattooed woman glared at them. 'Just imagine if Tuula showed up at Sunset Grove, that would be something, wouldn't it!'

'Umm, well . . . the retirement centre is responsible for this task, the packing, so if you take it from here, Sinikka, and tell us what time and resources you have allocated for this,' Jerry Siilinpää mumbled, gazing at his work of abstract art. He wrote SUNRISE GROVE PLUMBING RETROFIT in capital letters at the top of the flip chart.

The meeting was of absolutely no use, but Irma and Siiri found it a rather pleasant way to pass the morning and a refreshing change from the usual attempts to activate them.

One woman with tangled hair thought she was at bingo and kept complaining that she couldn't hear the numbers. Margit's snoring was growing louder and louder, despite Anna-Liisa's elbowing her in the ribs. But the Ambassador had little to say, which was peculiar, since he was typically alert and active on such occasions.

'Maybe he doesn't dare open his mouth, now that Anna-Liisa's got him under her thumb,' Irma suggested.

The young doctor with the tattoos demanded services every chance she got, such as a ride to her summer cottage, where the garden demanded regular attention, and there was no way she could travel alone, because she had kidney trouble that demanded heavy doses of daily medication. As she spoke, she threw in a smattering of medical jargon that no one understood but that made her garden and her kidneys sound like a matter of life and death. Gradually, the seniors lost interest, since neither Project Manager Siilinpää nor Director Sundström had the answers to the simplest of questions. No one even had any idea how long the retrofit would take and how long they would have to manage without water.

'No one's going to die of thirst,' Director Sundström consoled her audience, with an unpleasant emphasis on the word 'thirst'. 'The plastic water jugs in the hallways will be filled as often as necessary, and meal service has been outsourced. Meals will be delivered directly to the apartments of those who want them. The service is subject to a supplementary fee, and you'll find the price list in the folder in the common room, on the bulletin board outside my office, and online. You can sign up for the service in Pro Tem Head Sievänen's office.' The director smiled happily, as if this expensive temporary arrangement were emergency aid being provided free of charge by the Finnish Red Cross.

'Our time window's closing!' shouted Jerry Siilinpää, pointing at his wrist where there was no watch. 'Shall we say one last question and then on to bigger and better things?'

'When and where is bingo being held?' asked the woman with the tangled hair.

'I can't open the door to my balcony. Can someone come and open it?' shouted the nearly bald woman.

'There's a hole the size of a grown man in the wall between our apartments, and no one seems to want to fix it. Who should we complain to?' crowed Irma in a penetrating voice that rose above the din.

'Is listening to the radio forbidden?' asked someone from the back row. Then it was quiet.

'Right, right,' Jerry Siilinpää said, looking thoughtful. 'Excellent food for thought, yup, yup. Thanks. Until next time!'

He ripped his explanatory illustration from the flip chart, threw it in the bin, grabbed the laptop he hadn't opened once during the meeting and slipped it under his arm, then stalked from the room in long, tennis-shoe strides. Director Sundström fingered the damp wooden cross at her throat and tried to start a round of applause for Mr Siilinpää. The tattooed doctor and the bald woman clapped so furiously that Margit woke up and asked Anna-Liisa in a loud voice when the plumbing retrofit was supposed to begin. Then Siiri noticed a pause in the rumbling and drilling. Apparently, the demolition men were taking a lunch break; it was the only peaceful moment of the day. For a little while, life felt heavenly and no one had any aches or pains. In honour of this sliver of paradise, they decided to enjoy a peaceful game of canasta for the first time in ages. Only Anna-Liisa looked fatigued, and the Ambassador nearly had to force her to the baize-covered table. Irma shuffled the cards and dealt nimbly; she was very skilled.

'I have a three!' Irma tittered, and at that moment a horrendous bang came from the direction of C wing. The card table shook, Margit squawked, one old woman outside the dining room fell to the ground, Siiri's head thrummed nastily, Anna-Liisa went white as a sheet, and over in the magazine nook, the doctor with the tattoos started cursing. She stood up and announced that she was heading out to the local pub, the Ukko-Munkki, for a pint.

'Care to join me?' the doctor asked, but none of their little circle of card players was in the habit of drinking beer in bars. They had only been to the Ukko-Munkki once, on the occasion of the Hat Lady's funeral, when the pastor played the saw and the wine was flowing. But generally speaking, they didn't feel such watering holes were appropriate places for old people. Especially at an hour like this – why, it was barely noon.

'Jesus Christ, what a bunch,' the doctor said. The old woman was still lying on the floor outside the dining room, and the doctor winced at the sight as she rushed past them and out the door. A couple of construction workers were entering the building at the same time and politely made way for the doctor by stepping over the old woman.

'What is she doing here?' Siiri asked as she watched the doctor leave. For the life of her she couldn't understand why a sixty-seven-year-old would pay through the nose to live at Sunset Grove when she could have lived anywhere she wanted, like a normal person.

'And why is she a doctor?' Irma asked, and she started to laugh.

They went over to help the old woman up, because there was no sign of any personnel. Since the dismissal of Head Nurse Virpi Hiukkanen, the revolving doors of Sunset Grove staffing had spun faster than ever. Miisa Sievänen had been named pro tem head of residents care, and there was no more need for a head nurse. Ms Sievänen wasn't a nurse by training; she was some sort of theoretical expert in the care-giving sciences. She had explained that no one in their right mind would come and work at a retirement home where there was a major construction project underway, which the residents had no trouble understanding.

And which was why, without asking for assistance, they lifted up the old woman and helped her onto one of the benches in the lobby. Irma was so rotund she had a hard time bending over, but Margit, as her husband's caregiver, had learned the proper holds, and she gave the Ambassador, Siiri and Anna-Liisa clear commands in this demanding operation. After much ordering about and huffing, the old woman was sitting upright. She was disoriented, and blood was dripping from her forehead.

'Oh how awful, how terrible!' a voice shouted behind them. Pro Tem Head Sievänen stood there, covering her mouth. She didn't cope well with blood. Irma dabbed at the cut with her lace handkerchief while Miisa Sievänen swiped at her phone, trying to order an ambulance.

'There's no need for an ambulance,' Siiri assured her. 'One doesn't go to hospital for a little cut. Look for yourself, it's not even bleeding any more, now that Irma wiped away the blood.'

But the pro tem head couldn't bear looking at the old woman's cut, which was precisely why she had chosen the theoretical track in the caregiving sciences programme at vocational school. She'd been instructed that any senior exhibiting abnormal symptoms needed to be immediately collected by ambulance and removed from retirement-home premises, and a cut, if anything, was an abnormal symptom. Otherwise someone might sue the retirement home for neglect, and no retirement-home owner could afford to take on such a burden. Ms Sievänen trembled nervously and screeched into her phone: 'We need an ambulance right away – yes, a head wound, fallen, an elderly woman, yes, very old.'

'What was that horrific explosion? That was why this woman fell, because of that horrendous bang. What was it?' Siiri asked the director pro tem after the call ended. Ms Sievänen didn't know anything about any explosions; she hadn't heard anything of the sort and looked at Siiri and her friends as if they had made up the entire retrofit.

'There's no point getting yourselfs worked up over nothing,' she said before wandering off.

'Over nothing!' Anna-Liisa barked unusually shrilly. 'I've spent my entire life weeding incorrect plural forms out of young people's mouths and this is the result!'

They looked at Anna-Liisa in astonishment. Generally, she didn't behave in this manner, no matter how much of a stickler she was for grammar. But Miisa Sievänen, who hadn't grasped that she was the object of Anna-Liisa's indignation, had already disappeared from view.

The Ambassador took his wife by the arm and gave her a tender smile: 'All right, Anneli, that's enough.'

'Don't you patronize me with your petting!' Anna-Liisa snapped, wrenching free of the Ambassador's grasp. This was rather worrisome. Siiri desperately tried to think of a new topic of conversation that would calm Anna-Liisa down, but her friend was off and running. She had moved on from irregular plural forms and was giving a detailed account of a plumbing retrofit she'd been subjected to in the 1970s. At the time, the whole building association had been provided with one pickle jar in the bicycle storage as a shared toilet, and Anna-Liisa had no intention of remaining at Sunset Grove to witness the resulting urinary free-for-all when the residents rolled down to the basement with their walkers to do their business in a pickle jar.

'Maybe they'll give us free diapers?' Irma suggested constructively, but Anna-Liisa paid no attention, and instead took her vexation out on the Ambassador.

'What about meals? What have you been planning on

eating when there's no water? Dried goods? Spelt straight from the jar?' Anna-Liisa shouted threateningly. She concluded her diatribe by stomping her healthier foot and shrieking hysterically, virtually in tears: 'Why don't you do something, Onni Rinta-Paakku?'

'I'll take you out to eat,' the Ambassador said soothingly, and he offered his wife his arm. The thus-mollified Anna-Liisa fixed her bun and straightened the hem of her blouse.

'What I'm trying to say is, we cannot live here during the plumbing retrofit,' she said, confining her rage to a quiet quiver in her otherwise melodic voice. Flames of fury no longer burned in her eyes, replaced by a fearful panic, and she clutched her husband's arm as if she were lost at sea and it were a life preserver. They started walking towards the canteen, which was nothing like a restaurant, but an unpleasant, brightly lit institutional room. There the residents sat at long, birch-veneer tables without saying a word, spooning porridge like children back when Finnish schools offered free breakfasts to all. At Sunset Grove, porridge was served for breakfast, lunch and bedtime snack, but rarely for dinner. At one point it had been accompanied by jam, but the jam had run out in April, and not even sugar had appeared in its stead. Director Sundström had taken the opportunity to enlighten her dissatisfied clients that sugar was unhealthy, one of the most common causes of death. And besides, the discretionary funds weren't sufficient to cover jam and other luxuries.

The old woman who had fallen was propped up in one of the lobby chairs, still confused, but they didn't wait around to see if an ambulance would deign to accept her as a passenger. Margit hurried off to her felting class, and Irma noted that the time had flown and she was already supposed to be at her cousin's for book club. Siiri was desperate for fresh air, and she tried to look busy even though no one was expecting her anywhere. She fetched her coat from her apartment because she didn't remember it was hot outside, and walked to the stop on Munkkiniemi Allée to wait for the number 4 tram. Wrapped in plastic, Sunset Grove gleamed in the sun and looked like a work of American art, quite handsome, actually. But the clank of the approaching tram drew her thoughts away from Sunset Grove and all of the unpleasantness, at least for a moment.

Chapter 4

'What's that? Gone off to the villa and left you here alone?'

Siiri couldn't believe her ears. Anna-Liisa seemed oddly unperturbed as she related this recent twist in her life, although she looked pale and grave. She must have been struggling to maintain a brave face.

'There are so many of his former wives and children there that I can't go. They'll look after Onni at the villa, and I'm sure he'll be much more comfortable there than here.'

Irma was burning with curiosity: 'How many of these former wives are there?'

But Anna-Liisa wasn't in the mood to answer. She simply snorted to indicate that the Ambassador's holiday was not an appealing topic of conversation and Irma might as well accept it.

Luckily, the card table was still in its place. The wall next to it was covered in plastic with a handy-looking zipper running down it. There was a hole in the wall, and the demolition crew kept stomping in and out through the zipper, forever interrupting Siiri's, Irma's, Anna-Liisa's and Margit's game. The big television in the common room was wrapped in plastic, the magazine racks and books had been taken away, and the residents had an impossible time finding any space for themselves in this madhouse. They were required to keep the doors to their apartments open, and the construction workers marched in and out, ripping out kitchen cabinets one day, measuring the placement of electricity outlets the next. Sometimes they simply spun around in the middle of the room, grumbled something that sounded like *Eugene Onegin*, and left.

'Like doctors!' Irma realized. 'The only difference being that these men walk in and out, while you have to crawl to the doctor's office yourself, no matter how old and sick you are. Why don't doctors here in Finland make house calls the way they do in France, where my cousin lives? Or like on British TV?'

More than once, lunch had been cancelled with less than two hours' notice. A note had simply appeared next to the elevators and in the corridors that read: *Lunch cancelled today, do too the retro fit.* Anna-Liisa had found temporary stimulation in these announcements, and, to Siiri's pleasure, held brief lectures on the appropriate use of commas and quotation marks, the confusion caused by misspellings, and the historical development of compound words. More often than not, these notes reached their intended recipients too late, after Sunset Grove's hunger-prodded residents had already shuffled down to the lobby to wonder where their food was. Sometimes Director Sinikka Sundström would make a personal appearance to apologize for the situation, but more often than not this thankless task fell to Pro Tem

Head of Residents Care Miisa Sievänen. She would inform them that lunch would be served as soon as the water was turned back on, in all likelihood 4 p.m., to which the hunch-backed veteran Tauno replied that only an idiot ate lunch an hour before his supper, especially when all that was being served was porridge. The pro tem head of residents care would pass out flyers for restaurants in the neighbourhood and the price lists for Helping Handz, a private home-care delivery service. While everyone understood that Director Sundström and Pro Tem Head Sievänen were not to blame for the unexpected water cuts, it was difficult to pull much good cheer out of one's positivity pouch, as the director had advised.

'So there I was in my birthday suit, with my hair lathered, when I realized there was no water coming out of the shower-head,' Margit told the others. Now that it was over, she was able to laugh at her tragedy, which had climaxed in two men in suits from the construction company marching into her apartment to measure the placement of the ventilation ducts. Margit had asked them to bring her water, but they had run off in terror.

'I must have looked frightful!' Margit howled, shaking her head. She'd had to sit and wait for two hours with the shampoo drying on her head before the shower started working again.

'And what do you think of these dry doo-doo boxes that our Jerry was advertising yesterday?' Irma asked.

'You cheated,' Anna-Liisa growled. She clearly saw Irma slip a card under her bottom.

'Aren't we playing cheat? We should play that one of these days, too; it's such a fun game. I always played it with my darlings when they were young. Oh, those were lovely times! Look, what an idiotic card I got. What would you have done with an ugly old king like this, if you had picked it up?'

'It fits your own canasta, Irma,' Anna-Liisa said tiredly. She was somehow listless and downcast, and it was no wonder. Siiri was so disturbed by the Ambassador's stunt, abandoning Anna-Liisa in the middle of the retrofit, that she had a hard time concentrating. What if things were steaming up between Onni and one of his ex-wives?

'They have running water and a toilet, too, beautiful tiles and everything,' Anna-Liisa sighed glumly. These were luxuries that residents of Sunset Grove could only wistfully long for.

'Are you ladies planning on taking the poop jars Irma was just talking about?' Siiri asked, to shift the conversation away from the Ambassador's villa. She hadn't been completely convinced by Jerry Siilinpää's animated presentation last Tuesday. Waxed locks quivering, the young man had introduced them to composting toilets meant for temporary use in urban settings, which he claimed were easy to use and didn't smell bad. Even emptying them was a 'piece of cake', which was why the residents would be privileged to take care of this operation themselves. Compared to the campground latrine Siilinpää was offering, the outhouse at any summer cabin sounded like the height of luxury.

'I don't suppose we have any choice? Or are you planning

on allowing yourself to become constipated?' Irma asked and told them about her cousin, who had gone ten days without defecating and was then taken to hospital for a rather laborious evacuation. 'So yes, I'd rather have a cat box in the corner. Isn't that one better than that pickle jar you had in the basement during the 1970s, Anna-Liisa? Anna-Liisa?'

Anna-Liisa's head had drooped, and her cards had slid to her lap. The other ladies panicked because Anna-Liisa looked sick, not sleepy. Siiri stood up and took hold of Anna-Liisa's wrist: a strong, rather rapid pulse. Siiri was relieved.

'She's not dead.'

'Is that supposed to be good news?' Margit asked, continuing to play, since it was her turn. 'I've been thinking quite a lot about euthanasia lately. What do you ladies think, should people be allowed to decide about their own death?'

'Heavenly days, you do ponder difficult questions in the middle of this chaos! Why would anyone bother doing retrofits if we all started killing each other during them? Or ourselves? Anna-Liisa, wake up before they shovel you into an ambulance and cart you off to the hospital!'

Irma had stood, and she and Siiri were able to shake Anna-Liisa enough to rouse her. She was still pale, and her eyes wandered for a moment, but then her usual stern gaze sparked in them again. At that instant, the zipper in the plastic wall opened and three angry-looking men marched past, carrying moving boxes.

Anna-Liisa was instantly on high alert. 'Who was that? They weren't wearing neon vests or coveralls. Those were not construction workers!'

Complete strangers had been tramping in and out of Sunset Grove with increasing frequency lately. It was impossible to say who was there to work and who was there to make off with the residents' belongings. Or medication. They had learned through the death of that sweet boy from the kitchen that their daily pills were valuable drugs.

'That Weasel Tail claimed that every employee would have a tag around his neck with his name on it. All their names should also be on some bulletin board,' Anna-Liisa griped. 'I've never laid eyes on any bulletin boards in this mess; we're drowning in packing plastic and tape here. It's like we're some ... some ... I don't know what. I don't suppose even chickens are stored vacuum-packed for months on end at a temperature of eighty degrees, are they?'

'His name is *Siilinpää*: Hedgehog Head, not Weasel Tail,' Siiri said. Having a chance to correct Anna-Liisa was a rare pleasure.

'Maybe broilers? Or chicks, in those incubators?' Irma suggested cheerfully. 'With the Ambassador vacationing at his luxury villa and all the other men dead, Sunset Grove has turned into quite the hen house. Cluck cluck!' Irma did a rather skilful chicken imitation, although crowing like a rooster was her bravura.

'A distinctly unproductive incubator, I'd say,' Anna-Liisa remarked leadenly, gathering up the cards that had fallen into her lap. Irma shouldn't have mentioned the Ambassador and his summer villa just when the sight of the suspicious visitors had perked Anna-Liisa up.

'Did you think those gentlemen with the boxes were thieves?' Siiri asked, to smooth things over.

'How should I know? They certainly didn't look like construction workers. Perhaps they were someone's relatives, although that seems far-fetched. No family members ever set foot in this place.'

'Not all the men are dead. Eino is alive,' Margit said abruptly. She had stopped playing and absent-mindedly slipped the cards she was holding into her handbag.

'Margit, those are my cards!' Siiri cried.

'Eino is in a dementia ward somewhere in eastern Helsinki. All residents of the Sunset Grove nursing unit were moved there. If anyone's in storage, it's him, not us. I don't remember the name of the place, it was some sort of home too, or even a nest . . . wait, the SquirrelsNest, all one word, capital S, capital N.'

Anna-Liisa shrieked in horror.

'I've only been to visit Eino once, and that time I went by taxi. But I can't be taking a taxi back and forth to Itäkeskus every week. Maybe it's best I don't go, it's so sad . . . Oh dear, here I go, crying again . . . I'm sorry . . . it's such an awful thing to see, when the love of your life is unrecognizable and helpless . . . Dirty, too, and smells foul; I have a hard time bringing myself to get close, and I don't know what to do with myself while I'm sitting there at his bedside, but I have a bad conscience all the time since I haven't been to see him . . .'

Siiri hugged Margit, who trembled as she sobbed. Irma urgently searched for her lace handkerchief, and no one knew what to say. Was this what had been on Margit's mind when she brought up euthanasia? That Eino would be better off dead? Perhaps she hadn't been talking about herself or the rest of them; they still had their health and their marbles and had the gall to complain about a retrofit while others had no hope. Siiri was ashamed of her stupidity. And yet it still chagrined her that Margit had pilfered part of her deck. Would she ever get the missing cards back? Once again, Irma read her mind.

'We can play cheat with an incomplete deck; you don't need all the cards for that,' she whispered as she gathered up the remaining cards. 'All right, my chicks, where were you planning on eating lunch today? What if we all went to the Sunset Grove canteen in honour of the fact that it happens to be open? Or have you all ordered meal delivery? My darlings tell me that it's scandalously expensive, but since they don't have time to bring me food, they paid for it for me. Treated me, the loves. Which was very sweet of them; they didn't need to do that, seeing as how I have quite a nice pension. My widow's pension and the various funds Veikko set up for me with an eye to old age, the sweetheart. He was such a good man, of high ethical calibre. Oh dear, how I miss my Veikko! My sweetheart lying there in his grave, I mean in that miserable urn behind that marble slab. That's where I'll end up, too. I'm sorry, I shouldn't mourn selfishly like this; Margit's situation is much sadder, since her husband is still alive. But we could go to the French restaurant on Laajalahdentie for lunch one day, couldn't we? We have to make sure we stay stimulated; we don't want to rot away here like boneless chicken breasts from the Low Price Market. They're vacuum-packed, aren't they? Have you ever noticed the unpleasant smell that wafts out when you open the package? I'd already thrown several in the bin because I thought the meat was spoiled, until finally I had the nerve to take the package back to the store. I complained that they were selling spoiled meat, and that's when I learned that it was the packaging gas, nitrogen or something, they say it's harmless but keeps meat from rotting. Is that what they're pumping in here too? Jerry explained that the dust won't get everywhere, because they're going to use a vacuum or something to underpressurize the entire building. Did you catch what he meant by "underpressurizing"?'

'Unpressurization is a technique that creates an air-pressure difference between a sealed space and the surrounding environment,' Anna-Liisa said, with a promising correction of posture. 'An air pump directs the air out of the room under construction through a hose, or so-called sock, creating a difference in air pressure; this exiting air travels through a filter that collects impurities. This purified air is then blown outside the sealed space, in other words here, where we spend our days. Of course this doesn't imply that we won't suffer from dust at all. I'm not nearly as concerned about televisions and our other plastic-wrapped belongings as I am about risks to our health. Cement dust is exceptionally fine and exposure to it entails a substantial risk of contracting lifelong asthma.'

Irma perked up as if she were already writing a complaint to the Loving Care Foundation, which ran Sunset Grove:

'Yes! Asbestos is life-threatening, and at the beginning of the retrofit Siilinpää said something about asbestos. What did he say?'

'I just remember him talking about action items and drawing arrows,' Siiri said.

Margit had stopped bawling and had pulled herself together. 'Maybe I should bring Eino here. I wonder if life-threatening dust would be the simplest solution to everything?'

'Lifelong asthma, is that what you said? I doubt anyone considers that much of a risk when the victims are over ninety. But can you die of asthma? Is that the opportunity Director Sundström and Jerry Siilinpää were lecturing about? *Döden, döden, döden.*'

'Not everyone here is as old as we are,' Siiri said. 'That tattooed lady doctor lowers the average age quite a bit.'

'Why does she have that ugly needlepoint all over her body? She's a beautiful woman, but she has an anchor on her neck and snakes on her shoulder; it gives me the heebie-jeebies.'

'Perhaps she likes anchors and snakes.'

'Could we please finish discussing the dust?' Anna-Liisa smacked both hands against the baize tabletop and looked at her friends, her dark eyes flashing. 'Has anyone else had a constant cough and intermittent trouble breathing? Sometimes I cough so much at night that I can't get any sleep. There's no doubt in my mind it's because of this retrofit, and that's why I made myself an appointment at the health centre tomorrow. If they find asthma, I am going to hold Sunset Grove responsible.'

'And you might die!' Irma cried, coughing before she could laugh. Suddenly all their throats prickled. First Irma started coughing, then Margit, then Anna-Liisa, and eventually Siiri. They coughed so hard that their throats ached. This was, of course, rather amusing, and a moment later their choral coughing had devolved into giddy guffaws that perplexed the men marching past with the moving boxes.

'These old bats aren't playing with a full deck,' the first one said.

'So much the better for us,' his companion muttered, picking up the pace.

Chapter 5

The city's decision to change the number 3T tram into the number 2 and the number 3B into the number 3, or whichever way it went, was utterly absurd. It wasn't going to make things the least bit easier for anyone. The routes remained as confusing as ever, and the drivers still had to change the numbers displayed on their trams at the Eläintarha and Kaivopuisto stops. Besides, like all long-term Helsinki residents, Siiri remembered that the number 2 once ran from Pasila to Kruununhaka and before that from Kallio to Töölö, but never, ever to Kaivopuisto. But that's the way life was: perpetual change. Siiri had read in the paper that companies reorganized every year, too, and there had been a lot of talk on the radio about constant change and lifelong learning. Evidently, not being able to get used to anything or count on anything kept you on your toes. And it was true, too. Siiri might never have boarded the number 2 tram on Aleksanterinkatu if she had thought it was an old number 3T. But the numeral 2 had blazed so dazzlingly on the front of the tram that Siiri couldn't resist hopping on.

It was empty and, thus, a little dull, as was often the case in trams during early summer, when the schoolchildren had started their vacations and the tourists hadn't arrived in Helsinki yet, to scratch their heads as they asked where to find the architect Alvar Aalto's office and the monument to the composer Jean Sibelius. Siiri felt sorry for travellers who'd been blown off course to her little town. There was nothing for them to do but gawk at an ugly church carved into a rock that didn't contain a single painting or work of art, stand at the Sibelius Monument in the rain, and hunt for the world-renowned architect's combined home and office. This last attraction was in bad shape and looked like a normal, poorly maintained home, actually rather small, because nowadays people lived in enormous glass fortresses. They wandered through them in solitude with all the lights burning, like terrarium lizards, not giving a hoot who saw what they were watching on TV in their sweatpants. There were such buildings in Siiri's neighbourhood, too, and Margit knew that the shores of Espoo, the wealthy suburb right across the bay, were chock-full of them. If you went walking on the ice in the wintertime, you got a living exhibition of Espoo family life. Compared to them, Alvar Aalto's office was modest indeed.

It was no wonder that most tourists didn't even bother to spend the night in Helsinki. Siiri was happy to while away a moment or two chatting with Japanese and American visitors after pointing them in the direction of Alvar Aalto's studio. One Philadelphia couple in sun visors and trainers had explained to her that nowadays they spent their lives crisscrossing the world. It was their second time in Helsinki, and also the second time they'd seen the rock church with the funny round copper roof. They called it 'the wok'. Their cruise ship was like a retirement home; it had gyms, swimming pools, spas, cleaning staff, hair salons, laundries, restaurants and medical services. They even played bingo and showed movies. Apparently, there weren't enough assisted living centres for the elderly in the United States of America, and the few that existed were so expensive that the couple had solved their problem – old age, that is – by moving onto a cruise ship. Which couldn't have been sensible or affordable. But then again, neither was life at Sunset Grove.

She decided not to change to a number 4 at the new opera house for the ride to Sunset Grove; instead, she continued on to Nordenskiöldinkatu and waited to see if some interesting outpatient would climb on at the Aurora Hospital stop. Occasionally, a more or less disturbing lunatic would board at the psychiatric hospital, but as a rule Siiri felt safe in the tram. There were always other passengers, and the driver could use the radio to call for help. Siiri had witnessed the efficiency of this system: one time a man had started arguing volubly with himself and been picked up by the police at the stop agreed on with the driver. It hadn't taken more than a few words on the radio. Voila, it worked like a charm, as Irma would have said.

At the Aurora Hospital stop, a young woman with green hair boarded and sat next to Siiri. The girl had covered herself in tattoos of flames and roses and was wearing an undershirt with an unsewn hem. Threads from the fraying fabric fell onto the girl's black trousers; an orange bra blazed beneath her undershirt.

'Nah, two,' the girl said, apparently into her phone, although Siiri could see no sign of the gadget, only a pair of earphones in her ears. But here she was, talking to herself as if she were talking to someone. This wasn't a sign of insanity these days; a lot of people did it. 'Totally fucking lame. One was like a one-bedroom, the location was OK, but the fucking kitchen was so fucking shitty. Brown fucking cabinets and just two fucking burners and the tiles were, I dunno, like fucking turquoise or something. I mean, please, fucking turquoise, like from the fucking nineties or something. I was like, this can't be fucking real. Fucking old-lady tiles. The owner says they're not going to do any fucking remodelling, so we'd have to fucking pay for it. Dad's never going to fucking go for it.'

Siiri pricked up her ears. Apparently, the girl was looking for an apartment and was having trouble finding one she liked. Did it really come down to the splashback tiles? Perhaps the rent was also too high but the girl didn't want to let on to her friend, which was why she talked about the ugly colours in the kitchen. The second apartment was too small, only thirty-eight square metres and too far, somewhere in Munkkivuori, not much more than a mile from downtown. Perhaps the girl didn't know Helsinki that well? Perhaps she was a student and just moving to the city. Siiri's mother had always had girl students renting out her extra rooms. It had been a mutually beneficial relationship: the girls gave her mother a hand and kept her company in the evenings and her mother didn't have to move into an old folks' home to suffer from loneliness.

'Isn't subletting done any more?' Siiri asked the green-haired girl, after she ended her call. The girl didn't know what subletting meant. She was from Nurmijärvi and had got into the practical nursing programme and there was no way she was going to travel twenty miles on a bus to college.

'I'd have to wake up at, like, fucking six in the morning every fucking day,' the girl said, smiling prettily. She had a metal hoop in her cheek and three bits of tin in each eyebrow. Siiri reflected that if she were still alive in a couple of years when the girl finished her schooling, the girl might well end up being her nurse at Sunset Grove.

'Umm, I . . . was planning on fucking specializing in, like . . . kids . . .'

'We have to wake up at six every morning,' Siiri said.

The girl looked horrified. 'What the fuck for?'

'We're having a plumbing retrofit. The workers fire up their drills at six in the morning, and once they do, you're wide awake, no matter what sort of sleeping aids you take.'

'Why don't you guys fucking move the fuck out of there?' the girl asked sensibly, eyes wide. She had drawn thick black lines that framed her eyes rather adorably, actually; she looked like a cute cartoon character. Siiri explained that moving wasn't easy. They would have to find a temporary place to stay and those were horribly expensive. And at her age, just the thought of moving felt exhausting – even more exhausting than a plumbing retrofit.

'But how can students such as yourself afford to live in

Helsinki these days? Rents are so high. Don't you have dormitories?'

'The fucking lines for them are fucking insane. I want to fucking move to Helsinki now, not in like fucking October or something,' the girl explained. 'Some friends and I might move into a fucking *kimppakämppä* together.'

'I'm sorry? What's that?'

'It's like a fucking commune. We rent some big fucking random apartment downtown and live there. It's a lot fucking cheaper than everyone living in some fucking studio apartment out in Munkkivuori.'

'That sounds like a good solution. And I'm sure it's more fun living with your friends than alone . . . out in the suburbs somewhere.'

'Exactly. Fuck.' The girl flashed a pretty smile, stood and bounded from the tram without saying goodbye. She vanished into the hubbub of the parking lot at the Linnanmäki theme park, where families from the countryside hunted for parking meters while trying to keep their herds of children under control. Siiri gazed across the street at the Alppila parish centre. The streamlined white functionalist building was right where it was supposed to be, more beautiful and serene than ever after a recent paint job. Unfortunately, someone had immediately added a troll face to the wall; not half-bad actually, with masterful use of colours and meticulous shading. Siiri knew that such trolls weren't *vandalism*, they were *graffiti*.

The tram stood at the amusement park stop for a long time, because swarms of passengers were boarding, including parents trying to squeeze strollers into the spots intended for them. A group of Somali women with three strollers filled the middle platform in the first tram car. A flushed, over-weight Finnish father refused to wait for the next tram. He forced his stroller into the aisle, despite the driver's announce-ments that this was not allowed: the aisles had to be kept clear. The flushed man started shouting vulgarities about immigrants and infidels. Siiri was mortified, and she was afraid the man's child would be scared by his father's sudden tantrum, but the boy was so calm and content, coolly shovel-ling candyfloss into his face with sticky hands, that this couldn't be the first time his father had caused a public scene. The Somali families apologetically climbed off the tram with their strollers while the man beamed victoriously. His too-tight T-shirt was emblazoned with a lion brandishing a sword, a variation of Finland's coat of arms. Siiri looked at the women in headscarves and at their children, whom there was no room for in a half-empty tram on a beautiful summer day. She felt like hurrying off, because a pall had fallen over the tram, but the driver sped off before he even closed the doors.

A lot of other passengers disembarked at the Brahen-kenttä stop with Siiri. She walked to the number 8 stop on Helsinginkatu and changed to a number 4 at the new opera house. She felt badly about what she had witnessed and above all that she couldn't stop thinking about this incident she had played no part in. Should she have intervened? How come no one stood up for the Somali women? Suddenly, Siiri realized she was partially responsible for the horrible way the refugees had been treated. Everyone who allowed such foolishness was complicit in it. How had she grown so passive and lazy? Could it be because of the plumbing retrofit? It wasn't easy living in an apartment where there was a hole in one's bathroom wall big enough for a full-grown man to walk through from her neighbour's apartment, even when that neighbour was her dear friend Irma.

And then there was Anna-Liisa with her weak nerves. The remodel seemed to be hitting her the hardest, and on top of everything the Ambassador had the nerve to abandon her to the chaos while he went off to be pampered by other women. Siiri thought about the sweet, green-haired girl with the filthy mouth who was looking for a commune downtown. Could that be the solution to their problems, too? Perhaps she should put an end to her aimless, exhausted drifting along tram routes, stop being ineffectual, and take action. That was it: she was going to find a home in one of Helsinki's lovely old buildings for all of them to share!

Chapter 6

Siiri and Irma had brought Anna-Liisa to the French restaurant on Laajalahdentie to take her mind off things. The place always had a lot of customers speaking French or Swedish, and the cuisine was unfussy and delicious. On warm days like today, the big windows were thrown open and people were eating al fresco. For Siiri and Irma and Anna-Liisa, it was as atmospheric as being in a real metropolis, such as the foreign cities they'd got a taste of on television back before their televisions at Sunset Grove had been shrink-wrapped in plastic.

'I do miss my Hercule Poirot,' Siiri sighed.

'You can always read the stories instead,' Anna-Liisa pointed out.

'Oh, it's not at all the same. They're rather childish books, but when they show those lovely cars and clothes and houses from the thirties – oh, I just love it. Anyway, I haven't read in weeks, not since I packed my books into boxes like Weasel Ears told us to. Those Latvian fellows stacked the boxes into a tower in the middle of my bedroom. There's no way I could dig a book out, no matter how badly I felt like reading. I don't dare touch the teetering thing, I'm terrified it will topple over.'

The chaos of the renovation had prevented Anna-Liisa from reading her favourite books, too. A pervasive, anxious emptiness washed over her. She pressed her clenched fists to her chest so that Siiri and Irma would understand just how acute the sensation was.

'I borrowed Sillanpää's *The Misery of the Meek* from the library last week, but even that did nothing to lift my spirits. My personal library has been packed up in Onni's shipping containers and hauled . . . hauled off somewhere. It was a horrendous undertaking. My arms and back ached for days; I had to take pain medication morning and night. I even went to the doctor, but it was one of those outsourced ones, dark-skinned, and he didn't understand a word of what I was saying when I explained to him the health risks resulting from the retrofit, even though I tried to use as many Latin terms as possible. And then he gave me pain medication, the kind you can buy without a prescription. It was an atrocious misuse of a doctor's professional skills. I was downright ashamed for him.'

'Admit it, Siiri, you love the way that actor with the dark eyes smiles. David Suchet. Did you notice, I remembered his name! Did you know he clenches a coin between his but-tocks to create the waddle Christie described in her books?'

'I see we weren't able to enjoy many spoonfuls of soup before Irma steered the conversation to the glutei maximi,' Anna-Liisa sighed, lowering her spoon. She looked pale and frail; sweat was streaming down her temples, and she was breathing heavily. Irma and Siiri couldn't understand how the Ambassador could be recuperating at the villa surrounded by a bevy of women without giving a thought to his wife, who was wilting from retrofit-induced asthma or heatstroke like a delicate stalk of grass. As her last name Petäjä indicated, Anna-Liisa had always been as stout and strong as an old pine tree.

'When is the Ambass— when is Onni coming back to town?' Siiri asked, trying to sound casual.

Anna-Liisa didn't reply. Instead, she shook her head slowly and at length, coughed with some effort, and cast a disgusted eye over the French onion soup, which Siiri thought was delicious: topped with a perfect crust and heaps of melted cheese, which stretched and stretched and made eating a little messy. Of course Irma had to announce that onions gave her gas.

'It doesn't bother me, though; I've always got some flatulence brewing in my stomach. I've learned that if I press from the left here under my pancreas, it lets out a big, lovely fart. And if I lift the opposite cheek a little, it doesn't make much noise, if any, and no one is the wiser.'

'Someone made off with all my jewellery. Except this wedding ring Onni gave me,' Anna-Liisa said, gazing at the diamond ring sparkling on her left hand.

'I knew those men without neon vests were crooks!' Irma cried, as if overjoyed by the news of Anna-Liisa's latest troubles.

Siiri and Irma had known that Anna-Liisa owned a considerable amount of valuable jewellery. She had kept it in a beautiful mahogany box on her bookshelf: gold necklaces, strings of pearls, a cameo brooch, a diamond pendant, several big bracelets, a silver medallion, and a few medals from the war. After the books and the other belongings had been carted off to the fields of Vantaa, the jewellery box had apparently stood enticingly on the shelf alone, and Anna-Liisa was vexed that she hadn't hidden it in time. It had crossed her mind more than once to conceal her miniature treasure chest from greedy eyes. And, this morning, it was gone.

'As you know, I don't normally wear jewellery. And since we never have any formal events other than funerals, I didn't miss the box or its contents – some of my jewellery is very valuable indeed. The robbery could have occurred at any point during the retrofit, although I only discovered it today.'

'It's been such a long time since we've had a funeral to attend. Who was the last one who died? For the life of me I can't remember. *Döden, döden, döden.*'

Irma was such an inquisitive and social soul that she loved funerals. She always enjoyed herself at them; they gave her a chance to meet people and listen to beautiful music. The refreshments were generally above par, too.

'Is it improper to wear jewellery to a funeral? I always put on my long string of pearls. I think they look nice with the black without being too showy,' Siiri said.

'Oh but you can't go to a funeral with no jewellery! I'd feel as naked as a jaybird without my diamonds.'

'I'm talking about a theft, and you two are babbling on

about funerals. Don't you understand: I've been robbed! A chest full of valuables has been stolen from me, and you're pondering appropriate funeral attire!' Anna-Liisa shouted in an alarmingly loud voice, and her demeanour was so threatening that Siiri felt sorry for all the children who'd had Anna-Liisa as a teacher. Three men in suits at the neighbouring table turned to look at them, and the young woman sitting on their other side stopped breastfeeding long enough to cause her baby to start to shriek. But Anna-Liisa didn't allow the curiosity of others to impinge on her outrage.

Irma was brimming with enthusiasm: 'You have to report it to the police!' She knew you could file a report on the Internet and so dug her green gadget out of her handbag right then and there. Siiri would have preferred to finish her meal in peace and to enjoy her French onion soup, now that it had finally cooled off and she could sever the strands of cheese neatly with her front teeth.

'These are my own teeth. Just think: that's something I ought to be grateful for. So many people at Sunset Grove have dentures, and some of them are so fancy that they look unnatural. You both still have your own teeth, too, don't you?'

'Yes, Siiri dear, my teeth are my own. Don't distract me while I'm surfing. This won't take a minute. You can slurp up your soup with your healthy teeth while we shoot off this report. Look, I'm already at the police station! "Report a misdemeanour electronically"; that sounds like what we want. Do you remember your social security number, Anna-Liisa?'

Anna-Liisa didn't. This was slightly perplexing.

'When's your birthday, Anna-Liisa?' Now Siiri felt silly; she couldn't remember the last time they'd celebrated Anna-Liisa's birthday either. Was it in the wintertime? Wasn't Anna-Liisa a little younger than she was? Born in 1919, perhaps? The more she thought about this utterly uncomplicated matter, the more garbled her memory of it grew. And Anna-Liisa's mind was a complete blank. Siiri's throat was dry and she felt an unpleasant ache in her chest.

'Matriculation . . . preliminary examinations . . .'

Was Anna-Liisa trying to remember the year she matriculated from high school? Siiri was so stunned that she couldn't even remember what year she had graduated in. It was definitely before the wars, but when?

'Argh, forget about birthdays and graduations. This is asking for some sort of dratted security confirmation. What on earth could that be? "Use mobile confirmation, a banking code, or security confirmation". Whatever will they think of next, the idiots!' Irma jabbed a finger at the picture of a phone and was pleasantly surprised: 'My phone number, that will work! I just have to enter it in that little box. Oh dear, what was it again?'

Siiri panicked when she realized that Anna-Liisa couldn't remember her birthday and Irma couldn't remember her phone number. She forced herself to drink down several gulps of water and finish her soup. The hammering in her head eased off a little; perhaps it had just been the hunger and the heat. It was particularly important to remember to drink lots of fluids on hot summer days. She filled their glasses – perhaps the others would take the hint and drink, too – and forced down one last glass of water while silently repeating her own birthday and phone number to herself. She had no trouble remembering either one. Just to be sure, she recited her bank account number, address, the names and birthdays of all her children as well as the dates of her sons' and husband's deaths. At least her memory was working, but that wasn't going to do Irma and Anna-Liisa much good.

'Maybe we'll file a report later; my soup is getting cold. It says here you can also do it by phone. You can call the police as soon as you get back to your apartment, Anna-Liisa. Can't you? Anna-Liisa?'

Anna-Liisa had a ferocious coughing fit and stood up. She pounded her chest dully and hacked nastily. Just when they thought she was choking, the coughing stopped, and Anna-Liisa started looking around for her cane, which she already had in her hand.

'I must go and correct my preliminary examinations. The students will want them before the weekend.'

And then she strode off briskly and rather resolutely, without saying goodbye to her friends or paying her share of the bill. Irma and Siiri were shocked. Would Anna-Liisa be the next one to lose her marbles? Siiri looked at her now-cold onion soup, stunned, and felt both an unpleasant lurching in her stomach and a dreadful dizziness in her head.

'We have to get in touch with the Ambassador,' Irma said firmly. They didn't have his phone number, but both of them were under the impression that he owned a mobile phone; he probably had it with him at the villa. Siiri thought

Rinta-Paakku was such a rare surname that they'd have no trouble finding him in the phone book, and before she could squeal, Irma had pulled out her tablet and was asking it for the Ambassador's phone number. But the contraption either didn't know or wasn't working; Irma claimed it was because she didn't have the proper apps, and Siiri started feeling dizzy again. She drank one more glass of water, cursed the restaurant's tiny water glasses, and stood to leave.

'We have to go after her. How did we let her fly off like that on her own to correct compositions? What if she gets lost?'

'Nonsense; it's a two-block walk straight down Perustie.'

They hurried to the corner and could see from a distance that an ambulance was parked in front of Sunset Grove, next to the construction-waste container, rubbish compactor and cement mixer. The ambulance's doors slammed shut and it drove off towards Huopalahdentie. Siiri and Irma stood there amid the detritus of Sunset Grove, beside themselves with worry; there wasn't a soul in sight they could ask about the emergency vehicle's passenger and destination. They made their way to the apartment Anna-Liisa and the Ambassador shared on the fourth floor of C wing, rang the doorbell, and stepped in, as all doors were kept open during the retrofit.

'Cock-a-doodle-doo!' Irma crowed.

An angry-looking, helmeted head appeared at the bedroom doorway. 'What do you want?' he asked. He was carrying a measuring tape and a large gym bag.

'Wonderful – you speak Finnish. We're looking for Anna-

Liisa Petäjä. She lives in this unit, but we're not sure about her health. Someone was just driven off in an ambulance, and we started getting worried that it might have been Anna-Liisa. Do you happen to know where she is?'

The man didn't know and didn't want to know. He began to shoo Siiri and Irma out of the apartment, because private premises were off-limits to outsiders. He wasn't wearing construction coveralls or the name tag all employees were supposed to wear, just a neon vest over his grey suit, and he explained that he was a project architect conducting a routine inspection. He stared, dumbfounded, as Irma wondered why construction workers had to wear helmets while wandering through Sunset Grove, but residents didn't have to protect themselves from danger.

'Are you afraid the ceiling's going to come crashing down, seeing as how you're wearing that funny helmet indoors? It did happen, you know, in Tauno's apartment, and he said that it was more frightening than the grenades exploding at the Battle of Ihantala. Perhaps you've met Tauno? He's a bit hunched and waves his arms, like this, to keep from falling over.'

The project architect was a man of few words; he refused to comment on Tauno's collapsed ceiling. He was oddly agitated and demanded that Siiri and Irma leave. As he pushed them out into the corridor, Siiri spotted a beautiful mahogany container on the kitchen table; it had to be Anna-Liisa's missing jewellery box. She picked it up for safekeeping, but when she did, the project architect cursed and tried to snatch it out of Siiri's hands.

'How dare you, you impudent scoundrel, let go of me! You are not going to butt into my affairs, you . . . you inspection expert,' Siiri shouted, clenching the jewellery box to her chest. 'This is my dear friend Anna-Liisa's prized jewellery box, and she's afraid one of you is going to steal it.'

Irma encouraged Siiri: 'Yes, better us than you!'

The project architect let them leave, taking the jewellery box with them, and went back to his measurements in Anna-Liisa's and the Ambassador's apartment. They didn't understand why he was carrying such a large bag if all he was doing was inspecting the place.

'Anna-Liisa was right, that man is the thief,' Irma said. 'He was going to take the jewellery box, and that's why he got so upset.'

'Don't be silly, we're the thieves here,' Siiri laughed, as they scurried to the elevator.

The common room was eerily still. Its lone occupant, the tattooed doctor, was fanning herself in the corner where they used to read newspapers and magazines. Subscriptions had been cancelled for the duration of the retrofit as a cost-cutting measure, Director Sundström had explained. It was as if she were trying to smoke out the last of Sunset Grove's tenacious tenants.

'Damn, it's hot,' the tattooed doctor said. Siiri noticed that she had a picture of a skull on her left breast. It showed through her flimsy summer blouse, which looked like an undershirt.

'Have you been sitting here long? Did you happen to see who just rode off in the ambulance?'

'It was that sour old lovebird, your friend, the know-it-all who looks like a skeleton. What's her name?'

'Anna-Liisa! Poor Anna-Liisa!' Siiri cried, lifting a hand to her forehead. She gasped for breath and felt a shooting pain on the right side of her head. She had seated herself next to this unpleasant new neighbour and lowered Anna-Liisa's jewellery box to the empty magazine rack. She listened in alarm to see if her heart had stopped. She couldn't hear anything under her breathing and felt her wrist for a pulse. Her heart was beating far too rapidly, but at a good rhythm, steadily. Her decrepit circulatory channels were doing their best.

'Hello, I'm Irma Lännenleimu, I don't believe we've ever introduced ourselves; generally, no one does around here. People come and go, and no one knows anyone's name. My friend here is Siiri Kettunen; I believe we're Sunset Grove's longest-term residents now.'

'Ritva Lahtinen.' The doctor didn't extend a hand, she just kept fanning herself. 'You wanna join me for a pint at the Ukko-Munkki?'

'Not today, thanks,' Irma said with a friendly smile, as if she were in the habit of drinking enormous pints of beer at the local pub, but the idea didn't strike her fancy at the moment. 'Do you happen to know where we might find Anna-Liisa?'

The woman stood and slipped the fan into the back pocket of her jeans. Siiri mused that Ritva Lahtinen must be the first resident of Sunset Grove who wore jeans. Siiri had never owned a pair herself. They must have been hot in summer weather like this; no wonder the sweat was dripping from Ritva Lahtinen's face. Her hair looked wet, too, as if she had just stepped out of the shower, which was an impossibility, because the water had been cut off since last night. The throbbing in Siiri's head had subsided and her heart had steadied, but her throat was prickling unpleasantly. Could it be an asthmatic reaction to all the asbestos dust? Perhaps Ritva could tell them more about asthma symptoms; after all, she was a doctor, jeans or no. Siiri looked on tiredly as Irma followed the tattooed doctor for a few paces without getting the tiniest assistance in tracking down Anna-Liisa. Instead, Ritva lambasted the health-care system in a few sharp, vulgarity-punctuated sentences, said she'd been a medical examiner because the best patient was a dead patient, and headed out for her pint.

Chapter 7

Siiri had spent several days riding trams aimlessly, racking her brains trying to think of ways to escape the purgatory of the retrofit. They still didn't know what had happened to Anna-Liisa, and Margit didn't seem to be dealing well with the abnormal conditions, either. Nor was there any counting on the Ambassador; if the worst came to the worst, he would never return to Anna-Liisa.

'For all we know, he's not even at the villa. Maybe he has a new mistress!' Irma said, as they were eating liver casserole which tasted a bit suspect and drinking cheap red wine.

'You're kidding, aren't you?' Siiri asked in disbelief.

Irma laughed gaily and drained her glass. 'Do you know what the best thing about a plumbing retrofit is? You absolutely have to drink red wine, because there's no water in the taps,' she said, and she reached over to pour herself another glass from the wine box. 'This tap never goes dry.'

A thought had been growing on Siiri ever since her encounter with the green-haired girl, and now she decided to test the waters: 'What if we moved into a commune?'

'What are you babbling about?' Irma said. It was a

relatively quiet moment; all they could hear was a faint pounding from upstairs and an unidentifiable buzzing from the other side of the wall. It was stifling indoors, and they were sitting in nothing but their nightshirts. Irma had unbuttoned hers. 'You're suggesting we become communists? Workers at a cabbage kombinat, goat herds at some kolkhoz?'

'No, Irma,' Siiri said gently, because she felt confident that her idea was a good one. 'A commune means we live in the same apartment.'

'Nonsense. Anna-Liisa and the Ambassador live together; you're saying their home is a commune?'

'They're a married couple. But if – single widows like you and me or, say, Margit, who, for all intents and purposes is a widow, although Eino is curled up in some nest somewhere – if we rented an apartment together, that would be a commune.'

'I suppose we already live in a commune, since a hole the size of grown man is connecting our apartments now. They could knock a hole in this outer wall, too; this heat is draining. Whew. You're not losing your appetite, are you, with my nightshirt unbuttoned all the way?'

Siiri told Irma that the girl in the tram had said life was fun and cheap when solitary people lived together, and that there were a lot of big apartments available for rent downtown. Unlike Irma, Siiri always read the real estate classifieds, because she was interested in architecture, and lately she'd noticed that nice units were available for rent nearly every day.

'You never know what sort of condition the apartments

are in, but we're probably not too fussy about the colour of the kitchen cupboards.'

'Goodness, we'd be fine anywhere!' Irma exclaimed. 'You'd be hard pressed to find anything worse in this heat than this shrink-wrapped retirement home. Where would you like to move? Töölö? I'd love to die in Töölö.'

Like everyone who oohed and aahed over Töölö, Irma was referring to inner Töölö. As far as she was concerned, outer Töölö was the sticks. But Siiri knew the flats in inner Töölö were overpriced, there wasn't much in the way of services, and the lone tram line ran down Runeberginkatu. Her curiosity about Punavuori had been piqued, and since Irma had also praised the neighbourhood's old buildings, that was what she now suggested.

'There's a showing at an enormous apartment on Pursimiehenkatu today,' she said, looking mysterious as she pulled a classified ad out of her handbag.

'"Traditional floorplan for demanding tastes or a larger family",' Irma read, and shook her head. 'This sounds fishy to me. What does "demanding tastes" mean? Are you thinking you plus me makes a larger family? Do we have to bring Margit along so our family will be large enough? She's so gloomy these days. Or were you planning on starting to entertain and to throw tea and Tupperware parties?'

Siiri sighed. Irma's momentary enthusiasm had got her hopes up. The classified ads were full of codes you needed to know how to decipher. *A larger family* meant that the apartment had lots of bedrooms, just like they needed. A *traditional floorplan* indicated a big living room and hall or other common spaces, which would come in handy if the bedrooms were small.

'Open house Sunday two to four p.m. by owner. That means there's no agency involved.'

'Hm. Well – what are we waiting for?' Irma said, licking the lingonberry jam from her plate. 'What tram do we take to get there? Or should we hop in a cab?'

They took the number 4 to the National Museum, where they switched to a number 10 and rumbled on. They walked down Merimiehenkatu, past the old boys' grammar school to the intersection known as Five Points. There they came to an old building, from the late 1800s, with arched windows on two storeys and a tower at the end. Siiri opened the heavy door to the dark stairwell. The first thing she noticed was that there was no elevator.

'At least we'll get a little exercise.'

'They could have mentioned it in the ad,' Irma panted, as they caught their breath on the second-storey landing. 'There must be some code for "no elevator", too.'

'I think the code is not saying anything about it. Generally, they mention an elevator if there is one in the building.'

A pair of gorgeous wooden double doors was open to the corridor, and Irma and Siiri stepped through, out of breath. The flat's entry hall was tall and spacious, and Irma crowed out a passage from the Queen of the Night's aria to test the acoustics. Just then, a heavily made-up woman stepped into the hall in red high heels, a tight sheath dress, and peroxided hair.

'Linda af Nyborg-Jussila,' she said by way of introduction, eyeing Irma and Siiri in distaste. Perhaps she hadn't anticipated two old women being interested in a traditionally laid-out home for demanding tastes. 'If you don't mind slipping covers over your shoes,' she said, pointing at a heap of blue plastic slippers in the corner. Siiri and Irma bent down to pick up the covers and spun around in confusion, looking for something to sit on while they slipped into their indoor galoshes. Madam af Nyborg-Jussila glanced around nervously and fetched a stool from somewhere.

'Please have a seat.'

Pulling the shower caps over their shoes was hard work, but to their astonishment Linda af Nyborg-Jussila squatted down to help them, and managed to do so without her dress splitting at the seams, no matter how uncomfortable the crouched position seemed. When this operation was complete, Siiri held out her hand.

'Siiri Kettunen, hello, and this here is my friend Irma Lännenleimu. We're looking for a temporary rental and saw your advertisement in the newspaper. Are you the owner?' Siiri asked, but Irma was so enthusiastic that she interjected before the woman could answer.

'Are you related to Ketty Viitakoski, by chance? She's a Nyborg by birth, the better side of the family, the counts or what have you, and Ketty was my classmate, but I'm not sure if she's still alive. She doesn't generally come to our class reunions. We have a reunion on the first Wednesday of the month, and the only ones left are a few doddering old ladies and me. I seem to remember Ketty being very ill several years ago, and now she's lying in some *konservatorio* for the Swedish-speaking elderly, if you understand my little play on words – or are you perhaps a Swedish-speaker yourself? I remember Ketty saying—'

'No relation. Which one of you was thinking about renting the place?'

'Both of us! And we might bring a few friends along, too. There's a plumbing retrofit at our retirement home at the moment, and although Director Sundström insists that the renovation is dust-free and noiseless and perfectly feasible to live through, we're gradually starting to lose our patience. The workers are completely unprofessional. Our neighbour's kitchen ceiling came crashing down yesterday, can you imagine? The plaster hit the floor so suddenly that poor Mr Tauno nearly had a heart attack, which, of course, would have been a happy event, because that's what we're all hoping for there, a massive heart attack that will kill us at once, so we don't have to worry about ending up in the clutches of Alzheimer's. On top of all that, there's been damage to the residents' property and now they're threatening to turn off the electricity. We've already been making do without running water or toilets. We've not seen anything of the project manager, Weasel Ears, in weeks, and rumour has it that he's been given the boot. His real name isn't Weasel Ears, it's Jerry Siilinpää, or Hedgehog Head, probably from an old Fennoman family, a Swedish name that's been transliterated into Finnish, but we call him Weasel Feet because one of our friends, who probably won't be moving here with us because—'

'Feel free to have a look about. Take your time,' Linda af Nyborg-Jussila said, slipping into a hallway that evidently led to the kitchen, because a small servant's room opened off it.

'Isn't it more normal to say have a look *around*, not *about*? I knew Finnish was her second language,' Irma whispered loudly to Siiri as she peered into the tiny bedroom. 'This is just like the room our maid Lyyli slept in!'

They meandered, enchanted, through the flat, which brought back memories of childhood and youth, the bloom of married life and times past, when apartments were big, walls were thick, floorplans convoluted, and ceilings at least ten feet tall. The closets were built into the walls, too, with charming old keys in the locks. They opened doors and tittered in delight. The bathroom was small, which was good. They couldn't wrap their brains around modern apartments where the bathroom was bigger than the bedroom. Irma claimed that it was the law, in case you had a guest in a wheelchair. It was called accessible design, and it might have been accessible, but it was far from aesthetic.

'This is the way to live!' Irma said when finally they found Linda af Nyborg-Jussila eating a banana in the enormous, light-filled room they planned on making the dining room. It had lovely double doors that you could open on Christmas Eve once the table was set, the tree trimmed and the candles lit.

'Why don't you want to live here?' Siiri asked. 'It's such a lovely home.'

Madam af Nyborg-Jussila jammed the banana peel into a

plastic bag and the plastic bag into her crocodile handbag, dabbed at the corners of her mouth with her left pinkie, which bore an impressive ring, and looked out the window. There was a stunning vista over the building opposite. In classified ads, this was called a *Parisian view*. The sun was shining on the black tin roofs, and the steeple of St John's Church rose in the distance.

'Divorce,' she said finally. 'My husband traded me in for a younger model and took the children with him.'

'Some men are incorrigible, like this acquaintance of ours, even though he's an ambassador,' Irma stated serenely, as one does when acknowledging an undeniable fact. 'What sort of fellow is this Mr Jussila?'

'He's a consultant . . . a Taurus . . . What exactly do you mean?'

'Oh, how . . . shameless,' Siiri said, incapable of coming up with anything else. 'And you're going to move into a smaller place by yourself? Won't the children be staying with you from time to time?'

'It's very important to maintain contact with children during a divorce,' Irma said. 'You mustn't just think about yourself. You'll be fine. We're both widows; we know what it's like living without a husband. It's not that bad.'

'I'd rather be a widow than divorced! I wouldn't have to watch his blossoming happiness,' Madam af Nyborg-Jussila snapped. She looked back out across the rooftops and stood up straighter, as if the steeple lent her strength. 'Well, are you going to take it? The rent is five thousand euros a month; I don't think it was mentioned in the ad. It includes water and attic and cellar storage, but no parking space. The deposit is six months' rent, paid at signing.'

'Jumping Jehoshaphat!' shrieked Irma. 'Do you think we've got that kind of money? That would be two thousand five hundred euros apiece! And here I thought it was impossible to find a more expensive place to live in in Finland than a retirement home.'

'It's the current market price. I hadn't planned on turning this into an old folks' home.'

'Is it normal to have to pay six months in advance?' Siiri asked, shocked. It looked as if her dreams of a commune had been lunacy. In addition to the apartment, they had to pay their rent at Sunset Grove, and the sums were ballooning to such astronomical levels that Siiri thought she would faint. 'I don't know these things; I've never rented before. Except at Sunset Grove, that is, and that's a slightly different thing.'

Then the sound of giggling and commotion could be heard coming from the entryway. Five girls and one boy were pulling shower caps over their shoes, losing their balance, falling, and unable to stop laughing. Linda af Nyborg-Jussila rushed out and was even more horrified than when she'd seen Siiri and Irma in her traditional home for demanding tastes.

'*Jasso*, hmm . . . you're interested in a large apartment for a family?'

'Hey, what's up, yeah, we're looking for a place to share,' said the first one to pull on her slippers, a perfectly nice-looking girl. She was dressed in a pink baby romper that was far too big for her.

'It's a one-piece jump-in. Cool, huh?' she said to Irma, allowing her to finger the onesie.

'You look like a darling little piglet,' Irma said, and everyone burst out laughing.

The young people scattered around the apartment, slid across the parquet in their shower-capped feet, and cried out in delight every time they found a new room or hallway. Linda af Nyborg-Jussila held back her tears in the entryway of her traditional home for demanding tastes and looked so miserable that Siiri gave her a hug.

'It's going to be just fine, believe me. I'm ninety-five years old, I turn ninety-six in September, and I've survived more than one desperate situation. I can guarantee things have a way of sorting themselves out, sooner or later. I'm sure you deserve a better husband than that worthless scoundrel who left you. There's no point crying over him. And once you scrub Mr Jussila out of your life, you can also lose that silly hyphenated name; just think how nice that will be. I think these good-natured young people are decent students and you should let the flat to them. There's no way Irma and I could dream of an apartment this grand, even though when we were your age, we also had big flats in old buildings on the tram lines. If you saw how we lived now, in tiny studios and one-bedrooms with low ceilings and plasterboard walls, the whole cheap mess wrapped in plastic just in time for the summer heatwave, and refugees tramping in and out wielding sledgehammers, you'd be so shocked that you'd feel better instantly, because then you'd understand how good you have it, after all.'

Linda af Nyborg-Jussila gaped at the white-haired old lady who had wrapped her arms around her and talked to her as if they were childhood friends. She thought about her real friends, all those who had vanished into thin air when Pekka had left her for their Peruvian nanny. The unanticipated divorce had driven old friends into a state of such profound consternation that they had dropped her and left her to struggle with her self-esteem alone, imagining that if you owned two hundred square metres in downtown Helsinki, life couldn't be too bad.

'It's so unfair . . . and that's why it feels good, you comforting me and reminding me that I can keep living my life without Pekka. I agree, I think he's a real shit, too . . .'

Irma and Siiri patted the teary apartment owner until she pulled a small bottle out of her crocodile handbag and sprayed a cloud of sweet-smelling mist on her face.

'I'm going to move abroad. To Spain,' she said resolutely, straightening her sheath dress at the side seams. For a moment, Irma and Siiri thought the Swedish-speaking divorcée would head to the airport then and there. But then the boisterous herd of good-natured students appeared in the entryway, giggling and wobbling as they stripped off the shoe protectors, which brightened the mood. The sole boy, a broad-shouldered lad with a bun on top of his head, got down on all fours, and two girls helped Siiri and Irma pull the shower caps off their feet as they took turns sitting on this makeshift bench.

'This certainly is a nice way to undress,' Irma said in her

tinkling laugh, and she praised the boy's back muscles, which were massaging her ancient derriere.

'Irma!' Siiri exclaimed reproachfully, because she was afraid the strangers would find Irma's lack of decorum offensive, but everyone laughed, even Madam af Nyborg-Jussila. They said goodbye to their new acquaintances, told the young people they hoped they'd enjoy settling into their beautiful new home, and started slowly descending the four flights of stairs. They were disappointed that setting up a commune hadn't been as easy as they had thought. On the other hand, Helsinki was full of big flats which it would be fun to go see, and the day had turned out to be truly unforgettable.

Chapter 8

In July, the canteen at Sunset Grove shut its doors. Director Sundström couldn't say exactly how long the renovation of the institutional kitchen would last, because Project Manager Jerry Siilinpää was on vacation. Almost all of Sunset Grove's residents had escaped to the summer cabins of friends and family at Midsummer, and the staff vacations had begun. Siiri and Irma enjoyed the quiet and rode around the city in trams. Helsinki was magnificent in July; they'd never experienced their hometown so deserted and lovely. A handful of lost tourists wandering down Mannerheimintie were the only people they saw. Everything was green, and the sun was shining like in those architectural renderings where it was always summer.

Home-care service Helping Handz delivered food three times a day to paying customers; breakfast consisted of yogurt and a cup of juice that resembled a urine sample. For lunch, they often served soup and a slice of hard bread, plus a pat of light margarine. Just hearing the words 'light margarine' sent Irma into a tizzy, and she refused to use the pat.

'I've never let anyone force-feed me anything I don't

want to eat, and I'm not about to start now,' Irma announced. She and Siiri were in the tram, en route to visit Anna-Liisa at the Meilahti Hospital.

'You can't exactly compare a pat of light margarine to being force-fed through hoses and tubes.'

'In both cases, it's a matter of quality of life. And the only thing that fits the bill for me is butter.'

They had tracked Anna-Liisa down to the Meilahti Hospital, which they called the Hilton because of its towers. The breakthrough didn't come until Irma and Siiri caught Pro Tem Head of Residents Care Miisa Sievänen sneaking off for a cigarette with a couple of the layabouts from the construction company. Siiri and Irma had laid into the pro tem head behind the junk heap, and eventually she'd confessed that Anna-Liisa had been shipped off to the hospital due to confusion. Her behaviour had started disturbing the other residents. She claimed Anna-Liisa had been shouting in the middle of the night, which was why Sunset Grove had ordered the non-emergency ambulance that had snatched Anna-Liisa up the day they'd been to lunch at the French restaurant. Irma had asked Ms Sievänen why an old woman's midnight cries for help were a disturbance while constant drilling and pounding on walls weren't, but the pro tem head had offered no response.

Anna-Liisa had been prescribed one drug after another during her stay at the hospital. It had started from Alzheimer's pills for her confusion and sleep aids for her insomnia, and when Anna-Liisa had refused to swallow them, she'd been prescribed sedatives to counter her aggressiveness.

These had made her feel dizzy, and the fourth medication was to treat that. It made her horribly constipated, which was why the doctor had given her a laxative. And one of these pills had triggered nausea as a side effect, and so the whole regimen was topped off by some anti-nausea medication.

'I'm exhausted from all the treatment I've been getting,' Anna-Liisa said in a voice so soft it was barely audible. She had lost weight and looked skeletal, swimming in a faded yellow nightshirt that was far too large for her. 'I don't feel one whit healthier than when we were sitting at the restaurant. No one is doing anything about my cough, even though I've mentioned it on numerous occasions.'

Siiri and Irma were standing at Anna-Liisa's bedside, feeling useless. They were at a loss as to how to cheer up their friend under the circumstances, but then Irma remembered the composting toilets that had been distributed to the residents of Sunset Grove because the sewer pipes were out of use for the foreseeable future.

'This Pro Tem Head Sievänen arranged a composting toilet training session for the residents, can you imagine? At the end they passed the jars out and we all trundled off, carrying our chamber pots to our apartments. It took Tauno all day. You're supposed to pee into a separate chamber, and for the life of me I couldn't figure out how to direct my stream into it. Fortunately, Ms Sievänen didn't provide a demonstration. Have you tried your potty out yet, Siiri?'

'Oh, it can't be that difficult,' Siiri said. 'We've all had plenty of practice using more primitive set-ups. Tauno told me that he didn't have his first indoor toilet until after the war, when he moved to the city to look for work.'

But their babbling did little to improve Anna-Liisa's spirits, and Siiri didn't dare pull out the mahogany jewellery box. She was holding a bouquet they'd bought at the best florist in Munkkiniemi, the one next to the upper Low Price Market, or UpLow. The florist always wanted to know who would be getting the flowers and what the occasion was, and when they'd informed her that the recipient was the ninety-four-year-old victim of a plumbing retrofit, she had whipped up a cheery orange bouquet. But there wasn't a vase in sight.

'I'll go and look for a vase; you keep Anna-Liisa company,' Siiri said. Irma dived right into a detailed description of the composting commodes, and Siiri stepped out into the corridor.

She heard cheerful chatter coming from the nurses' desk, where six staff members sat at the computer, watching videos of cats doing silly things. Siiri watched one with them. It was of a cat falling into a bathtub, trying to climb out, and panicking as it kept slipping back in.

'Excuse me, where could I find a vase for this bouquet?' she asked, once the video was over and the cat had made it out of the tub, looking sheepish. A pretty nurse with dark skin rose and showed Siiri a cupboard where she could have her pick of tin jars. Siiri chose one and the nurse filled it with water and put the flowers in it.

'Who are these for?'

The nurse knew Anna-Liisa, and said she was a good patient.

'What makes for a good patient?' Siiri asked out of curiosity.

'I mean, Anna-Liisa is very nice to us nurses. Not everyone is. That's all I can say; we have to respect patient confidentiality.'

Siiri went back to Anna-Liisa's room and nearly had a heart attack when she stepped in. Irma was sitting at the window, and the sun-bronzed Ambassador was standing next to the bed in his summer suit. He had materialized from out of the blue to visit his spouse, who was sound asleep and, thus, oblivious to the return of her Peer Gynt. Siiri felt like giving this deserter a piece of her mind, but the Ambassador gazed at his slumbering, emaciated Anna-Liisa with such attentiveness that the words escaped her. Several weeks of rest at the villa with his kin had clearly done Onni good; he radiated sunshine and bracing sea air. Siiri glanced at Irma, who simply raised her eyebrows and spread her hands in bafflement. Apparently, the Ambassador hadn't explained his unexpected reappearance. He stroked Anna-Liisa's cheek tenderly and bent down to give her a peck on the forehead. Then he turned to Irma and Siiri.

'Shall we go for coffee? Let's leave Anna-Liisa to sleep off her worries.'

Worries, was that all they were? Siiri had read in the newspaper that many illnesses were psychological in nature and resulted from the patient being in a bad mood, stressed out, unhappy, or otherwise off-kilter. Perhaps the gutting of Sunset Grove was reason enough to send an elderly woman into a state of confusion. But where did the path out of this situation lie?

'*Döden, döden, döden,*' Irma trilled in a dramatic vibrato, and then pressed the elevator button that would carry them down to the hospital cafe.

'Everything will be fine, my dear ladies,' the Ambassador said with a winning smile. Siiri could smell the Ambassador's aftershave in the confines of the elevator, and it reminded her of her own husband, and suddenly she was unbearably sad. She followed Irma and the Ambassador up to the counter with heavy steps, took a tray, and stood there holding it, feeling like a fool. Were coffee and a sweet bun going to do anything to ease an old widow's longing?

'Why not?' Irma replied cheerfully, slapping a plate onto Siiri's tray. It held a doughnut with light-green frosting. 'Everyone's eating these, these days, why don't you try one, too?'

A smattering of wan patients dotted the canteen; there wasn't a single visitor in sight. Apparently, July wasn't any busier in the hospital than it was in the rest of the city. The Ambassador told them stories from his villa, and how he'd caught a decent-sized pike that he'd thrown back into the lake because pike didn't make for good eating. Irma disagreed vehemently and tried to remember a good recipe for pike, and when she couldn't, she pulled her green flaptop out of her handbag. The Ambassador was intrigued by Irma's iPad, and they got sidetracked by a lengthy conversation about how wonderful it was, without ever finding the fish recipe Irma had meant to look for.

'You bake the pike after stuffing it with all sorts of delicious ingredients,' she remembered, licking her lips. The Ambassador was engrossed in playing cards on Irma's tablet and was pleased when he beat himself twice in a row.

'We have to move out of Sunset Grove,' Siiri said, to put a stop to the stasis of the moment; it was what Anna-Liisa would have done. With Anna-Liisa missing, they were in constant danger of wandering off onto rhetorical side-paths instead of concentrating on the essential. The Ambassador gave the tablet to Irma, put his reading glasses in his breast pocket, and gave Siiri a sly look. Siiri had never noticed how penetratingly blue the Ambassador's eyes were; they were exactly how she'd always imagined Jean Sibelius's eyes. Many descriptions of the famous composer dedicated a line or two to them, how they were sky-blue, deep blue, delicate blue, or ice-blue, their gaze exceptionally intense and wise.

'My dear ladies,' the Ambassador began, 'as you might be aware, I'm involved in a variety of enterprises, including several apartments I own in central Helsinki. They're currently leased for various purposes, but, with a little rearranging, I might be able to free one temporarily so that we could escape the plumbing retrofit at Sunset Grove.'

Irma practically squealed in delight. 'All of us? Move into some communist ménage, like Siiri's been dreaming about?'

'I knew it was a good idea, but you never took me seriously!' Siiri said jubilantly.

'It depends on the flat, of course. But at the moment it's looking as if a sizable set of rooms at Hakaniemi may be freeing up in the near future. I was thinking that with Anneli in such poor shape, it might be best if several of us are looking after her.'

'You want us to be Anna-Liisa's caregivers?' Irma asked. She was a nurse, although she hadn't worked since the 1960s, when the last of her darlings was born.

'That's not exactly what I had in mind,' the Ambassador said, pondering for a moment. 'I haven't thought it all the way through yet. But it's plain we can't live at Sunset Grove any longer. Anna-Liisa's condition is such that if they throw her out of the hospital, she'll die at Sunset Grove. And I can't . . . I'm not prepared . . . something has to be done –' He gulped and wiped his tears with a tissue. Siiri gathered that the Ambassador was having a hard time solving the problem on his own. This man, who had always managed his affairs with such a firm hand, needed their help and was visibly embarrassed at having gone soft. Siiri regretted suspecting Onni of engaging in hijinks while vacationing at the villa. He was exceptionally warm-hearted and fair. He must have his reasons for seeing his heirs from time to time.

'I've been wanting to live in a commune all along,' Siiri said cheerfully. 'It will be fun. And it would only be temporary. The renovation can't last forever, can it? We'll be able to stand each other for four months. That's a shorter ordeal than the Winter War. Or is it?'

'A little longer. But much easier, I'm sure. After all, we see each other every day at Sunset Grove, too,' the Ambassador said, already more chipper.

'Did you say the flat was in Hakaniemi? North of the bridge, the Pitkäsilta, where the Reds and labour unions hole up?' Irma asked. She looked as if Hakaniemi were the most exciting thing she'd ever heard of. She'd refused to set foot north of the Pitkäsilta her entire life, and she found the opportunity to defy her own strictures invigorating, like everything else a bit naughty. 'How big is this flat?'

'It's very large and quite unusual, but unfortunately I don't have a very good grasp of the particulars. These apartments are investments for me and linked to my other businesses, so I've never set foot inside this specific unit. But to the best of my recollection, there are several bedrooms. Four or five.'

They started calculating that even three bedrooms would be enough for them. If there really were five, they could rescue a few more residents of Sunset Grove, too.

'Shall we bring Tauno along? I like him,' Irma suggested.

'Or Margit, preferably? She's in quite a jam, with Eino at that CrowsNest in eastern Helsinki.'

'SquirrelsNest, Siiri. And Margit . . . Well, she's a little unpredictable, and I don't believe Anna-Liisa has ever enjoyed her company much.'

'Hakaniemi is so much more convenient than Munkkiniemi. There's a metro stop, several trams, and almost all the buses stop there at the square.'

Siiri had always liked the market at Hakaniemi Square. Sometimes she would hop off the tram at Hakaniemi with no particular destination in mind, wander through the market hall, and browse the stalls outside on the square. The place had the ambience of times past, somehow. And what could suit them better, ancient relics that they were?

'And then there's Ritva Lahtinen,' Irma mused. 'But she is most definitely not invited.'

'Who's that?' The Ambassador's curiosity was piqued, but when they explained that Ritva Lahtinen was a sixty-seven-year-old, tattooed corpse-cutter, his enthusiasm foundered. 'I don't suppose we can save everyone. No need to start playing Noah's Ark.'

This was rather cleverly put. They shared a jolly laugh, finished their coffee, and continued out into the heat. They had a rollicking tram ride home, planning their new life in Hakaniemi. And their brilliant idea would, no doubt, breathe new life into Anna-Liisa, too.

Chapter 9

On a scorching July day, Siiri, Irma and the Ambassador were sitting in the courtyard at Sunset Grove, surrounded by old toilets, shower basins, bathtubs and grimy lengths of pipe. One of the nurses had carried out a table, a bench and a glass jar that was now brimming with cigarette butts, and this was where they were now having their rendezvous, because the Ambassador had looked into the Hakaniemi rental unit and had heard good news: the apartment could be vacated with very little warning. On top of that, it was already furnished, so the move would be easy and effortless.

'Anna-Liisa needs her books; at least some of them. Or is there already a bookshelf? One with books?' Siiri said. 'Some people fill their bookshelves with knick-knacks and photographs.'

'No, there aren't any bookshelves. To my understanding, the Kallio Library is within walking distance. I'm sure Anna-Liisa can find herself plenty to read there.'

Anna-Liisa would be coming home from the hospital perhaps as early as the end of the week. The Ambassador had got right down to business and had acquired his wife's medical records. Three of the documents were written by the nurses and read 'Treatment Notes' at the upper edge. The collated thoughts of the doctors had been copied on a separate sheet of paper, called a Report, even though it was clearly a discharge summary.

'These nurses' observations are quite funny,' Irma said. Anna-Liisa had been highly praised in the Treatment Notes. She was friendly and polite, didn't have much of an appetite and slept a lot, appeared confused on occasion. But when she'd refused to take all her medication, a shift in tone had appeared: 'Remains recalcitrant and uncooperative'. Anna-Liisa had refused the mood boosters and other nonsense, and for this reason the nurses had gradually started to treat her like a psychiatric patient, and a hopeless case at that. Which had, naturally, offended Anna-Liisa. According to the nurses she had started acting increasingly aggressively and suspiciously.

'Listen to this,' Irma cried. '"Patient is delusional. Claims to have seen people in her room at night and can't remember where she is. Constantly asks when she'll be going home, without any comprehension of her present state." And why do you think that might be! She's ninety-four years old, locked up in a hospital room with loads of other patients, and pumped full of drugs. Then they sneak around, spying on her at all hours to see if she's keeping up with what's going on in the world. It's a wonder they don't wake her up in the middle of the night and ask who the president's spouse is. Those are the kinds of stupid questions they use at the at the health centre to find out if you've got a screw loose.' Irma glanced at them uncertainly. 'It is Jenna, isn't it?'

'Jenni Haukio,' the Ambassador said, pleased to be the only one who passed the test.

'You only remember her because she's young and pretty. I'm sure you'd have had trouble remembering the previous spouse's name.'

'You don't remember it, either,' Siiri said.

'Of course I do: Pentti Arajärvi.'

'He's not the president's former spouse!'

'No, silly, he's the former president's spouse. You're certainly getting featherbrained, Siiri. Besides, you're leading this conversation off onto the wrong track completely.'

Irma was furious, not with the Ambassador, but with the hospital for questioning Anna-Liisa's mental health. After she had cooled off a little, the Ambassador told them that Anna-Liisa had, indeed, taken fright in the middle of the night: numerous people had been walking in and out of the room. As a rule, nights at the hospital were extremely quiet; certainly there weren't any nurses around if a patient happened to wake up and call for help. These nocturnal intruders had assumed that Anna-Liisa was sleeping, and she hadn't dared say anything; she had just lain there stunned and completely still. From the nurses' talk, Anna-Liisa had later deduced that the patient in the next bed had died earlier that night. That was why people had been running in and out, first a couple of nurses, then the doctor, and then several orderlies to remove the body. One of them had bumped Anna-Liisa's bed, but she'd been too scared to say anything.

And when she woke up again the next morning, a new, living patient was lying in the bed.

'Then Anneli made the mistake of mentioning the incident, and she was pronounced insane,' the Ambassador said and he laughed, because, in his eyes, the entire situation was the height of absurdity. In the end, Anna-Liisa's name had been added to the list of patients waiting to see a psychiatrist.

'Quite a punishment for demonstrating that you're still sharp,' Irma said.

For a moment no one spoke; they grew sombre at the thought. The construction workers were on their lunch break, and an unusual silence had fallen over Sunset Grove. They could hear chaffinches and chickadees singing, and that hadn't happened in ages. Siiri tried to see which tree the songbirds were in, but she could only spot a scruffy crow croaking from the gutters of Sunset Grove. A middle-aged woman, presumably one of the staff, stood smoking a couple of yards away. The nurses no longer wore white coats while they were on duty; there was surely a good reason for this. Irma suggested that perhaps the idea was that if the staff wore striped T-shirts, it made Sunset Grove seem like a home, not an institution. The downside was that the residents couldn't tell who was a nurse and who was a janitor.

'It doesn't matter; there aren't any janitors here any more,' she said, rummaging around in her handbag and pulling out a cigarette. Generally, she didn't smoke until evening, but the clouds the employee was exhaling aroused Irma's degenerate urges. She said her nose was stopped up from all the fresh air, which was why it made sense to smoke one nostril-opening cigarette. She searched for her matches and reported on this hunt so volubly that the woman in the striped shirt came over to offer her a light. A pair of spectacles, a key chain, a handkerchief, a pack of cards, a wallet, a bottle of whisky, a tube of lipstick, and a package of nylons already lay on the table. The Ambassador discreetly trained his gaze on the horizon.

'We nurses have red stripes. The practical nurses have green ones, and the supervisors wear blue,' the nurse explained.

'You don't say? So there's a system to it? Isn't that something, I never realized. I've just been thinking you all look like jailbirds, although I'd say we're the prisoners here.'

Irma managed to light her cigarette and she waved the smoke out of Siiri's face, where a lazy breeze persistently steered it. The nurse said she'd overheard their conversation. She thought that what had happened to Anna-Liisa was nothing out of the ordinary, 'totally normal', in fact. They shouldn't let it shock them.

'There's that word again!' Irma cried. 'Normal this and normal that. That's what my darlings always say, too.'

'She probably has a urinary tract infection; it's common among older people,' the nurse said. 'It can be asymptomatic. Sometimes patients get a fever, and confusion is very common. It's a typical symptom.'

'Wouldn't that mean the infection isn't asymptomatic?' the Ambassador asked. He wasn't pleased that this cigarette-smoking nurse was butting into their conversation.

'There are symptoms and then there are symptoms. Confusion can be a perpetual state. But if residential staff know their clientele, they'll notice the change, they'll notice that the confusion is temporary or a new development, which means they can look into the causes. I think we should be able to take urine samples at retirement homes; it's so simple and a major cause of confusion for many old folks. It makes no sense for them to take a cab to the lab or lie around in a hospital for weeks just for that.'

'That sounds sensible. But you don't know your clientele. You don't know us,' the Ambassador said emphatically. 'If you're such an expert at pinpointing problems, why don't you do something about it?'

The nurse grunted and stubbed out her cigarette in the glass jar. 'That's what's so frustrating.' She pulled chewing gum out of her pocket and started working her jaws. 'No one hires permanent employees. A permanent gig is too great a risk for employers; you can't fire them when times are tough or when you restructure your organization. I'm a temp worker, like all nurses. Here today, somewhere else tomorrow. Last year I was a whole three months at the same place in Porvoo, and it was a big deal. Just when I was getting a feel for the place, the work dried up. Yesterday I was at Riistavuori. It's one of Helsinki's biggest old folks' homes. It was like working on an assembly line, washing and showering. Do you think I have time to ask everyone whose dirty bottom I'm washing, what their name is, what their life's been like, what their favourite food is?'

'I see. I'm sure you can't,' the Ambassador said gravely. 'I suppose we're barking up the wrong tree. I assume you've spoken about this with your employer and the other nurses? If the staff aren't satisfied and the clients aren't either, then who is?'

'Yeah, well. That's the million-dollar question. HSS is a curse word these days and care of the elderly has snowballed into such a mess that the decision-makers are lost, the employees are demoralized, and the clientele . . . Well, you don't have much of a choice. The second you end up in hospital for the wrong reason, you lose any agency, and they pass you around like the ball at a Barça match.'

They had all heard of HSS. It was the abbreviation that was on everyone's lips these days, and meant the unpleasant obligations – health and social services – that gobbled up every penny of public funding. Irma had come across the phrase *alternative attitudes to municipal accountability* in the newspaper and they had all had a good chuckle over their instant coffee. It sounded like it was promoting the idea of municipalities shirking their responsibilities.

'But I'm drawing a blank from matchmaking balls. What's a barsa?'

'It must be some new trend,' Siiri said.

The nurse wished them a nice life, coughed for a moment, and then, pounding her chest, went back inside, where the racket of the remodel had resumed.

By now the combination of jackhammering, drilling and banging had taken on a hominess; there was something familiar and regular about it, so that when it was missing it felt odd and put you on edge. The days had taken on a new rhythm at Sunset Grove. At six o'clock in the morning, the building filled with men in neon vests who revved up their machines and started swinging their sledgehammers about. That was when all the residents woke up, the lights came on in the tiny units of the tightly wrapped house, and the restless wandering down corridors to the lobby began. The aimlessness lasted until eight o'clock, when the construction workers took a coffee break and the old folks retreated to their homes for a rest. They knew the moment of silence was brief and enjoyed it for all it was worth. Siiri generally lay down on her bed, shut her eyes, and listened to the thrumming in her head without falling asleep. Sometimes she turned on the radio and listened to the Morning Show until the noise came back and drowned everything out. The pounding continued until eleven, when the highlight of the summer day began: an hour of silence and rest. The disoriented residents gathered around the tables or retreated to their cubby-holes to gather up their strength in the way each deemed best for the final ordeal, which could be protracted indeed. The construction crew worked until six, but lately there had been increasing amounts of evening work, which meant residents weren't blessed with a moment of rest until late at night. The wiring and HVAC companies were overbooked during the summertime, and they fit in the work when they could. Just the other day, one poor young fellow had been poking about Siiri's kitchen at 10 p.m., even though he had three small girls at home waiting for their daddy. Siiri had offered him a glass of wine. He had refused, because he was on the job, but he gladly accepted a slice of pound cake and tea and sat down with Siiri for a chat during this little break.

'Weasel Face did promise we'd get used to the noise and other annoyances caused by the renovation,' Irma said, popping a Mynthon pastille into her mouth so that the cigarette wouldn't taste so harsh. 'But I bet he never guessed the boldest of us would make friends with the workers. Do you suppose he got fired?'

'Who? My electricity man? For eating pound cake on the job?'

'No, Jerry Siilinpää.'

Now this was news. Irma had heard it from Tauno during Director Sundström's information session on the plumbing retrofit. These sessions were a weekly event, generally held on Tuesdays at 10 a.m. Siiri had stopped attending before Midsummer, because they inevitably ended in cacophony and she never came away any the wiser.

'I haven't heard anything like that about Jerry Siilinpää,' the Ambassador said.

'Was Director Sundström the one who said Weasel Head got the boot?' Siiri asked. Irma was sharp, *all there*, as she herself liked to put it, but now and again she'd allow herself to get caught up in foolishness before looking properly into a matter. And then, of course, there were those days when her memory failed her and she mixed everything up. But such things happened to everyone on occasion and were no cause for alarm.

'She didn't say anything about anyone getting fired, but

Tauno knew. He wasn't the only one wondering why Weasel Tail was missing in action and Sundström had no explanation. Just went on and on about the project's various phases and a challenging, changing landscape. She certainly loves that word! The poor thing is starting to sound like a consultant herself, now that she's spent so much time in Weasel Back's company.'

'Are you going to keep coming up with different versions of Jerry Siilinpää's last name? Or should we get down to the matter at hand, the reason why we're gathered here at this construction refuse recycling point?' the Ambassador chuckled. Siiri and Irma had completely forgotten that, after meal delivery, the Ambassador had indeed called them together at the staff smoking area to negotiate the possibility of moving temporarily to Hakaniemi. He didn't have a floorplan of the flat, so Irma wasn't able to assign rooms, but the Ambassador promised that they'd be able to go and see the place in person, perhaps quite soon.

'It's possible you ladies won't find it suitable,' he said.

'Nonsense, do you think we have any standards at all after living at Sunset Grove? A garage would be better than this sewer-line storage centre. Look around! Here we are, refreshing ourselves next to a mountain of old toilets. Luckily, they can't talk and tell us what they've seen! I think I know which one is mine, actually. The lid broke once and I bought myself a new one, since our beloved director informed me that the board of the Loving Care Foundation could possibly be persuaded to grant me a new lid if I submitted an application that included a written report explaining what had happened to the old one. Well, I wasn't about to wait for those alms. They had all sorts of toilet seat lids at the Etola on Huopalahdentie, and I picked that pretty flowered one. Can you see it? It's there halfway up the pile, to the right; my dear old toilet!'

'If we had some red wine, we could toast the memory of all the good times you two shared,' Siiri laughed.

'Shall I go get some? I have a box that's barely been cracked on my nightstand. I keep it there, because there's always some helmet-head rummaging about in my kitchen.'

'Don't! Be a good girl and stay put, please. I didn't realize so many people here had bathtubs. Why, there are half a dozen old tubs there. You'd think a tub would be dangerous for old folks. Irma, do you have any funny videos in that flaptop of yours? Cat videos are popular; I saw one where this pitiful, bedraggled poor thing, a cat I mean, tried to climb out of a tub. Shall we watch it right now? I'm sure it would make you laugh.'

Before they knew it, Irma's green device was on the table, and she jabbed at it vigorously, bracelets jangling. But the Ambassador wasn't interested in modern technology today; he wanted to talk about money.

'I've been thinking I'd cover the rent in Hakaniemi. After all, you'll have to keep paying your expenses at Sunset Grove, even though we're living somewhere else. That's enough of a burden for you ladies.'

The Ambassador had tried to challenge Director Sundström over the rent being charged residents who had moved out during the retrofit, but she had remained resolute. All expenses, including service fees, had to be paid, even if you spent months living elsewhere because of the construction. The Ambassador wasn't wholly convinced of the legality of this arrangement.

'My attorney is on summer vacation, so I couldn't consult him,' he said.

'You have your own attorney? My husband did, too, but he died a long time ago; the attorney, I mean. And of course Veikko did too, my dear husband. As a matter of fact, Veikko died first, or was it the other way around?' Irma said and squealed when she found the cat video Siiri was hoping for. 'Is this it? I typed in *cat* and *bath*, and this is what my iPad came up with. He prefers to speak English.'

'He who?' the Ambassador asked, slightly irritated.

'My iPad.'

They watched the video, which was not the same one Siiri had already seen, but funny all the same. The Ambassador wasn't as thrilled as the ladies; he started clearing his throat impatiently. In the end, he stood, bid farewell to the coffee-morning group, even though they hadn't had so much as a sip of coffee, and announced that he was going to have a nap and then head off to the Hilton to visit Anna-Liisa. He promised to be in touch as soon as he heard when they could go and see the apartment. The Ambassador took his leave in his light summer suit, with his cane hooked over his arm, and Siiri and Irma watched six more cat videos before growing bored.

'Did the Ambassador really say he would foot the bill for this exodus of ours?' Irma asked. She gathered up her belongings from the table and put them back in her handbag, laying the tablet tenderly on top.

'Yes, that's what he said. I presume he hasn't talked to Anna-Liisa about it yet. We'll see how things go. It could be that the apartment is completely impossible and there won't be enough room for us, that we'll just be underfoot.'

They sat there on the bench and amused themselves by watching two Polish workers quarrelling vehemently. Arms were waving, the saliva was flying, and a vein started to bulge threateningly on a forehead. Suddenly, the shorter man punched the taller one in the face. Then the taller one was angry, too, and a moment later the men were engaged in a full-on brawl. Irma and Siiri didn't know what to do. When a third man ran out and jumped into the fray instead of separating the brawlers, Irma and Siiri slunk off the back way. This was one thing they had learned during the Sunset Grove renovation: they had no business sticking their noses into the affairs of professionals.

Chapter 10

'Shall we take the fast way or the fun way?' Siiri asked.

'The fun way, of course,' Irma said, not allowing the Ambassador any say in the decision.

'That means the number 4 to the number 8 to the number 6. First transfer at the new opera, and then again at Kurvi.'

The air was abuzz with excitement as Siiri, Irma and the Ambassador took their seats at the front of the number 4 tram. They were on their way to Hakaniemi, to see the apartment that soon might be their new home. None of them said anything, but they all wore happy smiles on their faces.

Suddenly, they heard a braying from the aisle: 'I was sitting in the back, wondering if that was you. And I was right!'

It was Margit. She had hurtled down the length of the car and stopped, out of breath, to inform them between gasps that she was on her way downtown to wander around; it was the best therapy she could think of. But she was curious as to their destination, of course, and for a moment they looked embarrassed, since they weren't sure making her privy to their intended move was prudent.

Siiri softened the story: 'It's just a silly little plan.'

'It's a stupendous plan, for heaven's sake!' Margit exclaimed, just as they had feared. 'Can I come with you?'

'Of course!' Siiri said. 'To see the Ambassador's apartment, I mean. It's always such a lark, going to see flats,' she added, so Margit wouldn't get the impression that they were inviting her to move into their commune with them.

The Ambassador didn't see what was particularly fun about transferring from tram to tram, but Irma and Siiri were having a grand time. The old Deaconess Institute was as beautiful as ever, and the Brahenkenttä soccer pitch was handsome. They remembered that Anna-Liisa had embarked on her illustrious teaching career at the Kallio School and spent a moment worrying about her present condition. Margit seated herself next to the Ambassador, in front of Irma and Siiri. She kept her eyes on the driver and looked as if she hadn't heard a word of what the others were saying. Maybe she'd left her hearing aid at home or in her handbag again.

'Anna-Liisa had an appointment with a psychogeriatrician on Friday,' the Ambassador said, trying to turn towards Siiri and Irma.

'A psychogeriatrician? That's a doctor who specializes in old people who've lost their marbles, isn't it? Is that supposed to be good news?' Siiri wondered.

'A psychowhatever like that could send Anna-Liisa to the SquirrelsNest for the rest of her life,' Irma cried.

'If you'll let me finish,' the Ambassador said. 'This psychogeriatrician is a sensible woman. She spent a long time talking with Anna-Liisa and declared the patient healthy in body and mind.'

The Ambassador looked proud as he related that, in this professional's estimation, his wife was more or less in possession of her faculties. Anna-Liisa's confusion had resulted from the urinary tract infection, just as the nurse smoking in the courtyard had guessed. Her anxiousness and aggressiveness resulted from her frustration at feeling ignored and helpless. In the end, the psychogeriatrician had ordered her to be taken off her mood enhancers, sleeping aids, and Alzheimer's medication. Anna-Liisa had been given a report that ended with the words: 'The patient is confident that she can manage at home. Release.'

'But that's spectacular news!' Siiri said, clapping with joy.

'This calls for a celebration!' Irma exclaimed.

Her enthusiasm prodded even Margit to life: 'What are your views on euthanasia?'

'My dear ladies!' The Ambassador raised his voice to bring his herd under control. He promised to throw a big party the moment Anna-Liisa was back at home, but before that, they needed to arrange a home to throw her a party in.

'Wonderful. Then we can celebrate my birthday at the same time. I'm about to turn . . . Hmm, what am I turning?' Irma paused to reflect.

'I think you're turning ninety-four,' Siiri suggested.

'That's very possible,' Irma said. 'It's not a hundred, I know that.'

'This is our stop. It's that building.' The Ambassador

pointed at a massive brick building with a neon sign that read OXYGENOL on the roof.

'Why, that's the Arena Building! Designed by Lars Sonck!' Siiri cried. She looked at the famous structure, practically a castle, with the round tower at each of its three corners. It took up the entire block. 'It's completely encircled by tram tracks. I never dreamed you were talking about the finest building in Hakaniemi.'

They hurried across Siltasaarenkatu and along the edge of the square, as if the triangular fortress would slip through their fingers if they dawdled. They paused in front of the building while the Ambassador searched for the right key. After going through his pockets, he starting rummaging through his brown leather satchel, which, based on its patina, must have been from the 1960s. Irma studied the display window of the art supply store and Margit let the light breeze caress her face.

For a second it looked as if the Ambassador had forgotten to bring the right key, but after numerous tries, one from his impressive set unlocked the door to stairwell A. The corridor was dark and cramped, nothing like the dignified lobby one would expect of a Sonck building. They rode an elevator with ugly steel doors up to the second floor and wondered why the lovely old scissor-gated models had been hauled off to the dump. The Ambassador was still in a fine mood; he was the first to step out, open a heavy door, and proudly present his property.

'Welcome to your humble refuge!'

They stepped into a big, round entryway where the walls

had been covered in red satin. A crystal chandelier, or some cheaper look-alike, hung from the ceiling – a rather tasteless fixture, but no one said anything. The Ambassador advanced briskly from room to room, clearly pleased with the flat's condition and furnishings.

The living room was enormous. It was broken up by two massive pillars, and the paned windows in the curving rear wall opened onto a magnificent view across Eläintarhanlahti Bay. The façade of Finlandia Hall gleamed in the sun with a singular beauty. Siiri experienced a flash of disappointment that Alvar Aalto's marble-faced master plan for Töölönlahti Bay had been abandoned during the 1970s' infatuation with concrete.

'But in this promised land of engineer-bureaucrats, no one had the vision to execute Eliel Saarinen's plan for Munk-kiniemi–Haaga, either,' Siiri huffed. She relented when she noticed the window-framed artwork in two generations: Heikki and Kaija Siren's circular building, Ympyrätalo, and the three-metre-tall steel ball at its entrance, by their son Hannu.

Yet something about the apartment seemed peculiar: there were mirrors and clothes hooks everywhere, along with unusual lamps and an ugly steel pole in the middle of the living room. The biggest bedroom had a closet the size of a small room, an en-suite, and a round bed. The smaller bed-rooms were different colours – one was mauve, another dark green, and someone had had the bright idea of painting the tiniest bedchamber blue – and the dark walls made the rooms look even smaller than they were. The living-room curtains were heavy, formally hung velvet, like the curtains of a stage. The bedspread for the round bed was shiny red satin and embroidered with sequins that glittered in the sun, casting strange patterns on the room's brown walls.

'How will you sleep in that?' Irma cried. It was a given that the biggest bedroom would go to Anna-Liisa and Onni. 'You're going to get seasick rolling around on that.'

There was no sign of a bookshelf. The living room was sparsely furnished, with only two low sofas better suited to lying than sitting, a gigantic television screen and large speakers dotted about. The overall effect was rather shiny. The bathroom was immense, more like a spa, actually. There were massaging showers, recessed lighting fixtures, a sauna and a big whirlpool tub, all of which the Ambassador pointed out enthusiastically.

'This remote controls the Jacuzzi, I imagine. It also appears to have a radio and speakers. And this one is for the lights. There's a starry sky in the sauna ceiling, rather atmospheric, wouldn't you say?' The Ambassador waved the remote around and twisted the knobs next to the sauna door; the starry sky started twinkling in and out rapidly. Suddenly the whirlpool tub's speakers burst out blaring awful rock music.

'Do something!' Irma shouted, grabbing the remote from the Ambassador. She jabbed at it hysterically as if it were a matter of life or death, until the music died. 'For goodness' sake. Are you trying to kill us?'

'Let's not get too dramatic,' the Ambassador said, with a winning smile.

'It's perfectly possible to die from fright. Or shock. It happens all the time in operas. Lucia di Lammermoor and Elsa from *Tannhäuser*, for instance, drop to the ground, dead as doornails.'

'None of you ladies are ever going to die,' the Ambassador continued breezily, demonstrating how to dim the shower's recessed lighting scandalously low.

'Knock me over with a feather,' Margit blurted. 'Is this where you're going to . . . for goodness' sake . . .' Evidently incapable of producing intelligible speech, she spun around in circles in the middle of the room.

'There's no washing machine,' Siiri said.

'But there are two bidets,' Irma noted mischievously. 'We can sit and spray ourselves side by side.'

'The laundry room is in here,' the Ambassador's voice echoed. He had stepped through the door next to the sauna into a chamber containing an immense steel washing machine and an even bigger dryer, as well as acres of room to hang laundry.

'Why, this is an institutional laundry,' Siiri said in surprise.

'We'll be able to wash our unmentionables in no time,' Irma laughed, and she tested to see how her soprano would resonate in the room. '"Siribiribim, siribiribim" – do you remember that song?'

There was no kitchen per se, just a corner of the living room with a small sink, a stove of sorts, and two big grey refrigerators, one with a contraption in the door which they eyed in perplexity.

'An ice machine, perhaps,' the Ambassador said. 'Unless it's a soda water dispenser. I'm not so familiar with the latest refrigerators.'

'Whatever will they come up with next?' Siiri said, examining the stove, a black surface with only one identifiable burner to the side, for gas. She opened the gleaming cupboard doors and found a tiny dishwasher behind one of them. How would they ever wash four people's dishes in that? This corner of the room seemed more like a bar than a kitchen. There wasn't even a dining table, just a narrow countertop surrounded by tall stools.

'Who's been living here?' Siiri asked finally.

The Ambassador didn't immediately respond. He looked at the stack of papers and keys that had been left on the counter and walked back towards the entryway, forehead furrowed.

'Hmm . . . well. I'm not exactly sure. I don't know much about the previous tenants. My understanding is that the apartment has been used for . . . entertaining. Embassies, import/export companies, and the like. All sorts of clients. As you know, I have many contacts at the Foreign Ministry.'

They all wanted to go to Hakaniemi Hall, the market hall right across the street. There was a well-known cafe on the second floor where former president Tarja Halonen, Finland's first female head of state, had a dedicated table. They seated themselves at the president's table, and the Ambassador carried over two trays loaded with sweet rolls and coffee. The coffee was served in mugs without saucers, and you had to stir in your sugar with a little wooden stick.

'At least you don't have to slurp your coffee out of a soup bowl, the way you do at the tram museum,' Siiri laughed.

In spite of their puzzlement at the flat's quirks, they were thrilled about the idea of moving. There were enough bedrooms, and the common spaces were much grander than anything they could have ever imagined. Margit sat in silence as they planned their new communal existence.

'Margit, what's wrong?' Siiri asked finally, but Margit didn't answer. She felt sorry for poor Margit, who had grown rather listless since her husband fell ill. 'Would you like to come and live in our commune, too? I suppose Onni and Anna-Liisa have no objection?' She gave the Ambassador a meaningful look and ignored Irma's below-the-table kick.

'Yes, well, why not, it's all still up in the air,' replied the Ambassador, who didn't appear to have anything against his flat having attained such popularity. 'We'd rather have you than Tauno.'

'So the harem is complete, and without the unpleasant Osmin!' Irma trilled. 'Isn't it a bit odd that in Mozart's *Abduction from the Seraglio* the harem guard Osmin is a bass, even though he's supposed to be a eunuch? Onni, you don't have to do any singing; Pasha Selim is a speaking role.'

Margit looked at them as if she couldn't believe her ears. Her deeply etched face revealed her age, but she still dyed her hair jet black. She must have been exceptionally beautiful as a young woman; she had fine features, good bone structure, and strong colouring.

'What are your views on euthanasia?' she asked. 'I'm at a

loss when it comes to what I should do. The one thing I'm hoping for is that Eino has a beautiful death. Don't you think it would be merciful if someone in Eino's condition were given a pill to set him free? Or an injection? I haven't looked into it enough to know how it's done. In Holland or Switzerland, Eino would be dead and happy already, and the funeral would be over.'

Their enthusiasm instantly deflated into an awkward silence. No one had a solution for Margit's angst or any words of consolation for her. Occasionally, they had discussed euthanasia without arriving at any consensus. Siiri approved of assisted death; the Ambassador put his trust in effective palliative care; Anna-Liisa felt that euthanasia was murder; and Irma's views changed by the week, based on what she'd heard on the radio or from her darlings over the phone. None of Irma's darlings visited her any more, now that Sunset Grove had been wrapped up for the retrofit. They found it such a bother picking their way through the cement sacks, getting their clothes grubby, and plugging their ears during the drilling. Irma's sole intentionally conceived child, Tuula, also had a plumbing retrofit underway in her building, and because there was no way Tuula could live in such chaos, she had moved to the family's summer cottage, which meant there wasn't room for Irma there.

'She needs her space; otherwise she won't have the energy to go to work,' Irma explained.

'How would you ladies like to divvy up the bedrooms?' the Ambassador asked brightly, to lift their spirits. He pulled the papers out of his worn leather satchel and found a floorplan of the apartment, which they spread across the president's table to begin planning their new life. Irma assigned the bedrooms, giving Margit the second biggest one, with the green walls, and herself the mauve one. Siiri was left the tiny blue one. They accepted Irma's proposal without complaint and started meandering about, oohing over the market hall, its butcher shops, fishmongers, vegetable stands, shelves of exotic spices, button sellers and handicraft shops. But they didn't buy anything. The group was brimming with the spirit of adventure as they crossed the square to the tram stop – even Irma, although she found the Metalworkers' Union building an atrocity and Oleg Kiryuhin's bronze statue *World Peace* an unpleasant reminder of the Soviet Union and the era of Finlandization.

'Giving us that ugly old albatross must have been one of the last things the Soviet Union did before Communism's house of cards finally came tumbling down.'

This even brought a smile to Margit's face and allowed her momentary respite from brooding over how best to murder her husband.

Chapter 11

In the end, everything happened so quickly that Siiri and Irma had a hard time believing it. The Ambassador's extraneous apartment had opened up as if by some miracle, and Anna-Liisa required no coaxing to get on board. The Ambassador told them he'd spoken with his wife about the plan on a couple of occasions while she was in the hospital, and the sole bone of contention had been Margit's inclusion.

'It was your idea,' Irma accused Siiri, as the number 9 tram drove past their future refugee asylum towards Porthaninkatu.

'I didn't remember at the time that Anna-Liisa doesn't care for Margit. Maybe she'll learn to like her; after all, we don't know her that well. Maybe she's a very sweet person.'

'Even I'm not that optimistic,' Irma laughed, and then *The Bear at the Anthill*, the sculpture that gave Karhupuisto Park its name, caught her eye. She started pondering who the sculptor might be. 'It must be Jussi Mäntynen, because all the animal statues in Helsinki are his. He got his start as a conservator's assistant at the university, which is why he can achieve such realistic representations in granite. Although I must say, that poor bear has an awful hump on his neck. Isn't it odd that this park has so few trees and benches? Are the fussbudgets in the parks department afraid that benches will attract drunks? Or senior citizens? Look, those loafers are playing that traditional game. Throwing sticks of firewood at each other.'

'It's called kubb,' Siiri said.

They weren't headed anywhere in particular. They had simply gone out for a ride to avoid the onerous business of packing; it was so hard to know what to bring along during their temporary flight. Siiri had come up with the idea of the number 9, and it was a wholly new adventure for Irma, despite the fact that the number 9 had been running through Hakaniemi and Kallio for a couple of years now. Siiri was particularly anticipating the bit from Fleminginkatu to Aleksis Kiven katu and on to Teollisuuskatu. That was sure to be new terrain for Irma, who had always given the city's old industrial areas a wide berth.

'It wasn't safe for a lady back then,' Irma retorted, and, of course, she was right. Siiri didn't feel completely at home in this part of town, either, but the area had been seen as a construction boom and had been cleaned up considerably since the turn of the millennium. Manufacturing was no longer profitable in Finland, and there was such an urgent need for housing that, despite packing every inch of shoreline with homes, vacated factories were being converted into residential flats, too. People preferred living alone to living together; that's what it said in the newspaper. Helsinki was full of lonely people, while families moved out to the sprouting suburbs in former farmlands and fields.

'Just because they live alone doesn't mean they're lonely. My darlings were explaining that it's a modern lifestyle choice. A lot of people prefer to live alone instead of ... of ... Yes, well, I suppose they really ought to find a spouse and raise children. But young women don't want to have children any more, because children get in the way of their careers. Oh, how folks fought over it in the Sixties, women entering the workforce. No one guessed it would lead to the decline of the entire nation.'

'We live alone and we're not lonely.'

'And we can kiss that bit of heaven goodbye, too. We'll have to put up with each other for God knows how long. What do you think, how long will the renovation at Sunset Grove last?'

They surmised that they might easily be spending six months at their asylum in Hakaniemi. Siiri didn't find the thought the least bit unpleasant, although she understood what Irma meant by kissing heaven goodbye and losing their freedom. Initially, she'd been sad when her children moved out one by one, leaving the house feeling increasingly deserted. Then she and her husband had bought a nice two-bedroom apartment in Meilahti, and when her husband died, the thought of living alone had felt confining and impossible. But gradually she had come to enjoy doing exactly as she pleased whenever she pleased, for the first time in her life, without having to worry about anyone else.

'Well, I'll be,' Irma said, admiring Aleksis Kiven katu,

which was, with its tram tracks running between two col-
umns of lindens, nearly as beautiful as Munkkiniemi Allée.
The former industrial area truly had taken on a new identity.
By some magic, the old Serlachius cardboard factory had
been transformed into a gorgeous apartment building; it must
be a marvellous place to live, with those big arched windows.
The former Pasila machine-and-metalworks stood opposite,
scheduled to become a little neighbourhood of its own.

'The only thing I can't fathom is why they couldn't come
up with a better name than The Machineworks. Just imagine
having to tell people you live at The Machineworks.'

The number 9 snaked charmingly through this peculiar
district, which was a rather neatly executed combination of
old brick warehouses and machine shops and new buildings
in brick instead of the typical glass and concrete. The door-
ways were adorned with pictures of trains, and even the odd
tree had been squeezed in. Siiri had read in the newspaper
that a large park was being planned near the old paint shop,
right at the heart of the new development.

'I simply can't understand why they kept Anna-Liisa at
the hospital for three weeks, pumping her full of drugs,
having her run up and down from the lab, when a course of
antibiotics would have solved all her problems,' Irma suddenly said, dabbing the perspiration from her brow with her
lace handkerchief. The heatwave had lasted all summer, and
it didn't seem as if August would bring any relief. Everyone
was revelling in the warmth and the sunshine – everyone,
that is, except ninety-somethings trapped in the middle of a
plumbing retrofit.

Siiri had also been baffled by the story the Ambassador had related about the run-around Anna-Liisa had got at the hospital. Things might have gone seriously wrong.

'Just imagine how much of the city's sparse resources and the staff's precious time could have been saved by applying a smidgen of common sense,' she sighed, 'and how little it takes for an old person to be labelled a dementia patient for the rest of their lives. If it weren't for that psychogeriatrician who happened to turn up, Anna-Liisa would be in line for some SquirrelsNest now. And we'd be thinking she just happened to be the next in line, that that's how it goes when you live too long.'

'The Ambassador handled that business rather deftly,' Irma said. Now that Anna-Liisa had been rescued and the flat in Hakaniemi conjured up out of thin air, she had stopped slandering the Ambassador for his other women and infidelities and joined Siiri in forgiving him everything.

When the tram turned onto Jämsänkatu, the landscape instantly changed. After the romance of The Machineworks, the depressing bunker architecture of the seventies felt so mean that it left a bad taste in Siiri's mouth; sour and acidic.

'Where did you put Anna-Liisa's jewellery box after you absconded from her apartment with it?'

Irma's question pierced Siiri's head like a pick: she felt a dreadful, stabbing pain and almost slumped from the force of the blow. The jewellery box! She remembered having been a little disoriented when she entered her own apartment with it, and had decided she'd stash the box in such a clever place that the construction crooks wouldn't be able to find it, no matter how much they poked about with their tape measures. But where had she hidden it? For the life of her, she couldn't remember. Irma wasn't worried in the least, though.

'You'll come across it while you're packing. Do you suppose the Ambassador will make all the arrangements for the move, like he promised? He seems to have contacts just about everywhere.'

'Yes,' Siiri said, still woozy, and she gazed up at the dreary concrete bridge that gave their present stop its name, Kellosilta, the bell bridge. What a desperate attempt to make this grim landscape sound beautiful, she thought, before being distracted by the sight of a woman wrestling with her stroller at the stop. No one helped her.

'Siiri, wake up!' Irma squawked. 'Did you hear what I said? One day I saw the Ambassador talking with two bearded men in helmets, as pleased as punch. Chatting away as if they knew each other. Now why would he do that?'

'Maybe he did know them,' Siiri replied lazily. The woman at the tram stop gave up the struggle and didn't board the tram after all; she just stood at the stop, looking as if she would burst into tears. The tram was fuller than one could have thought possible; there were already two strollers on board, and a large group of Asian tourists was packed into the aisles. They were all wearing dust masks, despite the fact that Helsinki's sole draw as a travel destination was the fresh sea air. 'Or not. That's just the way he is, friendly with everyone. Listen, do you know, I don't think I ever told Anna-Liisa that we stole her jewellery box for safe-keeping . . .'

'*You* stole, you mean,' Irma corrected her, and she laughed out loud at the sight of the Expo and Convention Centre; she thought it was such an amusing colossus. 'So that's where everyone goes to worship on Sundays: the food, travel and fitness masses. Don't they all have their own conventions? You can tell Anna-Liisa after you've found the box and returned it to her. And after she's released from the hospital.'

Which wouldn't be long now. The Ambassador had told them that Anna-Liisa would be moving straight from the hospital into their new home, at about the same time as them, on the first weekday in August. And that was the day after tomorrow.

Chapter 12

'I can't believe this; you must be kidding!'

Anna-Liisa stood, flabbergasted, in the foyer of the Hakaniemi flat, one hand gripping her cane, a wedding present from her husband, the other said husband's arm. The others waited with bated breath to hear her sentiments on their new communal home. After eyeing the curved satin walls, Anna-Liisa took a deep breath and advanced into the flat's interior. She was having difficulty walking, and the Ambassador had to offer a steadying hand as she stepped across the threshold and into the living room, where she stopped to admire the vista opening up beyond the window.

'Well,' she finally decreed, with a glance at the bar-kitchenette, and then she announced that she was going into the bedroom to have a rest.

'Have a look at the bathroom first. It's . . . it's immense!' Irma said.

Anna-Liisa paused at the door to their spa and took in the bidets, massaging showerheads and starry sky.

'Whatever will they come up with next,' she said dully, then she coughed and asked to be allowed to rest. As the

Ambassador helped her into their round nuptial bed, Anna-Liisa finally let out a little chuckle. 'Quite the pornographic lair you've found for us, Onni dear.'

The move had gone surprisingly smoothly, with the Ambassador conjuring up four Estonians from somewhere to move their scant effects from Sunset Grove to Hakaniemi. As the lion's share of their personal belongings had, at Project Manager Jerry Siilinpää's orders, been packed away in boxes in June, it hadn't been much trouble deciding which boxes to take and which to leave behind in the chaos of the retrofit. Irma had brought nearly all her earthly possessions, and now she was having difficulty fitting them into her room, which had neither shelves nor a desk. She arranged her darlings' photographs on the windowsill and crammed the rest of her unnecessary bric-a-brac into the closet.

'Hopefully, we'll be back home at Sunset Grove before the weather turns. I only brought my summer clothes.'

'Oh, Irma, we can always buy you a pair of wool trousers. It's just a hop, skip and a jump to town!'

Siiri had fewer belongings, but she'd brought a box of books that refused to fit neatly anywhere, so they remained in their box next to her bed. The bed was already made, like at a hotel. Margit had been first to finish unpacking in her green boudoir, and had already barrelled on over to the kitchenette, where she was familiarizing herself with its pots and pans.

'Everything is brand new, barely been touched. Three cupboards full of glasses!'

The Ambassador collapsed on one of the sofas, shaking

his head. All this fussing about was exhausting, and he no longer looked as tanned and rested as when he'd arrived from the ministrations of his former wives at the villa. He was still worried about Anna-Liisa, who had been released from the hospital under the condition that she received regular in-home care.

'The doctor wrote a referral. Does that mean we'll have to use public in-home care? Which health-care district do we belong to, now that we're living here?' he asked the flock of females fluttering around him.

'We're still in the Western district. That hasn't changed, because this home is temporary, correct? So either pay through the nose and hire a private nurse or get in at the back of the line for public care,' Irma replied. 'And for that you need to have enough points, otherwise you'll be left high and dry. It's a little like trying to get into the school of your choice. I was ordered all sorts of involuntary treatment after I was sent home from the hospital last year, do you remember? I gradually rid myself of them, when they realized that I manage perfectly well with assisted living and am wholly capable of making my own coffee in the mornings.'

'Maybe Anna-Liisa will perk up,' Siiri said hopefully.

In the doctor's estimation, Anna-Liisa needed in-home care for just about everything. For assistance with daily routines, the judgement decreed, including washing, dressing, getting about, rehabilitation, and taking her medication.

'I suppose someone needs to cook, too; I'm hopeless in the kitchen. A representative from the municipality will be here to figure all that out within the next seven days.'

The Ambassador looked a little uncomfortable, and they weren't sure what he found most disconcerting: confessing his lack of culinary skills, cataloguing Anna-Liisa's daily difficulties, or preparing himself for home visits from a perfect stranger.

'We needed to talk about meals anyway,' Margit said, quitting her pot-clattering. 'It looks like we have most of what we need to cook, and it would be a good idea to agree on kitchen duty. It doesn't make any sense for everyone to start fending for themselves, does it?'

In that moment, they realized that a commune wasn't all fun and games, as they'd imagined in their excitement. Margit was right. Although they were still paying for them, they were going to have to make do without Sunset Grove's services. And shopping and cooking for five every day was a whole new ball game to heating up a little liver casserole for lunch, despite the fact that Siiri and Irma had both run large households fifty years earlier, in the days before pre-packaged meals. They stared about glumly, wondering what might be the most sensible solution to the predicament. In the end, Irma pulled a slip of paper and a pen out of her handbag.

'Oh, you still use those. And here I thought you'd dropped everything old-fashioned in favour of your new tablet,' Siiri said a little sourly, unsure herself why.

'Let's make a chart,' Irma said briskly, and she started drawing lines across the paper. 'This is going to be our list of chores. It will tell us whose turn it is to do the shopping, cooking, cleaning and laundry. What am I forgetting?'

'I'm too busy to do much. I have to go out to see Eino at the SquirrelsNest every day, not that it does anyone much good. But I have to. I won't be able to stand myself if I don't,' Margit said. 'What are your views on euthanasia?'

'Anna-Liisa's out of the game for the meantime,' Siiri quickly interjected, to keep them focused on the topic at hand. 'And Onni, I don't suppose you're planning on participating in these household chores?'

The Ambassador seemed to have fallen asleep with his eyes open. When Irma gave him a friendly nudge, he started but didn't say anything.

'We'll release the sultan from household responsibilities,' Irma laughed cheerfully. 'After all, he's footing the bill for our little harem here. So that leaves two names on my chart, Siiri. Yours and mine.'

'I see, so you and I are going to do everything? In that case, I don't suppose we need to assign chores or make any lists.'

Irma crumpled up the chart and shoved it back into her handbag. She seemed to be looking for something in her bag, but when she couldn't think what it might be, she walked into the kitchen and started opening the cupboard doors. Margit said she was going to take a nap, the Ambassador was dozing on the couch, and Anna-Liisa was snoring away in her boudoir, at a respectable volume for such a frail convalescent. A faint drumbeat pounded from somewhere, a low, steady thump. Apparently one of the neighbours was listening to rock or some other racket. That was one thing there had been no need to grow acclimatized to at Sunset

Grove. Siiri joined Irma in the kitchenette to close all the cupboard doors her friend had just opened.

'So this is going to be our labour camp,' Irma said casually. 'Do you have any red wine stashed away? I could use a healthy swig.'

'Didn't you bring your box of wine with you from Sunset Grove?'

'Not that I remember. Which was silly of me, because, of course, those louts are going to drink it all up. But let's go and have a look, shall we? Perhaps it's waiting for me in my bedroom. Do you have a big mirror in your room, too? Isn't it a little . . . disconcerting? I'm startled every time I see my ugly old face in it. And what about when it's time for bed and you have to get undressed in front of the mirror!'

They went to Irma's room and she rummaged about in her boxes and continued jabbering without waiting for Siiri to comment. 'I've been thinking we ought to dig a little deeper into the Sunset Grove retrofit. Something about it strikes me as fishy. All those men in suits skulking around with gym bags, and none of the workers speak Finnish. Did you happen to see Anna-Liisa's jewellery box while you were packing?'

Much to her surprise, Siiri had indeed stumbled across Anna-Liisa's treasure chest among her underclothes. Of course that was where she'd put it: a ninety-five-year-old's unmentionables were the last thing of interest to a robber. She had added them to her moving load just as they were, so the jewellery box remained in the soft shelter of her bras and panties.

'How droll!' Irma said. 'But we won't tell Anna-Liisa until she's had a chance to settle in after the move. Have you been wondering where that young consultant, Jerry of the waxed head, suddenly vanished during the renovation? I think that bears looking into as well. Although I don't suppose we'll have much time to go out investigating retrofit-related shenanigans, seeing as how we have three lazybones to wait on. Oh, this does remind me of the best years of my life, those days when the house was full of strapping young men who were always starving and leaving their dirty laundry strewn across the floor. That's what they were like, my darlings, I must say, even though eventually they grew up to be fine, upstanding individuals. But! Some funny instinct is telling me that I packed a box of wine here in my lingerie – and here it is! A completely untouched box of smooth, supple red wine!'

Irma rose laboriously from her haunches and proudly presented the box of wine to Siiri as if it were the rarest of treasures. Just then, the doorbell rang.

'What was that?' Irma cried shrilly.

They didn't realize that the nasal warble was an indication that someone was at the door. They looked for a phone, but when they found it on the bar, they discovered it wasn't ringing. They wandered about the kitchenette, wondering what device could produce such an alarm, until they had the sense to roam into the entryway. The demanding warble burst out again, growing unpleasantly louder.

'You answer it,' Irma said to Siiri, nearly squashing her flat against the door. Siiri opened it warily, as if it were safer to crack the door open an inch at a time instead of opening it all at once. The corridor was dark, and she couldn't make out who was standing on the threshold. For a moment, everything was still; the only sound was the thump of the drumming from upstairs, louder than before.

'Hasan here?' asked the low voice of a man dressed in a well-cut suit from the midriff down. Then the voice took half a step backwards, which meant that not even that much remained visible; all Siiri saw was a gold tie-pin glittering in the darkness.

'Did you say Hasan? Is that a name? If so, there's no one here with that name. But we just moved in today.' Siiri studied the man curiously. He seemed agitated; he kept shifting his weight and jingling the coins in his pocket. He was wearing expensive-looking, polished dress shoes.

'My name is Siiri Kettunen. How do you do?'

The man did not take Siiri's hand, nor did he offer his own name. His right hand waved restlessly, and Siiri caught the bright gleam of a trio of fat gold rings. Irma crept up timidly behind Siiri, and even she wasn't able to get a word out.

'My mistake. Sorry to be a bother,' the voice eventually said, as the click of dress shoes receded into the darkness.

They never did see his face.

Chapter 13

Now that the plumbing retrofit wasn't waking them up at 6 a.m., they quickly settled back into their usual rhythms. The Ambassador and Anna-Liisa lounged in bed for hours, Irma slept like a baby thanks to her pills, and Siiri generally woke at nine. But Margit was an early bird and started flitting about the flat in her tattered nightshirt well before eight. She cursed loudly as she battled with the gas burner, finally got it to light, and made herself coffee and an egg. Then she hunted for the paper, wondered why there were four identical copies, took one, lowered her bulk into the enveloping sofa, and ate her breakfast as she lazily flipped through the news. After an hour of this, she grew bored and tried to turn on the TV. A protracted struggle with the five remotes ensued, culminating in her activating the television, much to her fright: the device bellowed, and the gargantuan screen showed a music video dripping with sex and gore.

'God save us. Help! How do I turn this off!' Margit squawked, jabbing remote after remote in a panic. This musical interlude was more effective than any diamond-drill cacophony at rousing the entire household. Only Anna-Liisa remained in her bed as the others stumbled into the living room in horror.

'Is that . . . why that's a breast,' Irma said, narrowing her eyes as she tried to make out what was happening on the wall-sized flat screen. 'And it has a gold loop with a ruby in it!'

'I doubt it's genuine,' the Ambassador said in a serious voice, as if he were an expert on piercings. 'Just a bit of glass. And definitely not gold.'

'This . . . this doesn't look like the Morning Show,' Siiri choked out. She tried to help Margit change the channel or at least mute the sound. The appalling screeching, drum-thrashing, and electric-guitar wails continued as a tiger appeared and started licking the woman. 'Oh dear, oh dear! This is just terrible . . . don't any of these remotes work? Do you suppose we should draw the curtains?'

They didn't know how to work the blinds or the television. Margit couldn't remember how she had turned it on, nor was there a power button on the device itself. The Ambassador tried to follow the power cable to tug it out of the wall, but it led into a tube along with a tangle of other wires, and it was impossible to say which one was the television cord. Irma and Siiri couldn't find any controls from where to pull or twist the blackout curtains.

'The curtains are on their own remote, of course,' Siiri said, giving up. 'But I don't suppose anyone is spying on us, trying to figure out what we're up to.'

'And perhaps we'll get used to what's coming from the television, just like we did with the racket from the renovation!' Irma said, going into the kitchenette to make her breakfast. She'd been too startled even to pull on a dressing gown.

'That's a pretty shade of toenail polish,' the Ambassador said politely.

Siiri rushed off to fetch her slippers before Onni started commenting on her craggy old toes. She decided to have her morning shower and dress while she was at it. It didn't feel appropriate to be traipsing about the commune half-naked, although both Margit and Irma seemed perfectly comfortable doing so. Thankfully, the Ambassador had donned ironed blue pyjamas and a stylish burgundy robe.

When Siiri stepped into their spa, the lights came on without her doing a thing. She looked at the tub, the shape of a stretched-out egg with a peculiar hollow in the middle, and decided to do her washing at the sink instead. But the tap had no visible method for releasing the flow of water. She tried pressing it, pulling it, and suddenly the water gushed out. When she moved her hand away, the water stopped.

'Oh, for Pete's sake,' she muttered to herself, testing the technology. Hands under the tap, water. Hands out from under the tap, no water. Very economical and efficient, to be sure. She didn't dare try the shower, but it appeared to work by a similar sort of mysterious logic and automatically knew when you wanted water. Suddenly Margit was standing behind her.

'Good grief, you gave me a fright! What are you doing in here? Can't you see I'm bathing, Margit?' Siiri cried, equal parts alarm and annoyance.

'I want to bathe, too,' Margit said, stripping off her thread-bare pyjamas and dropping them to the heated floor, then removing her hearing aid and slapping it down at the edge of Siiri's sink before marching into the shower as if mysterious, mind-reading robots were nothing new. Siiri found the sight of Margit standing before her in all of her unclothed, corpu-lent glory disconcerting. She modestly wrapped herself in her dressing gown and snuck off.

Outside the living room, she ran into a woman she had never seen before. This stranger, an adult, had bangs that were chopped far too short, like Siiri's children in their school photos from the 1950s, when she used to cut their hair herself. The woman had packed her thick thighs into a pair of geometrically patterned stockings and topped off the ensemble with a loosely knit sweater.

'And here's another one. How many of you live here?' the woman asked, without looking at Siiri.

'Five,' replied the Ambassador, who appeared to know who the woman was. The television was still spewing music videos. Just now, a man with a long beard was using a chainsaw to chop a dog in two on the roof of a car, while three topless women swayed and panted English-language sentiments into their microphones.

'I'm Siiri Kettunen, hello.'

'Jemina Koutamo-Navaglotu from the municipality,

hello. I'm the Temporary Part-Time Director for Western Health-Care District In-Home Care; the director is on job alternation leave.'

'She's here for Anna-Liisa. As you already know, Anneli has been ordered to receive in-home care,' the Ambassador explained, knotting the belt of his silk bathrobe more tightly. They were still a little shell-shocked after their rude awakening, and none of them had imagined in-home care was so efficient. Why, Anna-Liisa had just been released from the hospital, and people were already showing up on their doorstep at the crack of dawn.

'Would you care for coffee and a sandwich? I made us breakfast,' Irma said amiably, setting out slices of bread on a plate. They were covered with thick slabs of real butter and generous sprinklings of finger-salt. 'Or is that why you're here, to make us breakfast?'

'No, thank you. And no. This is an assessment visit. The idea is to evaluate the need for in-home care and support services with the client and those responsible for her well-being. Which one of you is the client, and who answers for her well-being?'

'Oh, we're all clients, depending on the situation,' Irma said, pouring coffee into cups. 'Or was it consumers? Isn't that what you call people these days, consumers? And we're all responsible for each other's well-being, in a way. Do you take milk or sugar? Unfortunately, I don't have any cream to offer you. We've just moved here to Hakaniemi; we're quite the refugees since a tribe of Huns attacked our retirement home. We call them crooks because they look like they're up to no good, and all sorts of things have happened there. Things go missing, the project manager disappeared, there are pockets of water damage here and there, the ceiling collapsed in one unit, and an enormous hole appeared in our wall, the wall I share with Siiri Kettunen here, and no one has bothered to repair it. They just taped some plastic over it. It all seems very illicit to me. Do you take sugar? Did I already ask?'

'No, thank you. And yes, you did. I wasn't given time to answer. Which one of you is Anna-Liisa Marjatta Petäjä?'

'She's sleeping in the round bed in the big bedroom. Imagine that, the bed is perfectly round, and there's a mirror on the ceiling above it. Have you ever heard of such a thing?'

Irma was astonishingly chipper, and it no longer bothered her that rock music was blaring from the television at an unbearable volume, along with horrific images of burning houses and blood-spattered heads with pigs' snouts and elephants' ears.

The Ambassador marched into his bedchamber to warn Anneli about the impending inspection. But Anna-Liisa had heard everything and had dressed as they recovered from their astonishment. The Ambassador helped his wife out into the living room and introduced her as if she were the object of enormous pride: 'This is your client. And I am the one responsible for her well-being. Her husband.'

The assessor with the complicated-sounding employment relationship at municipal In-Home Care looked Anna-Liisa up and down like an experienced judge eyeing candidates at a dog show. She flipped through her papers, tried to seat herself on a bar stool and refused yet another offer of coffee from Irma. To her horror, Irma realized she was barefoot and in a nightshirt and vanished into her mauve bedchamber in a torrent of apologies.

The representative from In-Home Care passed out colourful brochures advertising the palette of services offered by the city of Helsinki and said that the doctor had ordered Anna-Liisa a service called 'convalescent care'. The aim was to help the client achieve normal health after an illness, and it included treating the illness, monitoring the client's progress, and exercises that facilitated activity and mobility.

'How awful,' Siiri let slip. For a moment, everything was quiet. The nurse was still scanning her papers, clearly trying to get a grasp on Anna-Liisa's illness and the minutiae of her case.

'Can you please explain what is meant here by achieving normal health?' Anna-Liisa asked, after browsing through the brochure. 'Seeing as how I'm a rather worn-down, ninety-four-year-old individual: how on earth can anything be normal in my case?'

'Yes. And no. Nothing is normal; you're right about that. We don't like to use that word, because it's stigmatizing. If something is normal, that means something else isn't, if you catch my drift.'

'I do. Are you testing my comprehension? Am I going to have to answer another battery of questions, like what day is it?'

'No and no. I'm not testing your state of mind, and I'm not going to conduct an MMSE on you. In this case, achieving normal health means managing everyday life without assistance, like prior to your falling ill. What sort of help did you receive at the retirement home?'

'Excuse me, I'm having a hard time hearing what you're saying with that horrible contraption shrieking in my ear. Can't anyone turn it off? You're young; perhaps you know how televisions like this work?' Anna-Liisa said.

'Yes. And maybe. I'll do my best.'

'Look, now that nun is taking off her clothes, and she's a man! Like in Rossini's *Le Comte Ory*!' Irma squealed shrilly. She had put on her blue summer dress, brushed her hair, dabbed on a bit of lipstick, and looked very presentable – unlike the rest of them. Margit was still in the shower; the Ambassador and Siiri were in their bathrobes. In her rush, Anna-Liisa had buttoned her shirt askew and slipped on mismatching shoes.

Jemina Whatshername marched up to the television, located some magic button along the bottom edge, and killed it.

'Ah, lovely. You're a genius. Thank you so much!' Siiri said in relief and seated herself on the sofa to drink her coffee. She could feel her strength ebbing, as the day had started off too quickly and she hadn't had time to eat properly. At least she'd managed to drink her two glasses of water in the bathroom before Margit barged in.

Having achieved momentary peace in the flat, the in-home

care assessor took hold of the reins. She began by quizzing Anna-Liisa on all manner of things; she had three pages' worth of questions, and she marked the answers with a tick in a box. Siiri grew squeamish eating her breakfast as Anna-Liisa gave a detailed report of her present circumstances.

'. . . my digestion is rather irregular, and lately I've suffered some bouts of constipation, which might have as much to do with the fact that I was lying in hospital for three weeks for no discernible reason as with my being the victim of an unvaried hospital diet. I don't generally have problems with urinary incontinence – under normal circumstances, that is – although lately –'

Siiri and Irma exchanged glances, and without further ado took their sandwiches and coffee cups and moved into the recesses of the kitchenette. But there was no table there, and so they lowered their breakfasts to the marble countertop and discreetly turned their backs on Anna-Liisa, the Ambassador, and the in-home care assessor so that they could probe the particulars of Anna-Liisa's need for assistance in privacy. A moment later, they heard a roar of horror from Anna-Liisa, and they turned round to see what had happened.

'Which door is the one to my bedroom?'

Margit was standing in the middle of the living room, nightshirt over one arm and hearing aid in the opposite hand, the water from her undried hair dripping to the parquet. She was as naked as the day she was born, and looked even more enormous than when clothed. She hadn't even heard Anna-Liisa's roar, which had been as impressive as any during Anna-Liisa's prime teaching years.

'If multiple residents at the same address require in-home care, it's best to coordinate visits,' Jemina Koutamo-Navaglotu said, casting her professional eye over Margit. The Ambassador clearly found the situation amusing and ogled Margit with interest, shamelessly allowing his gaze to linger over the details. Anna-Liisa was annoyed by the interruption, and Siiri rushed over to help Margit, who didn't appear to have a clue as to what was taking place in the living room.

'Come on, dear, let's go to your room so you can get dressed.'

Siiri led, or rather dragged, Margit out of view as quickly as possible. Margit's room had a dreary exposure that received no direct sun, even on a hot August day. Siiri studied Margit's hearing aid in order to help her friend slip it on, but found its workings as impenetrable as the flat-screen television and automatic blinds of their temporary lodgings.

'Give it here,' Margit said, sounding brusque because she was talking too loudly. She put on the device; it squealed unpleasantly for a moment and then everything was back to normal. She started digging into her moving boxes, looking for clothes, and getting everything wet with the water-drops from her hair.

'This woman is here to survey Anna-Liisa's needs for in-home care. It's a normal process. It seems as if public in-home care is working efficiently this time,' Siiri explained.

Margit wanted to rest for a moment. Siiri spread a towel

out over her pillow and left her lying in bed. There were no curtains, just a roller blind that Siiri didn't even try to operate, other than waving a hand half-heartedly just in case the curtain understood that she wanted it to descend. Nothing happened. Margit said she had no problem napping in daylight and it made no difference to her if someone from across the courtyard saw her in her underthings.

'Yes, watching all those music videos we had the pleasure of waking up to must have tired you out,' Siiri said, laughing a little so she wouldn't sound nasty and then she returned to the living room to see how things had progressed there.

Irma was clearing up the remains of their breakfast and washing the dishes with a deafening clatter. The others had disappeared.

'They went into Anneli and Onneli's room to discuss the practicalities,' she said, clearly chagrined at not having been included in the evaluation.

Siiri helped Irma finish the washing-up. This was tricky, as they only had a tiny sink and a rag, no scrubbing brush. Luckily, there weren't many dishes. They moved over to the couch to browse through the brochures describing the palette of in-home services and only then remembered the existence of the dishwasher.

'I don't suppose it did us any harm to get a little exercise,' Irma sighed in her defence, before concentrating on the brochure. 'Now this is interesting!'

She started picking out services as if in-home care were some sort of spa. Why, they would even help you go to the sauna! All sorts of mundane pleasures were on offer:

cleaning, lotioning, shaving, putting in hair curlers, laundry service.

'I wouldn't say no to some of these!' Irma laughed.

'Yes, you do have those long hairs sprouting from your chin. I bet the cleaning isn't of professional quality. This calls it tidying up, and only mentions vacuuming and dusting.'

'Humph, tidying indeed. But so-called cleaners never clean properly these days, as we know from Sunset Grove. I wonder how things are going there? Should we pop by and conduct a little assessment of our own?'

'Not yet, Irma. Do you suppose Anna-Liisa's condition is poor enough to warrant grocery shopping service for the household?'

'I doubt it. But maybe this automatic meal dispenser. It's called a *menumat*.'

The menumat was a combination freezer and oven, a real convection oven, according to the brochure. Eighteen meals were delivered to the dispenser at a time, which the client then had to heat up in the oven.

'Should we request one of these?'

'I doubt the food is edible.'

Then Irma found a list of equipment one could request free of charge: a turning board with standing support, a wooden walking sledge, a portable electric suction device, a motion aid, and a sock-puller. They didn't have a clue what you would use them for, but they made superb word games.

'Did you use to play Words in a Word with your children? Where you're supposed to think of as many words as possible from one word? We could start, say, with *antiphar-maceutically*. What do you say? It has twenty letters.'

Siiri agreed. Irma dug a dog-eared slip of paper from her handbag and they started thinking of words they could make from *antipharmaceutically*. Meanwhile, they couldn't help hearing the conversation taking place in Anna-Liisa and Onni's room.

Apparently, Anna-Liisa and Onni had decided on a relatively light repertoire: help with washing and dressing morning and night, as well as a rehabilitation programme and an exercise plan, but no meal service, cleaning service, or other comforts that would have lightened Siiri and Irma's load.

'How many words do you have?' Irma asked, when she was too tired to think of any more.

'Eleven. Wait, I have one more. Do you want to read yours?'

'Ace, pace, ache, achy, acne, acme, accent, air, airy, pair, care, thrill, trill – do you see how rhythmic this is, like a poem, and then some random ones: rye, tamale, captain, rectum –'

Irma hadn't made it to the end of her list before the door to Anna-Liisa's room opened and the entire committee emerged: Jemina striding out briskly at the vanguard, then Anna-Liisa, wan and unsteady, supported by Onni, who brought up the rear. Anna-Liisa looked dejected. The municipality's temporary part-time substitute in-home caregiver stopped in front of Irma.

'Did you say Captain Rectum?'

'Oh, no, I didn't, first captain and then rectum. Two separate words. This is just a little game of ours.'

Jemina asked no further questions, but she wanted to see the bathroom before she left. The Ambassador showed her all of its finest features, from the dimming lights to the massaging whirlpool tub. In the meantime, Anna-Liisa studied Irma and Siiri's word-game lists as eagerly as during her healthy days.

'I can think of a few more: allium, yeti and plateau.'

'Your apartment is not suitable for elderly residents,' the in-home caregiver said, rather curtly, after continuing on to the kitchenette. 'We will monitor the patient's progress, and if there are any problems, the need for assistance will be reassessed.'

'Could we have foot rubs and help putting curlers in our hair?' Irma asked from the couch, from which, despite her best attempts, she found it impossible to rise. 'Or a hand with the household chores? And perhaps you could help me up?'

'No. And yes. There you go.'

Jemina Koutamo-Navaglotu hoisted Irma up from the sofa with a practised hand. She drily explained that in-home care was a doctor-prescribed service that, despite being public, was not cost free. It was not a spa treatment. The first in-home care specialist would be there that very evening and one would appear three times a day from then on, until further notice.

'Thank you and goodbye.'

She pulled out her smartphone, reported that her visit had

come to its conclusion, shook hands with Anna-Liisa and the Ambassador, and made her exit with a rustle of her geometrically patterned stockings.

Chapter 14

'Oh, it's heavenly here; it's like paradise,' Siiri sighed contentedly.

Unlike weekdays, Hakaniemi Hall was packed to the gills on Saturdays. Siiri and Irma meandered around the ground floor, basking in the ambience, taking in the smells, admiring the delicacies. Customers here didn't have their noses in the air the way they did at the Stockmann delicatessen or the downtown Market Hall, where Siiri felt ill at ease. Irma liked popping into Stockmann for smoked salmon and fish roe herself, but even she had to admit that the atmosphere at Hakaniemi Hall was special. People of every description strolled the aisles, lively chatter permeated the beautiful old building, and no one seemed to be in a hurry or a bad mood. Best of all, there were plenty of salespeople, several at every counter. The merchants were pleasant and talkative, served their customers cheerfully and without pushing their wares too aggressively.

'I can't stand it when I go to the mall and I make the mistake of stepping into a store out of curiosity. Those salesgirls pop out like jack-in-the boxes: Can I help you?' Irma complained.

They watched a handsome, foreign-looking butcher prepare oxtail for an elderly customer according to the latter's instructions. The saw shrieked, filling the air with the smell of burnt bone as the pieces fell to the wax paper. The butcher expertly cut longer slices from the tip of the tail, shorter bits from the butt-end.

'Do you girls know how to make oxtail stew?' the old rascal asked them flirtatiously, and then started boasting about his prowess in the kitchen. Irma was so stimulated by the exchange that she bought two kilos of oxtail, a kilo more than the randy old fellow. The foreign-looking butcher wrapped her purchase in wax paper, put it in a plastic bag, threw in a marrowbone for free, and wished them a nice day in perfect Finnish.

'Oh my! This certainly is different to the Low Price Market in Munkkiniemi,' Irma said, pleased. 'Veikko used to love my oxtail stew, although I haven't the foggiest what I put into it. But it mustn't have been too complicated; as I recall, I used to make it for him nearly every week. Oh, dear, he was such a lovely man, and now I miss him again.'

'Are you going to be able to haul all those bones home?' Siiri asked, concerned. She was also unsure whether the oxtails would fit into the pans at their luxury lodgings. Their cookware was all so very small.

'Pshaw. We'll just divide them up into smaller pots and season them separately,' Irma said with a dismissive wave.

The rarest delicacies appeared to be comfort food for Hakaniemi Hall's shoppers. No one else seemed to find any of it – the pullets swimming in a herb bath; broiler livers, hearts and gizzards; weeping Toholampi Emmental; Muscovy duck thighs; whole pike heads; or French champagne brie – the least bit strange. But Siiri and Irma stopped, peered, squealed, stepped closer, frowned and asked questions like tourists at a Marrakesh bazaar.

'Or at a Persian market! Like in that Albert Ketèlbey song about the dawn of time they still play sometimes on *Saturday Wish List*.'

They tried to piece together the song, but it was no use. They remembered that it began with percussion, flutes, piccolos and the rumble of a male chorus, and that the cello solo during the languid bridge built into a beautiful melody. But how did it go?

'It's always hard remembering a tune without the lyrics,' Irma said. 'Theo Mackeben's "Warum" is much easier. It goes like this.' She started warbling long passages of German in a shrill voice that climbed higher and higher, like Miliza Korjus at the apex of her career. 'It ends in a vocalize, doesn't it?' She continued trilling without words and then jumped back into the chorus.

'The Berlin Nightingale! Wasn't that what they called her?' Siiri interjected, hoping to bring Irma's street concert to a rapid conclusion.

'Yes! And Jenny Lind was the Swedish Nightingale. We don't have a Finnish Nightingale, unless you count that singer from Pakila who whistles, what was his name . . . Look,

Siiri! A whole rabbit! Which park do you suppose they caught it in, Tokoinranta or Karhupuisto?' Irma was laughing so hard that the tears streamed from her eyes. No, on further reflection, the beast was too scrawny to be one of the well-fed bunnies that had overrun Helsinki's parks. It was only when Siiri didn't join in that Irma realized her friend had turned away and was standing stock-still, watching a butcher hold up an enormous, pale, bloody slab with a pair of tongs for a black fellow to inspect. The slimy pancake went on and on until it dangled high in the air, revealing the nasty stub of some severed tube at the bottom. The black man looked pleased. His head was crowned by a pot-holder that looked like a beehive and jiggled precariously as he nodded.

'It's beautiful! Thank you, I'll take it,' he said.

Siiri leaned in to see what this foodstuff might be. 'Beef oesophagus and lungs, three euros thirty a kilo. Oh my.' She had to cover her mouth, so as not to look idiotic as she gaped at the black man's purchases.

'Cheap, tasty food,' he said, flashing a dazzling white smile.

'I'm sorry – is that for your dog?'

'I don't have a dog!' he laughed, waving the plastic bag containing the cow's lungs and oesophagus in Siiri's face. 'I'm going to cook lung stew, it's easy to make. The best place for spices is a couple of blocks away. The African grocery at Hämeentie five.'

'Is there one of those here, too? An African grocery?' Siiri marvelled.

Now it was the black man's turn to be surprised. 'You must not be from the neighbourhood. Where are you from?'

Irma was clearly put off: 'We're not from anywhere but right here. Our families have lived in Helsinki for ten generations, which you clearly cannot say for yourself.' She was quiet for a moment and then smiled. 'But we don't know Hakaniemi that well.'

The man laughed a deep, rumbling laugh so that the beehive on his head trembled.

'You can find anything you want in Hakaniemi; this is the best place in the world! We have a Chinese grocery, Indian, Moroccan, Japanese, African, you name it. You can get anything you want, and for a good price, too. Are you familiar with halal?'

'Who?'

'Halal. The best meat in the world, like kosher for Jews, but the Muslims say halal. There's a little shop nearby that sells excellent halal meat for a much better price than those plastic-wrapped pork chops you get at the supermarket.'

'How interesting! I don't particularly care for pork myself,' Siiri said. 'You must be a cook?'

'Me? A cook? No, no!' The man laughed loudly again. 'But I do cook for my wife and children every day. Do you live far from here?'

Siiri explained that they had recently moved to Hakaniemi. Irma launched into a detailed account of the sordid particulars of the Sunset Grove renovation before a reproachful look from Siiri silenced her. The man in the funny hat was as nice as could be and thrilled when he saw how much oxtail Irma had bought. He wanted to know how they planned on preparing it and recommended a recipe that called for raisins, pine nuts and chocolate.

'Why, that sounds crazy!' Irma laughed, but the man was serious. He pulled a piece of paper from his pocket and jotted down the recipe for them. 'You make it a day in advance, do you understand? This is not fast food, it's slow food. It needs to stew in the oven overnight. You add the chocolate at the very end.'

'Do we have an oven? I don't remember. But the one thing we have plenty of is time!' Siiri said.

'You can also do it on the stove, no problem.'

After accepting the recipe for chocolate stew, Siiri and Irma thanked the man and introduced themselves. Their new friend had come to Finland years ago from Nigeria, lived just a few blocks away, and was called Muhammed Haani Abubakar. He had to write the name down for them, because Irma and Siiri could make neither head nor tail of it, even though he tried to say it slowly and repeated it three times.

'Muhammed, this is my first name. In Finland everyone calls me Muhis. Haani is my middle name, it means happy and content. Look at me: I'm happy and content!'

He spread his arms and laughed his deep laugh. They wished each other luck in the kitchen, and then, lugging his bag of lungs, Muhis disappeared into the hubbub of Hakaniemi hall, his colourful hat bobbing among the drab Finns.

Chapter 15

Upon returning to their temporary lodgings, Siiri and Irma were greeted with a surprise: two men in their entry hall. At first they thought the men were in-home caregivers, because the City of Helsinki Western Health-Care District In-Home Care sent nurses of every description who let themselves in with their own keys at any hour of the day. Siiri and Irma no longer flustered easily; their refugee asylum had turned into Grand Central Station now that the doctor had ordered in-home care for Anna-Liisa. One day, three caregivers had appeared within an hour of each other, all claiming to be from different shifts: one from the morning, one from the day, and one from the evening. The caregivers had too many clients, which threw their schedules into disarray. The time spent with clients counted towards their workdays, but travel time didn't, and Anna-Liisa's living in Hakaniemi, although she belonged to the Western Health-Care District, created an extra burden, which meant many of the caregivers started or ended their shift with her.

If you could call it caregiving, that is. Occasionally, the caregivers were so young one felt sorry for them; frequently they were so angry one was afraid of them. They were slaves to their mobile phones, as they were required to constantly report their comings and goings and doings to their employer. One girl of Somali extraction had been frightened to death after spending three minutes more than the allotted time washing Anna-Liisa's bottom.

The two fellows purported to be policemen. They were just boys, actually, young and very nice-looking: blond, strapping Finnish lads. Both were neatly dressed, although not in police uniforms; they were wearing dress pants and dress shirts buttoned up all the way. They tried to slip out into the corridor, but Siiri stopped them on the doorstep.

'Who died? Anna-Liisa?' Siiri asked grimly, although she could feel her calcifying heart beating in a rapid arrhythmic syncopation. She'd heard that if an old person died happily in her own home, you were supposed to call the police to verify that it hadn't been a homicide. Would they be interrogated about Anna-Liisa's death now, like in one of Hercule Poirot's escapades? What other business could two police officers in civilian clothing have in an old folks' home?

'Anna-Liisa?' asked the quicker of the pair.

'Our friend Anna-Liisa, the one caregivers are traipsing in and out all day to look after. Or are you fellows actually from in-home care?'

'If you're looking for Hasan, he doesn't live here any more,' Irma added.

'We're detectives. To our knowledge, no one has died. We came to retrieve a jewellery box that had been reported stolen.'

'So Anna-Liisa reported it! Fantastic.' Irma was thrilled. 'We were right, those construction workers are crooks.'

She shot Siiri a victorious look and dropped two kilos of oxtail to the parquet. The policemen gaped at the heap of bloody bones. When the taller of the two lads bent down to see what exactly it was that had appeared there on the floor, Siiri and Irma could clearly see he was holding a mahogany box behind his back.

'That's Anna-Liisa's jewellery box! Where did you find it?' Irma cried.

'And where are you taking it?' Siiri wondered.

'We're not at liberty to discuss the details . . . the investigation is still pending, we're collecting evidence . . . as ordered. We'll be inspecting it more closely at police premises.'

Siiri started growing suspicious of this pair, skulking like a pair of naughty boys who'd been caught red-handed. Who had let them in, and why were they trying to sneak out like this, taking Anna-Liisa's jewellery? Siiri hadn't told Anna-Liisa about saving her valuables yet, because life at Hakaniemi had got off to such a hectic start and Anna-Liisa had spent most of her time convalescing in her room. Siiri had forgotten all about the jewellery box in the turmoil. How had these men found it in the chaos of Siiri's belongings? Had they rummaged through her underwear drawer and made a mess of the delicates she had finally got around to carefully organizing? The longer she looked at the discombobulated duo and thought about the jewellery box, the more irked she grew. In the end, she couldn't control herself. She snatched the box from the taller policeman, who hadn't foreseen the attack and was caught completely off guard.

'Beat it,' Siiri ordered, pointing at the still-open door. 'We may have one foot in the grave, but we're not suckers. Anna-Liisa's jewellery box belongs to Anna-Liisa, and if a single cameo has gone missing, I'm going to report you to the police. And you'd better believe it!'

The astonished men left, slamming the door behind them. Irma looked at Siiri in admiration, and wrapped her in a big, sickly sweet, perfumed embrace.

'Oh, Siiri, you are a rock! How could I ever live without you? *Döden, döden, döden.*'

They gathered up their oxtails and went into the living room. Irma crowed several cock-a-doodle-doos, but the Ambassador and Margit were out and Anna-Liisa was too feeble to respond from her bed. They stashed Irma's bag of bones in the fridge and went in to present the missing jewellery box to Anna-Liisa and to explain what had happened. At first she was overjoyed that the box had been found, and Siiri had saved it so cleverly, but then she went white as a sheet.

'Am I to understand that thieves, complete strangers, have been creeping about our apartment and I didn't hear a thing?'

Irma tried to lighten the mood, since the worst was over: 'Would it have been better if the thieves had been someone you knew?'

'Like your darlings, you mean?' Anna-Liisa parried, eyes flashing. 'They robbed you back at Sunset Grove while you were in the hospital, presumed to have dementia. No, but . . . how can . . . Jesus, Mary and Joseph!'

Anna-Liisa had opened the box. Her valuables were intact and were now spread across the bed. But beneath them, at the bottom of the box, was an enormous wad of five-hundred euro bills. It must have added up to tens of thousands of euros. They gaped at the money, flummoxed, and Irma admired the currency's violet tones.

'Look how pretty. It's modern architecture of some sort . . . Can either of you make out what building this is?'

'Is that your money, Anna-Liisa?' Siiri asked hesitantly. Anna-Liisa looked as if she would die then and there. She was breathing in tiny, shallow gasps, unable to speak. Finally, she started coughing and nearly vomited. Irma scurried off to the spa to fetch a bucket, while Siiri slipped pillows under Anna-Liisa's back.

'It's not my money,' Anna-Liisa said finally, in a barely audible voice. 'And I never reported the theft to the police.'

Chapter 16

Irma and Siiri made a chocolate stew from the oxtails based on Muhis' recipe. They started by simmering the bones for a couple of hours with root vegetables and onions; Siiri scraped the foul-looking foam from the surface with a strainer. Irma grated carrots, celery and onions, grumbling why Muhis didn't just let her dice them. But Muhis had written: 'Must be grated, otherwise the sauce will be too thin.' Siiri patted the boiled bones dry with a towel and browned them in two pans. Irma sautéed her grated vegetables in a third, and stirred them in with the bones. Then they added generous splashes of white wine, chopped tomatoes and soup stock, until the bones were covered. Irma was suspicious of Muhis' spices, but Siiri sprinkled in the pepper, cinnamon, cloves and salt. Then they put the pots in the oven they discovered embedded in the wall and let them cook overnight, adding chocolate, pine nuts, and raisins the next day and letting the black gruel simmer down until smooth.

For once everyone was present, even Margit, whose schedule diverged drastically from the routines of the rest of the household. After waking up early and watching morning television for a couple of hours, she generally left for her clubs and other activities, ate lunch who knows where, visited Eino at the SquirrelsNest and didn't come home until evening, utterly exhausted. The lack of synchronicity was actually a good thing, as Margit was the only one who had mastered the television's complicated remote controls and had an unfortunate habit of letting it blast if she were at home, even when she wasn't watching it. She had other unfortunate habits as well: she would wander about naked, forget to flush the toilet, leave her belongings strewn haphazardly about the flat, and doze off on the sofa with her reading glasses on, snoring heavily.

The Ambassador was a meticulous, tidy fellow; he gave his co-lodgers no cause for complaint. He was surprisingly busy, with any number of appointments, errands and engagements in town, fraternal organizations and the like, but no set schedule. He spent quite a bit of time in the bedroom with Anna-Liisa when she was too tired to rise from her bed, reading her the poetry of Saima Harmaja or *The Tales of Ensign Stål* in a pleasant voice. If Anna-Liisa was feeling livelier, they would entertain each other by listing noun cases and German prepositions. But the Ambassador found the presence of the caregivers so disturbing that he always tried to slip off before their arrival. If a caregiver happened to appear suddenly in their living room, the Ambassador would immediately remember somewhere he needed to be; once, when he hadn't had time to dress, he panicked and retreated to the spa in his silk dressing gown and spent over an hour sitting there in the unheated sauna.

Irma and Siiri got along famously with the caregivers, and they had already come to know a few of the more faithful rehabilitators. On occasion they would join Anna-Liisa on the mandatory outings included in her mobility plan. Paasivuori Park had become a favourite destination; the little square in front of the massive headquarters of the Social Democratic Party was peaceful and had sturdy benches. From this vantage point, they would spend a moment gazing at *The Boxers*, the simultaneously dynamic and static statue by Johannes Haapasalo. Irma never failed to mention that Haapasalo had studied with Rodin, at which point the conversation generally died, because Irma loved Rodin's statues but Anna-Liisa found them crude. Anna-Liisa could barely manage the walk to the park and, after a brief rest there, the return journey home. Somehow she wasn't putting on any weight, despite the fact that Siiri and Irma were feeding her like a growing child.

'Not bad, I must say,' Irma said, after her first sip of the chocolate stew. She slurped the broth from her spoon and smacked her lips as if it would bring out the flavours better. They were perched in their now-familiar places around the awkward bar-counter. The stools didn't support their backs, and Irma said the upholstery buttons were digging into her rear end.

'Is it supposed to taste like a Christmas dish?' Anna-Liisa asked. She hadn't touched her spoon yet; she was still sceptically eyeing the mounded stew Siiri had doled out into her bowl. Margit was gobbling down her helping, sucking loudly on the bone marrow.

'This is scrumptious!' she bawled.

The Ambassador fell in love with the chocolate stew, too. At first he nibbled warily, then with increasing gusto, until he stopped, closed his eyes, and purred in satisfaction. Anna-Liisa also praised the dish, and was the first to take seconds.

'It's so lovely cooking again,' Siiri said. 'I can never be bothered to cook for myself, but now that there are so many mouths to feed, I'm enjoying it. I think I'll try Muhis' rabbit stew next week.'

Siiri and her Nigerian friend often happened to be at Hakaniemi Hall around the same time, tennish, when things were relatively quiet and there was room to move. They'd got in the habit of talking about food, what they were planning on preparing that week, and how. Siiri had picked up a few exotic dishes from Muhis, but had yet to try her hand at stewed okra, corn porridge, or deep-fried yam, despite her friend's detailed instructions on how to cook and serve them.

Muhis' unquenchable enthusiasm for innards and all manner of stewed dishes had taken Siiri back to the foods of her childhood. She'd grown up cooking with tongue, blood and kidneys back when most Finns didn't even dream of beef. She had stumbled across a copy of the *Hard Times Cookbook* in one of the stands in the hall; it was sold as a joke these days, she supposed, and when Muhis saw it, he had chuckled his deep chuckle and read long passages out loud.

'"Blood milk: Place pieces of blood pudding in a pot and

cover with milk. Bone fat: remove meat (if any) from the bones and set aside for other purposes. Put the bones in a pot and simmer on a low heat for six hours."'

Siiri had been a little offended by Muhis' chuckling, because the book's recipes were familiar from her own life. Not many decades had passed since Finns had eaten that way.

Anna-Liisa and the Ambassador had their doubts about Siiri's Nigerian friend, and had no interest in being forced to eat Third-World finger-food. Irma defended Siiri and explained what a nice man Muhis was and how he always helped them carry their groceries home.

'What was the other boy's name, his friend? The one with the kinky hair who walks around in sandals?'

'Metukka. Muhis and Metukka are both from Nigeria and speak Finnish so well that even you would be surprised, Anna-Liisa.'

Muhis had introduced Irma and Siiri to his friend Metukka, whose real name was Mehdi Fuad Emeagwali. Muhis had jotted it down in the margins of the recipe for stewed rabbit and explained that Fuad meant heart and that Metukka had a good heart.

'Whatever will they come up with next,' Anna-Liisa said. 'Although this is delicious, I must admit. Was it this Muhammed who taught you how to make this?'

'It was him. My friend Muhis,' Siiri said.

'I see.' Anna-Liisa continued eating with a healthy appetite, until suddenly she dropped her spoon and looked at Siiri almost angrily. 'So are Muhis and Metukka your new Mika

Korhonens? Are they going to become our guardians, too, until they disappear, never to be heard from again?'

Mika Korhonen! A stabbing pain shot through Siiri's head and she started feeling so light-headed that she had to take hold of the countertop with both hands. Anna-Liisa certainly knew how to strike at the most corroded circuits of her calcified heart. How many times Siiri had tried to reach Mika Korhonen after he had fixed everything at Sunset Grove! But she had never got through to him, not once. Mika's phone number was no longer in use, and he had vanished into thin air. This had convinced Anna-Liisa that he was the most dastardly drug dealer of all, more hardened than even Erkki and Virpi Hiukkanen, and had been sentenced to a life behind bars. Siiri was having none of it. Perhaps Mika had moved abroad, or gone off to school and moved away. But she missed Mika often, and Anna-Liisa hadn't been far from the mark in teasing Siiri about her new young male friends.

'We don't have any reason to believe Mika won't be back. Maybe he has a new girlfriend,' Siiri said tiredly.

'What do you need guardians for anyway, now that everything's in order and no one is dying?' Irma said cheerfully, then sang the praises of the oxtail stew as if she'd completely forgotten she'd made it herself.

'Eino ought to die,' Margit said.

'Anneli doesn't need a guardian any more because she has me. A husband will take precedence over such upstarts in any court,' the Ambassador said. He had already eaten two servings and now helped himself to a third. Siiri was pleased; she hadn't expected the dish to be such a big success.

'But he's not dying. What am I going to do if I die before he does?'

'Margit! What sort of problem is that? You won't do anything, because you'll be dead. Or do you suppose you'll be flying back to the RatsNest in the form of a housefly to torment him?' Irma huffed, helping herself to more stew.

'I'm worried, can't you understand? Eino might end up lying there in that institution for God knows how many years without anyone knowing who he is, what his likes and dislikes are, and what he was like back . . . back when he . . . he was a person.'

'Yes, I suppose that's a good reason for you to not die. But you're not as old as the rest of us, are you?'

'I'm eighty-seven,' Margit said dejectedly.

'So young! Think about us, we're all well past ninety. *Döden, döden, döden.*'

'Sometimes I think I'll die from sheer depression. From not being able to see any hope for Eino. Every time I visit him, I feel guilty he's alive. Eino always said he doesn't want to lie around like a vegetable and be a bother to anyone, and I'm letting it happen every day. But what am I supposed to do, since this country doesn't recognize the mercy euthanasia offers?'

They all fell silent, their chewing slowed. Swallowing was hard; the cheery ambience had evaporated. Siiri racked her brains trying to think of something positive to say, but her mind was blank. She started gathering up bowls and clearing away their lunch. Then she remembered Muhis and Metukka and how they'd been a little taken aback when they discovered where Siiri and Irma were living. Apparently, they shouldn't be surprised if unusual characters came around knocking at their door.

'Onni, are you sure you don't know what this place was being used for before we moved in? I gathered from my friends that it has quite a reputation—'

That was as far as Siiri got, because the phone rang. This was a rare event. Irma had her mobile phone, as did the Ambassador, and no one ever called any of the others. Siiri's great-granddaughter's boyfriend Tuukka, who handled Siiri's banking on his computer, had learned to call Irma when he needed to speak to Siiri, and that wasn't often. Sunset Grove had tightened up its invoicing after the previous year's events. Irma dashed over to the phone and got there first, although the Ambassador did his best to be able to take the unexpected call.

'Hasan? Hasan again. Who is this Hasan?' Irma asked angrily, holding the receiver away from her ear to indicate how unpleasant the person shouting at the other end was. 'This is Irma Lännenleimu and I don't know any Hasan. Are you the fellow with the gold rings who was at our door asking about Hasan? Please tell your friend— the impudence! He hung up on me!'

Irma was so outraged that she fetched her whisky from her room and poured a healthy splash into a milk glass. The Ambassador took a tumbler from the vitrine and a couple of ice cubes from the ice machine with a practised hand. Of the apartment's countless appliances, it was the sole one he had mastered.

'Onni! Are you drinking?' Anna-Liisa asked in horror.

'I'm just having a little digestive, dear. Would you like one too?' the Ambassador asked, with a tender pat of his wife's back.

'Yes, I don't suppose there's any rush to get anywhere,' Irma said. 'Does anyone want to play cards? I have a pack here somewhere . . . I'm sure I had one . . .' She reached into her handbag and emptied its contents onto the kitchenette counter.

Siiri wasn't feeling well; all of this was making her woozy. This time it wasn't only thrumming in her ears and the hammering in her heart; now her stomach had done a somersault, too, and she felt nauseous. Perhaps she'd eaten too much. She thought about her missing friend Mika Korhonen, what Muhis and Metukka had implied about the infamous flat where she and her friends were now living, the well-dressed strangers who had come around looking for Hasan, and those two lads posing as policemen who had tried to make off with Anna-Liisa's jewellery box. Why hadn't Anna-Liisa said any more about the roll of cash she had found? What had happened to it, or was Anna-Liisa so out of sorts that she didn't recall the entire incident?

Irma, Anna-Liisa, the Ambassador and Margit were already deep into their canasta game and paid no attention when Siiri withdrew to her bedroom and fell asleep. She had a disturbing dream where their refugee asylum was a den of all sorts of unsavoury activity, a bit like Muhis and Metukka had insinuated. Gold rings flashed as pimps slunk about amongst the pillars, and in the middle of it all, Siiri tried to make blood pudding.

Chapter 17

'Hel-lo? Heya . . . Is Anna-Liisa here?' a young voice yoo-hooed tentatively from the round, satin-lined entryway. Siiri had never heard the voice before, but that was no surprise, because Anna-Liisa's rehabilitators and caregivers were, for the most part, one-time visitors and she never got a chance to know them. At the beginning, she'd rushed out to shake hands with each new arrival, but she'd come to learn that the caregivers had no interest in getting to know their charges, let alone their charges' flatmates. And so now she just carried on in the kitchenette, making broth from a pike-head she'd bought and cleaning herring. The herring required no con-centration; after all, she'd cleaned mountains of the fish for her family hundreds of times, and apparently this was one of those skills that, once learned, one could do in one's sleep, or at the age of a hundred.

'How are we feeling?' the shy voice called out, now from the living room, without noticing the old woman busying herself behind the counter. Siiri quickly washed her hands and wiped them on her apron. She had come across it in the bowels of the kitchenette; it was too tiny to offer much protection and read 'Queen of Fucking' across the front. She rushed over to the young girl, who looked lost and generally the worse for wear.

'Oh you poor dear – is everything all right?'

'Hi, I'm Emilia, from the City of Helsinki Western Health-Care District In-Home Care. Sorry I'm late, I don't have a driver's licence. I didn't know how to get here because I've never been to Hakaniemi and had to take public transport. Our head nurse said you can't find parking in Hakaniemi and all the parking money has been used up for the month. Not that it matters, because I don't have a driver's licence.'

'I see. But . . . now you're here. Would you care for something to drink? It's rather hot out there, isn't it?'

The girl collapsed on the sofa in a sweaty heap and panted there until Siiri handed her a glass of orange juice. She held it in two hands, like a child, and drank in big, greedy gulps.

'Thanks a mega ton.'

Emilia looked around as if she had just dropped by for a visit, oohed over the enormous television and its numerous pointless speakers, and wondered out loud why the place seemed so familiar. Then her mobile phone howled and trembled and brought her back to the task at hand.

'Oh yeah, I'm supposed to go for a walk with –' She swiped feverishly through her phone, just like Irma at her tablet, looking for Anna-Liisa's name.

'Anna-Liisa Petäjä,' Anna-Liisa said. She was leaning on her cane at her bedroom door, neatly dressed and looking chipper, curiously eyeing the wisp of a girl who had come to rehabilitate her.

'Yeah, wait just a sec.' The girl was still focused on her smartphone, apparently unable to believe that the voice behind her could belong to her next client. 'Now I found you, yeah, Anna-Liisa. Hi!' She turned to look at Anna-Liisa with her weary eyes and rose unsteadily from the couch.

'Good day,' Anna-Liisa said stonily. Today she seemed like her old self, full of vim and vigour. Her condition swung from extreme to extreme: sometimes she would loll in bed all day and even be a little muddled, and then there were these lovely late-summer days when it seemed Anna-Liisa's hard times were a thing of the past. 'Master of arts and instructor of Finnish.'

The girl's already-unfortunate posture slumped further, as if coming face-to-face with a teacher had instantly taken her back to a middle-school oral exam on the finer points of Finnish grammar. 'Yeah, so well . . . I'm, like, Emilia, in-home caregiver.'

'And I'm Siiri Kettunen, a perfectly healthy old woman. What I mean to say is that I don't use in-home care, but I live here, too.' Siiri started explaining the background of their peculiar living arrangements, and Emilia seemed to perk up a little when she heard about the shady goings-on at the Sunset Grove plumbing retrofit and the afternoon intrigues involving bespoke-suited men who came around looking for Hasan.

'Wow,' she said. Then she fainted. Simply collapsed to the ground, like a criminal shot dead in his tracks, or a senior who'd just suffered a merciful heart attack.

'Goodness gracious!' Anna-Liisa cried, rapping her cane

against the parquet and looking at Siiri as if she ought to do something. Siiri crouched down next to the in-home caregiver, patted her cheek, and lifted her eyelids.

'She's alive,' Siiri reported, and went to get more juice from the kitchenette. By the time she returned, the girl had come to, and didn't understand what had just happened. Margit had appeared at her side, naked, and apparently the water dripping from Margit's hair had revived her.

'For heaven's sakes, Margit, don't you have any manners?' Anna-Liisa snapped, turning away to avoid the distastefulness of having to gaze upon her enormous white bulk.

'I just took a shower,' Margit said, a little hurt, as she fitted her whining hearing aid over her ear.

'Yes, we can see that,' Anna-Liisa said, still refusing to look at her. 'But were you actually raised in such rude circumstances that you've never heard of a bathrobe?'

'I can't find it; I must not have brought it from Sunset Grove. But we're all friends here. Except this child. Who is she?'

'This is Emilia, the in-home caregiver who is here to rehabilitate me. She never gave a last name; apparently, doing so is contrary to the professional ethics of the caregiving field.'

Siiri glanced at Emilia, who blinked. She probably thought she was having a nightmare. Because the girl was in no immediate danger, Siiri decided to look after Margit first, and led her off to her bedroom to dress. But Margit didn't want to put her clothes on. She said she liked being naked.

'Yes, we've noticed!' Anna-Liisa shouted from the living room, yet again demonstrating the acuity of her hearing.

Margit started to cry. She sobbed silently, sighed, and clenched her fists to her chest.

'I can't take this any more. I just can't. I'm tired, I'm always tired, and I never want to get out of bed again.'

'Oh, you poor dear.' Siiri sat down next to Margit, not caring that her clean dress and borrowed apron were getting wet. 'This is odd for all of us, and a little difficult since we're not in our homes and conditions are what they are. But I've tried to think of this as an adventure. It won't last long. The renovation at Sunset Grove will be finished by October and that's only . . . Is that less than two months now? A little over a month, that's not much.'

'That's not what I'm talking about!' Margit wailed. She buried her face in her hands and rocked her head from side to side, like a disturbed child or a tropical animal at a European zoo. Siiri had seen such scenes on television, when she still had some control over what she watched. At Hakaniemi, what came blaring out of the flat screen at any given time was a complete surprise, but typically something inappropriate in the extreme: car chases, bedroom scenes, brawling teenage girls, sports.

'I'm talking about Eino,' Margit eventually said, very softly. Siiri felt a rushing in her head and almost fell off the edge of the bed. Euthanasia. Now it would start again, and frantically she thought about how she could get Margit to dress and start her day so that they could skirt round the unpleasant subject.

'Eino is very dear to you. I'm sure you had a wonderful life together,' she began. Margit stopped rocking and marvelled, moist-eyed, at Siiri. 'I had a lovely life with my husband, too, all the years we had together. I still think about him every day; he was such a wonderful man and so good to me. Maybe you should remember Eino the way he was not too long ago. Is there anything for you to wear in this pile of clothes? It seems it will be quite warm and sunny again, although it's already September. Would you like to come shopping with me at Hakaniemi Hall today? Then I could come with you some day to see Eino, couldn't I? To the SquirrelsNest.'

Margit smiled so that the unvarying white of her capped teeth gleamed prettily. She didn't say anything; she just slowly dried herself on her towel, pulled a jar of lotion from the pandemonium on her dresser, and started greasing her vast carcass.

Anna-Liisa's commanding voice echoed among the living-room pillars: 'Hello! Help is required out here immediately!'

Margit nodded at Siiri, giving her permission to go. Out in the living room, Anna-Liisa had settled into the sofa to read the latest issue of *Language Matters*. Emilia the in-home caregiver was still on the floor, this time face down. 'She fell when she tried to get up. Hit her head on the corner of the coffee table,' Anna-Liisa reported without so much as a glance at Siiri.

'Goodness!' Siiri exclaimed. 'Where's Irma? And what about the Ambass— Onni? Is he off taking care of business again?'

Anna-Liisa lowered her magazine to her lap, irritated at having to pull herself away from her fascinating article on morphophonological apophony.

'Onni's meeting with his lawyer. I'm not certain about Irma; but my understanding is that she's off at water aerobics somewhere. Do they offer it at the Allergy Institute? It's a horribly long way from here.'

'It's incredible that some people can make time for hobbies,' Siiri muttered to herself as she examined the cut that had appeared in the caregiver's forehead. It didn't look bad, but the girl was petrified with fear, since a tiny drop of blood had dripped to the floor. Siiri went into the spa and retrieved a bandage from her toiletries, pasted it to the caregiver's forehead, helped her onto the couch, and forced her to drink an entire glass of orange juice.

'How is it you're in such delicate condition?' she asked, when the girl finally appeared to have pulled herself together.

'I dunno. Maybe I'm pregnant, I dunno.'

'Pregnant?' Siiri cried, her voice rising until it was as shrill as Irma's, no matter that she had never taken voice lessons in her youth. She had always imagined that Irma's shrieks and screeches were the result of her operatic schooling and vocal training. 'How is it possible you don't know for sure, you silly thing? Isn't it a simple thing these days, a pregnancy test?'

'Yeah, I haven't had time. All I've got time to do is work and sleep.'

Anna-Liisa's eyebrows rose furiously, and she tried to sink even more deeply into her article elucidating the causes of inflected-form root variation. The caregiver told Siiri that she'd missed two menstrual cycles, but because she'd been working double shifts to gather enough money for a hiking trip she was planning in Peru and Bolivia, she hadn't had time to really think about the whole thing. She'd been feeling a little nauseous lately and had lost consciousness a few times. She had no idea who the father of the child could be. She related all this as nonchalantly but amiably as everything else she said.

'There's a pharmacy right nearby,' Siiri said. 'I'm going to go and buy you a pregnancy test; I suppose I can buy them without a prescription. In the meantime, you rest. Maybe you and Anna-Liisa can talk about what you should have been doing during rehabilitation today. It doesn't look like you'll have time to actually do it.'

Emilia suddenly remembered that she was an in-home caregiver. She jumped up, went white as a sheet, and toppled back to the couch, afraid she would faint.

'I've got to submit a report . . . I'm supposed to be in Pajamäki . . . oh no, what time is it . . . can you do my report for me?'

'Could you please submit,' Anna-Liisa said emphatically. 'How does one draft this report?'

'With my mobile phone, it's a simple app. Here. I gotta sign out on all my visits.'

'Register; I need to register. Seriously, it would be better to say register.'

The girl looked at Anna-Liisa, drained, and handed over her smartphone with what appeared to be her last ounce of strength. Anna-Liisa fiddled with it, a tremor of disgust playing across her face. Siiri didn't wait around to observe how this budding relationship between an in-home caregiver and an elderly client in need of rehabilitation would develop; she scurried off to the pharmacy.

She had to ask the pharmacy assistant for help, since she wasn't able to find the pregnancy tests herself. The woman gaped at her and repeated, 'Pregnancy test? You said pregnancy test?' to ensure she had heard correctly. Siiri patiently explained that the test wasn't for her but for an in-home caregiver who was lying half-stunned in their temporary asylum centre in the Arena Building. She remembered that one of Irma's cousins had been forced to fill out an insurance reimbursement form for diabetes treatment, where the first question was whether the ninety-two-year-old client was pregnant. Irma's cousin had answered: 'Not to my knowledge.' The pharmacy assistant asked no more questions after this, just obediently sold Siiri three pregnancy tests in case administering the test was tricky and they needed to practise.

When Siiri returned to the apartment, Anna-Liisa and Emilia were engrossed in the Sudoku puzzle from that morning's paper. Emilia never read the print version and hadn't realized it contained Sudokus and other things to do. Her smartphone shimmied and shook on the table, but neither of them paid any attention to it. Apparently, Margit had drifted off, because the faint rumble of her snores could be heard from her room. Siiri ordered Emilia into the spa to do the pregnancy test and gave her all three sticks. The girl obeyed.

Anna-Liisa said that Emilia had perked up during the Sudoku and told her all sorts of things about her work and other troubles.

'They have unreasonable schedules,' Anna-Liisa stated unequivocally, as if Emilia's problems had given her a boost. Each client, which in this case meant old people who needed help, was doled out eight to twelve minutes per visit. Caregivers weren't paid for trips between clients, as if they could zip like holograms from Pajamäki to Hakaniemi. To top it all off, they had a monitor in their phones that set off an alarm when the client's time was up. The only way to turn off the alarm was to sign off on the visit, in other words, to report that the visit was complete. Emilia had reported four visits during Siiri's absence, even though she hadn't budged from their sofa.

'The poor thing is a nervous wreck. It's as plain as day that she can't keep up, but in this instance I don't believe she's to blame.'

Then the caregiver in question stepped out of the bathroom. The stick in her hand showed two blue lines, but she didn't appear particularly overjoyed about the fact that she was pregnant.

Chapter 18

Although days at the Hakaniemi commune could be hurried and hectic as everyone went about their business, Siiri and her friends had a habit of gathering together in the evenings. After dinner, they would generally sit in the living room playing cards and drinking wine, and if the Ambassador sometimes preferred a whisky-soda on the rocks and Margit wanted the occasional gin-and-tonic, Siiri, Irma and Anna-Liisa stuck to red wine.

'I'll have my whisky when I turn in; the doctor has prescribed me a glass of whisky at bedtime for my ailments,' Irma said every night, as she shuffled the deck and refused the whisky the Ambassador offered, although on occasion she forgot her principles and joined Onni for a whisky or two while she played cards. But Siiri appreciated the repetitiveness of certain rituals and the sense of security they brought.

Siiri had prepared fresh sausage soup for dinner, and it had been a big hit. Muhis and Metukka had been intrigued by the fresh sausage, and so Siiri had written down the recipe for them and warned them that in all likelihood the sausages contained pork. But the boys weren't sticklers for the rules and had promised to make sausage soup for their families that very day.

'They thought *siskonmakkara* was such a funny name,' Siiri said. 'I've always thought it a strange word myself: "sister's sausage". They wondered if it was because fresh sausage is pale and soft, like Finnish women.'

'That's not the origin,' Anna-Liisa said. Her recovery from the urinary tract infection and her subsequent hospital-induced collapse was nearly complete. She sat up straighter, placed her cards face down on the table, and commenced her lecture. '*Siskonmakkara* is an erroneous translation, in other words, a pronunciation-derived adaptation, if you'll allow me to use a non-scientific term so you can grasp my meaning more easily. Raw sausage originated in France, where it is known by the term *saucisse*. It spread to Germany under the name *Sausichen*; a Germanic diminutive, then, of a French root. It was adopted in Sweden in the form *susiskon*, a rather unusual word and one that is, perhaps, unfamiliar to you, as in Swedish the name spread in the form *siskonkorv*, of which our Finnish *siskonmakkara* is a partially onomatopoetic translation: *siskon*, which happens to be the Finnish for *sister's*, and *makkara*, which is a direct translation of the Swedish *korv*, sausage. Quite the etymological adventure, wouldn't you say?'

'Are spades trumps?' the Ambassador asked merrily, in the hope of getting the game going. He had a good hand if spades were trumps. They played for a while, until Irma grew tired of waiting for her turn and remembered that she'd dropped by Sunset Grove that morning before water aerobics.

'It was horrible; it didn't look like the renovation had advanced at all, utter annihilation everywhere you looked. The electricity has been cut off in part of the building, and there was water damage everywhere. And then I ran into Tauno – you remember, that veteran who's as crooked as a corkscrew?'

Irma spoke of Tauno as if the flat-capped veteran were a top-notch private eye. It was also possible, of course, that Irma was embellishing her story a bit, but she claimed that Tauno had used his superlative spying skills to uncover the workings of the enemy and had discovered that the Estonian company Fix 'n' Finish had a Finnish owner, an extremely wealthy and respected individual. 'And Jerry Siilinpää wasn't fired, he just disappeared and then reappeared, hair as waxy as ever. But Tauno has been battling it out with Director Sundström, who continues to insist that residents pay full price for services that don't exist.'

'Yes, and we're paying for them, too, even though we're living here,' Siiri said. Her great-granddaughter's boyfriend Tuukka had wondered about this practice and had sent Siiri a record of all the direct debits that had been withdrawn from her bank account. Several thousands of euros, enormous sums, every month. 'We shouldn't even be paying for electricity under the circumstances,' Siiri continued, before getting distracted by the thought of poor Tauno alone in the unlit building without water, a toilet or food, like the sole survivor in some bombed-out city.

'He's not alone; that tattooed body-chopper is still there.'

Tauno had reported that the medical examiner didn't have a summer cottage or much other property to speak of, because she had drunk it all away, and that she was living at Sunset Grove on the city's dime, or, in other words, collected public assistance of some sort.

'Did she seem to be in a bad way?' Irma asked.

'She's not exactly fresh in the face.' The Ambassador's assessment was undeniably accurate. 'Considering her age. Isn't she the same age as our children?'

'What are your views on euthanasia?' Margit asked. Siiri had started to worry that Margit was depressed, had really taken ill from melancholy, like the lovelorn young ladies in Russian novels or the despondent Hermann in Tchaikovsky's opera *The Queen of Spades*, as she had less of an appetite every day and spent significant amounts of time lying in bed.

'Listen! I made fruit soup for dessert. Would anyone care for some?' Siiri bounded into the kitchenette in her apron to bring out the dessert she'd made the previous day. That would surely cheer up Margit. She even found some cream in the fridge, and there was sugar in the cupboard. Siiri set it all out on the bar, along with bowls and small spoons. Irma had followed her, looking for wine.

'Are you sure that will taste good with the fruit soup? It's gooseberry soup.'

'I'm not fussy,' Irma said, and Siiri knew she was waving her hand dismissively, because she could hear the jangle of the bracelets behind her back. 'Hellfire and brimstone, someone drank all my wine again. Is there any in your room, if I go and get it?'

Siiri didn't remember having stashed any bottles in her room, but Irma had already barrelled past on the hunt. She had barely opened the door when they heard a shriek. The in-home caregiver! Siiri had forgotten to tell Irma that they had laid the exhausted caregiver down on Siiri's bed for a nap. Was she still there, the poor girl?

'I'm coming, I can explain!' Siiri cried, running into her bedroom. The caregiver was more discombobulated than ever; she didn't know where she was or what time it was. It was lucky she remembered her name.

'Emilia, I'm Emilia,' she stammered in reply to Irma's barrage of questions. Siiri quickly explained that the girl had come to rehabilitate Anna-Liisa but had ended up in their care because she was pregnant.

'Don't you know who the father of your child is? How is that possible? Do you have that many bedmates?' Irma asked the girl as she helped her up. 'You could have caught some dreadful venereal disease.'

'Yeah, I know, or I mean no. We were on a cruise and I can't remember everything. But I'm not, like, hanging with anyone.'

Irma's curiosity was piqued. '*Hanging with anyone*. Is that what you call sex these days?'

'Hanging with anyone, dating, I'm not.'

'You're not what? A virgin?'

'I'm not with anyone! But you don't have to be, to have sex.'

'Oh, for goodness' sake. You must have hopped into bed with someone, unless this is the second coming of the Christ. Siiri, I must say, you've found another cross for us to bear.'

'Would you like some fresh sausage soup?' Siiri asked.

'Huh? What's that?'

They managed to get the caregiver to her feet and interested in a bowl of fresh sausage soup. The Ambassador rose politely when he saw the young lady enter the living room. Anna-Liisa nodded in greeting, but Margit paid no attention to the newcomer; she just kept staring at her playing cards, although the game had come to an end ages ago.

Emilia had a healthy appetite and ate two bowls of sausage soup, which provided Anna-Liisa with a second opportunity to present her etymological lecture, this time to a distinctly more receptive audience, as Emilia found the story of *siskonmakkara's* journeys from France to Finland via Germany mega-fascinating. The Ambassador was amused indeed when he understood that this frail urchin was his wife's in-home caregiver.

'So we're paying for this service, is that correct?' he said and smiled at Anna-Liisa, who now found this aspect of the whole affair amusing enough to warrant laughter.

'It looks like I won't be needing in-home care much longer,' Anna-Liisa said melodiously, wiping the tears from her eyes. 'At least this sort of care.'

Margit emerged from her reverie and pointed rudely at Emilia, who was sitting on a bar stool: 'Is that the caregiver?'

Irma's eye fell on the bowls Siiri had set out on the counter: 'Is anyone else hungry for fruit soup? I know I am!'

'Anneli, fruit soup? Don't get up, I'll bring you some,' the Ambassador said, getting up to serve his wife dessert. Siiri was pleased that her leftovers were so popular. Apparently, no one remembered they'd eaten the same fruit soup the day before.

Emilia helped herself to a third bowl of sausage soup. Margit's eyes were glued to the girl and followed her movements like a hawk. When the third bowl was empty, Margit walked up to the caregiver but didn't seat herself, as climbing up onto the stools required too much effort.

'You're a nurse. Are you also responsible for administering medication?' she asked brusquely.

'Um, well, yeah. I have to administer medication to clients who need it. And I pick up prescriptions from the pharmacy. I give insulin shots and stuff; I like it.'

Margit narrowed her eyes and looked at Emilia even more intently. She bent closer to the girl and spoke into her ear, imagining this would prevent the others from hearing her. But her stance caught their attention, and even with a hearing aid Margit spoke in a very loud voice. So they were all listening, frozen still, when Margit blurted out, in a supposed whisper:

'Can you tell me how euthanasia is done? What kinds of drugs will ensure that an old person will definitely die in his sleep?'

The silence continued. Weakened by the early stages of her pregnancy, the in-home caregiver stared, wide-eyed, at Margit, unsure of what this weary old woman with dazzling white teeth was getting at with her talk of euthanasia. Siiri had the urge to explain that Margit's husband was lying in a nursing home somewhere in eastern Helsinki in a state of profound dementia without the slightest hope for a better life, but she didn't have time. Margit grabbed the caregiver's pale, slender wrist, gripped it, and repeated her question. 'I need to know. My husband cannot suffer a single week longer than he already has.'

A healthy flush rose to the girl's cheeks. She looked fearfully at Margit, and then at the other elderly people, who nodded encouragingly.

'You can't do that. It's a crime in Finland.'

'I know. But haven't you seen any of these horrible fates as a caregiver? An old person lying in a filthy bed year in, year out, a living corpse waiting for one thing and one thing only: death!' Margit's agitation intensified alarmingly, and the Ambassador stepped in.

'Let's consider it on a purely theoretical basis, shall we?' he said, taking both the in-home caregiver and Margit by the hand. 'Let's forget about the legal aspects and only consider whether it would be theoretically possible to grant a loved one a merciful death without a doctor's help?' He trained his warm but penetrating blue Jean Sibelius eyes first on the caregiver and then on Margit. They calmed down; Margit stopped talking, and the in-home nurse frowned slightly as she concentrated on formulating an answer to this merely hypothetical question.

'Umm, like if my grandma was like . . . mega-demented and she had, like, certain medication, I think I could help her out.'

'And how would you get your grandmother to consume the necessary amount of medication?' the Ambassador asked, as if this were the current affairs programme *Tough Talk* and he were Jan Andersson, the handsome, polite young host who posed his questions, even the difficult ones, in a clear, pleasant manner.

'I think that . . . that I'd, like, put it in her food maybe . . . oatmeal or yogurt or something . . . if he's, like . . . if my grandma were able to eat.'

'And if she weren't?'

'Then it would be harder, although I'm pretty sure that, with certain medication, you can, like, dissolve them, so you could, like, put it in a drink, but then there are some that . . . if, like, my grandma couldn't even drink, then wouldn't she die anyway, from lack of nutrition?'

'Yes, I believe that's an alternative,' the Ambassador said, and concluded the conversation with a warm thanks to the in-home caregiver. Margit seemed very calm, and she went to her room without saying another word. Siiri and Irma loaded the dishwasher, but as only some of the dishes fit, they continued with their favourite activity, washing dishes. It had gradually become a bit of daytime fun for them. They loved soaking their hands in the warm water and soft foam, and it also gave them a nice opportunity for a cheery chat. Although at the moment, neither could come up with anything cheery to say. Emilia politely carried her bowl over to be washed and prepared to make her departure.

'It was mega-chill the way you guys helped me out and fed me and let me rest,' she said, with a peculiar little curtsey.

'Promise us you'll go to the prenatal clinic first thing tomorrow,' Irma said, and the in-home caregiver replied cheerfully that tomorrow was her day off, so at least she'd have time to call.

Chapter 19

Despite the continuing warmth, the trees of Tokoinranta Park showed signs of autumn. For a brief moment they thought the hot weather had ended and lovely, cool autumn had set in, but then another heat wave struck. When it did, old folks talked about Indian summers and everyone else talked about climate change. Luckily, their refugee asylum had air conditioning; Irma had accidentally set it blasting once when she thought she was turning off the television, and since then they'd learned to use it. All one had to do was press ON on the grey remote and then remember to press OFF at some point, too. Irma had written 'COOL AIR' on the remote in a red marker so that they'd remember which the right one was.

'Would today work for you?' Margit asked brightly one morning, when she and Siiri were the only ones awake. The television was blaring by itself, and the two of them were on the couch, eating boiled eggs and reading their newspapers. Initially, they'd thought it was silly for four copies of the paper to be forwarded to Hakaniemi, but they quickly realized that the thought of giving up their personal paper at breakfast was impossible. 'You promised to visit Eino at the SquirrelsNest with me, remember?'

Siiri thought it was a fine idea, her first adventure in ages, never mind that a home for dementia patients wasn't the most uplifting destination. She'd been spinning her wheels in Hakaniemi for weeks now, trapped at the stove of their refugee asylum and attempting to get occasional stimulation by visiting the farmers' market, the market hall, the parks, and the exotic shops. The days had passed in housework, grocery shopping, having coffee at the farmers' market with Muhis and Metukka, and endless cooking, which she had grown rather fond of. But Siiri hadn't set foot on a tram in weeks. A little outing would surely do her good.

'How will we get there? What tram line goes to the SquirrelsNest?'

'There's no tram, but we could take the metro. How does that sound?'

The metro! Siiri couldn't even remember the last time she'd been on the metro, and they had a horrendously ugly metro station right outside their window. This was going to be exciting. Just to be sure, she packed the things you never knew you might need; hunted for her handbag and her reading glasses before discovering them in her bedroom cupboard, swept up a random assemblage of other items from the table, dropped them in her handbag, and pulled on her beige poplin coat.

'I probably don't need a hat, do I?' she said. She was holding a blue beret, not quite sure if it was hers or Irma's.

'I'm going to wear a scarf,' Margit said, and that sounded like a good idea to Siiri, too. She searched for her scarf without remembering what it looked like, and in the end gratefully accepted one from Margit's abundant collection. It was green with gold curlicues and smelled faintly of Margit's musky perfume.

They walked to the Hakaniemi metro station in the mild autumn breeze and down into a vast, desolate hall. They wondered what the purpose of all the extra space was – construction was horribly expensive, after all – or if it served as a bomb shelter, although bombs no longer seemed to be used during wartime the way they were back when Finland was at war. Since then, bombers had turned into tiny, toy-like gliders controlled from some tower at a safe distance; there had just been pictures in the newspaper. Siiri and Margit made their way down an empty, echoing corridor that led to an escalator that took you down to a landing, where you boarded another escalator. By this point, their expedition through the subterranean wasteland had them in stitches.

'Couldn't they use this space to sell little doodads and snacks, like everyplace else? Peanuts and umbrellas?'

'Yes, or liquorice ropes, or those colourful lumps that it's impossible to tell if they're candy or soap!'

When they arrived at the platform, it was impossible to say which track led east and which one led downtown. They hesitated for a moment, until they heard a deep voice calling from down the platform: 'Siiri! Siiri, my love!'

Why, it was Muhis, waving at Siiri with both hands, the familiar colourful beehive teetering on his head.

'Is that him?' Margit asked, her voice leaden with suspicion.

'Muhis! Oh you, blessed man!' Siiri squealed and introduced her friend to Margit, who maintained her air of prejudiced reserve and stepped backwards even though Muhis was chuckling his hearty chuckle and revealing a mouthful of enviably healthy teeth.

'How's it going, Siiri? Where are you headed?'

Siiri explained about the SquirrelsNest and Eino and their planned metro escapade, and Muhis showed them that the eastbound metros left from the right side of the platform. He was on his way to the Itäkeskus Mall himself, and promised to ride with them.

It wasn't long before the orange plastic metro pulled up with its unmistakable whine, and they stepped in, Siiri and Muhis side by side, Margit trailing at a safe distance and seating herself on her own bench.

The metro ride was incredibly smooth, like gliding on air, and the combination of the peculiar smell, the whine that rose more than a sixth during acceleration and braking, and the automated announcements made Siiri feel futuristic indeed. 'Sörnäinen, Sörnäs,' the smiling female robot announced, first the Finnish name of the stop and then the Swedish, doing a superb job of differentiating between the Finnish and Swedish ways of pronouncing the *ö*. Anna-Liisa would have appreciated that. Not long after pulling out of Sörnäinen, the metro emerged from the tunnel, and then they could enjoy the autumn vistas just as if they were riding on a tram. On the Kulosaari Bridge, Siiri told Muhis and

Margit about her grandmother, who had lived in the forests of Kulosaari Island in the 1800s and had rowed across to the Market Square every day to do her shopping. Muhis didn't believe a word of it but laughed cheerfully; Margit's eyes were glued to the window. Muhis was on his way to meet his cousin. He explained that most members of his sizable family were scattered across Europe and the United States; other than him, this cousin was the only one who lived in Finland. Their relatives couldn't fathom how Muhis and his cousin could live in a dark country where it was always freezing. Which sounded particularly silly at the moment, since a blazing sun had been beating down on Finland for the past four months, making life difficult for the elderly.

'What are you planning on cooking this week?' Muhis asked, as always.

Siiri told him that she had picked up some Jerusalem artichokes and was going to make a soup from them. It was a lot of work peeling the little tubers, since they were so lumpy, and Muhis told her that the French had developed a smooth variety. Siiri had a hard time believing this.

'You can buy them at Hakaniemi; I'll show you tomorrow,' Muhis chuckled. 'And after the soup?'

Siiri had already thought about that, too. After the soup, she would serve globe artichokes with melted butter.

'Everyone will get their own cup of butter they can dip the artichoke – for goodness' sake, what are they? Scales? Shells? – in. It's a messy business, which is why it's such fun. Irma likes it, at least. And at the end, you eat the artichoke heart with a knife and fork; it's quite the delicacy. But you need an enormous pot to cook them in. I might have to cook them in several batches.'

'Let's go and buy you a big pot tomorrow. You need the proper tools, Siiri, my love. Or should we buy you one right now, at the mall? There's a Stockmann there, your favourite store!'

But Siiri refused to haul some ten-litre cauldron to the SquirrelsNest, so Muhis made her swear to buy a big pot at her earliest opportunity. Those were his very words: 'at your earliest opportunity'. He spoke excellent Finnish, much better than many consultants, luxury flat-owners, or pregnant in-home caregivers Siiri could think of.

'Otherwise I'll bring you mine. But just one; I have many. A plethora!' And once again, he laughed so loudly that his headwear nearly toppled into Margit's lap.

The Itäkeskus Mall was a vast leisure complex. There were dozens of department stores, a food court, boutiques, shops and hallways leading off in every direction, with a roof over it all so the weather didn't hamper the general loitering. Everyone seemed to be killing time; no one was in a hurry. Old people sat on benches, young people on the ground, and immigrants gathered in their own clusters. Siiri would have lost her way in this enchanted universe in a matter of seconds, but Margit trod purposefully down a convoluted path that led them out of the commercial jungle, across a few streets, and eventually to the nursing home known as the SquirrelsNest. They had left Muhis behind not long after the metro escalators had deposited them in the mall. Siiri barely had time to say goodbye to her friend, Margit was in such a rush.

The SquirrelsNest looked like most retirement homes. Eerie doors that opened by themselves, big windows, high, echoing common rooms and a courtyard in the middle that someone had tried to turn into a garden – but since the trees were newly planted saplings, the space bore an unfortunate resemblance to what it really was, a poorly cleaned construction site. Was this what the yard at Sunset Grove would look like, too, once the renovation was complete?

At the end of a hopelessly long corridor, they reached the dementia unit, which could only be entered by tapping a code into a box next to the door. Margit couldn't remember the code. She rummaged around her handbag at length, searching for her notebook; it took another few minutes of scouring her notebook before she found the slip of paper where she'd jotted down a column of codes.

'It's probably this second-to-last one ... hmm, that doesn't seem to work. Well, maybe if I try this one at the top, yes, I think that's it ... hmm, that didn't work either. Am I supposed to press that pound sign at the end, too, I wonder?' Margit looked fearfully at Siiri, as if she believed this was another mystery Siiri had the answer to.

'Press the pound sign,' Siiri said. There was a faint squeal, and then the door clicked and slowly started to open, as if they were in a haunted house. They panicked and jumped aside, trapping themselves behind it, but they managed to circle around the stupid thing before inevitably it started closing, even though Siiri hadn't crossed the threshold yet.

The dementia ward had a living room that was supposed to feel cosy. You could tell because the furniture was mismatched and on the shabby side, ugly needlepoints decorated the walls, heavy, ruffled floral curtains hung at the windows, and a plastic cactus teetered on the windowsill. There weren't any real houseplants, because a resident had been caught munching on leaves once. A tiny old woman sat on the couch, holding two stuffed animals, a dog and a unicorn. Three feet from her face stood the television, where a heavyset woman was lecturing the helpless parents of an unruly brood of ill-behaved children. A woman in a nightshirt and a pair of colossal spectacles was dozing in an armchair. The dining table was unoccupied, but a foreign-looking man was working at a computer in the glass cubicle opposite. Margit stuck her head into the office and said hello.

'Do you know him?' Siiri asked, surprised, because she couldn't believe someone worked at a nursing home long enough to get to know the residents' families.

'Not really, but he's here quite often, at the computer. Maybe he's the boss.'

Margit turned the corner and walked straight into the last room. They could hear loud singing coming from one of the other rooms, a shrill female voice belting out a lullaby with very coarse lyrics.

'Go to hell, you son-of-a-bitch, a-as, rock-a-bye-baby, you goddamn son-of-a-bitch, go fu—'

'I see they do a splendid job of maintaining folk traditions here,' Siiri laughed, but Margit was glum. Evidently, she had started ruminating over Eino's suffering and loss of dignity the moment she stepped through the automatic doors.

Like everyone in the dementia unit, Eino shared a room. There wasn't much daylight; all you could see out the window was the concrete wall of the building next door, and it blocked nearly all the sun. The walls were grey, which was, no doubt, a practical choice in terms of cleaning, and the sole pieces of furniture were the two hospital beds and a lone plastic chair evidently intended for loved ones. Margit settled into the chair and leaned in towards Eino, as if listening to determine whether the shrunken, lifeless-looking man lying there – her husband – were still alive. Siiri stood at a respectful distance and wondered how it was possible that Margit's and Eino's daily sexual interludes had, so recently, been so loud as to cause general consternation at Sunset Grove. Eino's slide into severe dementia had been surprisingly fast; here he was, a withered old man, barely recognizable. Siiri understood Margit's depression and gloomy talk better now.

The neighbouring bed was occupied by a slightly younger-looking woman in incontinence pads whose hands were strapped down. Margit explained that the woman was very restless and occasionally aggressive, because she'd come out of her fog intermittently and understand where she was.

'So they had to medicate her and tie her down like that. Or that's what the nurses told me. Is it really the only alternative? I wonder. No one comes to visit her; no one fights for her rights. She might end up in the basement; that's where they put those in the worst condition who don't have any loved ones.'

Siiri looked at the sedated woman and felt sick to her stomach. She remembered Irma in the same state and all the awful things that had happened at Sunset Grove a year ago. Had it only been a year? It all felt so distant. She sat at the foot of Eino's bed and held her head in her hands to make the stabbing pain go away.

'Look, Eino, Siiri came to see you today, too. Siiri is sitting on your bed, Eino.'

Margit spoke in a tender, low voice to her husband, who opened his eyes and looked at her fearfully, recognizing nothing but her soothing tone. Margit continued chatting, talked about falling leaves and the sunshine outside, told him about the delicious meals Siiri had prepared, and this was the first time Siiri learned that Margit enjoyed the food she cooked and perhaps even appreciated the fact that everything was served to her just as at the most expensive retirement homes.

'Siiri always sets the table so beautifully for us. Just yesterday we had bright green napkins in our glasses folded into cute little fans. Oh, Eino, you would have loved the moose soup Siiri made. Just think, Hakaniemi Hall is right across the street from our new home, and you can get whatever you want there. Who knows, maybe Siiri slipped in a few bulls' balls, too.'

Eino whimpered, and it genuinely seemed as if he were trying to laugh. Siiri glanced at Margit, and she was smiling broadly, too. For a moment they seemed oddly happy, a husband and wife who had journeyed through a long marriage together hand in hand, although one of them couldn't remember who he was. But the idyllic scene didn't last long: Eino's room-mate's eyes flashed open and she started shrieking. Her shrill, piercing wail even drowned out the foul-mouthed lullaby from the neighbouring room.

'Help, help, help, help me, help me, goddammit, can't anyone hear?'

Siiri rose, patted the hysterical woman on the hand and tried to stroke her head, but the woman spat on Siiri's hand and kept screaming. Eino shut his eyes and grimaced, as if in pain. Margit marched out of the room, pulling Siiri behind her.

'This is what it's like here. It's intolerable. We have to get the man at the computer to give her another shot. Every time I come I go away feeling just as bad.'

They found him in the nurses' office. He didn't look up from his computer when Margit stepped in; he just kept on working.

'There's an acute situation in room seven. The woman woke up and is being aggressive and crying for help,' Margit said in a tired voice; apparently, she had delivered this same message dozens of times. Siiri thought about Eino, lying in the same room with the woman shrieking like a banshee, and felt weak. The male nurse calmly rose, opened the medicine cabinet, took the needle, and made for Eino's room. He left the medicine cabinet open.

'Is that where . . . they keep all the medication?' Siiri whispered in surprise.

Margit had wasted no time making her way over to the medicine cabinet and examining its contents. Every patient – or resident, as they were called here, to create a homey ambience – had their own plastic basket. Eino's basket contained eight different bottles. Siiri recognized two pain prescriptions and one anti-depressant. Margit knew the others were anti-inflammatories, sleeping aids and medication for Alzheimer's disease.

'And those are morphine pills. For pain.'

'Are they still giving him Alzheimer's medication? Why on earth?' Siiri wondered.

'Force of habit. It comes with the territory here,' Margit said, and started writing down the names from the bottles.

The dementia unit was uncannily calm, although it wasn't quiet. The old lady with the big glasses was still sleeping in the armchair, and the tiny zookeeper was nodding off at the flat-screen TV. The programme had changed: now viewers could observe how a group of young people locked up in a room together would react when served too much alcohol. A bit like watching the surveillance cameras in a dementia unit, although here they poured drugs down throats instead of booze. The lewd lullaby echoed in the distance, and Eino's room-mate was still crying for help. The nurse must still have been administering the shot to her.

Suddenly, Margit took fistfuls of pills from three of the bottles, dumped them into her handbag, and put the bottles back in the cabinet. She eyed Siiri steadily to make sure her friend wouldn't do anything stupid.

'Let's go. There's nothing we can do here,' Margit said dejectedly. And in that instant, Siiri remembered that today was her ninety-sixth birthday, but she didn't say a word.

Chapter 20

The evening-shift caregiver was washing Anna-Liisa in the spa, and Margit was solving her crossword on the sofa — pondering the answers volubly, as always. She readily took up the substantial space her ample presence required. At first Siiri had found Margit's habit of talking to herself irritating, but she didn't let it bother her any more — nor the fact that Margit never cleaned up after herself, wandered around in various states of undress, suffered from flatulence, and forgot barely chewed wads of gum on the coffee table. But Siiri still couldn't get over the way Margit used any old toothbrush she happened to come across in the bathroom. Siiri had started keeping hers in her bedroom closet, which induced Irma to accuse her of being paranoid, in other words, practically senile. Irma hadn't noticed that Margit had ever used her toothbrush.

The Ambassador had escaped for an evening walk well before the caregiver's arrival. Before leaving, he had sung the praises of Siiri's blood pudding, which had taken him back to the 1970s and his suspenseful years as a diplomat during the Cold War. The compliment irked Irma, who had been skipping out on kitchen duty to an inexcusable extent, and Anna-Liisa, who had often cooked for her husband during their time in Sunset Grove without receiving any particular thanks.

'Stop scrubbing me with that potato brush! My skin is very dry; you're going to tear it!'

It was Anna-Liisa's voice. The amount of noise coming from the bathroom tonight was altogether peculiar. Anna-Liisa had already told the caregiver to close the window, because otherwise she'd catch pneumonia and die. The sound of the running shower was accompanied by a hissing and rasping and the occasional loud bang, along with groans from Anna-Liisa. Irma and Siiri were sitting on the sofa; Siiri was reading *Buddenbrooks* and Irma was playing Sudoku on her green flaptop. They glanced at each other, unsure if the situation were dire enough to call for intervention. Margit appeared to have forgotten her hearing aid on her nightstand. She paid no attention to the racket coming from the bathroom, just wondered out loud, coughing and clearing her throat, whether Jari Litmanen was a soccer star and if the answer for 'Eeva and Jari' might be 'Litmanens'.

'I HAVE THE RIGHT TO SELF-DETERMINATION!'

The shout cut through the living room's diversions like the crack of a whip. Even Margit stopped talking for a moment. Anna-Liisa's voice was tremendously defiant, furious. What on earth was going on in the bathroom?

'It's spelled out in the European Union Convention on Human Rights, haven't you ever heard of that? I get to decide what anyone does to me! You cannot force me to do this! An elderly person needs to be treated with as much respect as anyone else!'

Anna-Liisa's voice slid into despair. Siiri set aside her family of bourgeois Lübeckers and ran to the bathroom door, but it was locked. She knocked powerfully, and felt calm and confident.

'Anna-Liisa, it's Siiri. Can you open the door?'

Another knock, firm and clear, like one of Anna-Liisa's. Siiri heard murmuring inside, a couple of bangs, and then the door was opened by a brawny woman, not a skinny young thing like the majority of the caregivers. They were usually either students doing their practical training or children who had just received their diplomas, too timid to open a stranger's door and look you in the eye. But this one had been scrubbing seniors for decades. She stood there in the blue homemade housecoat that, apparently, was her uniform and a pair of rubber boots, stumpy legs spread angrily. 'What's this, another old lady who needs a good scrubdown? Or are you about to poop in your pants?'

'I . . . I'm just Siiri Kettunen and I live here, hello –' Siiri said uncertainly, and the woman steamrolled through this tentative introduction.

'Yeah, this is a pretty unique living arrangement. In all of my years of bum-washing I've never seen anything like it. But the only one on my list at this address is this Anna-Liisa Marjatta Petäjä, and there's no room for anyone else in here. I have three minutes to get Ms Petäjä tidied up and tucked in. If you can't hold it, I can give you a pad, courtesy of the city. You can pee in that.'

The woman looked over at the gargantuan bag that served as her portable toolbox. She was holding a coarse, old-fashioned scrubbing brush, the kind still sold at farmers' markets during the summer and upstairs at Hakaniemi Hall year round. Siiri had always thought they were for washing rugs. Pink drops dripped from the woman's brush to her big boots. In her other hand, she held a grey rag Siiri wouldn't have used to wipe the stairwell floor during an October sleet storm.

'Siiri, you came to rescue me!' Anna-Liisa wailed from the dim depths of the bathroom. She was sitting on a washing stool, bloody legs draining into the shower. Water was beating down on her frail shoulders. The window had been flung wide open, and a brisk autumn breeze was blowing in. No doubt it felt lovely to the caregiver, as she was doing heavy physical labour and smelled sharply of sweat. Without loosening her grip on her scrubbing brush, the woman raised an elbow and wiped away the perspiration beading up on her forehead, then gave Siiri a murderous look and turned towards her client.

'That's the end of this bath, then. Time's up.' The woman yanked Anna-Liisa up from the plastic stool and started rubbing her down violently with a scratchy linen towel. Where on earth had she found it? Siiri and Irma had discovered an enormous linen closet behind the front door, but it only contained soft, white terry cloth towels and endless piles of white sheets, like in a hotel. Anna-Liisa trembled and cried like a child at an orphanage, fearfully holding back the tears between her silent sobs. She must have felt humiliated, in addition to which it looked as if she were hurting all over.

'I came, I thought –' Siiri stammered, still not daring to step into the bathroom in her shoes. She wasn't comfortable going without shoes indoors, especially here in Hakaniemi, where the apartment was more or less a public thoroughfare.

'Hold your water. The john will be free in a sec,' the care-giver said, dragging the dripping Anna-Liisa along to her room. 'Put a little Vaseline on those cuts and tomorrow you'll be good as new!' her voice boomed from the bedroom, and a moment later she had stomped off to care for the next unlucky senior somewhere in Helsinki.

'Good heavens!' exclaimed Irma, who had been following events from behind one of the living-room pillars. Margit had fallen asleep on the sofa and barely noticed that a strange woman had been terrorizing Anna-Liisa in their bathroom. Siiri helped Anna-Liisa into her dressing gown and led her over to sit on the round bed. Anna-Liisa was still sobbing. Her body was covered in scratches; the worst wounds were on her legs. She was holding a jar of Vaseline but her hands were shaking so badly that she couldn't open it. Irma and Siiri tried to comfort their friend, which compelled Anna-Liisa to pull herself together into her usual composed state; Anna-Liisa didn't care to be the object of anyone's pity. She hurled the jar of Vaseline to the floor, which it struck sharply. It spun for a second, and then opened.

'The fact is, I can't use Vaseline. It irritates my skin. I have very thin, very dry skin, and scouring it the way that woman did is violence. If, on top of everything else, she had forced me to put Vaseline on my wounds, I would have been making the rounds of Helsinki's hospitals and health centres in an ambulance again before some dermatologist would have figured out what was going on. Thank God you came to save me, Irma.'

'Actually, it was . . . ' Siiri began, but then decided not to correct Anna-Liisa, because Irma was already graciously returning the gratitude in her inimitable style, downplaying the significance of her role; she was certain that Anna-Liisa's courageous mention of self-determination and the laws of the European Union had been more decisive in putting a stop to the unpleasant situation. In Irma's mind, nothing frightened a Finn quite as effectively as the European Union.

'Nothing like a supranationalistic-intergovernmental organization to put the fear of God into them. Wait, I think that might be a record – thirty-five letters, but there's the hyphen in the middle . . .'

'Indeed,' Anna-Liisa said, giving Irma a perplexed look. 'But do you know what that woman had the gall to say to me? That she's not some overindulgent lullaby-crooner; she's the old-fashioned type of caregiver whose job is to keep things as clean as a whistle. As if she were a garbage truck or a vacuum cleaner. Her superiors probably think this visit met the criteria for high-quality caregiving and assistance.'

'On computer it did,' Siiri said. 'I'm sure she'll report that the visit was successful.'

'*Döden, döden, döden.*' Irma shook her head and tugged the wrinkles out of the bedspread. 'Where did this come from?' She was holding a thick roll of cash she had discovered on Anna-Liisa's and the Ambassador's bed. 'It's not from your jewellery box. These are hundred-euro bills; those were magenta.'

Anna-Liisa looked at the roll of bills, snatched it out of Irma's hands, and slipped it into the desk drawer so swiftly that it was hard to believe she received in-home care.

'It's Onni's money. I don't know anything about it.'

'Good evening. Maija Saaripolku from Western District In-Home Care.' A friendly, experienced-looking woman was standing in Anna-Liisa's doorway. They all turned to look at her in astonishment. Her hair was tumbling out of a sloppily knotted ponytail but she radiated enthusiasm. Anna-Liisa tugged her dressing gown around herself more modestly, looked guilty, and shut the drawer where she had just hidden the large stack of cash. 'What are YOU doing here, pray tell?' she frostily. 'Your colleague just left, and I have yet to recover from her manhandling.'

Now it was the woman's turn to be bewildered. She pulled a mobile phone out of her well-worn handbag and consulted it.

'I was assigned – what is this phone doing . . . I was supposed to – oh, it was the morning shift. Did anyone come by this morning?'

Anna-Liisa, Siiri and Irma exchanged another round of astonished looks. This morning? Suddenly none of them could remember what had happened that morning. What day was it, even? Wednesday, perhaps? The in-home caregivers whirled in and out their front door at such a frenetic pace that they no longer paid much attention to who was coming and going. And since their home was teeming with complete strangers seven days a week, it was impossible to ever know if it was a weekday or the weekend. The days couldn't avoid becoming a jumble. Or were they supposed to be keeping a log of the caregivers' visits?

'I think I've mixed up my notes in the system,' the woman said, and jabbed at the phone's touchscreen, her forehead deeply furrowed in concern. 'Blasted piece of junk!' she shouted surprisingly violently, flinging the phone back into her bag. Across the bed, Anna-Liisa had gone rigid, as if to ensure that no other caregivers would be molesting her today.

'Why don't we step into the living room,' Siiri said, and the caregiver followed her through the pillars towards the bar stools. She felt like she was starting to get the hang of this caring for caregivers.

'This is a very unusual apartment,' Irma began, and Siiri knew Irma was about to drown her discomposure in a verbal deluge. Siiri went into the kitchenette, filled the pan with water to make some tea for the caregiver, and let Irma babble. It took her a few tries, pressing different spots on the smooth black surface of the stove, to get the red numbers to come on and the correct burner to start glowing.

'. . . and some think that this apartment is some sort of pornographic lair. I believe Anna-Liisa was the first one to say so out loud; the rest of us found the matter too delicate because the owner is her husband, the husband of my friend you're here to care for, who is an ambassador and apparently some sort of businessman as well, very wealthy, although we don't know much about his affairs, since we only met a couple of years ago at Sunset Grove, our retirement home, which is being gutted at the moment. Do you know anything about the renovation there? We've been getting rather suspicious about the whole thing; nothing is ever finished and everything just gets worse and worse and not a single one of the workers speaks Finnish, not one! Do you speak Finnish?'

'Yes,' the woman said, moving over to the sofa and gratefully accepting the cup of tea Siiri offered her. It wasn't a cup, actually, it was an ugly mug that read 'Hot drinks for hot girls'. Everyone seemed to drink coffee and tea from big mugs these days. In Siiri's day, coffee and tea were served from different kinds of cups: coffee from smallish ones and tea from a wider-rimmed variety, and that was why she found drinking from tankards like these off-putting. You lost the pleasure of the third cup, too, when filling two mugs emptied the coffee pot. But what were you going to do, when your own belongings were lost amid the wreckage of Sunset Grove, unless they had been stolen and sold off at a flea market in Tallinn? Which is what some claimed.

Over on the sofa, Margit snorted and woke up. She wasn't the least bit disturbed to find a complete stranger sitting next to her, sipping tea; she just cheerfully asked Siiri to bring her a mug of something hot, too, and some *pulla*, too, if there happened to be any.

'*Pulla*? You think I have time to bake for you, too?' Siiri muttered as she shuffled off to get Margit's tea. She was growing increasingly irritated with her new status as servant, which she had unintentionally accepted when she made the mistake of taking on the cooking. She remembered Muhis had asked about the *pulla* that grown Finnish men ate, tears in their eyes, then washed down with milk like little babies. Muhis wanted to learn how to bake *pulla*, and Siiri seemed to have remembered promising to show him. Where was she ever going to find the time? At Sunset Grove she'd cursed the fact that all she had was time, time, time, time, and now she didn't have time for anything. But Muhis and Metukka were sweet boys, good-natured and helpful, and Siiri felt herself perking up in their presence. She found an old packet of cookies in the cupboard and set them out on a plate on a cloth napkin. It looked very nice. She had bought the napkin upstairs at Hakaniemi Hall from a charming old woman who was, no doubt, decades younger than Siiri herself.

Irma was thrilled when she saw the cookies. 'Oh, we have cookies, too! Can you bring me a mug, too, since you're already up?' She was ensconced in the low sofa and unable to extract herself without assistance. Generally, the Ambassador pulled the women up one by one, but they couldn't rely on the courtesy of his arm at present.

'Get it yourself,' Siiri blurted rather rudely to Irma, who looked at her in sincere surprise.

'What's got into you?'

Siiri saw Anna-Liisa shuffling slowly out of her room; she had her cane and kept pausing to steady herself against the wall. She was wearing a beautiful dress but no stockings, and the cuts on her legs looked frightful. Siiri poured three mugs of tea, thought for a moment, and decided to leave Irma without. She could get her own tea herself.

Margit was already engaged in a deep discussion about euthanasia with the caregiver, who believed it should be allowed for those who suffered too much. She spoke about sedation and pain reduction, palliative care, end-of-life care, and who knows what. The real problem was that old age wasn't viewed as a factor that resulted in death.

'Old age isn't a disease,' the caregiver said. 'Although these days doctors talk about "frailty syndrome", because it sounds like a diagnosis. It's absurd, isn't it?'

'Goodness, what blockheads! What does frailty have to do with being old?' Irma laughed and sneezed loudly into her lace handkerchief. She didn't even seem to notice that she hadn't been served any tea. '*Döden, döden, döden.*'

'So "frailty syndrome" is code for "old age"?' Anna-Liisa asked.

'Yes. Or you know, if an old person doesn't contract some diagnosable disease, they'll still gradually grow frail and die. But doctors aren't the ones keeping an eye on the elderly; we practical nurses are. That's why there's no treatment available, although personally I believe all dying people ought to receive care, and those in the most pain ought to receive help, if you understand my meaning.'

'We understand!' Margit shouted in praise, raising her hands heavenwards. Finally, she had met someone to discuss euthanasia with, even if semi-directly. This nurse, Maija Saaripolku, was her saviour. Nurse Saaripolku had seen the deaths of many old people and didn't approve of patients in decline being moved by ambulance to a health centre or hospital.

'They want them out of sight, so they'll die somewhere else. Retirement homes don't want you dying on the premises, although they claim just the opposite in their brochures. "You can even die here!" That's what they advertise when they're trying to attract clients. But if granny's breath starts to rattle or she gets a touch of fever, the practical nurse who's been left alone to cover the shift panics and calls an ambulance. That's the way it goes, every time. They even have instructions on how to outsource responsibility for a patient's death.'

Margit told Nurse Saaripolku about Eino and the Squirrels-Nest and everything else, their long marriage, her own fears and agony, the room-mate strapped to her bed. Nurse Saaripolku listened with interest, taking the occasional sip of tea and fixing her ponytail. She said she knew the SquirrelsNest, had done 'gigs' there herself, and said that the pay there was a little better than average. 'But of course there aren't any doctors there. There aren't anywhere, except health centres. And the ones at health centres are too young, or else there aren't enough of them.'

'I don't think a doctor is going to do Eino any good. Euthanasia is a crime, after all. Or do you think there might be someone who might agree to – to help, you know . . .'

According to Nurse Saaripolku, assisted suicide was legal in Finland. It wasn't talked about much in general, and it was never discussed when it came to the elderly. Sometimes with cancer patients or others suffering from other terminal illnesses, some very progressive doctor would write the necessary prescription. Morphine, mostly, in sufficient amounts. The other alternative was to give a patient a lethal dose of sleeping medication and call the procedure sedation.

'I've never met the doctor who's treating Eino, although the head nurse at the SquirrelsNest has said there is one. I'm starting to feel like the doctor is some sort of imaginary being. Sometimes I'm afraid that even the staff in the dementia ward have lost their grip on reality . . .'

Nurse Saaripolku chuckled.

Margit edged closer to her; this woman was her only hope. 'I have a list of Eino's medication in my handbag. Could you help me?'

Maija Saaripolku looked at Margit matter-of-factly, as if the old woman had asked for help solving a crossword. She drained her mug of tea, rose to her feet, helped Margit up, and went with Margit into her room. She strode briskly, as if the opportunity to assist in the mercy killing of an old dementia patient were the best thing ever to happen to her during her career.

Chapter 21

'Use your hand to test if the milk is warm enough,' Siiri said to Muhis. He looked doubtfully at his grey-haired friend, who had wrapped the curious undersized apron around her to protect her clothes. A large porcelain bowl stood on the bar, and two pans of milk were heating on the stove.

'Are you saying I should put my hand in the milk? And how do I know if it's the right temperature?'

'It's supposed to be room temperature. You'll be able to tell. Then we add the yeast but not in one big chunk, in little crumbles.'

Muhis obediently followed Siiri's instructions, tested the milk with his hand and pronounced it the right temperature, poured the warm liquid into the bowl and broke in the yeast. He had never touched yeast before, and he got a kick out of its squeaky, crumbly texture. He didn't need to stir the milk long before the yeast had dissolved. The mixture was an unpleasant grey, but Siiri looked at it in satisfaction.

'Why didn't Metukka come over to bake? I thought he wanted to learn how to make *pulla*, too?' Siiri asked.

'He got a job for the day. We have to take any work we can get.'

'Where do you boys work?'

'All sorts of places. Mostly construction. Sometimes I clean, sometimes I work banquets, and I've driven a taxi a couple of times. Under the table, of course; otherwise, you lose all your benefits.'

'Don't stir the milk. Now, "under the table" means you don't pay taxes, is that it?'

Muhis explained that foreigners had two options in Finland: either be unemployed or have a permanent, full-time job. As far as the authorities were concerned, nothing else would do. And so Muhis and Metukka and other refugees were forced to do the little work they could hidden from the tax office's eyes. Muhis claimed that many Finns preferred to work under the table, too, since taxes were so high in Finland and welfare benefits were so good, but Siiri didn't believe him. Taxes had to be paid; otherwise there wouldn't be any trams, schools or hospitals. And Finns were a hard-working, respectable people. Many worked so hard they ended up on rehabilitation leave or disability in the prime of their life. All the practical nurses tending Anna-Liisa were being crushed by the weight of their burdens.

'Most Finns pay taxes the way they're supposed to,' Muhis admitted. 'But believe me, there's one Finnish businessman who's been running quite the under-the-table amusement park in this apartment. Bad things don't always come from abroad. What do we do now that the yeast has dissolved?'

Siiri handed Muhis a teaspoon of cardamom and two

decilitres of sugar and sprinkled the salt in herself, measuring it with a wooden spoon from a big box. Irma had brought it from her apartment at Sunset Grove; it was an old salt box that had been passed down in her family from mother to daughter, with a wooden lid and the word 'Salt' on the side in ornamental writing.

'Now crack an egg into it. Not everyone does, but I think the dough is better if you add an egg.'

'The incredible edible egg!' Muhis chuckled, cracking the egg neatly with one hand against the edge of the bowl. It was plain from every movement that he was used to cooking and baking. The bowl was an old piece of Arabia porcelain Siiri had found in a funny little junk shop on Toinen linja. The sign outside the store said 'Antique Shop' and the young, toothless salesperson claimed that the dish was vintage, which was why Siiri had been forced to pay twenty euros for a simple bowl. Irma thought it was highway robbery, and she claimed the salesgirl was pulling the wool over their foolish old eyes, but Siiri knew that they would get a lot of use out of the bowl.

'And then you can start adding the flour, but don't put in too much. You have to add it little by little, just like that, and keep stirring. Stir, stir! The dough needs air!'

Muhis stirred. There was no electric mixer in the commune, so he had to use a whisk. Muhis was wearing a shirt with no sleeves, and his coal-black skin accentuated his muscular arms magnificently. Siiri had offered him her apron, but when Muhis saw what was written on it, he laughed and politely declined. Only a queen should wear a queen's apron, he said. Now Siiri was afraid his shirt would get messy as he whisked with big, rapid movements.

'Do you want me to take off my shirt?' Muhis laughed. He stopped stirring and stripped off his shirt so quickly that Siiri barely had time to squeal. Muhis continued stirring more furiously than ever, and flecks of white batter splattered onto his black skin.

'What now? What are you thinking, Siiri?'

Siiri was distracted, marvelling at this man who could bake: 'I'm sorry, I wasn't thinking about anything. Right, you were adding the flour. You pour; you can put in almost all of it, but leave a couple of decilitres.'

It was impossible to know how much flour it took to make a good *pulla* dough. You had to feel it. Suddenly, Siiri remembered the butter; she had bought some lovely hand-churned butter from Hakaniemi Hall, and the salesperson had wrapped it prettily in wax paper. Siiri looked for the package, first in the fridge and then on the messy counter, where a sweaty shirt now swam among the ingredients and eggshells. The butter was hiding under the shirt, of course. Carefully, Siiri moved the shirt to a bar stool. She let Muhis test how the butter was supposed to feel, soft enough so that you could blend it into the dough when you start kneading.

'Needing?'

'Knead. K-N-E-A-D. There's even a joke about that ... how did it go ... What did the dough say to the baker? I need you to knead me.'

Muhis laughed but looked at Siiri quizzically, because he still didn't know what kneading was. Siiri told him to twist, fold and punch the dough with his bare hands until it stopped sticking to them. Kneading could take a while; baking *pulla* was not something to undertake when you were pressed for time. Muhis said that Africans always had plenty of time, and Siiri laughed merrily, because if that were true, Africans and old Finns were in the same boat: nothing but time on their hands.

Muhis dived right into the kneading as if he'd been baking *pulla* his entire life. Siiri looked on in admiration as her friend wrestled with the dough. Muhis' movements were swift and elegant, simultaneously sharp and fluid, like those of a wild cat. Siiri had never seen any cats in the wild, but she had never seen a man baking at home, either. If one of her sons had ever cooked, it had consisted of standing at a smoking grill with a bottle of beer in one hand, scorching sausages. No wonder they had died before retirement of gluttony, alcohol and other affluenza-related diseases. Muhis sang and laughed; the soft dough was fun to slap around until it grew pliant. The pale, late-autumn sun fell on his back muscles, which tensed splendidly in time to his kneading. And before long, the dough was pulling away from the sides of the bowl.

'There we go. Knead until no more kneading is needed. I'll make sure we knead out all the looseness,' Muhis said, continuing to abuse the dough. 'Doesn't "loose" refer to the kind of woman who's bad in some way? The kind that used to hang around here before you moved in?'

Siiri was embarrassed. 'You must mean loose lips, but that

can be a man just as easily as a woman. Someone who has a big mouth. That's enough, Muhis! Stop!'

Muhis obeyed as promptly as if he were one of Anna-Liisa's students. Siiri tested the dough. It was almost perfect: firm, quite thick and stretchy. 'Now we add the rest of the flour. I think one decilitre is enough.'

As Muhis finished kneading the dough, Siiri rummaged through the drawers in the kitchenette, looking for the linen cloth she'd bought the day before, the one with the little pigs on it. She didn't find it in the drawers and continued her hunt at the coffee table and the chairs in the entryway. She wandered through the cavernous apartment without seeing a trace of the towel. Then she spotted it in the spa, on Anna-Liisa's bath chair. Siiri couldn't grasp how her nice new kitchen towel had ended up there, and she hoped from the bottom of her heart that Anna-Liisa's in-home care-givers hadn't seen fit to use it. She lowered the towel over the bowl of dough and placed the bowl in the corner cupboard. It was in front of the radiator and a little warmer than the other cupboards.

'Then we just wait for the dough to rise. In the meantime, we can have a cup of coffee,' she said to Muhis, clicking on the coffee machine.

They seated themselves on the bar stools and sipped hot coffee, gazing out at the vista, across Tokoinranta Park and Hakaniemi market, the trains travelling past in the distance and the trail of souls wandering into the metro tunnel. Siiri wanted to know more about Muhis' life. It was a pity that a man as fine as Muhis wasn't allowed to work. Muhis told her

he'd attended very little school in Nigeria, because his parents couldn't afford to educate all their children and Muhis
was the second youngest of nine sons. He told Siiri he'd run
through the fields barefoot and lived very humbly.

'I had a wretched excuse for shoes during the war, too,'
Siiri said. 'Can you imagine, we made shoes out of newspapers and cardboard, and children wore them in temperatures
so cold your spit froze.'

Then they drifted into talking about food again, as always.
Muhis' unvaried diet in Africa hadn't been so different from
Siiri's memories of Finland during the depression. Siiri got a
kick out of the fact that she and the young Nigerian man had
been through such similar experiences.

'Of course I've always been privileged, even on a Finnish
scale. I was able to attend as much school as I wanted. Our
family always had work and food. Many of my contempo-
raries spent their childhood in deprivation and poverty like
you. But you need to work. And you're a well-bred man,
even though you didn't have the chance to attend school in
Africa.'

'What's a well-bred man?'

'A man like you,' Siiri said, looking amiably into Muhis'
coal-black eyes. 'You're kind to other people. You listen
and care; you're considerate and courageous. And then you
speak many languages and learn things quickly. You take
care of yourself and adapt to difficult conditions, even here
in Finland. And you have a good sense of humour. Doesn't
that make you a well-bred man?'

Muhis told her that he dreamed of owning his own restaurant. He used to help out in the kitchen of a friend's
kebab-pizzeria, but the tax office had raided the restaurant
and the friend had been forced to shut it down. Muhis had
done most of his work in construction, although most of the
men working in the field were Russian and Estonian.

'It's a mafia. If a Finn is in the construction business, he
has to have good connections in Eastern Europe.'

'Mika talked about the mafia, too, but it was the gay mafia,
as I recall. There were all sorts of messes at Sunset Grove
involving Russians, drugs and ice hockey. And now they're
using Russian and Estonian men on the renovation. Is that a
bad thing?'

Siiri tried to remember the name of the company doing
the construction work at Sunset Grove, but all she could
think of was the cleaning product Spic and Span, which took
her back through the years to an old television advertisement for Black and Decker: 'A pair of hands and a Black and
Decker is all you need to make dreams come true.' Diverting
as these anecdotes may have been, they weren't much use,
since she couldn't remember the name of the construction
company, even though she was singing a bit of the Black and
Decker jingle. That reminded her of Jerry Siilinpää and his
information session for the residents of Sunset Grove. She
mimicked Jerry, which amused Muhis.

'The name of the construction company is Fix 'n' Finish,'
Muhis said, growing serious. 'Unless it went bankrupt for a
change and switched names again.'

Muhis knew all about Fix 'n' Finish, even though he had

never worked for them. He thought it was one of the worst companies in the business, and Siiri wasn't sure what he meant by 'worst' in this context. After all, Muhis didn't pay taxes himself: what right did he have to be judging companies that did business under the table, or hired foreigners?

'Fix 'n' Finish isn't just a construction company. Its tentacles reach everywhere. Including this apartment,' Muhis said, looking around Siiri's living room. Just the way he was looking made its heavy pillars, curving walls, coloured chandeliers, bar and other eccentricities take on a suspicious cast. Siiri had grown used to the apartment and, after her initial bewilderment, no longer wondered why someone would choose to decorate their apartment in this fashion, and add floor-to-ceiling soundproofing to boot. The Ambassador had held forth proudly on it once, the floor mats, triple windows and the like, thanks to which the noise didn't travel up to the apartment from the street or from one apartment to another, the way it did in most old buildings in central Helsinki.

'Do you know someone named Hasan?' Siiri asked after a long silence. The mysterious, sinister-seeming men who came asking for Hasan had been nagging at her.

'I wish I didn't, I really do. But do you know what that pole is for?' Muhis pointed at the metal pole that they had imagined was a support of sorts. 'It's for dancing.'

'I thought dancers' barres were horizontal? Ballet dancers lean on them while they practise their leg lifts,' Siiri said.

Muhis laughed gleefully yet again, and told Siiri the poles

were all the rage, now that even your average housewives were practising Indian pole-dancing.

'So I suppose it has uses that are other than pornographic.'

Siiri nearly choked on her coffee. She lowered her mug to the table and started coughing nastily. Muhis pounded her on the back a little too hard and the coughing just grew worse. Then Muhis made her stand up, wrapped his strong arms around her, and spoke in a low, soothing tone.

'Everything's fine, Siiri, everything's fine. Don't worry, don't be afraid, even though the world is a crazy place.'

'I beg your pardon,' Anna-Liisa's voice suddenly said. Apparently, she had roused herself from her nap and stood there, one hand clutching her cane and the other the dancing pole. To Siiri's eyes she looked like a naughty housewife about to start her daily exercise routine, and Siiri giggled. But Anna-Liisa wasn't smiling.

'Siiri Kettunen!' she cried, as if the commune's living room were the auditorium at the Kallio Comprehensive School. 'Sit down and calm yourself. What on earth are you doing? And who is this . . . topless individual embracing you in the middle of our living room in broad daylight?'

Siiri hurried to introduce Muhis and Anna-Liisa to each other. She had told Anna-Liisa about her Nigerian friend, but never in her wildest dreams did Anna-Liisa think that one day a black man in a hat bigger than a bucket would be standing in her home, groping Siiri.

'We're making *pulla*,' Siiri explained, immediately understanding that this explanation would not suffice. 'Muhis wanted to learn how to make Finnish *pulla*. We already kneaded the dough; it's rising in the cupboard. As a matter of fact, it might be ready.' She scurried into the kitchenette, opened the corner cupboard and shrieked. The dough had risen over the edges of the bowl and spilled onto the shelves of the cupboard. The sight made Muhis laugh; Anna-Liisa was disgusted.

'I'll clean this up,' Siiri said. 'You two have coffee in the meantime. Muhis, please pour some for Anna-Liisa.'

Muhis didn't have to speak with Anna-Liisa long before the ice had melted. His elegant, fluent Finnish caressed Anna-Liisa's ears and his pleasant manner pleased the Ambassador's wife; and since Muhis was capable of discussing literature, Siiri could hear Anna-Liisa's purr of approval all the way to the corner cupboard.

'. . . and I use alliteration to teach the comitative, *kissan kanssa, kissoineen* . . .'

The three of them decided to use the *pulla* dough to make *korvapuusti*, cinnamon buns, and Anna-Liisa was no longer the least bit bothered that Muhis remained bare-torsoed as he rolled out the dough. She buttered the dough energetically, Siiri and Muhis sprinkled on the cinnamon and sugar, and in the end Siiri rolled the dough into a tube and showed Muhis how to cut the slices the right thickness with a sharp knife.

'Then we pinch them like this, so they spread at the bottom, and brush egg on the top to give them a nice shine,' Siiri said. Anna-Liisa brushed on more butter, and Muhis got to sprinkle the pearl sugar on top. He said it reminded him of snow. Anna-Liisa corrected him: more like hailstones, actually.

'Hail can consist of sleet or pure ice. And it's true that hail formed of sleet can resemble snow, even though it's something different. But this cinnamon is rather reminiscent of the sands of the Sahara, don't you think? Do you have as many words for sand as our indigenous Sami do for snow?'

'I have no idea.' Muhis smiled. 'I'm not from the desert; I'm from the jungle.'

Anna-Liisa laughed, tickled by the thought, and started to muse on which of them, her or Muhis, was from deeper in the forest. Siiri hadn't been aware that Anna-Liisa was born in the backwoods of Karelia, at the end of a dirt track, and Anna-Liisa hurried to point out that her parents had moved from the jungles of Karelia to the city of Joensuu when she was quite young.

'The point being that I attended school in civilization and was raised in furnished rooms.'

When the cinnamon rolls were in the oven, Anna-Liisa taught Muhis how to braid four lengths of *pulla* dough into a loaf of coffee bread. She was very adept at it, and Siiri was quite awe-struck by Anna-Liisa's skills.

'When I was a girl, it was my job to bake *pulla* every Saturday. Oh, how I hated it then, but I'm rather enjoying it now!'

Irma and Margit came home from water aerobics, utterly exhausted, just as Muhis was pulling the last sheet of cinnamon rolls from the oven. The aroma of baking *pulla* filled their pornographic lair, and Irma started singing old Schlager songs and waltzing around, so thrilled was she about Siiri's surprise.

'I'm not the least bit tired any more! That just goes to show: exercise is exhausting, but *pulla* perks you up,' Irma said, twirling around the pole one last time and flinging herself onto the sofa, where she waited to be served warm *pulla* and cold milk. Margit retreated to her room.

'Muhis knows the company doing the construction work at Sunset Grove, and he thinks it's involved in illicit human trafficking,' Siiri said, once they were ensconced on the soft sofa, eating fresh-baked *pulla*.

'What do you mean by "human trafficking"?' Anna-Liisa asked; the way she sat up straighter indicated that she found this topic interesting in the extreme.

'It can be almost anything,' Muhis said, mouth full of *pulla*. They waited with bated breath for him to finish chewing. 'Bringing people into the country illegally. Forcing them to work under the table. Construction work, restaurant work, but also prostitution. And, of course, drugs are always involved.'

Irma and Anna-Liisa shrieked as one. The memory of the drug ring run by Virpi and Erkki Hiukkanen out of Sunset Grove was still fresh in their minds. They had learned the hard way that, in the eyes of a drug dealer, a retirement home was paradise, because young people wanted to get silly on old people's medication. But hadn't they moved beyond all that, now that Mika Korhonen had so masterfully exposed the Hiukkanens' malfeasance? Siiri felt a powerful throbbing in her head and couldn't swallow. The *pulla* had turned to cement that filled her whole mouth; she started feeling repulsed. She looked out at the bleak view and, breathing calmly, chose a point to focus on: the letter M on the Metal-workers' Union headquarters.

'This *pulla* is divine!' Muhis said. He ate with his eyes closed, drank his cold milk, allowing it to mingle with the hot, soft, sweet dough in his mouth. He wasn't worried about human trafficking or drugs at the moment, because now he knew what Finnish men in pubs meant when they reminisced about eating warm *pulla*, straight from the oven in their mother's kitchen. After devouring three large *korvapuusti*, he pounded his chest rhythmically, stood, and said he had to go.

'I'm in a hurry,' he said, without further explanation. Anna-Liisa was about to make some snide remark about African notions of time, but a sharp glance from Siiri brought her up short. After all, he had spent all day with them without complaint. Siiri packed up one of the braided loaves for him, and with that Muhis vanished into the dark stair-well, the freshly baked *pulla* under his arm. As Siiri was closing the door, she heard Muhis run into someone on the stairs, with whom he engaged in a brief but intense debate in a language that wasn't Finnish, perhaps English.

After that, all was silent.

Chapter 22

Doing laundry at the commune was quite an operation. Luckily, a large room behind the spa-cum-bathroom had been dedicated solely to this purpose; it had enough room to pull the sheets taut before folding them and still line-dry clothes for five. The washing machine was as big as a hospital's, spacious and powerful, and next to it there was a dryer and a rotary iron for pressing the sheets. The latter was surprisingly easy to use. Siiri and Irma would first stretch each sheet flat by hand, then fold it, and in the end Siiri would hold the sheet while Irma slipped it into the rotary iron and pressed the button.

'Hocus pocus, and out comes a flat sheet!' Irma said, watching, eyes gleaming, as the pressed sheet appeared at the far edge of the device. They would fold the hot, smooth sheet and add it to the pile of clean linens. No one else had time to do laundry, so naturally this task as well had fallen to Siiri and Irma. Siiri was pleased that Irma liked using the rotary iron, because otherwise her friend might have shirked this responsibility as lightly as she did the cooking and cleaning, and she said so.

'Nonsense, I've gone shopping with you I don't know how many times, and even help out with the cleaning now and again. Does it make any sense to mop a clean home every day? Why, just yesterday I scrubbed both bathrooms, including those stupid bidets, although I'm not sure who's using them,' Irma responded.

It was true. The day before, Irma had participated in the weekly housework by pulling on a pair of pink flowered rubber gloves and the lace-trimmed housecoat she had sewn herself. Then she had stormed the spa and attacked it for over an hour, splashing and singing, because she loved the way her high soprano echoed in the vaulted space. Meanwhile, Siiri had dusted all the surfaces, taken the duvets out to the balcony to air, wiped the doors and jambs with a damp rag, and vacuumed the entire apartment while listening to Irma's arias. Irma had brought her tour de force to its conclusion by singing a rendition of Violetta's death scene from Verdi's *La Traviata*, collapsing to the couch and gasping with the last of her strength: '*Döden, döden, döden.*'

'You're folding the sheet wrong. They taught us at the Nursing Academy how to do it properly,' Irma said to Siiri, as they pulled the sheet flat prior to sliding it into the rotary iron. The sheet-stretching was fun; you could lean back into emptiness as long as you trusted the other person to keep you from falling. Siiri leaned with all her weight and closed her eyes. She felt unusually tired, a little weak, as a matter of fact; running a large household might not be suitable for an old woman. She sighed deeply. Just then, Irma's nose started to itch, and she let go of the sheet. Siiri crashed to the ground and hit her elbow nastily on the corner of the dryer.

'For calamity's sake! What have you done, you silly goose?' Irma cried, and bent down over Siiri. Irma huffed as she tried to help Siiri up from the floor, but she didn't have the benefit of in-home caregiver training, and so she plopped to the floor, too. There they sat on their backsides, bewildered, until they looked at each other and started laughing so hard they peed in their pants. There was a faint knock at the door, and a dark-skinned girl in a long robe peered in quizzically at the old women giggling on the floor.

'Are you all right?' the Somali-Finn asked shyly.

'Yes, yes! We're just resting for a moment before we finish up the laundry,' Siiri said. Her arm didn't hurt the tiniest bit any more.

'We have under-floor heating, would you like to try? It'll warm your bum right up!' Irma cried at the in-home caregiver, and they burst out laughing uncontrollably again. Irma felt around the sleeve of her housecoat for her lace handkerchief, found it in the pocket, and wiped the tears from her eyes. 'Under-floor heating and laundry rooms, of all the things people come up with when they don't have anything better to do!'

The shy caregiver explained that she was looking for Anna-Liisa and continued on her way. Siiri and Irma climbed up stiffly, stretched their aching limbs, and looked at the mountains of dirty clothes and clean sheets surrounding them.

'This is impossible,' Irma said, grabbing items at random and shoving them into the washing machine's gargantuan drum. Her in-house dye-shop had already turned out clothes in a variety of tints, generally pale pink. But even the Ambassador didn't chide her; he just bravely slipped on the shirts Irma had tie-dyed, as long as they were clean and ironed.

'Ironed, on top of everything else,' Siiri huffed. She knew men wore permanent press shirts these days, but the Ambassador refused to buy them. His were custom-made by a tailor who lived somewhere on the other side of the world. The Ambassador had sent the tailor his measurements, and once a month he would pick up a package from the post office containing a new shirt or trousers, sometimes an entire suit. Luckily, Anna-Liisa and Onni's suite had a separate room for clothes. Siiri set up the ironing board in front of the window and turned on the iron.

'Do you suppose the Ambassador's shirts are made under the table? I mean, is it possible Onni had this made somewhere inexpensively the way you're not supposed to?' Siiri asked, as she ironed the cuffs of a hand-tailored shirt.

'It's all the same to me where he has them made; I just wish he would take care of this rigmarole himself. My husband certainly didn't change shirts every day. Why, Veikko and all of my darlings put together produced less laundry than Onni does by himself. Oh, my dear husband was such a sweetheart. And now I miss him again!'

They spent a moment reminiscing about their husbands, dried their tears on Irma's lace handkerchief, and got back down to the task at hand.

Irma had been to Sunset Grove a month ago, to retrieve

her winter clothes in good time, but Siiri had nothing warmer than an autumn coat. October was well underway and the first snow could come at any moment. Irma said she had run into Tauno again, who was swaying amid the devastation like the last of the Mohicans. And when Irma had stepped into her apartment, she had found three hairy brutes moving her belongings around.

'I tried to give them a piece of my mind, but the blockheads didn't speak a word of Finnish. I switched to shouting in Swedish, German, English and French, even a couple of words of Latin, although I think those were the scientific names of plants, but all that did was improve my mood. I even let them have it in Italian, with a few musical terms and operatic phase. *Perfidi*, what a wonderful curse word. That's what Count Almaviva shouts in *The Marriage of Figaro*, and that's the best opera in the world. Oh dear, Mozart, you were an amazing man, even more amazing than my dear Veikko. Those demolition dolts just gaped at me as if I were a madwoman.'

Irma had retrieved her warm clothes from the moving boxes while the gorillas looked on. Just to be sure, she had slipped her kitchen silver in among her wool knickers, because she was thoroughly convinced the men were after her valuables.

'Not that I have any valuables left, since my darlings already divided everything up,' she said casually, as she carried the stack of pressed sheets to the linen closet, which was bigger than her bathroom at Sunset Grove. '*Döden, döden, döden.*'

'Should we go to Sunset Grove and have a look around?' Siiri asked. She had stopped ironing after pressing three shirts into presentable condition and was following at Irma's heels like a faithful dog. She discovered Irma was as enthusiastic as she was about the possibility of getting to the bottom of whatever major scandal was lurking in the shadows of Sunset Grove's retrofit. Besides, it would be lovely to ride the tram again; it had been such a long time.

Irma quickly packed the necessities: playing cards, a miniature bottle of whisky, two lace handkerchiefs, her tram pass, wallet, keys, cigarettes, lozenges, spare stockings and the iPad. They were already in her handbag, but Irma took everything out and laid it on the entryway console to make sure that nothing was missing, and then dumped it back in with both hands in no particular order.

'Now we can go. Oh, but where's my beret?'

She spun around in circles in the entryway, unable to decide on a sensible place to start looking. Siiri checked the hat shelf, but only found the Ambassador's felt hat and Anna-Liisa's red spring hat, the grand symbol of their love. Then she rummaged around the umbrella stand and picked up the newspapers from the chairs, in case Irma's beret happened to be under something. But it wasn't.

'Siiri, you're wearing it! You've stolen my beret!'

Irma snatched the blue beret from Siiri's head. Siiri was sure that the hat she'd happily been using for weeks was hers, but Irma held her ground. She placed the beret on her grey curls and eyed her reflection in the dim entryway, satisfied.

'Look! Just like Garbo . . . all that's missing are the sunglasses.'

Siiri opened the top drawer of the entryway console to pull out the scarf Margit had given her, and lo and behold, discovered Irma's light-blue beret.

'Yes, well. I believe that one's mine after all. Give it here. I thought this one was a little flat,' Irma said, handing the dark-blue beret back to Siiri.

Now they were ready to leave.

Chapter 23

As abominable as the weather was, waiting at the tram stop was still good fun. A cold wind skimmed across the faces of the waiting passengers, and the drizzle was so fine that no one bothered using an umbrella, despite a sure soaking. That was Helsinki in October for you. But there were so many different kinds of people wandering around Hakaniemi that Siiri could have watched them forever, these strangers who were all in a hurry to get somewhere. Siiri and Irma tried to guess where they were going, who they were, what they did for work, what their families were like. And where their elderly parents spent their days while these folks rushed around with stony looks on their faces.

They took the number 9 tram downtown but didn't get off at the train station, because Siiri wanted to roller-coaster up her favourite route: climb Simonkatu, take a sharp right onto Annankatu, and then immediately left onto Urho Kekkosen katu. They were sitting at the back of the tram, in the last row, where the winding curves gave you a lovely feeling in your tummy. Irma sang her 'Siribiribim' high and hard and laughed out loud. They exited the tram at the Electric

Building, designed by Gunnar Taucher and ruined by Alvar Aalto, so they wouldn't end up at the West Harbour.

'We're breaking the rules now, walking from stop to stop,' a slightly irritated Irma remarked, and then admitted that the superfluous hill-climb had done them good. Just as they were crossing the street to make their way to the number 3 stop, a number 9 came from the direction of the harbour, and they hopped on, delighted to spare their tired old legs, and followed the serpentine route back down the hill. From the train station, they walked to Mannerheimintie, since they had already violated the beautiful principle of transferring trams without ever having to change stops.

'Look, it's one of the new trams!' Siiri cried, as an LED-lit number 10 slid silently up to the stop. Two trams custom-built in the backwoods of north-eastern Finland had been delighting the residents of Helsinki for some time now, but Siiri hadn't had a chance to test them yet. Such a rare opportunity could not be passed up; they would have to adjust plans and take the number 10. They entered the tram from the front, but to their consternation did not find a ticket scanner there, and so they had to push their way through the wall of humans to the middle door.

'That's what you get when you let bumpkins design your trams,' Irma huffed.

Two polite young men stood when they saw the old women, which gave Siiri and Irma the opportunity to try out the seats, too. They were very nice, just the right height, and pleasantly firm, with a hint of softness. The windows were large and offered a beautiful view of the landscape racing past. The tram was nearly soundless but rocked rather violently, which Siiri found alarming and Irma amusing. A digital screen advertised the tram as being more environmentally friendly and reliable than the old trams, because it was made in Finland and would run in the foulest weather without any trouble. This was, of course, a jab at the trains. The State Railways had gone and ordered trains from Italy, which got jammed up by wet leaves in the autumn, couldn't take the summer heat, and got stuck in the snow during the winter. Far too many people had been late for work, and demands had been made for the director of the railways to resign. A smaller screen announced the tram's destination and the next stop, but here our northern Finnish engineers had pulled a real boner, as Irma put it. The sign was far too small. It read 'Central Railway Stat' and 'National Pensions Insti' because the rest of the letters didn't fit. 'But the driver's cabin certainly is handsome,' Siiri said.

The driver was perched in lofty solitude, and the glass-walled aquarium he sat in was larger than the nurses' office in your average dementia unit. A schoolchild who was trying to pay for her trip had to stand on tiptoes to reach the slot where transactions with the driver took place.

'He looks like the captain of a ship, piloting the tram from up high like that. Luckily, these aren't being automated like the metros,' Irma said.

'Don't the metros have drivers any more?' Siiri exclaimed. 'If I had known that, I would have insisted on taking a taxi to the SquirrelsNest that time I went there with Margit.'

The little girl finally succeeded in paying for her ticket

when a Russian woman sitting nearby offered her assistance. The Russian woman was wearing a full-length fur, even though it wasn't winter yet. Finns didn't dare wear fur coats any more, even on the most frigid January days, because young animal rights activists stained and cut them. Siiri and Irma had quietly packed up their old minks and forgotten them in the attic at Sunset Grove, from where, presumably, they had been snatched before being sold to Russians well before the July heatwave.

'Putin is a good president,' the Russian woman said, as she seated herself across from Siiri and Irma. The new trams had the same sort of four-person tables as the low-floor trams, with two benches face to face.

'Is he?' Irma's curiosity was piqued, because she was under the exact opposite impression. 'He certainly is rather fit and apparently gets a lot of exercise.'

'Marriage is for a man and a woman,' the woman continued in relatively fluent Finnish. 'I think it's ugly, very ugly, when two men . . . *patamusta* . . .'

'You're the one with a black heart,' Irma said, although she gathered full well that the woman had slipped into Russian, where *patamusta* meant 'because', not 'black-hearted', as it did in Finnish.

'Excuse me?' the woman said and started explaining over again. She thought Putin was a good man because he didn't allow gay marriage. Siiri knew how much Irma loved her homosexual darlings, her grandson and his beautiful boyfriend. Irma had been ready to march in the Pride parade on their behalf, but at the last minute her darlings had put the kibosh on the idea, because marching on behalf of gay rights was even more dangerous than traipsing about in a fur coat. You might take a tomato or a smoke bomb to the head.

'Don't we need to transfer to the number 4?' Irma said. Siiri pressed the glowing red button that, to her disappointment, wasn't as responsive as she would have wished. They rose and exited the tram at the University Pharmacy stop. Through the tram window, they could see the fur-clad Russian move across the aisle, doggedly trying to convert Finns to homophobia.

'Damned Russki,' Irma said, sparking a squabble with Siiri about the use of the word. Siiri felt that you shouldn't say it, because it had the same unpleasant tone as 'the n word' used in reference to black people. But Irma stoutly defended Russki.

'We've always called Russians Russkis. There's nothing wrong with it. I'm not about to start learning my language over again at the age of ninety-three just because some upstart language police is sitting around, sniffing out politically incorrect attitudes in perfectly acceptable words that have been around for ages. Or am I ninety-four already?'

The number 4 came quickly, and they forgot all about Russkis and other ugly words and concentrated on observing the wretched youngsters on their way to the narcotics clinic. Irma had heard that you could get drugs for free at Meilahti Hospital and that was how they kept drug addicts clean and in line.

'They have to be sober when you go there; that way they don't contaminate themselves with dirty needles. But it's nonsensical to me that they're given drugs instead of being taught how to live without them.'

Two young people sitting in front of Irma and Siiri were complaining that their weekly government-funded dose was too small, because they had the flu and were taking antibiotics and the drug didn't hit them the way it was supposed to. Irma was just about to engage the young people in conversation, but they exited at the Hilton hospital stop. Siiri sighed with relief. They rode the remainder of the trip in peace, and as the tram sped across the Paciuksenkatu Bridge, she felt her heart leap; it was so lovely coming home to Munkkiniemi.

'No matter how we feel about Sunset Grove, this is my home,' she said, clenching her hands to her breast, revelling in the joy the yellow-leafed lindens and little boutiques of Munkkiniemi Allée brought her. There was Max's Cafe, and people were still sitting outside, even though the weather was lousy and the air chilly. And before long, Raikka over at the hardware store would put up his window display for Christmas, the miniature village with a train running through it. One year Raikka had run out of money and hadn't done his traditional Christmas window, but the neighbourhood had felt so badly about it that they had gathered a collection to pay the electric bill and other expenses.

'That's right; I suppose it will be Christmas again soon,' Irma sighed, as if the holiday were some onerous burden to be borne. Which it was. For as long as they could remember, they had baked, cooked, crafted, decorated, knitted and wrapped for weeks on end so their families would enjoy a proper Christmas. Of course, this year they hadn't imagined they'd be celebrating Christmas on the wrong side of the Pitkäsilta in a Finnish businessman's private entertainment venue.

'Perhaps the remodel at Sunset Grove will be finished by Christmas,' Siiri said, trying to lighten the mood, but this time not even Irma could join in her optimism. And when Siiri passed through the automatic doors and entered the lobby of Sunset Grove, her good mood swirled away, like rainwater draining into a kerb-side gutter and into the bowels of the earth.

Sunset Grove was a sad sight, downright heart-breaking. They had seen ruination of all sorts of during wartime and vividly remembered the February 1944 bombing of Helsinki, yet the construction site yawning before them struck them as ghastlier than any of their memories. The lobby was dark and cold; evidently the electricity had been cut off for quite some time. Walls had been ripped open, the ends of wires and various coloured pipes stuck out everywhere, and the floor was strewn with bags of cement, a cement mixer, ladders and all manner of construction material scattered haphazardly about. A pair of men with black beards and safety vests were leaning against the wall, smoking cheap cigarettes, as calm as you like.

'That's a familiar smell,' Irma said, as they walked past the men.

They had to advance carefully because the floor was treacherous, littered with mines they might trip over. Not real mines, of course, which they'd also had to pick their way through during their lifetimes, but, nevertheless, the floor was full of traps. The elevator didn't work, which meant they had to brave the stairwell.

'Halt!' a shaky, slightly hoarse voice rasped from the landing opposite.

They squinted at the voice in the gloom and recognized a familiar figure. Tauno was standing there in his cap, eternally hunched, flailing his arms more furiously than normal. Apparently, he didn't recognize them, and was defending his fortress from enemy attacks with those tactics still available to him.

'Cock-a-doodle-doo! Tauno, it's just us, Irma and Siiri!'

Irma's password sufficed. Tauno was visibly happy to see old friends among the hunks of concrete. He reached for his hat and tipped it politely.

'My dear girls! You're still alive!'

He bobbed his way over to Irma and Siiri as quickly as he could, gave them both awkward hugs, and started babbling like a pot of boiling beans. He hadn't had anyone to talk to for weeks, and that wasn't even the saddest thing about his life amid the annihilation of Sunset Grove.

'This is no normal plumbing retrofit,' Tauno said, with a shake of his head. He had conducted scouting expeditions around the entirety of Sunset Grove and discovered walls between units being knocked down, entire kitchens demolished, doors carried out to dumpsters. Floors had been jackhammered up and balconies removed. Director Sinikka Sundström had fled to India to care for orphaned children with funds she had raised during a campaign she had organized at Sunset Grove. He had seen neither hide nor hair of Jerry Siilinpää since September, when the worst of the destruction had begun.

'So he wasn't fired?' Irma asked.

'No, although he should have been.'

'So where are you living?' Siiri asked, horrified, as it seemed all the flats had been demolished in the name of the renovation.

'And what happened to our belongings?' Irma shouted.

They rushed to their hallway with Tauno at their heels, and there was no need for them to dig around for their keys, because there was no door to their apartments. Their homes had been emptied. Every plastic-wrapped item of furniture and decorative object was gone, as were the moving boxes in which they had packed their dearest and most prized possessions. They gaped at the unrecognizable wastes of construction debris that had once been their homes. The kitchens and living rooms had been turned into one big room; the cupboards and fixtures had been torn out. The room looked oddly small; it was hard to imagine all the things it should have contained fitting in it. There was no longer a hole in the bathroom wall, because the entire wall had disappeared. Their bathrooms had been melted into one big cement cave with pipe-ends jutting oddly out of the walls.

'Is this . . . are they turning these two apartments into one big one?' Irma asked slowly, as she wandered around in the darkness, perplexed.

Tauno continued his incessant jabbering, as for him the

sight was nothing new. He told them he had moved his scant belongings from one room to the next as the construction work advanced. He had two old suitcases and a mattress, that was all, so a camp life had been more or less manageable.

'But now I'm staying in the last room at the end of the corridor. If they don't finish the first apartments soon, I'll be out on the street. That pathologist spends all her days at the Ukko-Munkki and sleeps wherever she can find a spot to lay her head. Who knows, maybe she's made it into some hospital, thanks to her connections? I haven't seen the old cow in a while, and I can't say that I've missed her, either.'

Siiri quietly corrected Tauno: 'She's a medical examiner, not a pathologist.'

'Heavens to Betsy!' Irma exclaimed. She was standing in the middle of her apartment, next to a heap of broken bathroom tile. 'Shouldn't they have . . . How can they just . . . Was this announced somewhere, that our apartments are going to be emptied?'

'On the Internet, apparently,' Tauno said. 'But since I don't have any way of accessing that magical world, I've been scouting around with my senses on high alert. I rescued this box from your room.' He dug into the old backpack he was hauling around and handed Siiri Anna-Liisa's jewellery box. 'I thought it might be valuable, or have sentimental value. Aren't women sentimental about jewellery?'

Irma and Siiri looked at the box in Tauno's hand, stunned. How could it be here in Sunset Grove when they had seen it in Hakaniemi just a short while ago in September? The day the two phony police had come sniffing around for it and Anna-Liisa had found the enormous wad of cash inside.

'Thank you, Tauno,' Siiri said finally, accepting the box. It wouldn't fit in the handbag she had brought, but she had the strength to carry it back to Hakaniemi.

Tauno wanted to show them his current foxhole, and they dejectedly followed him down the deserted hallway. The same annihilation had afflicted every apartment, as if they had been bombed.

'At least most of the walls are still standing,' Tauno said. 'Bombs usually take out the whole building.'

In the last flat, the plastic flooring was still in place, but the toilet, shower stall, shower and sink had been torn out of the bathroom, and the kitchen cabinets had vanished. The pipes jutted out of the wall and the lights didn't work. Tauno had dragged his dusty mattress over to the windows; he claimed it was still bright enough to read there during the daytime, even though the building was wrapped in plastic and this time of year there weren't more than a few odd hours of sunlight anyway. Tauno's pair of old cardboard suitcases looked like artefacts from a museum. They contained his clothes, winter boots, a hunting knife, a water bottle and a copy of Väinö Linna's *The Unknown Soldier*. He read it to himself every day, although he already knew it by heart.

'I'm holding the line here, the last man. What would have happened at the Battle of Ihantala if everyone had abandoned their comrades and run off? You'll never make a deserter out of me,' he said proudly, and Irma and Siiri gathered that he took heart from the notion that he'd ended up in World War Three.

'Tauno,' Irma said in a serious voice, taking hold of the hunchbacked man's perpetually swinging hands. She held them for a moment and looked Tauno in the eye, then glanced at his field gear. Tauno had an old green canvas backpack, the kind Siiri's sons had had back in the fifties when they went camping as scouts. Siiri was relatively sure Tauno had packed it with a camp stove, a mess kit, matches, a flashlight, rope and other necessities for survival.

'Tauno dear, you can't stay here. You're coming to Hakaniemi with us. There's room for you, and you won't need to drag that filthy mattress around any more. We have so many clean sheets that we need a room bigger than this apartment to store them in.'

But Tauno refused. He reminded them that Finland wouldn't be an independent country if everyone had jumped on the milk train home at the first sign of trouble. He opened his backpack and showed them everything Siiri had predicted was in there, along with hard tack and enough dehydrated food for weeks — or so he claimed. Irma started talking about the delicious meals Siiri prepared every day, what a fancy whirlpool tub they had in their spa, and how lovely it would be to be able to warm up the sauna and sweat out the grime and stench of the renovation.

'Thank you, Irma, but I can't leave,' Tauno said. He lowered his voice and started sharing secrets with them: how he'd delved into the operations of Fix 'n' Finish, eavesdropped and spied on the construction workers, and discovered a thing or two. Most of Tauno's revelations were familiar, as he had already divulged them to Irma.

'I speak Russian, you know,' he whispered, continuing his tale. Fix 'n' Finish was owned by a prominent Finnish civil servant who'd had shady business dealings in former Soviet countries for years. 'They're based on contacts he made during his career; apparently, he worked in many Warsaw Pact countries.' Tauno was sure the possessions of Sunset Grove's residents had been sold, and their bank accounts had in all likelihood been emptied, too. He had seen the construction workers exchanging thick wads of cash, and he firmly believed that drug dealing and money laundering were somehow involved. Siiri started wondering if Tauno was all there.

'But there aren't any drugs here any more, because there aren't any old people,' Irma said. She didn't seem to believe all of Tauno's ranting either.

'Mark my words, the taps are flowing,' Tauno said, looking enigmatic.

'There's not a single tap that works in the entire building!' Irma cried in vexation.

'The taps of illicit drugs. Of illicit money. Any tap you can think of,' Tauno said, still enigmatically, whirling his arms as if he were trying to take off in flight.

'This can't go on forever,' Siiri said. 'The renovation was supposed to last four months and so far it has lasted – how long has it been?'

'Five months, two weeks and six days,' Tauno stated. He tightened the straps on his backpack, fastened the leather loops, and, handling it as tenderly as a kitten, lowered it to his miserable excuse for a mattress. 'It's lasted longer than the Winter War. But I've lived through two wars, from the first trench to the final battle, and I'm not about to surrender now.' He asked Irma and Siiri to leave and laboriously laid himself down on his mattress.

Siiri and Irma sat in silence for the whole ride back to Hakaniemi, at first on the number 4, then the number 9. Irma clutched her handbag in her lap as if it were the last thing on earth she owned, and Siiri clenched Anna-Liisa's mahogany jewellery box.

Chapter 24

Anna-Liisa looked at the jewellery box and sighed. It was on the bar, lid open. Inside were three pieces of jewellery – two pearl necklaces and one cameo brooch – as well as a wad of cash. The rest of the jewellery had been lost or stolen, stolen and sold on the black market.

'Tauno was right, women place a lot of sentimental value on jewellery,' Irma said, trying to sound chipper. She placed a hand on Anna-Liisa's shoulder and gave it a consoling pat.

'Could you please refrain from pawing me,' Anna-Liisa said. 'This has nothing to do with sentiment. What we have here is a crime, and not your average robbery, either, but something bigger. Why on earth is my jewellery box being used to transport money?'

Irma flinched and pulled her hand away. She looked in alarm at Siiri, who started making coffee. Siiri had learned from one experienced hospice nurse that making coffee was the most effective ritual in the world. When the nurse visited the homes of the dying, where the loved ones sat around, too stunned to speak, everyone instantly felt better when she started making coffee. And this wasn't even a matter of life or death, but of one jewellery box.

'No, this is a much more significant affair. My jewellery box is but a tiny detail that symbolizes a bigger mystery. The mystery of the Sunset Grove renovation,' Anna-Liisa said, her voice trembling.

Irma popped into the kitchenette to lend Siiri a hand, although the coffee machine was perfectly capable of brewing the coffee on its own. She and Siiri opened cupboards, peered into the fridge, closed drawers the other one had opened, and bumped into each other. Siiri felt like whispering to Irma to move out of the way, but she didn't want to get into it.

'Did someone say death?' Margit peered out from her bedroom, her hair a fright. She had slept until noon again, gone for a dip in the whirlpool tub, and after that dragged herself back into bed to read princess stories in her Swedish women's magazine. She whiled away an unbelievable number of days in this manner, never mind that in the spring she had been more active than the rest of them put together.

'It would be inaccurate to say we were discussing death, although the word was uttered,' Anna-Liisa reported, casting a critical eye over Margit, who had emerged in nothing but a ratty pair of pyjama pants and a black bra.

'Oh. That's too bad.' Margit paid no attention to the jewellery box. She scratched herself drowsily, turned her back on Anna-Liisa, and hauled herself into the kitchenette. 'I so wanted to talk about death.'

'*Döden, döden, döden.*'

Irma was trying to lighten the mood, but she herself realized the inappropriateness of her slogan at this moment. The final utterance died on her lips, and she coughed loudly, so the unfortunate fade-out would sound like a mistake.

'Margit, could you please arrange these cookies prettily on a plate? We're going to have a little afternoon coffee,' Siiri said. Margit took the packet of cookies but remained standing there, as stout and still as Viipuri Castle.

'Isn't there anyone here but us? Not a single immigrant or in-home caregiver?'

'Anna-Liisa, where's the Ambass— Onni?'

'Oh, he's . . . Onni had a meeting in town, business. He's very conscientious about his affairs, as you might have noticed.'

'Right. Do you have any idea what those affairs might be?' Irma continued inquisitively and, in Siiri's opinion, a little too boldly. Presumably Anna-Liisa wasn't 100 per cent up to speed on her husband's activities – or else she didn't want to talk about them. She picked up the wad of cash and started briskly counting the money. This time they were yellow two-hundred-euro bills.

'I suppose I should look into Onni's affairs,' she said reflectively. 'As you know, we don't have a prenuptial agreement. That's the way Onni wanted it. So this curious apartment is my property, too, isn't it?'

'But that means you could do a little digging and find out what that Hasan who lived here before us was up to!' Irma exclaimed. Margit was still holding the cookie packet and didn't seem to grasp what the others were talking about.

'Absolutely not. I trust my husband, and it would be an incredible affront if I started digging through this apartment's – previous uses. Or his personal finances; I have no need to do anything of the sort. Nevertheless, I find myself rather surprised that this matter of much greater consequence, namely, the mysterious wanderings of my jewellery box and the altogether questionable renovation of Sunset Grove, have not sparked greater inquisitiveness in the two of you. This is fifteen thousand euros in two-hundred-euro bills.'

Margit looked at the money and dropped the packet of cookies to the floor. Siiri picked it up, took a plate from the cupboard, spread a poppy-print napkin across it, and placed the cookies in an even ring around it with excessive reverence. The situation was very odd. Anna-Liisa gave no clue as to whether or not she knew anything about the Ambassador's business affairs. Margit, on the other hand, was fixated on euthanasia again and appeared more depressed than ever, downright apathetic, in fact. Irma was hustling and bustling about without actually getting anything done. And on top of everything else, Siiri was fretting about Tauno, who was at Sunset Grove alone, sleeping on the floor on his filthy mattress.

'There's enough money here for me to take Eino to Switzerland or the Netherlands,' Margit said, fingering the bills in Anna-Liisa's hands. The more she fingered them, the tighter Anna-Liisa's grip grew, until her knuckles were white and her mouth an impervious line.

'As if anyone had the time to travel,' Anna-Liisa said

finally. She yanked the bills back, shoved them into the box, snapped the lid shut, and carried the token of criminal activity off to her room. 'It's been over a year since Onni and I went to the spas in Estonia on a veterans' organization trip. Oh, what lovely times those were!'

Irma poured coffee for all of them and managed to seat Margit on one of the stools. This was no simple task, with the stool being as wobbly as it was, and Margit's backside so immense. Before long Anna-Liisa returned; she reported that she had hidden the jewellery box in a safe place, and none of them dared ask where. After drinking a big mug of coffee, Irma suddenly remembered her beloved green flaptop, pulled it out of her bag, and set it on the table.

'I'll just have a look and see what my trusty friend knows about the company doing the renovation work at Sunset Grove. What was it called again? Kling and Klang?'

'Don't be silly, those are the policemen from Pippi Longstocking,' Siiri said. But she couldn't remember the name of the company either.

'So they are! That was so funny when Pippi didn't want to go to the orphanage and the police chased her up to the roof. Or when they went round and round on the carousel so many times that they got dizzy and everyone thought they were drunk. I read Pippi to my darlings all the time, even though my mother and many of my friends thought she was a bad example. And then later we watched the Swedish television series, which was so nicely done. Do you remember, there was that one episode where nothing else happened except Pippi danced around the attic and there was this horrible, atonal harpsichord playing in the background? My darlings always watched it, spellbound. I don't suppose a show like that would catch the attention of these restless computer kids. Now that I think about it, I'm not sure if it was my children or grandchildren whom I watched it with. Didn't the series start until the 1970s? Shuffle and cut, now I know! The name of the construction company was Skweekee Kleen, wasn't it?'

They put their heads together and racked their brains. Everyone remembered one funny name or combination of words, but none of them were right. Irma lost interest and started playing Sudoku. Anna-Liisa also grew tired and took the Swedish-language crossword from the sideboard, but Margit perked up visibly after loudly slurping down three mugs of coffee. That was another thing Siiri found annoying about Margit: she ate and drank loudly, smacked her lips, belched, and talked with her mouth full. Crumbs flew across the table, and she never bothered to wipe up after herself. They were lucky if she remembered to take her dishes to the sink. From where, of course, they always loaded themselves into the dishwasher.

Chapter 25

Margit slammed the newspaper down on the counter, making Siiri jump. Margit was still naked after her shower and had a peculiar look on her face; she narrowed her eyes at Siiri as if the sun were shining directly in them on this rainy October afternoon.

'We could go to the SquirrelsNest today. We don't have to take the metro, I'll spring for a taxi in honour of the celebration.'

They were alone in the apartment, because the Ambassador had taken Anna-Liisa across Hakaniemi Square to a hotel brunch; he was trying to placate her after the strain and stress produced by the jewellery box. Irma had rushed off to water aerobics at the Allergy Institute first thing that morning.

'Celebration? What celebration?'

'Eino's celebration. I need to get dressed, wait a minute.'

'Is it Eino's birthday today?' Siiri asked, but Margit had already vanished. She cleared away the mugs, a little peeved, and loaded and turned on the dishwasher. Why did it always fall on her shoulders, loading the dishwasher? It was convenient, the only convenient contraption in this household. She had never owned a dishwasher in her life, and now she intended on making the most of this ecologically unfriendly luxury that spared her from the daily mountain of dishes. A press of the button, and the machine started working for her. She took off her 'Queen of Fucking' apron, put it back in its place in the bottom drawer, and started gathering up the belongings she might need on an expedition to the Squirrel-sNest. Her cane and handbag, that was about it, now that she knew the place.

Margit emerged from her room surprisingly rapidly, looking utterly different to a moment ago, when she'd been drinking coffee in her usual house-wear – without a stitch, that is, unless you counted threadbare underwear. She had brushed her hair up into a tidy bun, put on a flowered head-band and a stylish navy-blue dress, and had even made up her face skilfully. Siiri couldn't be bothered to use make-up any more, but Margit occasionally felt the urge. She looked classy, and somehow dignified.

'I called us a cab. It will be downstairs in a minute,' she said.

It was grey and rainy outside, and the taxi was waiting for them by the pavement, just outside the door. The vehicle was disappointingly compact and not at all fancy. Siiri was used to a taxi ride being a touch of luxury; in the past, the cars were new Mercedes that smelled of leather and the drivers opened the doors with a tip of their caps. But this jalopy was mud-stained and cramped, and advertisements played in the headrest in front of you, making you queasy. The driver stayed slouched in his seat and didn't so much as glance at his customers, even in the rear-view mirror, the way Mika Korhonen had done fatefully so long ago. Siiri felt like ages had passed since their encounter with that dratted angel, even though it had only been a year or two. In addition to a mild nausea, she felt a profound wistfulness, and she was wrenched by a strong, vague spasm like you had when you missed someone. What had happened to Mika, why didn't he have a phone any more? She and Anna-Liisa could have certainly used him to look after their interests through this fresh spate of mix-ups.

Upon their arrival at the SquirrelsNest, Margit paid for the taxi with a debit card, had no trouble remembering her PIN code, and was otherwise very sharp, contrary to her usual demeanour at the Hakaniemi flat. She marched briskly down the corridor, entered the access code for the dementia unit without having to check the combination on her Post-it, purposefully pulled open the heavy automatic door before it started to open itself, audibly greeted the foreign male nurse in his glass cubicle, and sat down next to Eino in his room. The other bed was empty.

'Did you know that that other woman is . . . Did they move her somewhere?' Siiri asked, not knowing which words to use.

'They took her off to the hospital to die, yesterday. Now we can enjoy a moment's peace and quiet before they bring in the next shrieking lunatic.'

Eino was asleep and looked even more frail than before.

His sparse hair was in messy tufts, his bushy eyebrows tangled, and his face hadn't been shaved. Margit stroked her husband's forehead, gazed at him tenderly, and talked to him in a soft voice, until Eino opened his eyes and looked at his wife as if he recognized her.

Margit smiled, continued stroking his forehead, and said: 'Eino, today is your special day.'

Eino closed his eyes again. Siiri was sure she saw Eino nod and smile slightly, as if indicating to Margit that he remembered his birthday.

'How much is Eino turning today?' Siiri asked, thrilled at her friend's reinvigoration.

'Oh, today isn't his birthday. Just the opposite.' Margit opened her handbag, took out a candle, placed it on the table next to Eino's bed, and lit it. Then she continued digging around in her handbag, pulled out a blueberry yogurt and a small jar of medicine. She calmly opened the yogurt, poured a huge pile of pills into it, and stirred it with a spoon she had packed along with it. She looked at Siiri with a calm certainty.

'Could you help me lift Eino into a sitting position?'

It was only now that Siiri understood what Eino's 'celebration' meant. Only now did she realize the magnitude of the trust Margit had placed in her, the incredible significance of what she was about to witness, and almost reverently she started helping Margit, who propped up her husband with movements that were tender but sure. Siiri slipped two thick pillows behind Eino's back, and now he was in an upright position, although he could barely sit without assistance. She and Margit went about their business without speaking, in perfect harmony, knowing what they needed to do and why.

Eino opened his eyes. There was a bright gleam in them, and he smiled at Margit again. Siiri instinctively took a couple of steps backwards, so she wouldn't disturb the married couple, as the wife started to feed the yogurt to her beloved husband. Eino opened his mouth as if he realized what was happening, accepted a spoonful of yogurt, swallowed, and grimaced. He clearly had a hard time swallowing. After the second spoonful, he was racked by a coughing fit and looked mournfully at his wife. Margit gave him some water, but drinking it looked torturous, too.

'Let's keep going, honey,' Margit said calmly, placing another spoonful of yogurt in her husband's mouth. Eino ate with a healthy appetite, or so it seemed, as he kept his eyes shut and focused on swallowing. But the fourth spoonful was too much. Eino started coughing again, sucked yogurt into his windpipe, and started to choke. Siiri wanted to go for help, but Margit hissed at her like a she-snake and told her to sit down on the empty bed.

'I need you to keep a lookout and make sure no one comes in.'

Eino coughed and hacked until he vomited; the carefully swallowed yogurt splattered all over the bed. Eino sighed deeply, whether out of disappointment or relief, it was hard to say. He gave Margit a sheepish look, like a child who hasn't lived up to his mother's expectations.

'That's all right. We'll start over again, honey.'

Siiri went off to look for something to clean up the mess.

She didn't have a clue where to search for a cloth, but she was happy to have an excuse to step out of the room. She saw a cleaning cart at the far end of the corridor, relieved it of a couple of cloths and a pail full of dirty water, and carried them into Eino's room. Together she and Margit wiped the vomit from the bed and Eino's clothes. There was still an unpleasant smell in the room, but Margit wouldn't let Siiri go and ask the nurse for a clean duvet cover.

'Then they'll come in and make the bed, and we can't have that.'

'But aren't we . . . can't you take a small break now that . . . now that you have to start all over again anyway?' Siiri opened the window, and the candle blew out. 'Oh, I'm sorry!'

She hunted for the matches in a panic, but Margit must have put them back in her handbag. Suddenly, nothing was going smoothly, and the entire idea of Eino's 'celebration' was unnerving. Siiri heard a tremendous thunk; she was afraid Eino had fallen out of bed, but it was Margit, who had collapsed into the chair as if all the strength had drained out of her. Hands trembling, Margit hid the jar of medicine in her handbag, dropped the handbag to the floor, and, holding her head in both hands, told Siiri to go and get the nurse. Siiri rushed from the room. The dementia unit was perfectly still; even the woman who yodelled dirty folk songs wasn't disturbing the morning idyll. The tiny old woman with stuffed animals was alone in the living room, rocking in her rocking chair.

She greeted Siiri brightly: 'Oh, are you here to see me?'

Siiri went over to her, stroked her and the unicorn, and said she was visiting Eino.

'Eino is my lover,' the woman said, beaming with happiness.

Siiri left the woman to her rocking and hurried into the glass cubicle, shook the male nurse awake at his computer, and got a clean sheet from him.

'Put the dirty one in the hamper. You know how to change the sheets, don't you? I'm just in the middle of something here.'

Margit was thrilled that the nurse hadn't bothered to come and help Siiri, and so Siiri rolled up her sleeves again. She had never been impressed by the supposed ingenuity of duvet covers. Slipping one over a blanket alone was incredibly difficult, and for a small person like Siiri, nearly impossible. The clean sheet swept across the dusty floor; Siiri struggled to find the right corner of the blanket inside the cover, and shook out the bunched fabric as best she could, trying to straighten it out. The end result was rather lumpy, but maybe that didn't matter now. Margit remained calm as could be throughout this operation, stroking Eino's forehead. Eino had fallen into a deep sleep.

'All right, here you are. A clean sheet. You can start . . . over again.'

But they couldn't rouse Eino. Margit had to shake her now-skeletal husband rather roughly before he opened his eyes, but this did no good, because there was nothing there. His gaze wandered aimlessly without recognizing Margit. He tried to say something, but his voice was so feeble Margit and Siiri couldn't make it out. Siiri remembered how Eino used to make off-colour remarks at Sunset Grove, much to his wife's chagrin, and then Siiri felt ashamed of herself, thinking about such things at such a solemn moment. Eino had stopped whimpering. His eyes bulged, and then he fell back to sleep.

'Do you suppose he's already had enough ... yogurt?' Siiri asked, but Margit huffed angrily. Eino had vomited up the contents of his stomach. His last warm meal probably would have come up, too, if anyone on the staff had had time to feed him one. He had no strength left, and it was due to lack of nourishment. In Siiri's view, this wasn't an exclusively negative development, considering the circumstances, but Margit was determined to proceed in her chosen fashion. Stubbornly she pulled out the yogurt and patted her drowsy husband into a sufficient state of consciousness for her to convince him to swallow a spoonful. And a second. And a third, even a fourth. Everything seemed to be going well, until Eino yelped and sucked in air so loudly that the yogurt went down the wrong way again.

'This is impossible. The nurse didn't warn me about this!' Margit groaned, patting her frail husband on the back. Siiri took an empty plastic bag out of her handbag and held it in front of Eino's mouth, in case he vomited again. And vomit he did, this time listlessly. The carefully administered spoonfuls slid tidily into the Low Price Market shopping bag.

They tried one last time, but with even worse luck. Eino was too tired to swallow, and after he had inhaled the yogurt into his windpipe for the third time, Siiri grew afraid, although she wasn't able to verbalize what the worst possible outcome here was.

'Maybe we should come back some other day? Maybe he'll have more energy, say, tomorrow? Is he usually more lively in the evenings?'

'It's impossible to know. You can't really ever call him lively any more. This is horrible. Oh, Siiri, thank you for coming with me!'

Margit burst into tears and flung her massive carcass into Siiri's arms for a hug. Siiri steadied herself against the edge of Eino's bed and did her best to keep from being bowled over. Margit cried loudly, properly bawled, and Siiri could see what incredibly important things were weighing on her friend. Margit had planned it all out carefully, which drugs were needed to ensure death and how much of each, as well as the best way of getting the cocktail down her husband's throat. But it was too late. Eino couldn't swallow enough. Or else it was just a bad day. Margit had also discovered through her research that it wasn't a good idea to mix Eino's pills with juice because they wouldn't dissolve sufficiently, and the danger in that case was that Eino wouldn't ingest enough of the drug. This was no cakewalk, participating as an amateur in another's death.

'This is a catastrophe,' Margit said, breathing choppily. Siiri wiped the tears and streaks of mascara from Margit's cheeks.

'I think it's time for us to go. We'll come back tomorrow.' Margit kissed her husband on the mouth, patted him on the hand, picked up the candle, and whispered something in Eino's ear. Eino lay there as if dead, which, unfortunately, he wasn't.

Chapter 26

Anna-Liisa's rehabilitation had progressed at such a remarkable rate that, in honour of the upcoming weekend, the Ambassador had asked her to join him in the whirlpool tub. They spent over an hour in the spa, lounging and splashing about at their favourite pastime, memorizing various pointless rhymes together. The townships of Finland from the 1970s and German prepositions echoed rhythmically into the living room, where Siiri was preparing dinner. She was tired but felt incredibly happy, in that profound way that warmed the belly. Their home in exile had not had a particularly beneficial effect on Anna-Liisa and Onni's marriage, and although Anna-Liisa had been dragged out for a walk and a bit of exercise now and again, there were days she'd been so weak that Siiri had feared that the rehabilitative care would gradually turn into the palliative variety. Irma had told her about a cousin who had no desire to be rehabilitated at the age of ninety-six, but in the end the family had arranged interim care at an expensive private treatment centre. Irma's cousin had obediently gone in to exercise for a week and died mid-exertions.

'So if we're being rehabilitated to die, it was a very successful stint indeed,' Irma had said brightly.

Siiri had bought zander fillets from the Hakaniemi Hall despite teasing from Muhis and Metukka; in their minds, only urban ninnies bought their fish cleaned and filleted. *Ninnies*. Where had those African boys picked up a word like that? But Siiri simply didn't have the energy to cook two warm meals a day from scratch, and Muhis and Metukka forgave her this.

'As long as you don't buy fish sticks,' Muhis had laughed, his beehive of a hat jiggling on his head.

'Just the occasional ready-made liver casserole,' Siiri said, and it was true. She and Irma still enjoyed sharing a moment over liver casserole while the others were running around or lying in bed, too tired to eat lunch.

Zander was Siiri's favourite fish, and she always fried it in butter. All it took was a sprinkling of salt, and oh, it was delicious. Irma materialized to inspect Siiri's labours, lifted the lid to peer at the boiling potatoes and announced she needed sauce, to which Siiri replied, rather snappishly, that those who wanted sauce could make it themselves.

'Gravy, sirs, if you please.' Irma was quoting her favourite scene from Runeberg's *Tales of Ensign Stål*, and she now improvised a new ending to it: 'But, alas, it pleaseth not.' She raised her hand dramatically to her forehead and retreated to the couch for a smoke. 'Remind me that I have something important to tell you,' she called out as she lit her cigarette.

'Why don't you just tell me now, while you still remember it?'

'I can't. Don't forget to remind me.'

Siiri had put four peeled and six unpeeled potatoes on to boil in good time. A variety of tastes required accommodation: the Ambassador and Anna-Liisa demanded their potatoes be boiled without their skins, Margit insisted on eating the skins, and Siiri and Irma preferred to peel theirs after boiling. The proper assortment had finished cooking at just the right time, as the Ambassador and Anna-Liisa's whirlpool-tub bliss was coming to an end. They emerged from the bathroom, cheeks glowing and eyes gleaming, wrapped in their bathrobes, and before long the living room was enveloped in steam. It mingled beautifully with the smoke Irma was exhaling.

At first Siiri had found it irritating that Irma smoked her cigarettes whenever and wherever she pleased, as if she were the sole resident of the apartment, but she had come to realize that three cigarettes a day wasn't much, and how incredibly important those moments were to Irma, almost a ritual of sorts. Irma would always settle in at the window, pop a Mynthon pastille in her mouth, and draw long, leisurely drags of her cigarette, chattering all the time. She generally began by reporting what a lovely job the cigarette did of opening up her blocked nose, and continued by lamenting that she was incapable of quitting, even though it was so dangerous, and in the end reflecting that, when it came down to it, a ninety-four-year-old no longer needed to worry about how many cigarettes she smoked every day.

Then she'd stub out the cigarette in the round brass ashtray and say, of course: '*Döden, döden, döden.*' But this time she smoked in silence, without jabbering.

Siiri crowed out a line from the drinking song Otto Nicolai penned for Falstaff: 'Ready now, provide!' The others knew what this meant. She carried the plates and utensils over to the bar and set them out in everyone's spots, which had been settled without explicit agreement: the Ambassador always sat at the window end, Anna-Liisa at his side, Siiri and Irma across from each other, and Margit at the bedroom end. At their age, even the smallest habits developed into meaningful routines they clung to, whether or not it made any sense. Like the Ambassador's compulsive need to read the newspaper back to front, or comb and trim his moustache in the kitchen with a little pocket mirror. Why couldn't he do it in the bathroom, or in the privacy of his bedroom?

'Come one, come all, come and get it!' Siiri shouted in a loud voice; this was how she had called her family to the table for decades, all those years ago. Her ceaseless toil in the kitchen reminded her of when she'd been in the prime of her life and her hands never at rest. Nothing was as easy as it had been then. She had seen a programme on television where famous old Brits in various stages of decrepitude spent a week living the way they had in the seventies, when they were still hale and hearty. The wallpaper in their temporary home was awful, big patterns and gaudy colours, the rooms were filled with wall-to-wall carpeting and ugly furniture, but the main takeaway from this human experiment was that the old people really did perk up as they were forced to cook their own meals, climb the stairs, spend time in each other's company, and think about what their normal lives had been like forty years earlier. Of course they'd been much younger than Siiri; in a similar experiment, she would have to remember back to the sixties, if not the fifties, and life before dishwashers, washing machines, and rotary irons. Oh dear.

As always, the Ambassador was the first one at the bar, nattily dressed and smelling nicely of aftershave. He boasted about how much fun he and Anneli had been having in the whirlpool tub.

'I suppose you've taken it for a spin, too, or have you been too busy running the household to make the time?'

'I might have had the time, but I'm not sure I understand what the point is in an oversized, bubbling bathtub.'

'Oh, Siiri, you must try it. It's like a massage! The warmth will do your stiff limbs good, and the alternating bursts of water and air massage away aches and pains. It's splendid, even more wonderful than the sauna, which the doctor has completely forbidden me from using.'

'Why on earth?' Siiri asked. 'Is your doctor afraid you're going to die in the sauna? Is that such an unpleasant thought?'

'Not at all, that would be wonderful. But my doctor is just a boy; as a matter of fact, he's the grandson of my real doctor. The first two already died.'

They shared a good laugh over the dead doctors, and Irma immediately interjected, explaining how Sibelius had noted that every doctor who had forbidden him cigarettes had died before him, which was why he puffed away with a clear conscience well past the age of ninety.

'I borrowed one of Tawaststjerna's books on Sibelius from the Kallio library, they're so cleverly written and amusing,' she said. 'Of course I can't always be bothered to slog through his music analyses, but what he writes about Sibelius the man is terribly fascinating.'

'Yes, I suppose you've forgotten everything since the last time you read it,' Anna-Liisa said. She was still red-cheeked and spry after her joint spa session with her husband.

'Where's Margit?' Siiri asked, and Irma said that a call had come to the apartment's landline from the Squirrels-Nest, reporting that Eino had a fever and an ambulance had come to collect him and take him to the hospital. Margit had turned the apartment upside down looking for Eino's living will and then had gone off to rescue her husband from the clutches of the hospital's doctors.

'Eino doesn't want anyone hysterically trying to heal him, but he probably isn't going to be able to say so himself.'

The Ambassador took advantage of this opportunity to gently criticize Margit's talk and behaviour. 'Eino doesn't want, or Margit doesn't want?'

He wasn't aware that Siiri had been on hand to witness the unsuccessful euthanasia attempt at the SquirrelsNest, but had nonetheless accurately intuited that something of the sort was in the pipeline. Siiri didn't mention the tragicomic incident – that was up to Margit – and was well aware that the role of trusted friend had fallen to her, although she wasn't sure why. Even now she should have been at the hospital, supporting Margit in her battle to keep Eino from being treated, and instead she was waiting on her healthy friends hand and foot.

'Did Margit ever find the living will?'

'No, but I wrote her one,' Irma said casually. 'I must say, I've never tasted a grander zander!'

Siiri couldn't wrap her brain around Irma's writing a living will for Eino. The document was supposed to express the patient's will when he was still in full control of his faculties, not the wishes of loved ones when they were feeling desperate. And Irma wasn't even a loved one, but a rather distant acquaintance who happened to be temporarily cohabiting with Eino's wife.

Irma laughed heartily at this. 'I'm not stupid enough to have written my own will on it!' She told them she had drafted an entirely new document in Eino's name. She and Margit had forbidden any and all involuntary treatment, even antibiotics administered through a drip, which, with the help of her trusty flaptop, Irma had found the proper medical term for on the Internet.

'IV antibiotics, that's what they call it,' she remembered. 'With capital letters, so it looks like a Roman four, even though it's not.'

At first Irma had written the wrong date – today's – on the paper, and they had to start all over again. Margit had carefully calculated when Eino would still have been capable of writing the living will himself, and in the end the document had been signed at Sunset Grove, with Margit and

Irma witnessing, on some pleasant day approximately a year and a half ago.

'The date was the last day they had sex. Margit had it marked in her calendar. She claims that Eino was very good in bed.'

'Yes, we're well aware of that,' Anna-Liisa said.

'Have you also –? You haven't –?'

'Silence! Don't you remember how much racket they used to make every afternoon at Sunset Grove? I don't suppose such sounds could be produced by anything but good sex.'

'I wouldn't consider that such an important criterion,' the Ambassador said, suddenly attentive.

'I suppose most of us have had to fool around quietly in the dark,' Irma mused, and the Ambassador began recounting a rather unusual story from the height of his diplomatic career in Romania. Something complicated involving the chauffeur, the embassy's cook, and a midday rumpus in the kitchen.

'Anyway, then I scribbled out Eino's signature on the living will on his behalf, since Margit wasn't up to it. It turned out rather well, quite manly, like Veikko's used to be,' Irma said.

'What was Veikko like in bed?' the Ambassador asked, and Irma started to praise her husband.

Siiri stood, gathered up the plates, and walked them around to the sink.

'I must say, this is one of Helsinki's finest restaurants,' the Ambassador remarked.

'You would know, wouldn't you?' Anna-Liisa said a little

sourly, without looking at her husband, although he had just treated her to a buffet brunch.

'Isn't life rather comfortable here in Hakaniemi, all in all?' the Ambassador asked his harem, directing a heartfelt smile at each of them.

The women didn't respond. Anna-Liisa was thoughtful; she must have wanted more time alone with her husband, who instead spent most of his days gallivanting around town. Siiri didn't know how long she would be able to take her daily drudgery, and there were many things Irma missed.

'Most of all I miss my music,' she said, sighing deeply. 'I'd give quite a lot to be able to listen to Mozart's clarinet concerto from start to finish.'

The workings of the apartment's complicated sound system had remained a mystery. They had found no sign of a radio or record player, so apparently the idea was to look up music on the Internet and, by some magic trick, make it play from all the ugly speakers sticking out everywhere you looked.

'And then I'd like to listen to that lovely piece for violin and viola, and the slow bit that's so deliciously erotic.'

'*Sinfonia concertante*. I thought the clarinet concerto was what you wanted to listen to while you were dying,' Siiri said.

'Yes, but I never grow tired of it. And in the evenings, when I'm lying in bed freshly bathed and lotioned and waiting for sleep to arrive and it won't and I'm tired of reading Tawaststjerna, at those moments I'd love to listen to even a moment of Bach. "Wohltemperiertes Klavier", say, performed by Andras Schiff. I don't understand why I didn't bring my CD player. Now it's been stolen and sold. I wonder if those thieves stole my records, too? Do you suppose they understand the value of Mozart and Bach?'

'If you're lucky, you can get a couple of euros for them,' Anna-Liisa said, as if she knew all about the fencing of stolen goods. 'I miss my playing cards and the rhythm of life at Sunset Grove. Tuesdays, stick-exercise class, Wednesdays, handicrafts, it lends a nice rhythm to the days, even if the activities themselves are tomfoolery. This in-home care is very disruptive and tiring, not to mention irregular. They show up whenever they please, and some don't even have time to say hello.'

The Ambassador looked stunned. 'Are you saying you want to go back to Sunset Grove?'

He'd heard so much griping about the way things were run at Sunset Grove and had been privileged to observe their brave battle against the criminal activity and non-existent services at the retirement centre that he never thought he'd live to see this day. He genuinely believed he'd arranged things in the most satisfactory way possible and in accordance with everyone's wishes when he had acquired the apartment in Hakaniemi for their use.

'I said I missed Mozart and Bach, not Sunset Grove in particular,' Irma said.

'Perhaps I was referring to the lifestyle. This is rather unusual, after all,' Anna-Liisa said. 'And you're away most of the time. We used to spend much more time together.'

The Ambassador gazed at his wife with his blue eyes and

patted her hand. He thanked Anna-Liisa for her having reminded him of the names of Helsinki's old townships during their shared bath.

'To be perfectly frank, I'm not much of a nurse. Your illness wasn't easy for me to take. And then with all these half-mute, overworked wisps of girls traipsing about, these in-home caregivers, I've thought that it's best to be out from underfoot. But now you seem like yourself again, Anneli. Do you need the caregivers any more?'

Anna-Liisa didn't know how to cancel in-home care. She had asked a few of the nurses, but one said that in-home care generally ended with the client's death and another one didn't know what the process was, because she just worked at In-Home Care. Irma was certain that a simple phone call to the offices of the City of Helsinki Western Health-Care District In-Home Care would produce the desired result. In-Home Care was horrendously understaffed, and if some crazy old bat thought she had suddenly been healed of her old age and no longer needed their help, it would be like a gift from heaven.

'Better than death! Maybe they could resource nine minutes per client if they didn't have to come all the way here to roll you over. Did everyone notice how fluently I used the word "resource"?' Irma said, rising into a tinkling falsetto again. 'Now what did you make us for dessert, Siiri?'

Siiri didn't have any dessert.

'Oh, so you lords and ladies would like dessert, too!' she snapped, perhaps too feistily. When no one replied, she got up and peeked in the refrigerator, to see if it might contain a dab of two-day-old fruit soup or the butt end of pound cake. But there was nothing that would serve as dessert. 'I'm afraid you'll have to be satisfied with your modest meal. Or do you suppose we'll witness a miracle tonight, like one of you actually fixing dessert?'

Irma looked glum, but the Ambassador came up with a solution that pleased everyone. He assumed his usual spot on the kitchenette side of the bar and asked the ladies what he could fix them to drink. Irma ordered red wine, Anna-Liisa was in such a boisterous mood that she took a gin-and-tonic in Margit's stead, pronouncing the gin as if it were English and the tonic as if it were Swedish. Siiri didn't know what she wanted. Irma pondered, and then exclaimed.

'Why, we'll make mojitos for everyone! What do you say, Siiri?'

Siiri had completely forgotten that Muhis and Metukka had insisted they buy mint leaves and limes for a cocktail that was awfully delicious. Miraculously, Irma managed to remember the recipe, and she wasted no time bustling about in the kitchenette. You started with crushed ice, which the Ambassador knew how to make using the magical machine in the fridge door, then poured a bit of rum into the bottom of the glass, a lot of sugar, slices of lime, and mint leaves, and mixed and mashed furiously, like pepper in a mortar, until the limes and mint were crushed and the flavours mingled.

'Didn't the recipe call for a little soda water, too?' Siiri asked.

'I believe so, now that you mention it. Let's add a splash.

There are those little drink stirrers around here somewhere, too, I know I've seen them. Do you remember the Three Robbers' looking song, when they can't find their pants or shirts? "Where are my trousers, where is my shirt, where is my lala lallallaa and at the end I'm sure I just saw them yesterday".' She sang and played the roles of the robbers and laughed merrily without finding the drink stirrers. But she did find some straws.

'Straws are what I should have been looking for anyway, not sticks!'

'They've been here this whole time,' Anna-Liisa said from the end of the bar. And, sure enough, there on the countertop, right under their noses, was a cup with a cluster of colourful plastic sticks poking out.

'There they are! This is going to be so much fun. Help yourselves! It's scrumptious, even though it looks like poison.'

They decided to gather around the television to drink their mojitos, and after a skirmish of sorts, the Ambassador managed to turn it on. There was nothing bizarre on this time; just the good old nightly news. They were all enamoured of their drinks, which tasted tart and sweet at the same time, and clouds of blithe banter floated across the room.

There was no news to speak of. At first the tired-looking boy of a prime minister spoke in responsible tones about budget cuts, then a heavyset opposition politician spouted a couple of populist idiocies, after which the anchors reported that the Finnish school system was the best in Europe but no longer the world now that Asians were being included in the comparison tests, too. A dejected expert explained that these measurements shone an unfortunately bright light on Finland's gradual chipping away at basic education. They chuckled at the story, because they couldn't understand why having the best schools in Europe wasn't good enough for the expert.

'Everything is so fancy at schools these days,' said Irma, who used to hear about school from her darlings when they still came to visit her. None of her darlings had had the time to pop by Hakaniemi, since they were so busy working and vacationing. 'And on top of everything else, my daughter Tuula is having a plumbing retrofit in her apartment building. Can you imagine! The poor thing.'

'We certainly can. You've told us quite a few times,' Anna-Liisa said. 'And a plumbing retrofit is the reason we're here, too, killing time on a swaybacked sofa in a sound-proofed, pillared hall. We're retrofit refugees. Have you already forgotten? What about your daughter's plumbing retrofit is so much worse than what we're experiencing at Sunset Grove, where they're gutting the place from floor to ceiling?'

'I have no way of knowing. But in any case, she has so much going on at the moment that I understand perfectly well why she doesn't have time to come and see me. Working life is very demanding these days. Why, even being on vacation is stressful, or so I understand. And what's there to see in me, an old woman!' Irma burst into such merry gales of laughter that they could all see the mint leaves stuck in her teeth. Her glass had been sucked dry, and now she was trying to scrape the dregs of the sugar into her mouth with her straw.

After reports on crises abroad, the news shifted back to Finland. The anchorman, who was crammed into a jacket that was too small for him, started reporting on a retirement home where a renovation project had been mismanaged. He asserted that numerous retirement homes ended up in trouble when building repairs were required. Then they showed pictures of walls that had been torn out, floors that had been jackhammered up, ceiling plaster that had come crashing down, and a yard mounded with toilets and bathtubs. A female voice recited a litany of horror stories about old people who'd been abandoned, whose rents and service fees had gone up even though their homes were uninhabitable. Most had cut their losses and decamped for parts unknown.

'St Pete's pants!' Irma exclaimed.

'Silence!' Anna-Liisa bellowed, rapping her knuckles against the coffee table. She was leaning forward, back straight, and listening attentively.

'Why, that's Sirkka! The woman who moved into a tiny closet on Riihitie before the retrofit began!' Siiri squeaked. Sirkka was explaining on television that she had run out of money and was queuing for public housing or a nursing home. More images of the renovation's aftermath were shown: close-ups of debris and piles of junk and wiring dangling perilously from walls. The female voice announced that many of the remodels involved illicit business, with work being farmed out illegally, making it impossible to monitor the chain of subcontractors. In addition, the work was unprofessional, so that in this particular retirement home, the new floors had to be ripped right back out due to moisture damage incurred during the remodel.

'Who's looking out for the interests of the elderly?' Sirkka wailed from the flat-screen TV, looking somehow comical.

At the end of the story, the female voice reported that it had found a brave veteran in the ruins of the retirement home who had refused to move out of his apartment, because he was paying thousands of euros a month in rent and other fees. It was Tauno standing there on the screen, next to his mattress, pack on his back and cap pulled down tightly on his head, squinting angrily in the lamp-light like a mole unused to daylight. The mattress had been propped up against the wall so that it would figure prominently in the shot. Tauno talked about the Winter War and white-collar criminals and deserters, swore he would fight to the end, and claimed that an international criminal league masterminded by a Finn was behind everything. After Tauno's dramatic outburst, the male newscaster came back on and said that the weather would continue to be exceptionally rainy for the time of year.

Siiri thought poor Tauno had been shown in the wrong light; he seemed dotty and more confused than he actually was. But where on earth had the reporters got the idea to use the Sunset Grove renovation as an example of all the horrible things that can happen to old people at a retirement home?

'All it takes is for one loved one to call the news desk.

Seniors are a media trend these days,' Anna-Liisa said. She had grown tired of every newspaper and every television broadcast reporting on abandoned, unhealthy old people whose incontinence pads no one was paying for and whose care was driving society into bankruptcy. 'It's the wrong tone, somehow. Old age shouldn't be some new phenomenon that has caught contemporary society off guard, a liability we have to rid ourselves of as quickly and cheaply as possible. That's the impression you get from these sensationalistic stories.'

Anna-Liisa was right, of course. They didn't recognize themselves in the portrayals of the elderly that appeared in the media. Nor did they see themselves as particularly exceptional. Why, they were completely normal people.

'That's asking too much!' Anna-Liisa laughed. 'People, ha! Toxic waste is what we've become.'

'Hmmm. That's not a very nice thing to say.'

Irma thought about Anna-Liisa's words. But she didn't have the mental stamina for much doom and gloom, even in matters that concerned her, like this old age no one could do anything about.

Siiri had read in the newspaper that a human life consisted of cell division, and during this process something called a telomere grew shorter every time a cell divided. In the end, there were no longer enough telomeres, which is when you died. 'Life keeps time in telomeres,' she said. 'It's that simple.'

'What time is it?' the Ambassador asked, looking at his

watch. 'Shall we play cards? Didn't we all say we missed our canasta club at Sunset Grove?'

Irma pulled the pack of cards out of her handbag and skilfully started shuffling them. She didn't need the table; she knew how to knock the decks against each other in her hands without a single card falling out. 'Who's in?'

Everyone wanted to play, and with Margit gone, for once they had the right number for canasta. The Ambassador had a good hand and was pleased. He laid out his first canasta right away, humming to himself. Even Irma managed to concentrate and didn't show her hand the way she normally did, and that made Anna-Liisa's game more tranquil than normal. Siiri had been dealt a bad hand and she found herself having a hard time concentrating, as much as she enjoyed the fact that they were all sitting there happily together, like old times, playing cards. But why hadn't Margit come home yet? And what had happened to Eino?

Chapter 27

Irma felt they ought to join forces and report their property that had gone missing from Sunset Grove during the renovation. She just didn't know whether they ought to lodge a criminal report with the police, or if a simple complaint with the Loving Care Foundation, which ran Sunset Grove, would suffice. At the very least, Project Manager Jerry Siilinpää and Director Sundström needed to be made aware of what was happening at the retirement home under the pretence of a remodel. The Ambassador didn't want to participate in their complaint, but Anna-Liisa was in such high spirits that she decided to help Irma and Siiri. Margit was at the SquirrelsNest waiting for Eino's rescue from pneumonia or some other infection.

Irma swatted at her device as if she were screaming obscenities in sign language, despite the fact that she was looking for information, officials, forms and addresses. Suddenly a wet, embarrassed-looking cat floundering about in a shower stall appeared on the screen. 'Now, where did you come from?' Irma muttered, and she tried to push the cat off the screen with a determined swipe. 'Dratted contraption,' she said, shaking her flaptop, and then, to her own surprise and the other's relief, managed to turn it off. 'So be it. You ought to be ashamed of yourself,' she said to her favourite toy, after setting it aside as a punishment.

Anna-Liisa sharpened a pencil to write a draft – she would pen the official document in ink afterwards – and Siiri made them all coffee and found some pound cake in the cupboard. They had already drawn up a list of all of the furniture and other belongings each of them had lost during the remodel. Or remembered losing. Irma had reminded Anna-Liisa about her missing jewellery, but Anna-Liisa didn't want it on her list, because she still had the roll of cash squirrelled away and it didn't really belong to her. She blushed and looked uncomfortable as she spoke about the jewellery box.

'Have you noticed how much better this drip coffee is than the instant kind we always drank at Sunset Grove?' Siiri asked, as she filled their mugs with the piping hot brew.

'You can say that again. Although at the time I never thought the coffee was bad. But cake is always delicious when you dunk it in hot coffee. Oh dear oh dear, it's important to know how to make the most of life until the very end. *Döden, döden, döden.*'

They decided to deliver a memorandum about the stolen items and furniture to Director Sundström and Jerry Siilinpää, send a complaint to the board of Loving Care Foundation, and file a criminal report with the police. It was Anna-Liisa's suggestion: in her view sufficiently robust and it followed a logical procedural hierarchy.

'What shall we say? We would like to call your attention to the fact that during the remodel at the Sunset Grove retirement home, numerous items have been removed from our apartments . . . Or should we say stolen?' Anna-Liisa looked at them questioningly.

They sat there thinking about the right term. The fact of the matter was, they weren't sure whether the furniture and moving boxes had been stolen or not. They had simply been removed without their knowledge, and who knew, perhaps the intent was to return them all one fine day. Regardless, residents should have been informed about the removal of their belongings somewhere other than on the Internet, and in this respect, their outrage was justified.

Irma started remembering the satirical vignette 'A loan is a loan.' In it, the Man with the Black Beard is accused of stealing Mr Rakohiili's gold watch, although it was only a case of multiple loans, first from Mr Rakohiili, and then on to someone else, who had lent it on again.

'Do you remember it? It's so funny that I used to know the whole thing by heart.'

Anna-Liisa raised her eyebrows in surprise; she wasn't the least bit upset with Irma, despite the fact that her friend had wandered off onto a side-track again. Just the opposite: Anna-Liisa was filled with deep respect. It would never have occurred to her that Irma was capable of memorizing long passages of silliness to keep her brain working.

'Let's hear it,' she commanded.

'Oh, I don't know it any more. But the Man with the Black Beard says to the judge: "Exaggeration, Your Honour,

I borrowed it." And then he explains that the watch may have ended up in Canada and says: "It is where it is; what's the sense in getting worked up over it?" That's the only bit I remember. I should read *Scenes from Olli's Life* again. I had a big collection, but I suppose it's at some pawn shop now, too, or at Mustamäe Market in Tallinn.'

'It is where it is; what's the sense in getting worked up over it?' Anna-Liisa remarked aphoristically, lowering her pencil to the table. 'Mightn't that be the right precept for us to follow, too? What difference do our chairs and books make at this point? We'll be leaving this place behind before long, and when that happens our treasures will be nothing but rubbish and trouble for our inheritors.'

'Nonsense, my furniture was new. I bought it from IKEA after my darlings divided up my Biedermeier set, the thirties couch from Stockmann, my hand-painted porcelain table, and the rest of my lovely belongings. Put down that a brand-new Bögen dresser, bed, table and chairs were misappropriated from me. At least four chairs. Or were there six?'

'Bögen? Doesn't that mean homosex—'

'I don't remember what they were called, some funny Swedish word. Put down Murran, doesn't that sound like a cosy IKEA name?'

'Misappropriated is quite a nice verb.' Anna-Liisa savoured the word and started writing again.

'Shuffle and cut! Misappropriated under the pretext of a loan!' Irma squealed, clapping so her gold bracelets jangled.

'Some funny instinct tells me I've heard that before,' Siiri said.

The presiding judge accused the Man with the Black Beard of misappropriation under the pretext of a loan. The Man with the Black Beard also loaned a pawn shop Mr Tikkumetso's fur coat, as well as a wall clock, bicycle and hunting dog from other acquaintances, but in the end the case fell apart because in 1927 the presiding judge had borrowed some book on the history of the Finnish justice system that he had never returned, because he had lent it on to someone else and it had never been returned to him. Siiri and Irma laughed so hard that they peed in their pants, but Anna-Liisa looked stunned.

'Can't you use that term in our report, misappropriated under the pretext of a loan?'

They burst into fresh gales of laughter. Irma wiped her eyes on her lace handkerchief and lent it to Siiri, too.

'In his stupidity, he gave me his gold watch – that's what the Man with the Black Beard said when he explained why Mr Rakohiili's watch had ended up in his possession,' Siiri managed to say between fits of laughter. 'Write: "In our stupidity, we left our belongings in our homes".'

'My dear friends!' Anna-Liisa raised her voice so that she sounded testy, although her words were kind. It was an old trick of the trade for teachers.

'Don't you like *Scenes from Olli's Life*?' Irma said, genuinely taken aback.

Anna-Liisa stared off into the distance and started jabbering robotically: 'The pronunciation of the Finnish language demands an antireciproicalpropsilarically acceptosuffobic approach insofar as it is animalistically rotundifolic, in other words overexpelled to the extent that it does not laryngicalize both the vowel *o* and the vowel *y* in the same contextual context, in other words sociology. This being the case, one cannot say, for instance, *olyt*; the correct form is *olut*, beer. Nor can one say *olympialaiset*, Olympics; one must say either *olumpialaiset* or *ölympiäläiset.'*

'What are you going on about?' Irma said.

Siiri was worried, too. 'Are you . . . how are you feeling, Anna-Liisa?'

They exchanged glances and knew they were both thinking about that hot summer day when they were having lunch at the French restaurant and Anna-Liisa abruptly excused herself to correct preliminary examinations and ended up the victim of a descending spiral of hospitalization and in-home care. Had their fun with the Man with the Black Beard permanently hurled Anna-Liisa into the abyss of dementia, and when she was on the cusp of her heroic recovery? At Irma's urging, Anna-Liisa had even called City of Helsinki Western Health-Care District In-Home Care and informed them that she had recuperated sufficiently from her hospital treatments for her to no longer require interns running in and out, disturbing her domestic peace. But nothing was ever that simple. Anna-Liisa had to wait for the head nurse to have enough time in her busy schedule to conduct a home inspection and patient evaluation; only after successful completion of both could treatment be voluntarily waived.

'That was "A Little Refresher" from *Scenes from Olli's Life*. Don't you remember?' Anna-Liisa said with a delicious laugh, leaning back and letting out tinkling staccatos like a young girl, so that her molars, which had clearly been filled on numerous occasions, gleamed brightly. She looked at the still-confounded Siiri and Irma in satisfaction.

'I don't remember that,' Siiri said finally.

'My husband Veikko always talked about drinking *ölyt*,' Irma pondered. 'I wonder if he got that from Olli? Have you noticed that almost all Finnish sayings come from the Bible, Topelius's tales, the *Kalevala*, or *Scenes from Olli's Life*?'

'The satirist Olli, in other words Väinö Nuorteva, was an astonishing writer. His vignettes grew funnier and funnier by the day, and they have never lost their edge. In his time they were exaggerated, of course,' Anna-Liisa said, sitting up straighter. Nevertheless, she refrained from launching into a long lecture; she wanted to return to the matter at hand, their reason for sitting there, and started turning out meandering sentences in the style of *Scenes from Olli's Life*, so that the authorities would understand in no uncertain terms that these compositions penned by hands well past the age of ninety needed to be taken seriously. She was convinced that the more tortuous and dreadful Finnish they wrote, the more attention their matter would receive.

'We need to use expressions like "the opaqueness of the project's sourcing framework" and "overestimated under-resourcing", for instance. And "deficit" too, an "accountability deficit" at least.'

They had a grand time cooking up bureaucratic language and managed to get a few terms down on paper that were so long and nonsensical that Irma had to count the letters.

Unfortunately, not a single one beat the previous record of twenty-six letters. Anna-Liisa brought her considerable experience as a Finnish-language professional to bear on their epistle, composing endless sentences heavy with participial phrases in which the noun being modified remained deliberately vague. That was the custom, evidently. In the end, she read the memorandum, complaint and report to Irma and Siiri in her strong, melodic voice.

'Bravo. I give ten points to all of them, but my favourite is the memo. I can make neither head nor tail of it, and I'm sure that will further our cause,' Irma said.

The criminal report relied heavily on main clauses composed of a clear subject, predicate and object, because they believed this was the type of text the police would prefer receiving. They boldly announced that their movable property had been stolen in toto. But in their letter to the Loving Care Foundation they marvelled that such practices were allowed, as they could not be sure whether their property had been robbed, stolen, temporarily moved to another location, or misappropriated under the pretext of a loan. They demanded an immediate written account of events and declared that the foundation suffered from a serious confidence deficit among residents. The letter to Jerry Siilinpää was priceless. Anna-Liisa had masterfully cross-bred Olli's impenetrable style and Siilinpää's consultant-speak into such a dense mat of cobwebs that even the wisest presiding judge wouldn't be able to determine if they were blaming Jerry or themselves for the fact that, in their stupidity, they had left their belongings behind to be stolen by others.

'Sign your names at the bottom,' Anna-Liisa said, after she had copied out each of the documents in her neat 1940s hand. Then they slid the folded sheets of paper into envelopes, printed out the addresses, glued the stamps in their places, lamented the fact that stamps were no longer lickable now that they had been turned into stickers, reminisced about the tang of postal glues past, debated whether the glue was made from bones and, if so, whose, and then headed off to deposit the letters in the mailbox, even though they knew it wouldn't be emptied until the following Monday.

Chapter 28

Not even the hardiest Finn drank her coffee outdoors at Hakaniemi Square on a sleety November day, despite the fact that the stands were tented and warmed by glowing heat-lamps and the air was oddly mild for the time of year. There was no hope of a proper snow, which suited Siiri and her friends just fine; they had endured enough mountainous snowbanks during their lifetimes and had no interest in frolicking through snowfields. Margit, Siiri and Irma had moved their daily coffee outing to the second floor of the Hakaniemi Hall in hopes that President Tarja Halonen, Finland's first and so far only woman head of state, would one day sit at the table permanently reserved for her, but no luck yet.

Margit had much to report. Her coffee cooled in its cup as she apprised her friends of her adventures in the jungle known as the Meilahti hospital complex. It had taken some time before she found Eino at the Haartman Hospital, abandoned in a hallway surrounded by belligerent, unruly drunks.

'Be grateful he ended up at Haartman. At least it's new and nice, compared to those old dumps where the plaster is falling down on the patients' heads.' Irma was informed, because she had made the rounds of nearly every hospital in Helsinki during her bout of temporary dementia.

Unfortunately, the hospital had managed to begin treating Eino before Margit's arrival: an IV drip was delivering liquids and drugs from two bottles into his arm, an oxygen moustache had been shoved up his nose, and his chest was full of electrodes or whatever those sticky magnets were called.

'Why on earth would they drive a man with a fever to the hospital when there's no room for him there anyway?' Siiri huffed in empathy, although they all knew the multi-hospital circus was normal practice, the Finnish way of doing things.

The living will Irma had written had proved effective once Margit got her hands on a doctor, which was no easy undertaking. If a member of the staff happened to sail past in the corridor, it was a nurse, and nurses had no interest in living wills or the concerns of loved ones. 'The doctor will be here soon,' they all said to Margit, and more than one had clocked out in the meantime. But Margit hadn't given up. Every few hours she had trudged off to the petrol station to chew down a dry, plastic-wrapped sandwich and returned to Eino's bedside, until a Russian doctor had suddenly appeared at her side the next morning.

'He barely understood a word of the living will except the bit about IV antibiotics. I said *antibiot nyet*, and he responded by nodding wisely.'

The doctor had exited without saying a word, after which Margit had waited a further two hours before a friendly Filipina nurse had come and disconnected Eino from the tubes, bottles and stickers. The nurse had clearly expressed her displeasure at not being able to treat such a lively old fellow, but these textbook sentiments, memorized during nursing school, had had no effect on Margit. The nurse had pushed Eino's bed into the lobby to wait for the non-emergency ambulance to arrive.

'It took another three and a half hours before a single non-emergency emergency vehicle was available in this city.'

'That's quite the contradiction in terms,' Siiri chuckled, glancing at the family that had occupied the next table. The exhausted mother pulled a plump, wool-swaddled baby out of a sleeping bag, the kind given to all Finnish parents in their government-issued baby box. The poor thing was dripping sweat and red as a beet but very good-natured. The infant patted its mother on the shoulder and peered brightly at Siiri, giving her a winning, albeit toothless, smile.

'It's a good thing there's someone who isn't in a hurry, even if that someone is an ambulance!' Irma chuckled, and they laughed merrily. The tired mother started feeding her chubby child unheated baby food, which brought Siiri's game of peek-a-boo to an end. Margit continued ploughing through her account, without skipping a single detail.

Eino was back at the SquirrelsNest, only in a new room, because his spot had already been released for some fresher dementee's use. It made no difference, because Eino didn't seem to understand where he was lying. Margit gathered that the doctors had poked and prodded Eino enough to find, in addition to advanced Parkinson's and a difficult case of dementia, heart failure and pneumonia.

'But that's wonderful!' Siiri cried spontaneously.

'How so?' Irma said.

Margit was very calm. She explained to Irma that she'd been hoping to expedite Eino's death for some time but hadn't come up with an effective strategy until one of Anna-Liisa's caregivers had advised she mix morphine tablets and sleeping pills in yogurt.

'And you were there, Siiri? You didn't say a word.' Irma seemed angry, but Margit looked at Siiri approvingly.

'We were too late. It was pretty macabre, since Eino wasn't able to eat properly any more,' Margit continued. Ultimately, it was a big relief that Eino didn't have to die from the yogurt she fed him. She hadn't completely thought out whether she'd be able to bear responsibility for the consequences of her actions.

'Besides, if they had done an autopsy they would have caught you,' Irma said.

'They wouldn't necessarily have performed one, but for that reason alone I would have had plenty of sleepless nights,' Margit said tiredly. 'Now we just have to hope that this case of pneumonia is merciful to Eino.'

Irma thoughtlessly started pondering out loud about the likelihood that Margit's force-feeding had somehow caused Eino's pneumonia, and could that be somehow detected through an autopsy. Siiri listened impatiently; this had occurred to her, too, but she decided to weed the notion out of Margit's mind.

'I don't suppose even the most eager medical examiner would want to open up a sick old man who died of an apparent illness to determine the cause of death. They must have better material,' she said.

'For teaching purposes, maybe?' Irma suggested. 'I'm leaving my old bones and organs to science.'

Margit didn't trouble herself over autopsies. 'My only concern now is whether Eino will be allowed to live out the time left to him at the SquirrelsNest. But they're not prepared to deal with dying seniors there; all they can handle are the kind that lie there without any symptoms and can be regularly medicated.'

Margit had engaged in many contentious conversations with the nursing home's head nurse, director and head of resident services on the topic. They had arrived at a truce of sorts when Margit agreed to pay out of pocket for a dedicated nurse to watch over Eino at night.

'Last night a frightened little thing with her face and ears full of spikes sat there at Eino's side. I'm sure she'll be an incredible comfort to me when I have to face my husband's death.'

'Look! Tauno's in the paper, too.'

Irma was browsing through the tabloid someone had left on President Halonen's table, and there was an entire spread on the retrofit at Sunset Grove and the steadfast veteran who refused to desert. There was nothing new in the article; it just rehashed the story from the weekend news with an extra dash of scandal. Facts about retirement home renovations were called out in a box to the side, and it said that most of the buildings were so new that Sunset Grove was a precedent of sorts.

'It reads here that the costs of the Sunset Grove renovation have tripled during the project, and it's the clients who will foot the bill. That means us.'

'Of course. They can raise the rents and the service fees as high as they want. And there's no law against it,' Siiri said.

'A Facebook group has been founded called "Save the Last Vet Standing", and thousands of people have already joined,' Irma read. It was a beautiful gesture; the intent was to offer Tauno help and moral support, but it didn't seem as if it had much practical effect. Irma had come to learn that the Internet was like the Shakespeare comedy *Much Ado about Nothing*.

'On Facebook you can like and poke and tell everyone what's on your mind, but what good is that going to do us or Tauno? Besides, Tauno isn't the only World War Two veteran who's still standing.'

'Siiri, my love!' rang out in a familiar voice, and in that same instant Muhis and Metukka were seating themselves at the table. The boys had been grocery shopping, and this time they planned on preparing something from veal kidneys. Eyes twinkling with enthusiasm, Muhis recounted what beautiful innards were available downstairs. He couldn't understand why Finns ate ready-made pizza by the yard and frozen French fries when fresh organs were available much more cheaply.

'Kidneys taste like urine to me,' Irma made the mistake of saying, and was repaid with a long lecture on how kidneys needed to be rinsed several times, stewed and spiced until they were succulent and delicious.

'Have you found work?' Siiri asked. She was concerned about her friends' unemployment and consequent drift into illicit activities. Muhis reported that he had spent a couple of days the previous week cleaning schools, and Metukka had lent a hand at an acquaintance's moving company. But nothing else had turned up, and they didn't have anything in store for the week ahead. Metukka drummed the tabletop restlessly and Muhis adjusted his hat; their beaming smiles had vanished.

Then Siiri had what she thought was a brilliant idea: 'Maybe you could come and work for us? We're too tired to clean, do laundry, press the sheets and cook every day. You could help us out, and we can give you a little spending money in return.'

As soon as she spoke the words, a wave of relief washed over Siiri, as if the burden of their blended household had been instantly swept from her shoulders. The boys liked the idea. Margit didn't participate in the conversation; she just gathered up her things, still muttering about Eino. The chubby baby at the next table had finished her meal and squealed cheerfully. She continued squawking insistently, until Siiri looked over and was rewarded with another exuberant smile. Suddenly Siiri felt as if the sun were shining through the roof of Hakaniemi Hall and straight onto her face, even though it was November.

Irma doubted whether they could afford manservants, but when Muhis and Metukka said that twenty euros an hour would be plenty, it stopped sounding so bad. Besides, it would be charity: they would be helping the boys, and the boys would be helping them.

'But isn't that what they mean by under the table?' Irma asked, lowering her voice conspiratorially. 'Might we end up in jail?'

Muhis and Metukka burst out in guffaws. Of course it would be under the table, but in Finland even ministers didn't need to report payments made for a little help around the house to the tax office. It was 'totally normal'.

'Or "hella normal", as my darlings would say,' Irma said in satisfaction. 'Have you noticed how everything is normal these days?'

Muhis and Metukka promised to come by that very week to clean the apartment and do the laundry.

'We know the place. We've done a few odd jobs there in the past,' Metukka said with a wink.

Chapter 29

Margit had spent five days at Eino's bedside, praying for a beautiful death for him. Every night, a paid nursing student had relieved Margit so that she could go to the Hakaniemi apartment to sleep. And every night Margit had lain awake, afraid that Eino would die while she was gone, with some spike-faced stranger ogling him. By the sixth morning she was utterly drained, but of course she couldn't stay home to rest, because if she did, someone might roll Eino out to an ambulance and send him back to the hospital. Every day without fail, Margit had to explain to the new workers at the SquirrelsNest why Eino was not to be carted off to the hospital or even the health centre, even though he had a fever.

'I can't take this any more. Why can't an old person just be allowed to die?' she mumbled tearfully to Siiri, who had woken up earlier than normal to Margit's clattering around the kitchen.

'Don't you worry, Eino will die,' Siiri said with such serene certainty that she surprised even herself. 'Maybe it will happen today.'

'That's what I've said every morning,' Margit muttered in

exhaustion. 'Could you . . . could you come with me to the SquirrelsNest today for moral support?'

Of course Siiri could. And so they set out together, right then and there, while the others were still sound asleep in their bedrooms. But when Siiri opened the front door, she and Margit were greeted with a surprise. A man was standing there with a key ring in his hand, clearly intending to enter their apartment. He was short, dressed in grey, and had combed his hair into a tuft in the middle. Siiri took such fright that she thought her heart had stopped and she'd gone blind, but when her vision returned, the man was still standing in front of her, just as startled as she was. Siiri couldn't help but be reminded of the scene in *The Magic Flute* where Papageno and Monostatos stare at each other, equally frightened. 'It must be the devil himself,' was how the old version of the libretto went, but that wasn't relevant in this instance.

'Excuse me, are you an in-home caregiver?' Siiri asked, after regaining her composure. 'Are you here to see Anna-Liisa Petäjä?'

'Yes . . . exactly, absolutely,' the man replied. There was something familiar about him; perhaps he'd been by to rehabilitate Anna-Liisa before.

'Go on in. I believe Anna-Liisa is still asleep, but I'm sure you know how to wake her gently.'

The man slipped into the apartment, and Siiri and Margit continued on their way. The street below was rather quiet and pitch-black, and the metro was practically empty. Apparently, at this hour on a Saturday morning, no one except in-home caregivers and old people waiting to die had any call to be awake. Luckily, there was no slush and it wasn't pouring with rain, the way it had been for nearly the entire month of November.

The ambience at the SquirrelsNest dementia ward was even more static than usual. Everyone was in a deep slumber. The sleeping aids were effective; the strapping male nurse dozing in the glass cubicle was the only one in the place enjoying a natural, fatigue-induced sleep.

Margit knocked softly on Eino's door, and she and Siiri stepped in. The room was just like Eino's old one: efficient and practical, in other words grim. A whale of a woman, surprisingly young-looking, snored in the other bed, and a slight, green-haired girl lay curled in a foetal position on the floor at Eino's side. She had bunched Eino's bedspread up into a pillow. Margit gave the girl an unfriendly nudge, vexed that the private nursing student she was paying out of pocket was sleeping instead of watching over Eino.

'Rise and shine, missy. How did Eino sleep?'

The nurse jumped, too groggy to grasp who Margit and Siiri were. Her body was decorated with tattoos, and steel balls pierced her face. She thought they were patients and spoke in a gentle, soothing voice as she got up.

'What are you naughty little things doing here in the middle of the fucking night? You should go back to fucking bed, because it's like fucking midnight right now and everyone is supposed to be fucking tucked in their beds like good fucking little girls and not like shuffling the fuck around.'

Siiri recognized the nurse: they had met in the tram months before, when the girl was looking for an apartment in Helsinki. But the girl didn't remember Siiri; she just looked at them with her round, kind eyes and tried to take hold of Margit's arm so that she could lead her back to bed.

'It's morning, and I'm your employer, Margit Partanen, not some midnight shuffler. I'm the one paying you to look after my dying husband.'

The nurse grew visibly alarmed. Nervously she pulled herself together, tugged her woollen scrap of a sweater straighter and raked her green hair into a tidier mess. Margit marched past her, stepped up to the bed, bent down to give Eino a peck on the cheek, and shrieked. It was a piercing, heart-rending sound that must have woken up everyone in the dementia unit and the majority of the population in the surrounding neighbourhood.

'Eino's dead,' Margit said a moment later, in a barely audible voice. She gave her husband another kiss on the cheek, this time more carefully and respectfully, placed a hand on his throat, then his chest, and then back on his throat. 'Eino's dead,' she repeated, pressing her head to her husband's shoulder. 'Eino is finally dead. Eino, my dear, sweet Eino.' Margit leaned against her husband with all of her substantial weight, quivered there silently, and cried soundlessly, not in grief, yet, but relief.

The nurse looked more flustered than ever. She didn't

have the slightest idea what time the patient had stopped breathing while she was stretched out on the floor.

'He was fucking sleeping . . . like totally peacefully . . . no one fucking told me that this was the kind of situation I had on my fucking hands. He ate a fucking ton, too, like a huge fucking ton, late at night, even though usually in the fucking terminal stage – Fuck!'

Siiri soothed the night nurse, who felt like she'd made a dreadful mistake. Siiri explained that this death was beautiful and long anticipated, that this was exactly the way everyone hoped to die, in their sleep, painlessly. And there was nothing a nurse or anyone else needed to do.

'OK,' the nurse said. 'Well, that's a fucking relief. What . . .what the fuck should I do now?'

'You could go and get the doctor. Or phone one; I don't suppose there's a doctor on call here at the SquirrelsNest. But we need a doctor to come and pronounce Eino dead.'

The green-haired nursing student who'd got this gig from the nursing agency didn't know where to call. Siiri went with her to find a phone, so Margit could spend a moment, however brief, alone with Eino – although, of course, they weren't alone, the whale of a woman was still sawing logs in the other bed, blissfully ignorant of the irrevocable, momentous event that had taken place in the room. Margit's scream hadn't roused anyone else in the ward after all. They found a phone in the glass cubicle and managed to bring the male nurse to a sufficient state of consciousness for him to be able to mumble which number they should call.

'One one two.'

'Silly boy, that's the emergency number. One of your patients died during the night and we need a doctor to come in and confirm the death.'

The slap-happy nurse kept insisting on the general emergency number. The SquirrelsNest didn't have its own doctor, and doctors weren't on call at health centres on weekends. That left the emergency number, where it was doubtful anyone would be sent to the dementia ward to look at a corpse, as first aid and hospice staff had better things to do with their weekends. Even the private sector didn't have doctors on call to confirm deaths, the nurse chuckled sourly.

'But you're welcome to use the phone if you want to try.'

Siiri hesitantly lifted the receiver and then lowered it; the nurse seemed to know what he was talking about. Siiri just didn't understand what she was supposed to do under the circumstances. Should they leave Eino lying there until the day after tomorrow, when hospice and health centre doctors would be on duty again? How could this be so complicated? Didn't old people die at the SquirrelsNest all the time?

'Sure, people die here, too, even though we usually try to spot the ones who are contemplating it and shunt them off to a hospital. Was it the old guy who refused to stay at Haartman?' The nurse flipped through an open folder on his desk. 'Eino Partanen? He should have just stayed at the hospital; he would have saved everyone a bunch of trouble.'

The nurse explained a little crossly that if you're obsessed with dying in your own bed, you ought to do it on a weekday, and preferably during business hours. Friday night or Saturday morning was the worst possible time to get it in your head to die in a nursing home. There was no morgue at the SquirrelsNest where they could store Eino; now they were going to have to start calling around to medical examiners and hospitals to see if someone would accept the body for storage.

'The police might help, or hearses, I mean their drivers. They're the ones who are going to come and move the body anyway. There's another patient sleeping in the same room, isn't there?'

Siiri started feeling wretched. She had to sit down and hold her head in both hands. The absurdity here was beyond that of any scenes from Olli's life: at first an old person isn't allowed to die, and then when he does, there's nowhere to put the body. Whatever happened to old-fashioned doctors you called any time, day or night, if grandpa passed in his sleep at home? What on earth was going through the heads of those who came up with these rules and procedures? What had happened to wakes and weeping women? Siiri took a deep breath, then an even deeper one, and listened to the arrhythmic beating of her heart. Out of the corner of her eye, she saw the night nurse with the green hair packing her things and preparing to leave, but then she sat back down. She didn't look the picture of health, either.

'This is so fucking horrible,' she said with sorrowful eyes. 'I'm so fucking . . . like really sorry.'

But the SquirrelsNest staff nurse was a more seasoned professional and didn't stoop to sentimentality. He reached for the phone and evidently called an old friend at the hearse service. 'Jaska here, hey – Yeah, we got one for you at the SquirrelsNest – *Bueno*.'

Then he dug a red candle stub out of the cabinet and strode off to Eino's room, clearly irritated about the extra work piling up during his shift. Siiri chased after him, and the spike-faced night-nurse trainee slunk off without saying anything to anyone, presumably to some big, boisterous downtown commune.

It was still dark in the room, and the whale of a woman was still rumbling and rattling in her bed. Margit was sitting at Eino's side now, holding his cold hand in hers. She gave the male nurse a beautiful smile, and he said something brief and intended as polite in a low voice before lighting the candle and placing it on the table. He stood at Margit's side for a moment, shifting his weight, before blurting:

'The body will be picked up in fifteen minutes and taken to cold storage; I'm not sure where yet. It will stay there until a doctor is able to confirm death, which probably won't be until late next week, if not the following. You'll get the burial permit after the doctor confirms the death. Those are the rules.'

The nurse left the room, and with that, end-of-life care had been delivered according to SquirrelsNest Nursing Home procedures. Siiri stood at the foot of the bed and looked at Eino, who looked exactly the same as he had a week ago: asleep. Even back then, he had looked more dead than alive. The fact of the matter was that dying didn't happen in a moment; it was a long process. Eino hadn't had to struggle, exactly. He had just gradually faded, unlike Siiri's husband back in the day. Had it already been fourteen years? Siiri didn't remember and couldn't be bothered to count. Margit was calm and unruffled, caressed Eino from time to time, but didn't say a word. The whale of a woman stopped breathing, and Siiri was afraid that they had another dying patient on their hands. She remembered having read a novel where death was an epidemic without any attendant diseases or illnesses. And then there had been José Saramago's fine story about contagious blindness, but that was different. Siiri felt disoriented and out of touch with reality; her thoughts meandered down odd paths, and she thought it all must be due to how tired she was. She hadn't looked at the time that morning, and now she pulled her watch out of her handbag. She didn't like wearing it on her wrist, even though it was a beautiful timepiece she had got from her husband long ago, on her seventy-fifth birthday. Goodness gracious, only six-thirty. What time had they left Hakaniemi? And had it really been a caregiver waiting for Anna-Liisa on their doorstep? The whale of a woman was snoring steadily again, so at least she wasn't dead. But Eino was, and that was a good thing. That had been the intention, and this was what Margit had been waiting for all summer and autumn.

The door popped open, and two men, one short and one tall, stepped in. They introduced themselves as father and son, and at second glance it was clear that the short one was still a minor, perhaps still in school. What on earth was he doing carrying bodies around? But the men had practised movements and practical tools. Without asking any questions or saying anything, they pulled the blanket off Eino, took hold of the grey plastic sheet, and, with a couple of neat flicks, rolled his body onto the shroud. Then they fetched a wobbly-looking stretcher from the corridor, lowered the rolled-up plastic to it, strapped it down tightly with three handy-looking cable ties, lifted the stretcher at either end, and were on their way.

Siiri and Margit looked at each other, stunned. Siiri felt like bursting into tears, but suddenly Margit started to laugh, riotously and uncontrollably.

'There he goes, the love of my life. Eino finally made it out of here,' she said. 'Poor Eino, I wonder if he's finally at peace . . .' She blew her nose, and her laughter slid into tears. Margit threw her arms around Siiri's neck and jiggled, cried and jiggled out all her muddled feelings. They stood there holding each other for a long time, and in the end, neither one was crying any more. Margit dried her face on a paper towel, blew her nose loudly, extinguished the red candle, and looked one last time at the bed where the only memory of her husband was a narrow hollow.

'That's that, I suppose,' she sighed.

They made their way back to Hakaniemi. By the time they arrived, the sun still hadn't come up.

Chapter 30

The big, peculiar apartment on the second floor of the Arena building was very quiet that November weekend. Eino's passing didn't shock or surprise any of them; they all knew that Margit had been hoping for a merciful death for a long time. But society's engineer-like practicality and efficiency in dealing with the body combined with the country's under-resourced and misguided health-care system put them in a reflective mood. They were all thinking about their own deaths and, above all, the unnatural consequences of that natural event. What sort of cold storage would they end up in, and for how many weeks, before someone had time to come and confirm that the death had taken place? And did it make any difference? What if you weren't really dead, and you ended up lying there in cold storage for no good reason?

'*Döden, döden, döden.*'

It was about all Irma was capable of saying. She shook her head and smoked what was at least her sixth cigarette, which was unusual indeed. Her whisky tumbler had already been filled twice, Siiri noted in concern. She was afraid Irma would start feeling poorly, although she understood that Irma had good cause for behaving the way she was.

The Ambassador and Anna-Liisa were sitting side-by-side on the sofa, holding hands. Anna-Liisa had an empty crossword in her lap, and the Ambassador was absent-mindedly fingering the black tie he had donned in memory of Eino. Margit was lying on the other sofa. She had covered her face with a copy of *Finland Today* which she'd been trying to read. It was impossible to say whether she was awake. She had been oddly calm and collected since Eino's death, and spent the bulk of her time sleeping.

With Margit in mind, Siiri had made such a generous pot of lamb-and-cabbage stew that it had lasted for days. She knew that, like the rest of them, Margit loved lamb-and-cabbage stew, and no one had complained, despite the fact that they had been eating the same dish for several days now. Siiri hadn't had the energy to even consider cooking on a gloomy November Sunday like today, when time simply didn't seem to pass and it felt like they were sitting in glue, unable to move on from Eino's death.

'Is it just a coincidence that so many people die in November? My husband died on 7 November. And both of my sons died in November,' Siiri said after a long silence. Anna-Liisa perked up at this. She set her crossword down on the coffee table and cleared her throat.

'The Finnish *marraskuu*, or November . . . The word *marras* refers to various death-related phenomena.'

Anna-Liisa held forth for what seemed like ages. She taught them that *marras* was of Indo-European origin, and the root word was presumed to be *martas*. She claimed that *martas* had travelled to Finland from ancient India, landing in Latin in the forms *mori*, meaning 'to die', *mors*, 'death', and *mortas*, 'mortal'. Anna-Liisa clapped her hands between the Latin words to facilitate reception of her message. She transitioned smoothly from Latin to English and French, making a detour to Spain and Italy en route. None of her listeners understood at what phase the ancient Indian *martas* settled in Finland, to describe the penultimate and over-whelmingly gloomiest month of the year.

'*Marras* also appears in any number of folk contexts. Its meaning is not restricted specifically to death; it can also refer to a dying soul or portents of death, as well as creatures of the underworld, imaginary creatures reminiscent of . . . elves,' Anna-Liisa said, bringing her lecture to a rather uncertain conclusion.

The Ambassador looked at her in admiration. Irma was on the verge of saying something, but Anna-Liisa beat her to the punch: 'Not a word of Swedish now, Irma.'

Siiri was still unclear if more people died in November than during the other months, or if her life was simply marked by peculiar coincidences.

'But if you're not sure whether or not you want to keep living, and you happen to look out the window in November, chances are you'll die,' Irma said, stumping out her cigarette against the bottom of the brass ashtray. 'Blech, this cigarette tastes bad. It's unpleasantly heating up the titanium ball bearing in my hip, too. Does anyone have any red wine?'

No one answered. They were loath to interfere in each

other's alcohol consumption, but it seemed plain that if Irma drank a glass of red wine in addition to everything else she had imbibed, she would be in less than optimal condition. Siiri made coffee for all of them and brought over some pound cake. This proved an effective ruse, and successfully distracted Irma from her wine. She was already digging around in her handbag to find her Amaryllie pillies, which she felt she had to take any time she ate something sweet.

'Since I have this touch of diabetes.'

'How does everyone want to die?' Margit asked, rising from under her magazine into a half-sitting position, looking refreshed indeed. Since becoming a widow in mourning, she had dressed in black more often than normal, and today she was wearing black loungewear consisting of a tunic and loose trousers.

'I'd like to die with all of you around me,' the Ambassador said and smiled. It was difficult to say whether he was being serious.

'It's all the same to me where I die,' Margit said. She had seen so much in the way of institutions, hospitals, mistreatment, pain, suffering and hopeless waiting that she had given up on the idea of dying at home. 'It's a fantasy, a utopia. Everyone says they want to die at home, but it makes no sense.'

'Yes. Everyone hopes they'll die of old age and without suffering, in their own bed and in the presence of loved ones,' said Anna-Liisa. 'But that would mean that even if the old person were fit as a fiddle, after a certain age their loved ones would have to gather at their bedside every night just in case they kicked the bucket in their sleep.'

'I don't think it makes any difference to the dying person where they die. Most of them are so medicated they don't even know they're alive.'

Pondering Eino's fate as she had, Margit had developed greater fluency in death-related statistics than the others. She had read a study concluding that 90 per cent of elderly Finns died in the inpatient wards of health centres, and under 10 per cent died in their own bed. Half of those who died annually were over the age of eighty-five, which meant that the death hadn't come as a surprise. 'Or shouldn't have. But the notion that an old person has to die drugged out in a health centre is idiocy. Just as idiotic as putting corpses in the deep-freeze for a week. Someone at Sunset Grove always used to say, "while I'm waiting for my turn at the crematorium", do you remember? Now Eino's waiting for his burial permit, and no one knows how long that will take.'

'I think what people are afraid of isn't death; it's pain,' Siiri said. She had poured coffee into their cups and brought a creamer and a sugar bowl to the coffee table. 'And they're not necessarily afraid of getting old, either, but of getting sick.'

'Alzheimer's! That's what everyone's afraid of. That's the real bugaboo,' Irma exclaimed. 'If you don't remember what day it is right away or some stupid PIN code, then everyone immediately panics: she has Alzheimer's! Boo!' She crooked her fingers and made a scary face. 'I've always told my darlings that I'm a scatter-brained old woman. It's completely natural to forget all sorts of things at this age. It's a blessing. Just imagine if you remembered everything; now, that really would be horrible.'

'Yes. Perhaps moderation in all things, after all,' Anna-Liisa said.

'Even sausage,' Irma cheerfully added. 'That's from one of Topelius's fairy tales: moderation in all things, even sausage.'

But Margit agreed with Siiri. She believed Eino had got by easier than she had over the past year. Eino didn't have the foggiest clue where he'd ended up and how he'd been treated. Margit was the one who'd suffered from the fact that her husband had lost his personality, lain in bleak rooms and been left alone in corridors, turned into a vegetable.

'Although Eino went through his share of difficult times as well. When he realized what was happening to him—'

'I don't approve of euthanasia,' Irma proclaimed. So this was how she felt today. 'At least for the elderly. Luckily, Eino didn't die from your yogurt concoction. If one of my darlings were suffering from some painful terminal illness, I might think otherwise. But there's no point with old people; we die just fine on our own.'

'It wouldn't seem so,' Anna-Liisa remarked frostily. She had been listening silently and seriously to the conversation. Maybe Anna-Liisa had her own fears and anxieties regarding death; there was no way the others could know. Or was Anna-Liisa afraid that her Onni would die and that she would have to give up something so precious a second time?

'Siiri, my love!' a carefree voice called from the entryway.

They all jumped. The voice indisputably belonged to Muhis, but where did he get the nerve to let himself in to clean and do laundry on a quiet Sunday afternoon, and while they were still in mourning? Although, of course, there was no way he could have known that.

'Eino? I don't believe I met him,' Muhis said, abashed. He apologized and offered Margit lovely condolences. When he heard how Eino had been moved into cold storage somewhere in the Helsinki central morgue, he was even more shocked.

'In Africa we don't . . . we do things differently,' he said. 'It's important to say goodbye to the dead.'

Muhis told them about his mother's death and how the entire village had stayed awake and mourned her, how beautiful his mother had looked dressed in her finest clothes and how good it had felt to be able to take his time bidding his mother farewell in the company of friends and relations. They had eaten and sung for three days, and then held the funeral, where they all danced joyfully together. The memory of it still moved him. Then he looked at Margit and took her hand. Margit let Muhis share in her grief, but she couldn't bring herself to look at him.

'It's not your fault Eino isn't here now and we can't say goodbye to him,' Muhis said.

'It's the welfare state's,' Siiri said.

And that's how she felt. She had almost started hating the welfare state, the endless abundance that had killed both of her boys at the age of sixty and thanks to which no one had time for anyone and the dead were swept off into cold

321

storage. The supermarket shelves were stocked with seven types of every snack and sweets, and it was impossible to know which eggs to buy, as every alternative promoted the well-being of the chickens who laid them or the humans who ate them in a different way, but healthy young people didn't have jobs and old people had no one to help them, and a law was in the works that would force children to look after their parents.

'Don't start claiming that everything was better in the good old days,' Irma said, with a laugh. 'It's not true, and besides, it smacks of desperation.'

'Nostalgia gilds everything,' the Ambassador said. 'Old age and death are the only things nostalgia cannot sentimentalize. That's why we're afraid of them.'

Muhis had come to clean the apartment by himself. Metukka had been offered a gig somewhere; Muhis didn't know all the details. He had brought a couple of microfibre cloths and a mop that looked rather handy. It had neatly trimmed strings and a fancy mechanism that squeezed out the extra water. The bucket appeared to be part of the same set, because it had a dedicated stand for the mop.

'But why on earth did you come here to clean on a Sunday?' Siiri asked, as she examined the miracle mop.

'Sunday? Siiri darling, today is Monday!' Muhis laughed his best laugh so riotously that Siiri was afraid his funny headwear would topple to the floor.

'Monday?' Margit cast a suspicious eye at the black man who wasn't perhaps as offensive as she had originally assumed. They all looked at each other, flummoxed, until Irma burst out in a merry falsetto, like a young soubrette soprano from an operetta.

'Alzheimer's, now we all have it! Boo!'

Since Eino's death, which had taken place early on Saturday morning, they had been wandering around as if in a fog and had spent most of their time sleeping. None of them had gone outside, turned on the television or read the newspaper. Siiri's lamb-and-cabbage stew was the only thing that had intermittently brought them together for mute meals. But had they really lost a full day saying their silent goodbyes to their friend Eino, who, with the obvious exception of Margit, hadn't been in their lives long? Eino, whose sad convalescence they had witnessed and whose death had been far too slow?

Muhis went and got the stack of newspapers from the entryway. There were four fat Sunday editions and four flat Monday papers.

'Land's sakes alive,' Irma said, and she started browsing her personal copy of the Sunday paper. 'I wonder if there are any funny obituaries today,' she said, true to form, without devoting much thought to whether this sentiment was the most appropriate for this specific extended weekend. 'Our dearly beloved district superintendent . . . Oh dear, so many people my children's age have died again . . . Hasan . . . what a peculiar name: Hasan Babenstuber, and he wasn't very old, either, the poor cross-breed. Was this the Hasan that all of those fishy fellows came creeping around asking about?'

Muhis' ears pricked up and he leaned in to read the obituaries over Irma's shoulder.

'Yes, that's Hasan. That's the one.'

Chapter 31

Irma had suggested a tram ride after their daily coffee hour on the second floor of Hakaniemi Hall, and because Siiri had noticed that a new route, the 6T, had just been added to Helsinki's selection of trams, she wanted to ride the entire route once. It would have made most sense to ride it downtown first, because it wasn't until after Hietalahti Market Square that the number 6T veered off from the number 6 route and ventured down new paths, but Siiri wanted to go a little further afield, to get away from it all, and Arabianranta felt like a sufficiently distant destination. Besides, the tram would make a quick loop there before continuing back to the long Hämeentie stretch, which all drivers hurtled down even faster than the number 4 did down the Paciuksenkatu hill on its way to Munkkiniemi.

Hauhon puisto was the stop after Lautatarhankatu. The park was known for its abundance of roses and fruit trees, which nevertheless brought no joy on this snowless December day. A few pooch-walkers were sheepishly scooping up their pets' droppings in plastic bags; other than that, the place was lifeless. Siiri had sat in the park the previous spring, when the blooming Cornelian cherries had formed a leafy arbour over the bench at the southern end. One year someone had hung recipes on all the branches; the idea had been that the recipes' ingredients could be found in the tree it was hanging in.

'But I didn't see it myself; Muhis told me about it. Those are handsome, those tall, colourful buildings over there on Hauhontie, although some people think they shade the park too much,' Siiri said.

'Hmm,' Irma mused absent-mindedly.

At the Vallila tram depot, Siiri started waxing rhapsodic over her favourite architect, Selim A. Lindqvist, even though the halls where the trams were serviced was quite the hotchpotch, and only its oldest part and the main façade were designed by Lindqvist.

'Just think, there used to be a market hall here in Vallila, too, a cute little wooden building that was torn down when the tram depot needed expanding,' Siiri said, but Irma's response wasn't particularly enthusiastic. Irma didn't put much stock in Vallila; she still thought of it as the city's old pasturelands. That's where the name came from, too: some manor house whose cattle spent their days chewing cud in the vicinity. Since then, it had, in Irma's eyes, been transformed into a neighbourhood primarily for rumrunners and the poor.

'Look, they even have potato patches.'

'Those aren't potato patches, they're allotment gardens planned by Elisabeth Koch. Charming little cottages and gardens, and still popular, even though no one in Finland is starving any more.'

To the left they saw St Paul's Church, a dreary brick building from the 1930s by Bertel Liljeqvist; dents and surface damage from the Winter War had been unrepaired as a historical reminder. Irma thought it looked more like a fire station than a church. But neither one of them had ever passed through its doors, and it might be the most beautiful building imaginable from the inside.

'Jumping jiminy, we are in the countryside now,' Irma said, as the tram passed the allotment gardens and drove on towards Arabianranta.

'I was supposed to remind you about something, but for the life of me I can't remember what,' Siiri said. Irma admired the old Arabia porcelain factory buildings and didn't remember what Siiri was supposed to remind her about.

'It was some time ago; I think it was before Eino died. You were very serious, you were smoking, and you said you had something very important to tell me but couldn't talk about it then.'

'Shuffle and cut, now I've got it!' Irma crowed, and just then the driver took the end-of-the-line loop at a clip and it elicited a small squeal of joy from both Siiri and Irma. The driver looked at his sole passengers in concern, and Siiri recognized him: it was the boy who generally listened to classical music as he drove.

'Why aren't you playing Bruckner or Wagner today?' Siiri called out.

'One of the passengers who got on at the Western Harbour complained,' the man said. 'But if you don't mind, I'll put some on now.' And so the familiar, sonorous orchestral thunder started building at the front of the tram.

'This is such childish music,' Irma whispered to Siiri, unnecessarily loudly. 'Cowbells and cuckoo-birds. Poor Mahler, I wonder what complex he suffered from.'

'What was it I was supposed to remind you about? Do you still remember?' Siiri said, to distract Irma from criticizing Mahler any further; after all, he was the driver's hero.

Irma remembered. It had to do with the renovation at Sunset Grove and the company responsible for carrying it out, and the time their whole household had unsuccessfully tried to remember the name.

'Well, I remembered it: Fix 'n' Finish. But I pretended that I didn't, because Anna-Liisa was there.' Irma looked a little uncomfortable as she explained that she had found several articles and comments from some crazy discussion forum on her flaptop about the company known as Fix 'n' Finish, and it had made for unpleasant reading. Quite a few plumbing retrofits had taken on a dubious cast when this company was involved. Someone writing under a randy pseudonym had claimed that Fix 'n' Finish was in the habit of changing its name whenever things got too hot.

'That's what Muhis and Metukka said!' Siiri cried.

'It's clearly a fishy enterprise, that's what everyone was shouting on the Internet. I suppose that means bankruptcies and fraud, all sorts of malfeasance. That's why people change their names, too. My poor cousin who moved to Oulu knew one such swindler, a Don Juan whose name changed every week. Luckily, my cousin jumped off that horse before things got any worse; all he got out of her was a gold watch. Imagine, how idiotic!'

'Sounds like something out of a novel.'

'Believe me, he was no romantic hero; he was a completely average, normal man from Oulu. Well, not normal, of course, but from Oulu. And then I found out on the Internet, as a matter of fact on the *Baby* magazine discussion board, that Fix 'n' Finish isn't necessarily just a construction company, that it's involved in . . . that site hinted that it's somehow linked to a broader network involved in human trafficking.'

'That's what Muhis said. He's been trying to warn us this whole time,' Siiri said softly. 'But why couldn't you tell me this when in Anna-Liisa's presence?'

'That's what's so awful.' Irma gazed out the tram window, and Siiri wasn't sure if she'd forgotten what she was talking about, or why she was holding such a long pause. Eventually, Irma turned back to Siiri, a distressed look on her face. 'You see, the name Onni Rinta-Paakku kept coming up.'

'But that's the Ambassador!'

'A Finnish businessman who, thanks to his past career, has connections to Eastern Europe and former communist countries.'

Chapter 32

Mahler's music echoed more and more loudly in Siiri's head, even though they had stepped off the tram. She felt so dizzy and so weak that she was afraid she would faint. Everywhere she turned, things looked ambiguous and incomplete, old warehouses and half-built apartment buildings, and she didn't recognize the neighbourhood.

'Let's take this number 9; it will bring us back to Hakaniemi,' Irma said firmly and led her friend onto the tram. 'Look, your favourite spot is free; sit there. I'll stand here next to you.'

Siiri didn't want to believe it. She thought about the Ambassador, who was such a charming man – debonair, as Irma said. Over the past year, Onni had become a real friend to Siiri, someone she had absolute faith in. Cooking was a joy because the Ambassador ate with a healthy appetite and purred in satisfaction whenever he tasted something delicious. Inevitably kind and considerate, he was an informed conversationalist, and had a sense of humour to boot; he dressed stylishly, smelled good, and demonstrated common courtesy. On more than one occasion Siiri had reflected how happy Anna-Liisa must be to have found such a man at the end of her life. Nor did it really bother Siiri any more that Onni trimmed his moustache and his eyebrows in the kitchen. It was good he took care of himself. And now she was supposed to believe that this fine man was a notorious Mafioso? Had she misjudged the Ambassador so badly? Or was it all just a big misunderstanding; what if Irma had muddled things while fooling around with her tablet? And why would the readers of *Baby* magazine know anything about it?

The number 9 was packed with drunken cruise-ship passengers hauling towers of beer-cases behind them on hand-trucks. Irma wondered how cheap the beer in Tallinn must be for it to make sense to sail across the Gulf of Finland to fetch it, and how much beer one had to guzzle to make the trip pay off.

'Maybe someone is celebrating their fiftieth birthday and is giving friends beer by the case. Even fifty-year-olds don't celebrate with much dignity these days,' Irma said. Momentarily, she harkened back to her own fiftieth, over forty years ago, when the darlings and other relatives had pitched in and bought her a freezer. 'I'm smiling next to it in my fiftieth birthday picture, surrounded by flowers, as if it were a coffin.'

Siiri couldn't stop thinking about the Ambassador's business affairs. She remembered what Mika Korhonen had taught her: first you did something illegal that brought in horrific amounts of money, and then you had to scrub the money clean in a legal company. That's what retirement homes and construction companies were for. It didn't seem likely that Fix 'n' Finish was the Ambassador's sole enterprise. What about the apartments he had scattered across the city? Perhaps they weren't normal rental units after all.

'That's where they conduct their filthiest business,' Irma said serenely. 'It's plain as day in our Hakaniemi apartment. It's no reception venue for the Foreign Ministry.'

'Do you think the Ambassador is aware of this, knows what's going on in the names of his companies? After all, he's a very cultured and ethically advanced individual.'

'That's the way the biggest crooks always seem, at least in the movies. Do you remember that charming gentleman thief they made that TV series about, Arsène Lupin?'

'This is much worse than Lupin's shenanigans,' Siiri said soberly.

They took in the arresting view at Ruoholahdenkatu. The disjointed effect arose from the wooden shanties from the 1890s, called 'villas' in real-estate agents' ads, which were now besieged by a mishmash of modern apartment and office buildings. Siiri felt like one of those dilapidated shacks that looked completely out of place in its surroundings, a memory, a relic that had been left behind, to which the Antiquities Board's preservation status offered cold comfort. To the left, before they reached Malminrinne, they passed a triangular sliver of park, the biggest in the neighbourhood, where hundreds of people walked past Emil Cedercreutz's statue *Apollo* without knowing that originally it had been proposed as a memorial to Finland's national author, Aleksis Kivi.

'Why didn't you tell me about Onni and Fix 'n' Finish earlier?'

Siiri couldn't understand how Irma had been able to forget such a devastating bit of news. She was hurt that Irma had known something so essential about the Ambassador and hadn't told her.

'Eino's death came at a funny time. And ever since Anna-Liisa has been feeling better, you and I haven't had a chance to talk privately. And sometimes I just forgot. That's what I'm like; my mother always called me a grasshopper, even though I don't think that has much to do with memory, more with an attitude towards life. There's that little story about it, too, the grasshopper and the ant. Or was it a bee?'

Siiri smiled. Maybe this was the reason she loved Irma so much. What were they supposed to do about it if their friends had got mixed up in unfortunate circles? The best thing would be to just die off.

'Does she know . . . have you spoken with Anna-Liisa?'

'No, I couldn't. Do you know, I found a photograph on my flaptop of the Ambassador with Jerry Herring Head, the one with the waxed hair who taught us how to use composting toilets.'

Siiri corrected her: 'Jerry Hedgehog Head, Jerry Siilinpää. So you think he's involved in all this, too? He was a fool, not a criminal. He was just a boy.'

Irma didn't believe Anna-Liisa knew anything about her husband's affairs, not even the fact that her jewellery box was being used to transport illicit gains back and forth between Sunset Grove and Hakaniemi. This last bit was just a wild guess of Irma's, of course; Siiri didn't want to believe the jewellery box had anything to do with anything. In the end, Irma had come to the conclusion that this business of the Ambassador's was nothing they needed to stick their noses into; they could leave the entire Sunset Grove renovation unprobed by their inquisitive minds. This wasn't at all like her; Irma was forever sticking her nose into everyone else's business. And this matter had, no doubt, been weighing heavily on her.

'But then I remembered the complaints and memos. We filed a criminal report, and Anna-Liisa's signature was at the top of the list.'

'Oh, poor Anna-Liisa!' Siiri said from the bottom of her heart, tears welling up in her eyes.

The number 9 had driven to Hakaniemi, but just as they were standing to get off, the driver announced that an accident on Fleminginkatu was blocking the tracks. He had been ordered to loop around the Arena building and drive back to the Western Harbour. Everyone travelling to Kallio, Alppila, or Pasila should get off now and wait until the track was cleared or a replacement bus arrived.

Siiri was thrilled. She knew trams rarely drove the Arena loop. It was a unique loop on Helsinki's tram map, because it was the only one to circle a single building: their temporary home, the formidable fortress designed by Lars Sonck. Suddenly, she also remembered how the Ambassador had told them the building was divided into two housing associations, so the OX from the neon OXYGENOL sign on the roof belonged to one of the associations, and the YGENOL belonged to the other. And that during the bombing of Helsinki in February 1944, some simpleton from Turku living on the YGENOL side had refused to turn off his lights, despite the blackout that had been declared to trick the Russkis. This fool from Turku had basked in his lamplight, but despite this, not a single bomb had hit the building. Siiri absolutely wanted to ride along as the tram circled the triangular, single-building loop.

'Yes, that's fine,' the driver said, after all the other passengers had stormed off. They would be late for their important engagements, and as far as they were concerned, it was the innocent driver's fault, which was why they took out their pointless frustration on him. Siiri and Irma rode ceremoniously up Siltasaarenkatu, slowly curved onto Toinen linja, even more carefully onto Hämeentie, and then pulled up at Hakaniemi Square again, only headed in opposite direction. It felt like a real victory lap. They were the only two passengers in the tram, and the finale to Mahler's Sixth Symphony rang out dramatically. The people on the street gawked; most understood that they were witnessing something out of the ordinary.

'Quite the feeling, making the round of our private prison,' Irma said.

'What do you mean?'

'We're imprisoned there, without any options, and thanks to our little secret, we're even more isolated than we were at

Sunset Grove. It's like being on a desert island that a lost ocean liner of a tram circles once every ten years. Only death can save us now. *Döden, döden, döden.*'

Chapter 33

'Good, you're back!'

Anna-Liisa hurried out on her cane to greet them in the entryway. She looked concerned, not the least bit tired or weak; a little grave, perhaps.

'Onni is ill,' she said in a low voice, articulating over-carefully, as if she were revealing a confidence. 'Very ill indeed.'

Just that morning the Ambassador had been his energetic self, as they had seen with their own eyes when they'd drunk their morning coffee, but after painstakingly reading the newspaper from the comics and the TV guide to the letters to the editor and the front page, he had started feeling fatigued and had retired to his room to rest, which wasn't in the least bit like him. The Ambassador had been in a deep sleep when Anna-Liisa's in-home caregiver showed up to twiddle her thumbs in the middle of the living room. Anna-Liisa had taken advantage of the situation and asked her to take a look at Onni.

'And this was no little girl, but an experienced nurse. One glance at Onni through the cracked door was all she needed to tell me that Onni needed to go to hospital.'

But Anna-Liisa hadn't obeyed; Onni didn't want to go to the hospital. Anna-Liisa was agitated and urged them to follow her. She spun around on her heels and started off, her cane cracking sharply against the parquet. Siiri and Irma silently stripped off their outerwear, damp from the December rain, and exchanged glances.

'Will this be the resolution to our problem?' Irma fixed her hair, swiped on a bit of lipstick, and smiled at her reflection, satisfied. Then she dropped her cane into the umbrella stand, because, like Siiri, she never used it indoors. Irma eyed the cane and raised a bossy forefinger: 'All right, Kalle, my trusty cavalier, I expect you to wait there patiently for our next adventure.'

It was dim inside the bedroom Anna-Liisa shared with her husband; the curtains had been drawn across the windows and the only light came from the mirrored dressing table in the corner. The Ambassador was lying in his big round bed, sleeping almost soundlessly. Anna-Liisa was standing at the dressing table, holding the jewellery box in her hand, an odd look on her face.

'Is he already dead?' Irma asked inquisitively.

'For goodness' sake, Irma, could you please be sensible for once, if for just a moment,' Anna-Liisa said, her voice trembling. She took two steps towards them, opened the jewellery box, and showed it to them without saying a word. They stretched out their necks to peer in, as if forbidden from taking a step.

'Land sakes! Will you look at that!'

The box was full of jewellery, most of it gold. Anna-Liisa's stolen goods had been restored to her!

'When did you notice that?' Siiri asked, nearly hoarse. She thought they were being asked in to help care for the Ambassador, but at the moment Anna-Liisa was more concerned about the jewellery box.

'I found it today when I was looking for the money; you remember that bundle of fifteen thousand euros. My thinking was that if Onni was in a critical condition and we needed a doctor or something out of the ordinary, I could use this stash, because I don't have access to my husband's bank accounts, and I'm nearly penniless myself. But there's neither hide nor hair of the bills, and instead ... All this jewellery ... And this isn't my jewellery; I've never laid eyes on it.'

They looked at the ropes of diamonds, gold chains and other pieces in the box without recognizing a single one. It was only at the very bottom that they came across Anna-Liisa's pearl necklace and cameo brooch. Siiri remembered the strange man she had let in the morning of Eino's death before realizing how early it was, and she started feeling weak again. Irma shot a glance at Siiri and took the reins.

'This is one devilish box, but jewellery is only an earthly concern, isn't it? Right now it's more important for us to concentrate on Onni.' She bent down at the Ambassador's side, placed a hand on his forehead, and waited for a moment. 'He has a fever. Are you sure he doesn't want to go to the hospital?'

Anna-Liisa was absolutely sure. She and Onni had last

discussed these matters after Eino died and had sworn a sacred oath to each other that if one of them fell ill, the other would make sure the doctors weren't allowed to interfere and they wouldn't start some three-hospital circus.

'Do you think . . . He was still in such good health just yesterday, do you think it's possible that he could . . .' Anna-Liisa had to search for the words, which was anything but typical.

'He's not going to die,' Siiri said confidently. She had regrouped thanks to Irma's energetic example; it wasn't going to do any good to start fainting now. 'Onni is a strong man, and this is just a touch of the winter flu. He needs to drink a lot, and he mustn't get too hot. Take off that heavy blanket and go and get a cold towel from the spa for his brow. I'll bring something to drink.'

They pulled together like seasoned nurses at a field hospital, and everyone rushed off to complete their assigned tasks with a brisk efficiency. Anna-Liisa pulled the big blanket off her husband, Irma popped into the bathroom, and Siiri made for her own realm, the kitchenette. As she poured apple juice into a tall glass, Margit appeared from her room, fresh from a siesta. Her hair was an untidy thatch and she wasn't wearing a stitch, other than a pair of nude underpants that reached up over her bellybutton, and she belched away as she inserted her hearing aid, calm as could be.

'Is that for me? Siiri, you're such a sweetheart!'

Siiri snatched the glass from the bar before Margit's greedy hand reached it and told Margit to pour her own juice. She explained that the Ambassador had a fever, but this intelligence was of no interest to her drowsy friend.

'You always have so much energy,' Margit sighed, and eyed the paper lying on the bar as if she didn't remember that she had read it thoroughly just a couple of hours earlier.

Siiri left Margit pondering life's mysteries in her underwear and brought the juice back to the round-bedded boudoir. Irma was already attending to the Ambassador; cold water trickled down his face from the wet towel on his forehead. Anna-Liisa had opened the window and folded the bedcover at the foot of the bed. The pallid Ambassador lay under the thin sheet, watching the three women bustle about him.

'What is my harem up to now?' he said in an uncharacteristically feeble voice, struggling to sound like his usual cheerful self.

'Onni, dear, would you like to try to drink some juice?' Anna-Liisa asked at a near-whisper, and the Ambassador nodded enthusiastically.

They helped the Ambassador sit, and Anna-Liisa held the big glass to his mouth. Siiri couldn't help but be reminded of Margit feeding her husband at the SquirrelsNest a few weeks earlier. She started trembling and had to sit. Luckily, Anna-Liisa's and the Ambassador's bed was so insanely immense that there was room and to spare for multiple attendants to rest themselves if one started feeling weak.

'Here they are,' Margit said, in an unnecessarily loud voice, opening the door for a balding man who stepped into the room, looking quizzical. He was clearly a little alarmed from the reception he'd received, as Margit still hadn't dressed.

'Hello, I'm director of customer relations from the Car-endo Company, and I'm here on behalf of the City of Helsinki Western Health-Care District In-Home Care,' he said in a reedy voice that was straining to sound energetic. He was one of those young men whose age was hard to determine. Judging by waistline and hairline, he was no spring chicken, but on the other hand he was wearing jeans, and a blazer that was too tight.

'Hello,' Anna-Liisa said, standing up. 'Don't you have a name?'

'Petri Ali-Möttölä, hello. Here's my card. City of Hel-sinki Western Health—'

'Anna-Liisa Petäjä, MA, Finnish teacher. I'm whom you're looking for, I presume?'

Anna-Liisa behaved like a suspect defiantly confessing a crime when finally caught by a detective who'd been tailing her for ages; she had no idea that her friends were feverishly thinking about the authorities and crimes and Anna-Liisa's husband, who now languished under the sheet.

'I'm here to conduct a patient evaluation, as I received a ticket that the rehabilitatee has recovered and treatment is overscaled at present, but apparently the situation isn't so rosy after all . . .' Petri Ali-Möttölä looked inquisitively at the Ambassador and nodded sympathetically at the loved ones.

'I have nothing to do with your home inspection; I'm just

the spouse. The patient is my wife here, who is caring for me,' the Ambassador said with a winning smile.

'We shouldn't tire him out,' Anna-Liisa said, leading the awkward public-private director into the living room. Irma and Siiri followed like Bill and Bull, the two foolish helpers from the Peter No-Tail books, even though the matter didn't concern them at all. When all of them were uncomfortably perched on the bar stools, Anna-Liisa explained the situation politely but firmly. She had been rehabilitated back to health, in spite of the in-home care she had received, and no longer required the city's services. Speaking in unambiguous main clauses, she hoped that this would be the last time she would have anything to do with the wide range of services offered by City of Helsinki In-Home Care.

'You can see for yourself, I'm perfectly well,' she said, concluding her explication with a sharp rap of her knuckles.

'And we're here, too,' Irma said. 'Helping out, that is.'

'And the Ambassador, I mean her husband, isn't terribly ill. He just has a fever,' Siiri added.

The man peered over his spectacles at them, allowed his gaze to meander over the stout pillars, dance pole, and home theatre and momentarily rest on Margit's half-naked carcass, which was snoring on one of the sofas, its face covered by a Swedish women's magazine. He twitched unconsciously several times, unglued his eyes from Margit, remembered he was in a client meeting, and pulled out his tablet. It was even smaller than Irma's.

'A few questions, and we'll be able to update your client record. In addition, you can fill out this customer satisfaction

form for a chance to win a fruit basket.' The man handed
Anna-Liisa a piece of paper he had pulled out of his brief-
case, marked with traffic lights and a range of questions.

'A fruit basket, of all the things!' Anna-Liisa cried, as if
she couldn't think of anything more idiotic if she tried.

'They're very popular business gifts now at Christmastime . . .' the man began, but immediately moved on to the
client record. Anna-Liisa answered all of his questions
quickly and fluently and finished by lying that she was very
satisfied with the services and staff of the City of Helsinki
Western Health-Care District In-Home Care.

'So are we clear now?' Anna-Liisa asked. 'I no longer
need to pay your invoices, and you won't send a single
burnt-out, incompetent, hurried, harried, recalcitrant individual incapable of normal communication at any time of
day or night to frighten myself and my friends?'

Petri Ali-Möttölä frowned and looked as if he didn't quite
follow. 'Are you talking about our services? Our employees . . . ? What are you talking about?'

'I mean to say that I no longer want your services. Is this
so incomprehensibly difficult to grasp?'

'Of course not, not at all. It's just rare for the client's need
for assistance to decrease at this age,' Petri Ali-Möttölä said,
and cheered up enough to see the positive side of things. He
called this a win-win situation, because Anna-Liisa felt like
she was in good shape and one less person required in-home
care. Then he remembered that Anna-Liisa's rehabilitative
services had been turned over to that function of Western
Health-Care District In-Home Care that had been privatized

and, after bidding, outsourced to the Carendo Company Ltd, which meant that Anna-Liisa's miraculous healing would mean a financial loss for a publicly listed international corporation.

'At Carendo, we are committed to caring for every client, which is why it is my responsibility to confirm that you're in full control of your faculties. So a couple of follow-up questions, Anna-Liisa. What day is it today?'

'My good man, you are not a sensible person,' Anna-Liisa said. 'Are you claiming with a straight face that I've turned into some sort of key client, when not too long ago I was an under-resourced HSS problem contributing to the sustainability deficit? At what point did this pendulum swing the other way?'

This outburst disconcerted the poor fellow, who started twitching oddly again. Margit coughed on the couch three times, which nearly sent Ali-Möttölä's thoughts permanently off the rails. But then he pulled himself together with admirable determination and swiped his miniature tablet a couple of times, as if rebooting himself.

'So . . . that is to say . . . this is nothing more than a simple market-economy phenomenon. When public-sector problems become private-sector enterprise, then what was a cost yesterday is a source of income today. It's no more mysterious than that; as a matter of fact, it's rather fantastic, don't you think? Old people are taken care of and shareholders get a return on their investment. What day is it today?'

'It will be your last, if you don't stop this foolishness.'

Anna-Liisa stood and knocked her cane against the parquet so fiercely that Petri Ali-Möttölä fell off his bar stool and staggered to his feet. Anna-Liisa had genuinely gone berserk, and was even frightening Siiri now. Cheeks flaming and dark eyes glowing with rage, she pointed her cane in the direction of the front door. 'Please leave. You will rehabilitate me over my dead body, and in this context you will allow me this cliché, because it is to be understood literally.'

The director of client relationships twitched for a moment, clicked his tablet's protective sleeve shut, grabbed his leather satchel, and turned to leave. As he passed Margit, he hesitated, took a few determined steps but then turned back around and said: 'I consider the client relationship ended. If you change your mind, you have my contact information. I'll leave my card here on the . . . on the coffee table. You'll receive an end-of-service agreement via email. You need to print it, sign it, scan it and send it back to me.'

'Madman,' Anna-Liisa huffed. 'As if I had email and a printer and whatever the third gadget was. What more is there to be said?'

They exchanged glances, and this time even Anna-Liisa joined in the chorus: '*Döden, döden, döden.*'

Chapter 34

Irma had penned a note in her ornate hand that politely declined advertisements, free newspapers and other junk mail in both of Finland's official languages and fixed it to the door. Margit hadn't wanted her to post it there, because she enjoyed browsing through the special offers and other postal debris that drifted in through the mail slot, but in this instance the majority opinion was so clear that Margit had to settle for grousing occasionally that she didn't have anything to read, which generally came to an abrupt halt when Anna-Liisa thrust Joel Lehtonen's *Hogweed Hollow* or some other equally stimulating reading material into her hands.

Not that there was much in the way of mail proper. Their bills travelled along the invisible paths of the Internet, and no one wrote letters or even postcards any more, despite the fact that Irma's darlings were constantly travelling the world for work as well as vacation to recuperate from work. So it was unexpected indeed when two letters addressed to Anna-Liisa Petäjä, MA dropped to the doormat on 7 December, the day after Finnish Independence Day. The sender of the first was the Loving Care Foundation, that of the second Fix 'n' Finish Renovations and Odd Jobs Ltd. Siiri looked at the letters in horror and instantly decided to ask Irma for advice. She knocked softly, so Anna-Liisa wouldn't hear, and opened Irma's door.

'Cock-a-doodle-doo!'

Irma was lounging on her bed in a state of dishabille, unable to rise, as she had just lotioned herself from head to toe and had to wait absolutely still for the oils to be absorbed. By some miracle, Irma had made the mauve room unmistakably hers: rose-patterned throw pillows from Sanderson were strewn about; the table was drowning in perfume bottles, pictures of her darlings and make-up; a box of wine and a purple orchid stood on the windowsill; and a faint sweetness permeated the space. She had fixed her husband's picture to the wall with masking tape; it was from the 1970s, when Veikko had been a spry, whiskered pipe-smoker.

'But you go ahead and read the letters, and I'll listen.'

'Irma! These are addressed to Anna-Liisa; we can't open them.'

'Of course we can. They concern all of us; we sent in those stupid complaints together. Considering the Ambassador's . . . shall we say status, it might be best if we never say a peep to Anna-Liisa about these letters.'

But they knew how pedantic and precise Anna-Liisa was. She would be sure to notice if no one ever responded to their complaints. If the letters never arrived, she would start digging into the dirty details of the Sunset Grove retrofit with intensified vigour. In the end, Siiri agreed to open the letters. She fetched a sharp knife from the kitchen and deftly slit the envelopes, as she knew Anna-Liisa would not look kindly on letters addressed to her being barbarically ripped open.

'Which one first?' Siiri asked Irma.

'Fix 'n' Finish. I'm dying of curiosity to hear what lies those louts have come up with to try and trick us. And if the blockheads know who they're sending their lies to.'

The letter was brief and completely incomprehensible. The main gist was to inform the recipients that their complaint had been received and processed and required no further investigation, because what had happened was normal. But the language was so funny that Siiri couldn't read the letter with a straight face. She had to constantly stop to collect herself and start over.

> *'Dear customer, thank you for the letter that we have investigated the information inside. We can sincerely guarantee that every process remodel in the year Sunset Grove has been completed in normal practices accordance with. There is nothing required to be worried. You will be informed when the project is complete in approximately all details your property and other questions mentioned to the letter.*
> *Sincerely, Yuri Ahkmatov, Lead Contractor.'*

'How splendidly nonsensical! Read it over again from the beginning!' Irma squealed and squirmed in such delight that the anti-aging cream spread all over the floral bedspread she had hauled to Hakaniemi from Sunset Grove. Siiri obeyed; this time she did a superb job of maintaining her composure and recited the gibberish in its entirety from start to finish as if it were prose deserving of serious consideration.

'It must have been written by a robot,' Irma said, once Siiri finished. 'Or Google.'

'What's that?'

'Google is . . . well, it's a kind of robot.'

'Oh. I thought it—'

'Listen, I know these Internet robots. I have an artificial brain here in my flaptop that tells me what an English-language word means if I'm not familiar with it. I just place my finger on the word, and blip, the translation appears. What about the other letter, is it as hilarious?'

Siiri glanced at the letter from the Loving Care Foundation, proprietors of Sunset Grove. It had been penned by Director Sinikka Sundström, who apparently still had a seat on the foundation's board, thus overseeing herself, although this arrangement had spawned complaints reaching as far as the parliamentary ombudsman.

'Dear Anna-Liisa, Irma and Siiri,' the letter began.

Irma interrupted: 'Blech, how revolting. Belittling and treating us like some little pets of hers instead of paying clients and independent citizens exercising our legal rights.'

The letter was unadulterated drivel. Director Sundström was terribly sorry about everything, yet she semi-maniacally went on and on about how normal the procedures and practices had been throughout the various stages of the remodel. Massive water damage turned into minor incidents of dampness; the theft of their personal property into attentive responsibility for residents' belongings. Director Sundström was so crushed by the renovation delays that she was nearly overcome with depression, and yet they were completely normal, as was the fact that the residents were responsible for both the costs of the renovation as well as their rent and any damage to their apartments that occurred during construction.

'Merry Christmas, one and all! Hope to see you soon. Hugs, Sinikka.'

'How convenient!' Irma said. 'Now she was saved the expense of sending Christmas cards, too.'

Upon closer reflection, Director Sundström's letter was rather disturbing. She insisted that everything that had taken place during the renovation was normal, even though their property had been destroyed and stolen and no one knew the full extent of the costs that were racking up.

Irma stood and slowly started to dress. Siiri helped her with her blouse and made sure her hair looked nice from behind, now that Irma's arms were too stiff to reach the back. Irma started telling Siiri about a cousin who was always in tip-top form: who was well groomed and even wore make-up.

'And then from the back, her hair was like a rat's nest and no one had the nerve to say anything to her about it. She would have had a heart attack if she'd known, and I mean that literally – which she eventually did, the lucky thing. She went instantly and never knew about the rat's rear-end on the back of her head.'

After applying a little lipstick and drenching herself in an excessive cloud of cloying perfume, Irma was ready to emerge from her chambers. They paused at the doorway, because Siiri didn't know what to do with the letters addressed to Anna-Liisa.

'Show them to her; there's no reason not to. No one intends to take any action, which, under the circumstances, is a big relief.'

'Are you referring to me?'

Anna-Liisa was sitting, back erect, on the white couch, listening to everything; she had very sharp hearing. Margit, on the other hand, was engrossed in a *Damernas Värld* article about the nocturnal shenanigans of the King of Sweden and his brother-in-law and didn't react in the least. Her hearing aid was on the coffee table next to a hairbrush and a hardened clump of chewing gum.

'Two letters arrived for you, or actually for all of us, seeing as how it was all of us who sent those complaints, which is why we dared open and read them.'

Looking guilty, Siiri handed over the unsealed correspondence, and Anna-Liisa eyed her reproachfully but said nothing. She read Director Sundström's warm Christmas card first, grunted sourly, and then studied Yuri Ahkmatov's enigmatic expressions with a frown.

'What an atrocity! "All details your property and other questions mentioned to the letter!"'

Siiri noted Anna-Liisa's piquing interest in the matter with concern and regretted not having discreetly thrown the letters in the bin.

'It's robot language,' Irma said. 'I thought you might find it interesting.'

'Irma and I were just saying that it seems both letters indicate that everything going on at Sunset Grove is normal. That's a relief, isn't it?' Siiri said, trying to smile naturally.

'Have you been complaining again?' The conversation had roused Margit's attention, as there was nothing novel about the escapades of Swedish royalty. She had popped the hearing aid onto her ear and the gum into her mouth. 'Don't you remember that's a sure shortcut to being locked up in the dementia unit?'

Irma blanched as she recalled events from a year ago. Siiri hadn't considered that possibility at all; she continued to hold on to the belief that Director Sundström was a sincere person and that all the bad things at Sunset Grove had been the handiwork of Virpi and Erkki Hiukkanen, who were now paying for their crimes. Suddenly she was overcome by an incredible longing for Mika Korhonen, her personal angel. They could certainly have used his help now.

'We also reported it to the police,' Anna-Liisa said matter-of-factly. 'And strictly speaking, we never approached this Fix 'n' Finish company; we addressed our complaints exclusively to the Loving Care Foundation. In addition, we informed Director Sundström and old Weasel Head about our intentions.'

'Hedgehog Head.'

'Yes, him. But now it turns out that our letters have

been passed from one hand to the other, and the matter has been foisted off on Director Sundström and this imbecilic, illiterate contractor.'

They were silent for a moment. In the ecstasy of relief, Siiri had forgotten the police report and everything else Anna-Liisa now stated so pointedly. Siiri was afraid they would end up in an even bigger pickle; Anna-Liisa didn't have the slightest clue about her husband's complicity and as a result was dedicating all the vigour of the recently healed and rehabilitated to ensuring justice was carried out. She was already casting about furiously for a pencil and sharpener in order to draft sharp replies to Sundström and the foreign robot she suspected of having a low IQ. How on earth could they extract themselves gracefully at this point? Siiri shot a helpless look at Irma, who returned her look equally helplessly. But it was Margit who came to the rescue.

'Oh for goodness' sake, stop while you're ahead,' Margit said with what was perhaps an unnecessary brusqueness, laughing at Anna-Liisa's activism. Margit thought that renovations and plumbing retrofits in particular were legally countenanced criminal activity it was pointless fighting against. 'Especially for old people living in retirement homes who scribble out letters in pencil.'

'I always copy out everything neatly in ink,' Anna-Liisa said, slightly offended.

Irma wasted no time backing her partner in crime: 'It's true. Anna-Liisa writes skilfully, and she has an exceptionally beautiful hand. But maybe Margit is right. I can't be bothered to tilt against windmills. And we don't even speak the same language as this half-Russki Fix 'n' Finisher.'

'Besides, we can always wait and see how the police react to our criminal report,' Siiri said, sounding far too unenthusiastic, because the very thought of starting a criminal investigation made her weak. She hadn't forgotten her previous interrogation at police headquarters in Pasila; she had fainted that time and found herself in the rear of an ambulance on her way back to Sunset Grove.

'How is Onni feeling today?' Irma asked, to brighten the mood, but she was humming the blood-chilling theme from the final act of *Rigoletto*, which led Siiri's thoughts to assassins.

According to Anna-Liisa, the Ambassador had been restless all night, but had settled down after drinking a strong cup of coffee and a glass of juice for breakfast. Now he was in a deep sleep, but unfortunately his fever hadn't gone down.

Siiri and Irma applied all of their arts to making the Ambassador's flu sound trivial and asked Anna-Liisa to join them for coffee at Hakaniemi Hall. They could flip through the tabloids in the second-floor cafe and learn the identities of the tarted-up peacocks they'd seen during the televised broadcast from the president's Independence Day ball. While they were at it, they could buy something delicious for dinner and look for Christmas ornaments. It was plain now that they would be spending Christmas at Hakaniemi, and a few straw ornaments, angels and elves would cheer them up.

'But there's no way we're dragging a Christmas tree up here,' Irma said, and everyone agreed.

Chapter 35

Much to their surprise, Eino Partanen's burial permit arrived well before Christmas. Some blessed, hard-working doctor who had a true calling for his work had managed to drop by the city's central freezer long enough to have a peek at Eino and verify that he was, indeed, dead.

Margit was invigorated by the funeral preparations. She said she was a member of the Lean-to Co-operative, even though there weren't any Lean-to stores any more, as it had merged into a larger retail chain long ago. But the Lean-to Funeral Home still existed and, wouldn't you know it, continued to offer co-operative members a 10 per cent discount on its services, which put Margit in a particularly good mood. And since the offices of the Lean-to Funeral Home were just around the corner on Siltasaarenkatu, the plans for Eino's funeral advanced as if it were a long-awaited party.

'You'll come with me when I go and arrange the details with the funeral home, won't you?' Margit asked Siiri.

Margit had grown so entwined with her husband that she didn't feel confident on her own. She needed someone at her side to approve her decisions and doings, even when she was acting decisively. During their stint as refugees at Hakaniemi, she had latched onto Siiri for an emotional security blanket, and Siiri had nothing against standing at Margit's side at difficult times. But Irma was hurt she hadn't been asked along. She was used to organizing big family celebrations and would have loved being able to pick out sandwich cakes and casket trim.

'I don't need anyone aside from Siiri. There's no need to turn it into a town meeting,' Margit said rudely, and left Irma sipping her morning glass of red wine on her bar stool. Since Eino's death, Irma had developed a new habit of drinking a small glass of red wine after breakfast, as if to counterbalance the evening whisky she partook at her doctor's orders. Her morning wine set the blood circulating, and in addition she had heard it was wonderfully healthy.

'It has flavonoids . . . they're anti-aging compounds,' she said. And before anyone could say anything to her about retarding the aging process, she laughed merrily: 'It's never too late to start looking after your health!'

All was quiet, calm and grey in the funeral home, as was befitting. The staff member who served them introduced herself as the director and spoke in a low voice, practically a whisper, and made generous use of passive forms in an apparent attempt to give a polite but not overly intrusive impression. At first Margit couldn't make anything out of the woman's consolatory, pronoun-free sighs, but this didn't really pose a problem, as the task at hand seemed rather straightforward. First they chose the casket. An intriguing miniature display of the selection of coffin style had been arrayed on the wall. Siiri and Margit fingered the toy caskets inquisitively as the branch manager related what she considered interesting details about the product selection.

'A classic casket in German oak is always popular. The very latest trend is this eco-casket, which is made without nails.'

'Without nails? Won't it fall apart?' Siiri asked.

'The eco-casket uses wooden dowels. They're made in Nakkila from Finnish pine and are suitable for all sorts of crematoria.'

'I'll take whatever's cheapest,' Margit said, and Siiri remembered how they'd discussed their own funerals on a trip once and Margit had announced that she wanted a cardboard coffin. Unfortunately, the funeral home's selection was not this extensive. The cheapest option was an apparently slightly un-ecological pine version made in Estonia of unfinished planks.

'It's a tad spare, isn't it?' Siiri felt compelled to remark, because without any fabric the coffin looked like a fruit crate.

'Let's throw in a black cloth to cover it. Something cheap, no draping or pointless tassels,' Margit said. The branch manager raised an eyebrow that wasn't an eyebrow, because she had carefully plucked out every hair from her forehead and painted brown lines in their place. Now these lines rose in bewilderment, because in Finland caskets were generally white.

'Eino has to have black. He looked so handsome in a tux,' Margit explained.

Next they needed to decide on the lining, which Margit thought was idiotic, because by this time her husband had got used to lying in a freezer drawer and it was doubtful that he expected much in the way of comforts during his few hours in the casket.

'No lining, then,' the funeral-home director whispered. 'What about the pillow, shall we say silk?'

'A pillow? What on earth are you going on about? We're not putting a silk pillow in there just so we can burn it.'

The conversation staggered on. The funeral home's agent wanted to dress Eino in his best clothes, but Margit announced that they'd been stolen ages ago from the closet at Sunset Grove. This made Siiri realize that her serviceable old funeral dress had also been swallowed up in the maw of the retrofit. She would have to buy new funeral wear, and it seemed a horrific waste, but Margit reminded her that she'd use it at least four times, since the rest of them would be following Eino and would need to be buried too.

'Why would I be the last one to die?' Siiri asked, and the branch manager cleared her throat in order to draw their attention to the glossy catalogue featuring a variety of funeral garb for the dead. She wasn't surprised when Margit chose the cheapest one, the option that looked like a paper sheet without any extras.

'The casket will be closed the whole time, won't it? No one's going to look inside,' Margit said.

For the urn, Margit wanted a grey cardboard box, even though the agent tried to explain that these were mostly used for the remains of dogs. Margit was sure her husband had wasted away so much by the time he died that he'd produce less ash than the average canine.

'You see such enormous dogs in this part of town, have you noticed?' Siiri said, as the mood was already rather tense. 'Real ponies! Imagine how much they eat in a day! More than the five of us put together.'

They were compelled to explain that 'the five of us' meant their little refugee community that was temporarily occupying an apartment in the Arena building. Siiri had already advanced rather deeply into her account, and although she didn't go into the suspected crimes at Sunset Grove, the funeral-home director looked at her watch and started talking about the pastor, the music, the obituary, the catering and the estate inventory.

'How awful, there's so much to remember,' Margit sighed, as the list was undeniably long.

They accepted the stack of brochures decorated with white flowers and promised to study them as they reviewed the responsibilities of kin with respect to funerals, and the funeral-home director didn't have all day to sit there listening to them speculate about which one of them would die last. They could no doubt decide the details themselves, seeing as how they were all experienced buriers of loved ones. Margit announced that she would be holding the funeral service at Kallio Church, in which she had never set foot.

'It's closest.'

'And it was designed by Lars Sonck, like the Tampere Cathedral and our very own Arena building. It might be quite lovely from the pews,' Siiri exclaimed, as she had never been inside the Kallio Church either. Its tower formed the central element of the city's horizon north of the Pitkäsilta, and you had a handsome view of it down Unioninkatu all the way to Kaivopuisto.

'Right. So what day were you thinking?' the brow-less woman asked, flipping through her desk calendar as if Margit ought to be happy if she could clear out thirty minutes for Margit's husband's final journey.

'It doesn't matter, just fit me in somewhere. My calendar is wide open,' Margit said. Nor did she care which pastor led Eino's funeral service, because she didn't know any and didn't much care for their sermonizing anyway. 'As long as they can stand there and speak intelligibly.'

'Do you mean soberly?' Siiri clarified.

'That, too, preferably.'

The funeral-home director swallowed a deep yawn and said the funeral home would pass on Margit's wishes to the parish.

'They'll be in touch. What was the phone number?'

This was a ticklish question. Margit didn't own a mobile phone, because she was hard of hearing and had never learned her way around them anyway. Siiri didn't have one, either. There was the landline at the Hakaniemi apartment, oddly shaped and electric blue, and it had taken them a couple of weeks before they realized that it was a phone, but they didn't remember the number, nor did they know in whose name the line was registered. They would be able to find Irma's number from information, because there couldn't be more than one Irma Lännenleimu in this world, but Margit didn't want random pastors calling Irma about her private affairs.

'That's just going to get messy. Could the pastor pay us a visit at home?' she suggested, and that was just fine.

'Unfortunately, our time here has ended,' the funeral-home director suddenly whispered, and true to her word, she drove them out of her office, even though they had only been sitting there for a little over an hour, and half the decisions had yet to be made. The stingy woman hadn't even offered them coffee; in quality funeral homes they always did. Siiri and Margit exited, a little offended, and had to turn right back around, as Siiri's walking stick had fallen behind the sofa and she had forgotten it there. The funeral-home director didn't lift a finger to help Siiri fish the cane out of the awkward spot, just picked at her cuticles, looking concerned.

'Pleasure meeting you, see you soon!' Margit waved at the woman, who stood waiting at the door to close it the second they stepped out, even though it was only two in the afternoon. The silly thing; in her line of business, they were the clientele she should have been after.

Back at home on the sofa, they related their adventures to the others and distributed the funeral home's brochures.

Anna-Liisa delved into a pamphlet that said you could turn a loved one's ashes into a diamond. The brochure was illustrated with images of smiling people wearing brilliant-cut blue stones in necklaces, bracelets, rings.

'This is macabre,' Anna-Liisa muttered.

'I think it's a rather fun idea,' Irma exclaimed. 'I'm wearing my husband on this finger and my mother on that one, and over here on my other hand I have my father, that's the biggest diamond because he was a very heavy man, and this little one here on my bosom is . . . let's say my cat!' Then she started missing her dear old Veikko again, but once the catering brochure was in her hands she forgot her husband just as quickly as she had remembered him. 'Oh, what delicious-looking cakesies, they're making my mouth water. Let's order lots just to be sure; I want some of this caramel cake at least, and Sachertorte. How big is your family, Margit?'

None of them knew anything about Eino and Margit's immediate family, let alone extended relations. It turned out that Eino's family was actually quite large, but Margit didn't care for their company. She claimed it was an 'in-bred mutual admiration society', and it didn't take much to deduce that Margit felt like she wasn't good enough for them. Her own siblings were dead, and she hadn't stayed in touch with their children.

'What about . . . Do you two have any children?' Siiri asked tentatively. After all, this was a matter that required clarification as well.

'Eino does,' Margit said. A long silence followed. Anna-

Liisa read the estate inventory advertisement, Siiri poured more coffee for all of them, and Irma racked her brains trying to think of a polite way to proceed in this matter, which was growing more interesting by the minute.

She finally settled on: 'Are Eino's children bastards?'

'Some are,' Margit answered matter-of-factly. She told them Eino had been married to another woman when he was young, before he and Margit had met at a workplace seminar. A torrid, blazing passion had immediately sparked between them, and even now Margit's cheeks started to glow as she remembered the early days of their shared life.

'As you know, having a forbidden love adds to the excitement,' she said, as if they had all jumped in the sack with married men as young women. She fanned her breast with a headstone brochure to cool herself off and remembered all the strange places, hidden from the eyes of the world, where they had urgently practised sex.

'All right,' Anna-Liisa cut off Margit's description, which had grown rather detailed. 'I've never experienced the pleasures of forbidden love, but I still haven't engaged in amorous behaviour in the presence of others.'

That put a stop to Margit's reminiscences. They were silent for a moment, until Irma started thinking which operas pertained to Eino and Margit's story. Wagner's *Tristan and Isolde*, of course, but would Strauss's *Der Rosenkavalier* or Verdi's *La Traviata* also apply? She wasn't sure.

'The Marschallin is married, so she would be Eino, and Margit, you would be the young Octavian. In *La Traviata*, Violetta and Alfredo are both free, but she is from the wrong class, and didn't you say that Eino's family has never accepted you, so I was thinking that might fit the bill, too. Puccini's *Madama Butterfly*, on the other hand, would not be suitable, because that blockhead Pinkerton consciously bamboozles the poor girl, and I don't believe we can accuse Eino of that.'

Irma looked at them, eyes aglow, proud at having come up with what she felt was such a good topic of conversation. But Anna-Liisa couldn't care less and Margit couldn't hear, so Siiri felt it was her obligation to comment on Irma's suggestions.

'Why don't we pick a story with a happy ending. I'm afraid we won't find too many in operas.'

'Of course we will! *The Marriage of Figaro*, *The Barber of Seville*, and all kinds of others. Of course I can't remember anything else at the moment. Shuffle and cut, now I've got it: Rossini's *Cinderella*, of course.'

Suddenly Margit was upset. As it turned out, she had heard everything and didn't see what Irma's frivolous operas had to do with her life with Eino, their dramatic love story, which had sprung out of sheer lust and matured into a deep affection once Eino's first wife finally understood and stepped aside, taking the children and every penny Eino owned.

'We didn't necessarily want to know all this,' Anna-Liisa said. 'The original question was regarding your and Eino's children, which is not, in my opinion, an unreasonable enquiry, considering the length of your marriage.'

'Or did this all happen just before you moved to Sunset Grove?' Irma asked with a chuckle.

'Yes, Eino had three children and some grandchildren from his first marriage, but he hasn't really been in contact with them. I don't have any children. I never needed anyone else in my life except Eino.'

'And then . . . there were still these . . . other children?' Irma asked.

'Yes. Eino acknowledged two others with two different women. But I've forgiven him everything.'

'Like the Countess in the *Marriage of Figaro*. What fun! So we'll be having a big funeral!' Irma exclaimed.

Margit didn't know what to do. She didn't want to invite any of Eino's relatives to the wedding, but the others felt that she couldn't discount the deceased's relations, at least his children. They convinced Margit to draw up an inexpensive and straightforward death notice, single-column and without poems, for the Monday paper. It would include an invitation to the funeral and memorial service formulated in such a way that readers would gather it was going to be an intimate affair. They spent some time thinking of a discreet way to word it. Irma suggested: 'Only those close to the widow invited', but the others found this inappropriate. In the end, the notice read: 'A small, modest affair.'

'It has to read "modest". I'm not about to start feeding that clan of gypsies,' Margit said.

'And you're not going to put "my dearly beloved agronomist",' Irma verified.

'Of course not. I'll just put "Beloved" with a capital B.'

After momentary conferring, it was plain that the memorial service would be held at the Hakaniemi apartment, but they would let a catering company take care of the modest refreshments. Siiri in particular was relieved. She'd been worried that, because Margit was arranging the memorial service for the love of her life on a budget, and a tight one at that, she might have expected them to prepare the refreshments together, which would have meant Siiri handling them on her own from start to finish. It would have been the death of her.

'Anna-Liisa! Anna-Liisa!'

The Ambassador was calling from his room in a surprisingly powerful voice. He was in bed for the fifth day straight, with a fever that would drop and then inevitably rise again. He had refused any treatment; he was too exhausted to go to the health centre and he didn't want a private doctor called in, even though Anna-Liisa had gone through a lot of trouble to find a doctor who belonged to the same Masonic lodge as he did. But he wouldn't stand for either. It was starting to alarmingly look as if, now that their household had recuperated from in-home care, they would be learning palliative care the hard way.

They rose as one when they heard his call, except Margit, who kept reading her crematorium brochures. They made the trek to the Ambassador's round bed, as it always put a smile on his face to see his harem, as he liked to say.

'Onni, dear, we were just planning Eino's funeral,' Anna-Liisa said, to cheer up her ailing husband.

But the Ambassador didn't appear to hear. He was worryingly confused, and a touch seemed to indicate that his fever had risen higher than ever. Anna-Liisa wiped her husband's brow with a cool towel and tried to get him to drink. His breath was rattling now, and he tossed his head from side to side, refusing the juice. They stood there stock still, not knowing whether they should stay to support Anna-Liisa or give the couple some time alone.

'Anneli, please forgive me,' the Ambassador said, and mumbled something none of them could make out. His eyes remained shut, but he grabbed his wife's hand in a powerful grip. Anna-Liisa looked at Siiri in alarm, and Siiri took a couple of steps closer.

'Forgive me, Anneli . . . your jewellery . . . it wasn't supposed to happen this way . . .'

Irma's senses sharpened at this, and she moved up right next to Anna-Liisa, who didn't appear to understand what the Ambassador was talking about. He no longer shook his head strangely as she stroked his forehead, but he kept his eyes closed and squeezed his wife's hand with both of his.

'Calm yourself, Onni, it's all right. I'm here.'

'The boys were just supposed to take care of the money . . . your jewellery . . . it was a horrible mistake . . . I beg your forgiveness, Anneli.'

'He's confused,' Anna-Liisa said, to Irma and Siiri's disappointment, as they were eager to hear more of the Ambassador's revelations. But Anna-Liisa was extremely agitated and didn't want them standing there, bearing witness to her husband's unconsidered, feverish ravings. Grim-faced, she drove them from the room.

'We're going to be alone now. This could be his last night.'

Chapter 36

Siiri and Irma had to go shopping for something to wear to the funeral. Margit always wore black, so the missing mourning garb didn't pose as much of a problem for her as it did for the others. It was clear that the Ambassador wouldn't be participating in Eino's funeral, and Anna-Liisa remained unsure about her own attendance, as she might have to keep watch at her husband's bedside.

'Come shopping with us; you need to get out of the house!' Irma said. 'You can always use whatever you buy at Onni's funeral if you can't make it to Eino's shindig.'

This argument was so sensible that Anna-Liisa agreed to join them. The Ambassador had eaten his lunch with a healthy appetite, hobbled over to the bar on Anna-Liisa's arm to join the others, looking much better than when he'd raved deliriously about Anna-Liisa's jewellery. Unencumbered by cares, the trio boarded the first tram headed downtown. They were cheerful and talkative, since none of them could remember the last time the three of them had been out on the town in such boisterous spirits.

That was another grand thing about Hakaniemi: five tram

lines stopped more or less right outside their front door, and all of them led downtown. This time the number 7 came first, and they took it as far as Aleksanterinkatu, where they climbed off at the university so that they wouldn't miss a single display window on Helsinki's main shopping street. Senate Square was packed with rows of huts, a German-style Christmas market of sorts, but Irma knew they wouldn't find anything in the shacks but expensive, hand-made knick-knacks for tourists; not a drop of mulled wine, even the non-alcoholic sort. A handful of Japanese tourists were wandering in the rain, looking in puzzlement at reindeer-fur booties and trolls glued together from rocks and taking pictures of themselves at the base of the statue of Tsar Alexander II. Siiri, Irma and Anna-Liisa glanced at the sad sight, pitied the tourists, and spent a moment admiring the gleaming white Cathedral, its apostles scrubbed and its gilding burnished to such a shine during a recent renovation that the church radiated light, even on pitch-black December days like today. They headed off to look at display windows on Helsinki's venerable high street. Irma remembered having strolled along Aleksanterinkatu – or Aleksi, as the locals called it – with her mother back when Stockmann was still in the little blue Kiseleff building at Senate Square, but they couldn't calculate if that was possible.

Aleksanterinkatu was a crushing disappointment. Not one store looked as if it sold funeral dresses for nonagenarians. It being Christmastime, there were plenty of sparkly mini-skirts, because companies were throwing Christmas parties and apparently women were expected to show up at them looking trashy. Siiri, Irma and Anna-Liisa made the mistake of plunging into the Kluuvi shopping centre and were so disoriented by the thicket of soap-and-nail-polish shops, Japanese restaurants, and purveyors of French bric-a-brac that they couldn't find their way out. In the end, Irma had the bright idea of exiting through the McDonald's, which had direct access to the street, but no matter how hard she tried to convince them, Siiri and Anna-Liisa refused to stay and eat greasy food with their fingers.

'You should try everything fun at least once,' Irma whined, in vain.

'We're not Africans and we don't eat with our fingers,' Anna-Liisa observed tartly, weaving her way through the cars parked on the pedestrian street.

Next they tried the department store Aleksi 13, which had once been a reliable and affordable place to shop. But it had experienced such violent upheaval that they couldn't find the escalator for all the suitcases and sporting goods crowding the floor, until a nice young Russian woman helped them. They glided a couple of storeys upwards and were lost again.

'So, like, what are you ladies looking for?' a cheerful sales-clerk asked, once they found women's apparel.

They explained that they required suitable funeral attire. When Irma started talking about the construction company carrying out the retrofit at Sunset Grove and the complaints they had sent in, Siiri grew alarmed that she would acci-dentally reveal the whole, horrible truth of the matter in Anna-Liisa's presence. But then some funny instinct came to

Irma's aid, and her reportage stopped as if at a brick wall. She announced that she was a size 44 and made herself comfortable at the base of a mannequin, waiting for various alternatives to be carried over for her to try on.

'So, like, it's the event season so, like, we have a bunch of stuff in black,' the salesgirl said, sweeping an arm through the air to prompt her customers to search for their purchases themselves.

'Event season? Are there a lot of funerals being held?' Siiri still believed people preferred dying in November.

'So, like, it's Christmas. Does it have to be, like, totally all-black?'

'Simply "black" will do nicely,' Anna-Liisa said, straining to sound even the tiniest bit polite.

They explained that any black dress that wasn't too loud would do nicely, and that they would even settle for the same dress, as long as the salesgirl could find them something with a hemline that wasn't too short or a neckline that wasn't too open and that wasn't drowning in sequins – and preferably had sleeves.

'So, like, unfortunately we don't have anything like that,' the salesgirl said, without lifting a finger. Apparently, their demands were completely unreasonable. Irma said she could wear something with a more generous neckline and she didn't really care about sleeves, because she could always yank a shawl over her shoulders, but the salesgirl wasn't as willing to compromise in these negotiations as Irma.

'So, like, unfortunately you're out of luck.'

'This is outrageous!' Anna-Liisa cried, rapping her cane against the floor.

'In that case, we'll have to take our business to Stockmann. *Där får man ju allt*, as my mother always said.' Irma adopted a snappish tone to drive home her point regarding the competing department store's incomparable selection, but the salesgirl looked just as cheerful as she had been throughout the entirety of their brief encounter.

'So, like, bye, and Merry Christmas and everything!'

They set off in search of the escalators that would take them down and out and, much to their surprise, stumbled across them right around the corner. The department store was full of cranky, working-aged people out shopping in the middle of a weekday, and they had to remain vigilant to avoid being knocked over in the rush. A dreadful medley of American Christmas songs was blaring everywhere, and Siiri was getting so hot she was afraid she would faint.

'I don't understand what has happened to young people's manners,' Anna-Liisa huffed as they rode the escalator down.

'The same thing that happened to black dresses,' Irma said.

'And common sense,' Anna-Liisa added.

The streets were as crowded as everyplace else, but at least the air was fresh. Siiri paused at the corner and breathed calmly for a moment. What luck that the winter had been so mild. Only a couple of weeks before Christmas and there was no snow on the ground, or any hint of frost. It was easy to breathe and get around, and yet in the newspapers people were demanding that the city build a frozen tube where people could ski year-round. Somehow they felt this was within the purview of the public sector.

'Whatever will they come up with next,' Irma said. 'My husband always said he'd only ski during wartime. He ended up skiing in the Alps, where he was quite the ace, since the others had never laid eyes on skis before. Oh, my dear, lovely Veikko!'

'I always liked skiing,' Siiri remembered. 'But I don't recall the last time I've had a pair on my feet. It must have been a horribly long time ago. I've managed just fine without them.'

'And there you have it. They can forget their skiing tube and use that money for something more sensible. Like a children's hospital.'

Everywhere you looked these days, funds were being collected for the children's hospital, which was unusual in Finland, where such things were publicly funded. The pharmaceutical companies were actually competing to see who could make the most impressive donation on behalf of sick children. This was called *branding*, as Anna-Liisa knew. She held forth at such length on this English-language marketing term that Irma kept thinking she wanted to stop off for a cheap cognac somewhere. Siiri had donated dozens of euros herself, dropping them in the collection box of a campaigner wandering around Hakaniemi Square. She had informed this disbelieving volunteer that this was the second children's hospital drive she had participated in during her lifetime. Siiri had educated the campaigner about the enormous push during the 1940s, which the whole city had participated in; she had sold tickets to a historical joint concert of the Gentlemen Singers and the Helsinki Workers' Men's Choir and helped arrange a raffle for coffee, in short supply after the war. While she chatted with the campaigner, she'd also been reminded of a well-known story about a benefit concert dating from the earliest days of the hospital's collection, back in the 1920s. Sibelius had composed a piece, and the manuscript was sold at an unusual auction: if you bid, you had to pay the sum on the spot, but the bidding continued. The one who ended up with the work was, of all people, the master chocolatier Karl Fazer, brother to the music publisher. The defeated-looking donation collector hadn't been able to get a word in edgeways.

'What do you think? What will happen to the old Children's Hospital when the new one is completed?' Siiri asked. She thought the building, designed by Kaarlo and Elsi Borg was, in all of its idiosyncrasy, rather handsome.

'Maybe it will be turned into a private nursing home,' Irma suggested. 'The old military hospital was converted into a pricy retirement home for the poor. Why not convert all the abandoned buildings unfit for human habitation into final repositories for the elderly? Did you all notice what a fine term I just remembered: *final repository*.'

The throngs at Stockmann were even worse than those at Aleksi 13. They packed into the elevator and rode up to the fourth floor, where they found a saleswoman in a dusty corner drinking imported French water straight from the bottle. Finnish and Swedish flags were pinned to her breast, as if there were any need to advertise the fact that she could serve them in both of the country's official languages. They stated their business to the parched saleswoman and were immediately led to an even more secluded corner, where a rack read 'Final Sale'.

'So, like, these might work for you,' the saleswoman said, pulling various old-fashioned, sensible black outfits from the rack.

They waited half an hour for the changing room before deciding that, when they thought about it, trying the garments on was too much trouble and actually rather unpleasant, as it meant gazing at themselves naked in the mirror in a cramped, dirty cubicle as complete strangers sighed impatiently on the other side of the curtain. Irma explained in a loud voice that she couldn't be bothered to wear a bra any more and it might be awkward to be caught topless in broad daylight. They decided to buy sizes that were large enough, roughly measured the length over their winter coats, and confirmed with the salesgirl that they could return the items if they proved completely unsuitable.

'So, like, returns are cool,' the salesgirl said, and they decided from her sunny smile that she had nothing against their suggestion.

Irma bought a pleated and only slightly shimmery party frock. The fabric was light and probably draped beautifully and didn't wrinkle, no matter how much they bunched the material up in their fists. Anna-Liisa found a straightforward, streamlined dress in a wool blend, to her mind a more sensible choice for a winter funeral than Irma's diaphanous gown. Siiri was so taken with a trouser suit the salesgirl showed her that she bought it, despite the steep price.

'Margit said I would still have all of your funerals to attend,' she said cheerfully as she claimed her loyal customer discount.

They rewarded themselves for their labours under the big cupola at the Fazer Cafe on Kluuvikatu, splurging on shrimp sandwiches because, as Irma noted, wasting a little money always did wonders for one's mood. Irma still had a few fifty-euro bills in her wallet, and she waved them around merrily to show that squandering on delicacies wouldn't break the bank.

'Besides, I can always withdraw more from the wall,' she continued. 'If I can just remember that stupid code. But mine is easy, it's . . . just a moment, I have it here some-where, I wrote it on a big yellow Post-it . . .'

'That's enough, Irma,' Anna-Liisa said, before the entirety of Irma's earthly possessions were strewn across their table.

And so they ordered a glass of wine apiece, too. They were sitting directly across from a young couple in love, whose tender whispers echoed across the domed dining room to their table more audibly than into each other's ears. But as Siiri and her companions knew the acoustics would, reciprocally, carry their sentiments to the other table, they exchanged glances without comment, despite the brazen woman's lunchtime lack of propriety. They weren't used to women taking the initiative.

'I have no intention of tolerating those robot-drafted

replies regarding the renovation at Sunset Grove,' Anna-Liisa said, to mask the indelicate whispering. Siiri felt herself growing dizzy and had to lower her fork and knife to her plate. This made an unpleasant clank; the woman on the other side of the room wondered what the sudden sound was. Days, if not weeks, had passed without anyone having mentioned the retrofit at Sunset Grove. Siiri had started hoping that Anna-Liisa had forgotten the whole thing.

'What else can we do? There's no point fighting with robots,' Irma said, looking genuinely unperturbed. 'I've had it on more than one good authority that complaining about plumbing retrofits is futile. Why, one of my cousins, Kirsti, lived in exile nine months, had two rents to pay, and didn't get a penny from the insurance company, even though she had paid through the nose for her policy. And when the renovation was complete, everything had been done wrong. In the end, she moved out and died. All of which was totally normal, of course.'

'Dying?'

'That, too, but especially the fact that there was a stupid shower stall where the bathtub should have been, and that they had forgotten to install an oven in the kitchen, and the water came out of the tap the wrong way.'

Anna-Liisa frowned. 'What do you mean, the wrong way?'

'Hot water from the cold tap and cold water from the hot tap. And a painting that was very valuable and had been in the family for generations got so dusty that it was ruined. Which was totally normal, of course, and my cousin Kirsti's fault since she hadn't had the sense to protect it properly. After Kirsti's traumatic tale we've always said it's impossible to make it through a plumbing retrofit in one piece. But here we are, alive and kicking! Skål!'

Siiri wasn't sure if Irma was telling the truth, but she was grateful to her gallant friend who managed to drag Anna-Liisa along with her chatter and made her forget retrofit rapscallions. Irma continued jabbering and suddenly dropped a genuine bomb. She had gone to Munkkiniemi after water aerobics and witnessed a miracle: the plastic had been peeled away from Sunset Grove, and its walls had been painted a cheery yellow. According to Irma, the sight had been almost festive. She claimed to have taken a picture of the freshly painted walls with her flaptop, but Siiri and Anna-Liisa didn't believe her.

'Don't you two know that you can take a picture with nearly any gadget these days? The boy at Stockmann showed me, you just press a button, and click, there's your photograph. I have five photos of that nice boy from Stockmann somewhere in the depths of my flaptop. I'd forgotten all about the camera until I was standing there, admiring the yellow wall at Sunset Grove, but then my brain shuffled and cut: I remembered it and took the picture. When I went in, I found Tauno amid the chaos; he was the same as ever, hauling that mattress around with his pack on his back, and he told me they might complete the renovation by February. I invited him to Eino's funeral so he'd have something to look forward to, too.'

'So only six months behind schedule,' Anna-Liisa said.

'Yes, that's not so bad. My cousin Pentti's plumbing retrofit in Töölö lasted eighteen months, can you imagine? And he's like Tauno, a tough old bird who stuck it out in his place for the whole hellish renovation, even though the construction company did everything in its power to chase him out into the streets. They didn't even give him a handy composting toilet; he had to do his business at libraries, swimming pools and restaurants.'

The lovebirds across the room had fallen silent and were gaping at Siiri's table, but she and her friends paid no mind. The new completion date had not been announced to the residents of Sunset Grove, Irma was sure, because she'd been keeping an eye on the Sunset Grove website with her flaptop, which she now dug out and set on the table, much to Anna-Liisa's distress.

'Irma, we're eating!'

Irma swept and swiped and suddenly brought up photographs of a freshly painted Sunset Grove. They barely recognized their dear old concrete bunker in all of its new yellow splendour. It looked lovely; the yellow brought it a pleasant lightness, and in one image it looked as if there were more balconies, those glass boxes that were pasted to the outside of old buildings these days. The tablet also contained a couple of pictures of a baffled-looking Irma. She claimed that the flaptop took pictures by itself and from both sides, which made her appearance on the screen understandable, even though the intent had been to photograph Sunset Grove. Irma's Internet didn't know when the renovation was supposed to be completed, and so they had to trust Tauno's intelligence. They did understand that if someone said everything would be finished in February, they should add at least another month, because there was no such thing as a renovation without unpleasant surprises.

They took the number 7 tram home and sat in silence all the way. Siiri was thinking about Hakaniemi and realized she felt wistful. She had grown used to her new neighbourhood and almost preferred Hakaniemi's bustling, exotic ambience to quiet Munkkiniemi. The thought of moving back to Sunset Grove felt unreal, but also oddly tempting. She was fed up with her status as slave, waiting on the others hand and foot, and her heavy housework; their life in exile was rather grating on her nerves. At Sunset Grove, she would have her privacy and eat when and where she wanted. And listen to music! That was completely missing from her present life. How wonderful it would be to lie in bed and listen to, say, Sibelius's Fifth Symphony or Schubert's String Quintet.

Maybe it would be nice to be back in her own home one day – not that Sunset Grove felt like home. So what was it, then?

'A final repository,' Irma said.

Chapter 37

The December Thursday that was the day of Eino's funeral was rainy but warm. It was as dark as the bottom of a bag, of course, because there was no sun, or any snow to reflect the light. Even those who weren't attending funerals were wearing black, and so the procession of Sunset Grove refugees trudging up Siltasaarenkatu to the church didn't really stand out. Their gait was slower than that of the overstressed majority of the population, it was true, and they used canes, and their bearing was no longer erect and proud – except Anna-Liisa's, who got healthier and more rehabilitated the feebler her husband grew. The Ambassador would not be attending the funeral, but because he had slept soundly the previous night and eaten breakfast in bed, sitting up without any help, Anna-Liisa had dared to leave his side for a couple of hours. Just to be sure, Siiri had asked Muhis and Metukka to come over and clean while they were gone and she'd told them about the Ambassador's illness. Muhis had promised to keep an eye on Onni and make sure he didn't die during Anna-Liisa's absence.

'It's just a flu,' Irma had told Muhis, even though she

didn't really believe it herself. After all, she knew about telomeres and frailty syndrome. In the end, cell division turned against itself, the defence mechanism became an enfeebling operation, and the old person died of some random, harmless infection. But of course the Ambassador's fever might go down, who knew?

The interior of the Kallio Church was too expansive and lofty for such an intimate affair; the pews could have accommodated a crowd of over a thousand. But Siiri found it beautiful, soothing somehow, and after the imposing entrance and granite exterior its whiteness and brightness did the soul good. Paavo Tynell's 1930s chandeliers and Hannes Autere's simple wood-relief altarpiece represented the brand of spare beauty that appealed to Siiri. Anna-Liisa gave a brief lecture on how the residents of the surrounding neighbourhood had served as models for the relief during the 1950s.

A surprisingly large crowd filed in, even though the death notice hadn't extended a warm welcome to anyone. Margit had listed herself as the sole mourner without a single one of Eino's children, who, nevertheless, formed quite a herd as they entered the church. Some looked exactly like Eino, two tall boys in particular, and according to Margit, one of them was the older bastard. She had somehow managed to communicate this in a rather soft voice as they stood outside the door, waiting to see if anyone would show up. Now Margit sat bravely in the front row, to the right of the aisle. Siiri, Irma and Anna-Liisa sat a couple of rows back on the left, as they weren't family. Row upon row of cheerful people of various ages gathered behind Margit, not all of whom knew each other. Irma guessed that the bastards hadn't been accepted as part of the clan, as she thought they sat a little apart from the others and weren't smiling as broadly.

The cantor commenced by pedalling a very nice rendition of the Bach chorale 'Jesu, Joy of Man's Desiring', which prompted immediate sniffles from the relatives' pews, even though none of the mourners there had ever been to visit Eino at Sunset Grove, let alone the SquirrelsNest. The power of music was miraculous, especially during ceremonies like theirs, so unfamiliar to so many. But having passed the milestone of ninety, Siiri and her friends had become funeral professionals, seasoned ceremony participants on whom the exoticism of the event had little effect. Even Irma didn't pull her lace handkerchief out of her little black handbag during Bach's endless melody, and Margit sat in solitude, still and stately as a statue.

For the hymn, Margit had selected 'For the Beauty of the Earth', which was a clever fit for Christmastime. Many knew it only as a Christmas song, even though Siiri had heard it played at funerals dozens of times. She didn't sing, because the organist took the tune too high, but Irma belted out her soprano blissfully and was, indeed, practically the sole singer, as all that could be heard from Eino's descendants were murmurs and uncertain groping for the tune. Siiri thought about which hymn she would like played at her own funeral, briefly considered Hilja Haahti's gorgeous lyrics to 'Abide with Me, Lord Jesus', then remembered that she didn't even belong to the Church, and started seriously wondering whether she ought to rejoin. Burying her would be such a bother for those responsible if they couldn't fall back on the rituals of the Church.

The young, long-haired female pastor spoke softly but with commendable brevity. During her visit to the Hakaniemi apartment, the pastor, who purported to be a vicar despite being far too young for the task, had been very shy. She had been accompanied by an elderly fellow who looked like he'd seen a thing or two and whom they had mistakenly assumed was the vicar, but the girl had introduced him as the substitute cantor. The young pastor had declined coffee and didn't bat an eyebrow when Margit told her to just recite the mandatory gibberish. And so today the pastor didn't start remembering a man she'd never met, as was customary. She simply wished a mournful welcome to all those who had come to bid farewell to Eino Juhani Partanen, prattled a couple of Bible verses, and then moved on to the blessing.

As part of her uncongenial invitation, Margit had forbidden flowers, and so they were spared the ritual where one spoke a few words and laid one's floral contribution across the casket. Margit had wanted to do away with the closing hymn, too, but the pastor and the cantor had exerted so much pressure that after the blessing Irma was able to trill again, this time the familiar notes of 'Spirit of Truth'.

In conclusion, the cantor did a masterful job playing Widor's Toccata, a stumbling block for organists if there ever was one. The representatives from the parish had been somewhat perplexed by Margit's choice of music, as the Toccata was known as a wedding recessional and in its exuberance was not, in their opinion, fitting for the occasion. But Margit had stuck to her guns, and it had been for the best. The irrepressible Toccata brought a unique ambience to the funeral, and when Siiri thought about everything Margit had reported about the love she and Eino had shared, and looked at the flame-red roses Margit had laid across the coffin in Eino's memory, and remembered the afternoon squeals that had reverberated in the corridors of Sunset Grove just a year ago, she understood that the only appropriate music for Eino's funeral was Widor's Toccata.

Six of Eino's descendants, apparently grandchildren, marched timidly up to the coffin in time to the music. The coffin looked unusually dignified, and the sight of the young men standing around it moved Siiri to tears, Irma to blast her nose into her lace handkerchief, and Anna-Liisa to rap her cane against the floor, as Irma should have exercised greater restraint at such a delicate moment. The young men glanced at each other, and when the boldest reached for the handle of the casket and placed the carrying straps over his shoulder, the others started searching for their fabric scraps. Carrying a casket was no piece of cake, and these fellows were clearly doing it for the first time. One of them put the strap on incorrectly and almost found himself permanently entangled, until he crumpled it up under his arm and made do with the handle alone. Eventually, the bold boy gave the signal, and they started off at a shuffle, lugging the black coffin of their estranged forefather down the long aisle of the Kallio Church as Widor's fireworks echoed in the grand, nearly vacant space. The guests trailed behind, with Margit at the fore. Once the casket, after much loud huffing, was safely loaded into the rear of the funeral home's hearse, its doors were shut, and the vehicle glided along the long allée to Castréninkatu, where it slipped in among the mundane rush-hour traffic. Siiri had to dab at her eyes; there was something quite arresting about the sight. She could make out the red roses from surprisingly far off, right until the vehicle disappeared from view.

'That's that,' Margit said, and she turned towards them with an endearing smile, and Siiri was reminded yet again of how striking Margit must have been as a young woman. No wonder Eino had fallen for her. Eino's relatives stood off in the distance; some were smoking, and none came over to greet the widow. Irma was outraged by such boorish behaviour, but Siiri and Anna-Liisa managed to calm her enough to keep her from rushing over and giving a piece of her mind to these country bumpkins.

'No, they're from Helsinki,' Margit said, still smiling blissfully. 'Let's go. They'll come if they come.'

And so they walked back down to the Arena building in the gloom, and not a single one of Eino's grieving descendants followed in the hopes of caramel cake. Irma wanted to know how Margit intended on arranging an estate inventory with such miscreants, and Margit said she'd turned the task over to an attorney recommended by the funeral home.

'You should never use them!' Anna-Liisa cried. 'Funeral-home attorneys are . . . they're vultures and thoroughly untrustworthy, absolutely undistinguished. You should have asked us; Onni makes use of several very capable and highly regarded lawyers.'

'I'm sure he does,' Irma let slip. 'He'd better.'

Anna-Liisa stopped and trained her steely eyes on Irma: 'What are you implying?'

Irma started rummaging around in her handbag in agitation. When she couldn't think of what she was supposedly looking for, she pointed at the display window they were standing in front of.

'Look, what a funny store. They sell clothes for giants.'

'For big and tall men, and there's nothing funny about it. What did you mean when you said Onni had better have good lawyers?'

'Oh, I just blurt out whatever pops into my head. You know that,' Irma said, managing a rather sincere laugh. 'I suppose I was thinking about Onni's property; you've said yourself he's a wealthy man. Do we get to eat everything, now that Eino's bastards aren't coming to the feast? This is going to be a fun party! It's too bad Tauno hasn't made it. There's no way I'd have had the energy to earn my cakesies by talking with compete strangers. Oh, I must remember to take a couple of Amaryllie pillies. I have this touch of diabetes, you know.'

They opened their front door to the sight of Muhis and Metukka bustling about. The big rug from the entryway had been carried out to air, along with the Oriental rug from the living room that they never would have been strong enough to budge on their own. Metukka was swaying, shirtless, around the living room with the vacuum cleaner, and

Muhis was clattering around in the spa. The sight of her friends cheered Siiri; she reflected that it had been an excellent idea to hire the boys as domestics. It was such fun sitting on a bar stool and watching the two dark-skinned men sing and work. But Margit's blissful smile had evaporated.

'I see it's going to be an interesting memorial service,' she said, clicking on the coffee machine Siiri had filled beforehand.

'Is it time for the funeral now?' Muhis asked, as he came in from scrubbing the toilets. He shouted a couple of funny words at Metukka, who turned off the vacuum cleaner. 'We're sorry, we're in your way. We'll finish later.'

But Irma was having none of it. Why, the very idea that the boys would bring in the rugs and then leave! She invited Muhis and Metukka to stay for cake, because there was no way they would be able to finish it all, even though the plan had been to keep the celebration modest. Margit was standing in the kitchenette and didn't say anything. Suddenly, the Ambassador appeared at his bedroom door in his silk dressing gown, looking chipper indeed and not at all in need of palliative care.

'Hello, everyone; are we going to raise a toast to Eino's memory?' he said, and slowly approached the bar. He let Muhis help him to the bar and, after giving his wife a peck on the cheek, started making everyone their usual tipple. 'What are you boys having?' he asked with a winning smile, but Muhis and Metukka said they were fine with coffee.

The memorial service proved downright unforgettable. It was, of course, nothing like what the man of the hour would have planned, as Eino had never set foot in the Hakaniemi apartment and had never met their Nigerian friends. Margit was mostly quiet and didn't eat anything; she just took the occasional sip of red wine. She was a stylish presence in black on the sofa, and radiated an unusual serenity and warmth. Sorrow had imbued her with a languid generosity, and she wasn't at all bothered when Muhis and Metukka related amusing anecdotes about African funerals and claimed that in some villages they threw a big party once a year, and after they had sung and danced for days, the elders of the village clasped hands, walked to the brink of a cliff, and jumped to their deaths.

'How convenient,' Irma said, and started thinking where one might find a ravine in Helsinki to solve the aging-induced prosperity deficit ravaging their recession-era society.

'There's a strong tradition of storytelling in Africa,' Anna-Liisa said, sparking a long, meandering debate as to whether oral traditions produced more implausible legends than written tales did. In her view, memory was the most fictitious of mankind's inventions. Irma agreed, which was why she felt bad whenever anyone doubted her memory or the accuracy of her entertaining anecdotes.

'Who can be bothered to tell dull stories?' she said, as always. 'And now I'm going to smoke one cigarette, otherwise I'll never die! *Döden, döden, döden.*'

She pulled her cigarettes and pastilles out of her handbag and politely stepped aside to puff. For a moment, the room was strangely still, almost like a memorial service, but Muhis looked restless. He kept shifting and glancing at the Ambassador and adjusting his beehive hat. He never took it off, despite the fact that Anna-Liisa had employed every method at her disposal to acquaint him with Finnish manners.

'Do you know what Hasan died of?' Muhis finally blurted out, eyeing the Ambassador intently. Margit lowered her wine glass to the coffee table, Anna-Liisa's back grew even straighter, and Irma and Siiri exchanged worried glances. Everyone tensed to observe Onni, who was as calm as if he'd been asked about his cholesterol values during a physical. He tinkled the ice cubes in his whisky tumbler, took another swig, even though there was nothing in the glass but melted water, and slammed the glass to the table with surprising force.

'Hasan was killed,' he said.

A heavy silence fell over the room. The stunned Anna-Liisa frowned, trying to remember who, exactly, was the topic of discussion. She had been caught up in the most frenzied maelstrom of in-home care when the parade of men, each shadier than the last, had come around asking for Hasan. Irma didn't dare breathe, Siiri didn't dare swallow, and Margit started playing solitaire. She laid out the cards on the table, cool as a cucumber, moving the glasses and plates out of her way.

'Yes, I heard,' Muhis said, smiling brightly, as if the Ambassador's confession had come as a huge relief. Metukka tapped his foot against the floor and drummed his fingers against his thigh.

'Good,' he said, without looking at anyone.

'What in heaven's name are you talking about?' Anna-Liisa shouted, slapping her thighs. 'Who is being discussed? What sort of person, in your estimation, deserves to be killed? And how is it that you, Onni Rinta-Paakku, know any such individual?'

'Calm yourself, Anneli,' the Ambassador said, wrapping his wife in an embrace. He patted Anna-Liisa on the shoulder and stroked her hand. 'I know all sorts of people. When you've spent forty-five years working as a diplomat in the Foreign Ministry, you see all sorts of things. This poor Hasan was a sad case.'

The Ambassador began speaking remarkably openly about Hasan, with whom he had not been personally acquainted. Some years ago, his property rentals had led to dealings with Hasan, who had a company that arranged reliable tenants for investment properties, including the very apartment they were sitting in.

'As I'm sure you're aware, tenants can cause all sorts of trouble.'

Muhis and Metukka listened closely to the Ambassador as he calmed his flock of females and explained that his acquaintance Hasan had ended up involved in unfortunate incidents that in no way related to the Ambassador's investments or other affairs. Siiri believed the boys knew at least as much about the matter as Onni, but discreet fellows that they were, they had no interest in inserting themselves any more deeply into the conversation. Why Muhis had wanted to bring up Hasan at Eino's funeral, Siiri had no idea, and she hoped she would remember to ask him at a better time.

'Are you embroiled in criminal activity, Onni?' Anna-Liisa asked, not the least bit appeased. Now the Ambassador took Anna-Liisa's concerned face in his hands, kissed his wife, and said: 'No, Anneli, of course not. It was a mistake to trust Hasan, but we don't have to worry ourselves about that any more.' Then he stood remarkably spryly and asked: 'Shall we have another glass of red wine?'

After they had toasted Eino's memory several times, eaten half the caramel cake and almost an entire sandwich cake, taught Muhis and Metukka to play Black Maria and say *death* three times in Swedish in rapid succession, and even succeeded in making Margit laugh several times, the Ambassador was almost falling asleep on the sofa. The boys helped him into bed, brought in the aired-out rugs from the courtyard, and promised to come and finish the cleaning the next day.

'You boys are so sweet,' Siiri said, giving each of them two ten-euro notes. The boys laughed their loud laughs, thanked their hosts for the party, and went on their way. Siiri watched them for a long time and wondered how she would manage without her good-natured helpers at the newly renovated Sunset Grove, with no one but old folks around.

'Oh dear, oh dear, what a smashing day,' Irma sighed, when it was quiet again and she was lounging on the sofa in her nightshirt waiting for Siiri to bring her her evening tea. 'I've always said funerals are such fun. And the cantor played so beautifully, even though he looked like a drunk.'

Chapter 38

Luckily they hadn't prepared for Christmas in vain. Siiri had thought she would buy a cooked ham and ready-made casseroles from the Hakaniemi Hall and bake some gingerbread cookies from frozen dough. They weren't in the habit of giving each other presents, and so that caused no excess fuss. Irma hadn't been invited to her darlings' this Christmas, because they'd all decided to travel to the ends of the earth together, to Madagascar, without Irma, to recuperate from the stresses of their own renovations. At least the gargantuan spruce erected at Hakaniemi Square, which made for a pretty sight from their windows, radiated a little Christmas spirit.

Amidst their listlessly commencing Christmas, other concerns arose. The Ambassador had been in rather good shape since Eino's funeral, and they'd started hoping that he'd beaten his flu. But on the Wednesday four days before Christmas Eve, the darkest day of the year, the Ambassador's temperature rose again. Anna-Liisa forbade anyone from calling in help, and they understood why.

The Ambassador spent most of his time sleeping with a

nasty rattle in his lungs, but it didn't seem to bother him. Siiri and Irma tried to gather pillows under his back to help him breathe more easily, but none of their tricks silenced the rattle.

'Phlegm and fluid in the lungs,' Irma said knowledgably. 'Pneumonia or heart failure is my guess.'

Anna-Liisa didn't say anything. She slid into a stupor, which was uncharacteristic of her, and acted instinctively but didn't dare stop to think how this all felt. If Siiri hadn't kept an eye on mealtimes, Anna-Liisa probably would have forgotten to eat. She lay or sat next to her husband around the clock and without speaking, unless she was reading something out loud. Now and again Onni would utter a couple of words to her, and then Anna-Liisa would stroke her husband, but he was rarely able to answer.

The hardest thing was keeping the patient clean. Irma had bought a little blue potty from Etola, which made life a bit easier for Anna-Liisa at night, but in the end they had to dig into Margit's stores for Eino's leftover incontinence pads and force the Ambassador into them. This wasn't easy. Anna-Liisa would have preferred to handle the task herself for reasons of modesty, but she'd been compelled to ask for the others' help. All this had been extremely embarrassing for the Ambassador, and he tended to snap at his helpers in irritation, which didn't make things any easier. He felt humiliated lying there in his nappies, and he scratched and tore at them in his sleep. Now and again Muhis and Metukka came by to lend a hand and the Ambassador was able to do his business, but they couldn't trouble the boys all hours of the day and night. While the boys tended to the Ambassador in the spa, Siiri and Irma changed the sheets on Anna-Liisa's and Onni's bed.

'These smell horrid,' Irma remarked as they carried the dirty sheets to the washing machine. They chuckled at the big, round sheet, but Irma grimaced as she took a suspicious sniff. 'They smell like death.'

'Do you think so?' Siiri whispered.

'Yes. Death has a very particular smell; I've smelled it before. Maybe it's best our problems at Sunset Grove and Hakaniemi are coming to an end this way.'

That's what Siiri had been thinking, too. The Ambassador would take their awful secret to the grave, and then no one would need to nose about in the less savoury details of the renovation or their property. Their biggest concern was Anna-Liisa. They knew she suspected something, but it was impossible to say how much she knew about her husband's questionable affairs. Anna-Liisa avoided discussing anything remotely related, seemed to have forgotten the jewellery box and the rolls of cash, and since the shrimp sandwiches at the Fazer Cafe, hadn't mentioned the renovation once. They left Anna-Liisa to her own devices, and when she wasn't keeping watch at her husband's side, she sat staring out the window, or even dozed off on the couch.

Since the funeral Margit had perked up again, and she spent a lot of time out and about. They didn't know where and were too preoccupied to ask. Margit came and went, sometimes she was on her way to her book club, others to the theatre, and one day she brought home a red clump she had felted herself, which was supposed to be a Christmas elf.

'Just like the handicrafts we used to make at Sunset Grove!' Irma cried and started remembering the Easter decorations they'd pieced together from toilet paper rolls and coloured feathers. The poor woman who led handicrafts had come up with this inanity to keep their minds occupied, and they hadn't had the heart to not participate in the leisure activity she had gone to so much trouble to prepare. It felt wonderful having a proper laugh, so proper that they peed in their pants. Life was so incredibly bleak in their temporary nursing home. Siiri was tired, and she didn't even have the energy to cook; she just bought liver casserole and pea soup from the supermarket.

On Christmas Eve, the Ambassador stopped eating. He shook his head in exhaustion when Anna-Liisa tried to spoon soup into his mouth, and she didn't force him. He did sip a little water and juice, but he no longer asked for wine, the way he had a few days earlier. Anna-Liisa diligently read to her husband, the paper during the day and P. G. Wodehouse's *Jeeves* books in the evening. The Ambassador seemed to enjoy listening, if nothing else, then at least to his wife's melodic voice and careful articulation.

On Christmas Day, the Ambassador no longer wanted to get up for the bathroom. He surrendered to his pads and didn't seem to need them any more either. Death's gradual march had reached the stage where the body's functions start slowly failing. His feet felt cold, despite the layers of blankets and the hot water bottles under the sheet. They made sure the room was aired and the Ambassador always had something to drink. There wasn't much else they could do.

'Touch is important,' Irma said, and held the Ambassador's hand while Anna-Liisa was resting on the couch. 'Touch is the last human sense to go.'

Siiri had read that in the paper, too, and people had known it forever. But nowadays science rigorously applied its own methods to proving obvious truths, and the results were then trumpeted in the newspapers. Studies had shown that if you held a dying person's hand, they needed less pain medication. Or that if a terminal-cancer patient had a beautiful view out the window, they suffered less. Simple things.

Suddenly Onni started bellowing. His eyes were shut, and he no longer seemed to be in this world. But he yelled for help and, surprisingly, God, even though to their knowledge he wasn't a deeply religious person. He tore his watch from his wrist, ripped apart his nappy stickers, squirmed and shouted. Luckily, Anna-Liisa didn't hear; undisturbed, she remained sleeping in the living room. Siiri and Irma held Onni by the hand, stroked his forehead, and tried to talk to him in a soothing voice. For a moment it looked as if they would be outmatched by the Ambassador's agony, but he calmed down from the fit as quickly as he had flown into it. He gripped his watch to his chest in both hands, and the nasty rattle reappeared.

'Did he take off his watch so that he could die?' Irma asked, mystified, but she didn't really expect a reply. She and

Siiri sat in silence next to the Ambassador's bed. Irma stroked his grey hair and Siiri tried to help him drink, but that also seemed like too much. The hours passed, and no one knew what time it was, because the Ambassador's watch had stopped. Siiri raised the blanket to feel Onni's feet. They were cold. Gradually, ugly purple splotches and depressions you could instantly tell weren't bruises formed on them; his blood wasn't circulating any more. His hands were cool, too. It wouldn't be long now.

She rose and went over to the sofa to rouse Anna-Liisa. She didn't need to say anything to her friend; Anna-Liisa could tell from the way Siiri looked at her why she had woken her. Leaning against each other, they went into the dim bedroom, where they could hear the slowing, rattling breath. Anna-Liisa kissed her husband on the forehead and cheeks, and Irma and Siiri helped her lie down on the bed, next to Onni. There they lay, next to each other, looking so serene and beautiful that Siiri was filled with an incredible joy. She tried to get Irma to leave the room with her, but Anna-Liisa didn't want them to go. Siiri and Irma sat down side by side and indulged in the rare sight: a happy old person taking his leave, surrounded by loved ones.

Sometime that evening, no one knew when, they noticed that the rattle had stopped. At first they thought the Ambassador wasn't breathing any more, but then he sighed deeply. After that, the breathing was different: short and choppy, pausing for long stretches. But whenever they thought it was all over, the Ambassador drew a deep breath and started gasping lightly again.

'Shall we sing?' Irma suggested.

'If you do, no hymns, please,' Anna-Liisa said, and Irma started from her childhood song 'Oh, my darling August.' It was an utterly silly choice for this moment, but they sang it from the bottom of their hearts, because somehow they needed to get out their feelings, or at least part of them that had welled up in them during the long wait. After they had sung about August four times, Irma started a round of 'Benedictine Monk Liquor', and Siiri and Anna-Liisa naturally came in on cue. This song suited to the mood better, and so they sang many rounds of it, and at times it seemed as if the Ambassador smiled faintly.

Suddenly Onni coughed, went dark red, almost purple, and something white dribbled from his lips. Siiri wiped his mouth and Anna-Liisa stroked the Ambassador's forehead.

'Let go, Onni; it's all right,' she said, and the deep flush disappeared from the Ambassador's face and he stopped breathing. They looked and listened for a long time, waiting for another gasp, but it never came. The Ambassador looked incredibly handsome; he had a faint, peaceful smile on his lips, and they could tell from everything that things were going to be fine. When his face was nearly white, Anna-Liisa kissed her husband on the forehead once more and whispered to him in a soft voice: 'Thank you, my love.'

Siiri and Irma left Anna-Liisa sleeping at her husband's side one last time. They remembered Eino's tragedy at the SquirrelsNest and absolutely refused to call anywhere to let the world know that a nearly centenarian veteran had died in his own bed in an apartment that was apparently his but that might have been the site of any number of unsavoury assignations. Siiri poured them glasses of red wine, pulled an old pound cake from the fridge, and they each laid down on a sofa. Margit's faint snoring could be heard coming through the door to her boudoir.

'Merry Christmas, dear friend!' Irma said, and it was only then that Siiri remembered that it really was Christmas Day. Irma dunked her cakesies in her wine, which was a new invention, and proclaimed it goodies, too. 'You should always try new things. How would I have ever known about this, if I hadn't tried?'

Siiri looked at Irma contentedly, thought about the married couple resting in the round bedroom, and felt unspeakable relief. She was happy about the beautiful death and felt privileged to have witnessed it at such close proximity. She thought it was incredibly wonderful that, at the age of ninety-six, she was surrounded by people like this, with whom she could share the most important things in life. And no longer would she have to investigate the Ambassador's criminal doings and dubious affairs. Now that Onni was sleeping the eternal sleep, it made no difference whom he'd rented his apartments to and what illicit activities had taken place in them. There was only one thing that still weighed on her.

'We need to get back to Sunset Grove.'

'We will,' Irma said, waving her hand so her gold bracelets jangled. 'Unless you keel over and kick the bucket first. *Döden, döden, döden!*'

DEATH IN SUNSET GROVE

Good detectives come in all manner of guises . . .

Siiri and Irma are best friends and queen bees at Sunset Grove, a retirement community for those still young at heart. With a combined age of nearly 180, Siiri and Irma are still just as inquisitive and witty as when they first met decades ago.

But when their comfortable world is upturned by a suspicious death at Sunset Grove, Siiri and Irma are shocked into doing something about it. Determined to find out exactly what happened and why, they begin their own private investigations and form The Lavender Ladies Detective Agency.

The trouble is, beneath Sunset Grove's calm facade there is more going on than meets the eye – will Siiri and Irma discover more than they bargained for?

Coming soon

The End of
Sunset Grove

Best friends Irma and Siiri are relieved when they can finally return home, but things have changed in the retirement home . . .

Sunset Grove is under new management, a sinister new organization that promises spiritual enlightenment in return for donations from its residents. And the staff seem to have disappeared, replaced by new technology that remotely takes care of all their needs, if only they could work out how to use it . . .

The Lavender Ladies are increasingly suspicious of the new order and plan an elaborate act of sabotage. But their last hurrah has some drastic consequences – will the Lavender Ladies get more than they bargained for?

extracts reading groups
competitions books new
discounts extracts
competitions
new
books
events books
extracts
new reading groups
interviews
discounts
new books events
events new
www.panmacmillan.com
discounts extracts discounts
extracts events reading groups
competitions books extracts new